June 6, 2014

Book Launch
&
Pre-pride
Party

ARCANE OCEAN

Copyright © 2013 by Nathan Dudley

2nd edition published by CreateSpace Independent Publishing Platform.

The following is a work of fiction. Events, people, places, and history may seem familiar but they are in no way to be considered fact. Any similarity between real people, events, or places are to be disregarded. If magic has returned, no one has yet notified me. The individuals characterized in this book are purely fictional, except Mercedes.

ARCANE OCEAN

Nathan Dudley

Forthcoming

Arcane Fire

Arcane Armageddon

In dedication to

Faye Dudley

You never let me stop believing

Arcane Ocean

Whispers of the Past

"I don't care if you're tired, Morgan, you've already had two breaks," Kaleb called over his shoulder.

Carefully, the trio picked their way over fallen branches and loose stone. The tall sinewy Kaleb was in the lead, followed by Nick, and panting behind was Morgan. Morgan carried a small cage that held their sacrifice: a white mouse they had picked up at Pet World. Nick had named her Lucy. Lucy seemed nervous.

Leaves crackled and twigs snapped underfoot. A lone owl called out to the chirping insects and the trees whispered their reply. A chilly and damp autumnal breeze greeted the three friends as they made their way through the woods. Winter had begun its annual harassment of fall, though not yet to the point of requiring more than a light jacket.

They had chosen Rosewood Park for tonight's ritual because of its remoteness, but that same rural quality meant the upkeep on the trails left much to be desired. Three weeks ago, a wind storm tossed around the contents of the forest floor. It would be another three weeks before the park rangers came out to clear the paths.

Morgan hiked up her peasant skirt as her short legs lumbered over the remains of an old tree stump; its frayed hem trailed behind her in the dirt. She wasn't a picture-perfect beauty by anyone's definition. Her long, strawberry blonde hair was a tangled mess, she was overweight, had no fashion sense, and sported the social skills of a cornered badger.

Kaleb quickly ascended the stone steps cut into the rock face. The stairs wound around a steep ledge and led to its peak. When Kaleb reached the top he looked over its edge and shouted at Morgan, "Keep up girl. This isn't our first midnight run through the brambles."

Her sides ached as she started her climb. Morgan resented the boys for making her carry the cage; she was already lugging a heavy backpack. They told her the exercise would be good for her. She grumbled to herself, "You wouldn't even be here if it weren't for me."

She thought about the double meaning of her statement. Aside from the fact that she was Kaleb's willing taxi, it had been Morgan who introduced Kaleb to the world of witchcraft when they were young. They did all the things that kids with Barnes and Noble spell books did: chatted with the dead, cast spells, and hung out in cemeteries. Occasionally, they found a spell that actually worked.

One of those spells happened to be the love spell that brought Kaleb and Nick together. Four years ago, on the night before the summer solstice, Kaleb and Morgan each cast a love spell. Not a spell to make someone fall in love with them, but a spell to bring them the man of their choosing. Kaleb learned from that spell that it takes more than a list of adjectives to make a relationship. Morgan realized to specify that the man of her dreams be straight.

Nick had been fresh out of high school and loved older men. Kaleb had just turned twenty-two and kept insisting that he didn't count as an older man. They bonded over a number of occult and mundane commonalities, but for all their mutual interests they only lasted two months.

At first, they had hard time remaining friends, but Kaleb insisted on staying in touch. He said he refused to let their failed attempt at love separate their love for the craft, and their love of magic. Morgan was very pleased that they stayed friends. Shortly after the breakup, Kaleb learned of Morgan's secret crush on Nick. It was mostly because he was tall, dark, and morbid. He wasn't quite at the level of model, but his beauty was enough to ensnare unguarded hearts.

From what Kaleb had shared with her, Nick wasn't entirely gay. At least, not from her understanding of the term. He had dated girls in high school, and from what she could tell he liked to surround himself with beautiful women, present company excluded. Kaleb never dated women in high school. Their relationship had always been like siblings. Nick was different. She could feel it in her heart whenever he looked at her.

The full moon cast its light on Nick's angular face giving it an elfish quality. His walnut-colored eyes held enough mystery to keep Morgan guessing at his sexuality. Morgan found herself day-dreaming as she followed close behind him. She stared at his strong but not overly muscled arms, the designer jeans cupping his butt, and his curly dark hair. She sighed.

Morgan tripped on a loose rock and fell face first into the dirt. Lucy's cage went flying into the air. Nick deftly caught the small metal cage in his hands before it could hit the ground. Kaleb walked back down the path to offer Morgan a hand, but she had already picked herself up and dusted herself off.

•⁊•

"You okay?" Kaleb asked, mildly concerned by her face-plant.

Morgan groaned as she rubbed her knee. "I don't know how much further I can walk tonight. I need to sit down and have a smoke."

"Well it's a good thing we're here," Kaleb said to her.

Surrounded by overgrown rose bushes was a circular concrete slab the size of a small car. A large tree limb had fallen onto the path, Kaleb walked to it and dragged it from the center revealing a compass cut into the stone. The compass was the centerpiece of three trails joining together.

He pulled the branch behind him as he walked to the ledge overlooking the river. Kaleb closed his eyes and took in the fresh breeze coming off the water. He ran his fingers through his platinum hair and sighed with contentment. When he had finished enjoying the beauty of the river, he left the branch where it lay and walked back to the center of the compass.

Kaleb waited patiently for Nick and Morgan to join him inside the circle. Morgan retrieved her dagger from her purse. It wasn't so much a dagger as it was an ornate letter opener that she sharpened, but it served its purpose.

When all three were in place they began as they had done countless times before. Nick was always first to begin. He stepped to the eastern point on the compass and drew his short sword from its sheath on his side.

Nick called to the starry night sky, "Hail to the guardians of the Watchtowers of the East. Guardians of the winds and of the mind. I call upon you. Be with us." He bowed to Morgan who took her place in the south.

Morgan pointed her dagger to the southern sky. Her voice was full of confidence as she called, "Hail to the guardians of the Watchtowers of the South. Guardians of fire and of passion. I call upon you. Be with us now." She motioned to Kaleb who stood ready at the western point of the circle.

"Hail to the guardians of the Watchtowers of the West," Kaleb said as he faced west and pointed to the sky with the best dagger in his collection. The blade itself was adorned with a knot-work pattern. "Guardians of water and of the emotions. Be with us tonight. I summon you." Kaleb lowered his dagger and motioned for the others to join him.

Kaleb, Morgan, and Nick converged on the northern point of the circle and in unison called, "Hail to the guardians of the Watchtowers of the North. Guardians of earth and of mother. We call upon you. Be with us."

Kaleb stepped to the center of the circle pointed his blade upward and called out, "As above." He then pointed his dagger to the center of the compass and completed closing their circle of protection. "So below."

With the circle complete, Morgan eased her way to the ground taking in a sharp breath when she bent her knee. She lit a cigarette and closed her eyes.

She had been a smoker for many years now. Morgan started smoking so a high school crush would notice her. David had been the football star, and she was just a lowly band geek with a trombone. She thought smoking would impress him, but just ended up becoming a smoker. By now it had become such an ingrained part of her life that Kaleb no longer tried to convince her to quit.

Kaleb arranged four candles around the compass points. He lit a stick of dragon's blood incense and used its flame to ignite the candles. Kaleb closed his eyes and inhaled the aroma. He had always loved the metallic and spicy scent. He placed twelve quartz crystals around them to represent the wheel of the year. As Kaleb placed the last of the crystals, representing the month of October, he felt a shiver run down his spine.

Nick picked up the cage holding the tiny white mouse and began speaking to the frightened rodent in baby talk. "Who's a good sacrifice? Yes, you are."

Kaleb crossed his arms as he sat down next to Nick. "Can we please focus? This isn't a joke. We've been planning this for months."

Nick stared into the mouse's cage as he addressed Kaleb, "No, my dear, *you've* been planning this for months. I'm just here to collect whatever death magic is left over from little Lucy here. Don't get me wrong it's a great ritual, but you wouldn't take any of my suggestions."

Morgan took a slow drag off her cigarette. "It's not like we could if we wanted to. You know how hard it is to get a virgin these days? You put in your order online and then you're on a three year waiting list."

Kaleb frowned. "Sorry if I take summoning Merlin's shade a bit more seriously. I don't know of any other Samhain that coincides with a lunar eclipse." Kaleb looked up to the moon. The earth's shadow was already starting to cover a large section of the disc. He checked the time on his phone. This all had to be timed properly and he was getting no help from his friends.

"Is it so hard to call it Halloween?" Nick said as he reached into the cage and pulled out the mouse. He caressed Lucy's soft fur. "I guess sacrificing people would raise too many questions. Lucy will have to do. I bet you're a virgin, aren't you, Lucy? Who's a good little virgin? Yes, you are."

Kaleb rolled his eyes at Nick, and Morgan snickered. Unfortunately, the only person who seemed to care about this spell tonight was Kaleb. It didn't seem to matter to either Nick or Morgan if the summoning worked. Once again, it was up to Kaleb to corral their wandering minds.

"Oh lighten up," Nick chided. "It's not like we're actually going to get Merlin's shade to visit us." Nick grabbed a quart of Hawkeye Vodka and a two liter of Diet Mountain Dew out of his satchel.

Nick mixed himself a drink while Kaleb passed around the pages of the incantation to them. Morgan squinted and then pulled out her lighter to get a better look.

"Whoa girl!" Kaleb said as he blew out Morgan's lighter. "You burn that and you can go wait in the car."

"It's not going to do any of us any good if I can't see to read it," Morgan said defensively.

"Good thing I brought these." Nick handed them glow sticks and cords. He strung one around his neck and waited for the others to follow suit. "Seriously, I try to help and nobody appreciates me."

Kaleb took the glow stick and strung it around his neck. After he finished arranging their offerings around the circle he started reciting the incantation. "Powers of the night, facets of light, we draw you down to us tonight. Powers of the night, keepers of blight, we call upon you tonight." He looked over to Nick and Morgan to join him.

Morgan donned her glow stick and slowly stood. Nick held the mouse in his hand as they all recited in unison, "Powers of the sky, remember. Powers of the earth, remember. Rise and join us."

It was Morgan's turn. "Hallowed ground, obey this sound, open your gates." She pulled a round loaf of pumpernickel bread and a plastic bear full of honey from her backpack. "Hallowed ground, obey this sound, accept our offering." Morgan placed the bread in front of her and opened the bottle of honey. She squeezed it all out onto the bread.

In unison they called to the sky, "Powers of the sky, remember. Powers of the earth, remember. Rise and join us."

"Powers of the night, facets of light, we draw you down to us tonight. Powers of the night, keepers of blight, we call upon you tonight," Kaleb repeated. He took a bottle of chardonnay in his hands and uncorked the top. "Restless River Styx, let your waters be still so that the dead may pass. Let the blood of the moon sate your thirst." He poured the wine onto the bread.

13

In unison they called to the sky, "Powers of the sky, remember. Powers of the earth, remember. Rise and join us." They looked up at the moon. It had turned a deep red color. A shiver ran down his spine. He looked around they circle and it appeared as though they each had felt it.

Nick crouched down next to the mess of honey and wine. The tiny rodent squirmed to get free. "Merlin, keeper of wisdom. Merlin, keeper of time. We summon you. With the blood of our sacrifice we call you. Cross the river of the dead and speak with us tonight." He thrust his blade into the diminutive creature, impaling it with his short sword.

The earth's shadow finished its slow crawl across the face of the moon, the four candles simultaneously went out, the air became still, and a silver mist seeped from the ground at the center of the compass. Each of their faces conveyed fear and disbelief.

A voice boomed into Kaleb's mind. "*With this message let it be known, the Ladies of Avalon have fallen. The wards holding high magic from this world have failed. Heed my words all who cast in these times. What you call magic is as feeble as a single drop of rain.*"

Kaleb's throat was dry. No words would come to his lips. His heart pounded in his chest as he looked around the circle. Time slowed to a standstill. The silver vapor snaked around the compass, stopping at each of those gathered. One by one they all fell down.

As it reached Kaleb, visions came flooding into his mind. They flashed too quickly for him to make any sense of them: six women at the top of a tower made of black marble, blood, a bright crack forming in a dark sky. When the visions ended, Kaleb found himself lying on his back. His left hand was sticky from the wine and honey. He had never experienced such strong visions before. Whatever had caused the mist to form was done. The earth's shadow was no longer touching the moon.

Nick was the first to recover his voice. "Well, that was ..." He trailed off into silence.

•ᵛ•

It was four in the morning by the time Morgan finally returned home. Her mind was crawling with questions. It didn't seem as though anyone was quite ready to discuss what had occurred. Nick had driven off without so much as a goodbye, and when she dropped Kaleb off at home he was distant and vacant.

Upon returning home to her small trailer, Morgan went to her bathroom mirror. She pulled globs of honey out of her hair and sighed. Tears ran down her cheeks and mixed with the dirt that was stuck there. The boys had gotten off easy. They landed far enough away from the center of the compass that the worst they got was sticky fingers. She had fallen head first into the pumpernickel.

She focused magical energy into her body as she had done countless times before. If there was some new magic that was like an ocean compared to the minuscule amount they had been using, she was going to dive right in. She lit four white candles and placed them beneath her bathroom mirror. Her tired hazel eyes stared back at her.

The bathroom was tiny and cramped. Mercedes, her black cat, sat on the toilet watching her. Morgan began repeating a short incantation over and over. "Power of the moon, power of the sun. Let me be born again. Born into the image I hold in my mind." The cat tilted its head to the side.

The soft fluorescent lighting flickered overhead as she covered her face with her hands. After several minutes of drawing and channeling mystical forces to her will, she withdrew her hands and sighed. Her image in the mirror had not changed. Her skin was still blotchy, her hair didn't morph into a waterfall of golden curls, and her body was definitely not an hourglass figure.

Mercedes watched as she tried again and again until the sun peeked through the heavy curtains she had erected to keep it at bay. She washed her hair and climbed into her small twin bed. She looked around her bedroom and took in its filthy condition. The tattered remains of a long ago discarded sewing project mirrored her tattered emotional state. She hated her life, her body, and her job.

The beige paint on her walls was cracked and peeling. As proud as she was owning her own place, she was still a glorified renter with the bank as her slum lord. She told herself that she would eventually get around to repainting.

Morgan groaned as the to-do list in her mind expanded into a to-do nightmare. After trying to fall asleep for several hours she gave up. Stretching, she unburied herself from a cocoon of blankets and made her way to the kitchen which, like the rest of her life, was in shambles.

The sink was a graveyard of dishes. Cups and plates went in, but never came out. She took the last two clean bowls out of the cupboard and yawned. She cleaned the sleep from her eyes as she handed Mercedes her breakfast. Morgan cursed to herself as she brought a spoonful of cat food to her mouth.

Mercedes was happily lapping away at her bowl of cocoa-puff flavored milk when Morgan corrected her mistake. She made short work of her cereal. As she placed the bowl with its fallen comrades and turned to go back to the bedroom, she heard a strange voice enter her mind. "*You're a bitch, you know that?*"

Morgan froze. She looked down at the cat who was looking up at her from the floor. "*You heard me. Don't stare at me with your mouth open and give me back the bowl.*"

Morgan's mouth hung open in disbelief. "Okay, so first a talking mist and now a talking cat. I'm insane. I'm officially insane."

"*Obviously!*" the voice said snidely. *"Now put the bowl back on the floor and go clean my box.*"

Without taking her eyes off the cat, Morgan slowly backed up to the sink and fished out the finished bowl of cereal, still full of chocolate colored milk. Carefully she lowered it to the floor. Mercedes went back to happily lapping the remaining milk. Morgan stared at the cat in a dumbfounded silence.

The cat's head slowly swiveled until their eyes met. "*Now, clean my box.*" Morgan stood frozen. The cat tilted its head. "*Seriously, it's fucking disgusting.*"

•⊤•

Kaleb courted sleep for several hours, but to no avail. Thoughts of magic kept circling in his head. For over an hour he tried to remember the flashing images he had seen. The memories from the vision seemed to be evading him. He knew they were there, but just couldn't reach them.

He tossed and turned while trying to piece together any sense of what had occurred. It was hard to focus. His mind felt like someone had put their fingers in and were playing with his brain like silly putty.

Austin crawled onto the brown threadbare couch behind him. He was slightly shorter than Kaleb, so they fit together on the couch nicely. "When did you get home baby?" He put his arm around Kaleb and kissed the back of his neck. "Why didn't you come to bed?"

Kaleb pulled Austin's arms around him tighter. "I got home really late. I didn't want to wake you."

Austin's tenor voice spoke softly into his ear, "You're so sweet. I have to start getting ready for work. Let me carry you upstairs." Kaleb smiled as Austin kissed him and then picked him up.

They were both attractive, though Kaleb needed more reminding than Austin. Kaleb was slender to Austin's muscular physique. Kaleb was pale, and Austin's olive complexion never required tanning. The body part Kaleb loved about Austin most was his biceps. Austin scooped him up and carefully made his way through their small house. He took great care not to bump Kaleb into the china cabinet that held Austin's collection of porcelain Japanese ladies.

Kaleb's blue eyes were locked on Austin as they made their way up the stairs and to the bedroom. He luxuriated in the feeling of Austin's muscular arms holding him and he pressed his head against Austin's shoulder. "I love you."

"I love you too. Did you have a good time with your friends last night?" Austin asked as he gently lay Kaleb down onto their bed.

Kaleb yawned. He tried to keep his eyes open, but they felt heavy. "I have so much to tell ..." Kaleb started but his sentence was overcome by a yawn.

"Goodnight," Austin said as he tucked Kaleb into bed. "Sleep well little prince." Austin turned out the light and went back to getting ready for work.

Kaleb rolled over in bed. He closed his eyes. More thoughts about magic came flooding into his mind before he could drift off. As tired as he was he still couldn't manage to fall asleep. Hours passed and he was no closer than where he started. It was well after noon when he finally decided to give up trying.

His phone rang. "Hey girl," he said into the phone. Morgan began to ramble quickly and incoherently. He tried to get her to slow down. "Now calm down, you're not making any sense. Slow down and start from the beginning."

Morgan had started over but still was speaking too quickly to make any sense. He yawned. When she was finished rambling he asked, "Do you need me to come over?"

After a long silence she finally replied, "No, I'll go over there. No, wait, I'll come get you." She paused again. Kaleb was growing impatient. Morgan's voice was hushed as she said, "She's judging me with her eyes."

Kaleb was confused, but he had been through enough Morgan-meltdowns to know she required him to take a ride on the crazy train before helping her find an exit. "Excuse me?"

"Have you been listening to anything I've said?" she asked.

Kaleb sighed. "I heard everything you said, I just couldn't understand any of it."

The phone went quiet. "Sorry. I guess I need to start from the beginning." She went over the events of her morning while Kaleb tried his best to refrain from laughing.

When Morgan had finished the retelling, he held in the giggles that threatened to erupt from him and said, "Put Mercedes on the phone."

The line went silent. After a moment she came back to the phone and replied, "She says that I'm the only one that can hear her."

Kaleb rolled his eyes. He had entertained her crazy story long enough. Kaleb tried not to sound irritated. "Now isn't that convenient? So I know we're all excited about what happened last night, but a talking cat, come on?"

"Okay. So I did this spell last night. I wanted to make myself ..." Morgan paused again. "I wanted to be pretty." He could hear the sadness in her voice as she spoke those words. "It didn't work, but I think it did something."

Kaleb was skeptical. "Go on."

"Wait." She paused again. "Mercedes says that I'm an idiot if I think I managed to do anything other than bore her. She says to tell you that I'm her human and she is my familiar. Wow, Mercedes, really?" The line went silent and suddenly Morgan shouted, "You really need to stop it with that mouth of yours!"

Kaleb's headache was beginning to return as Morgan continued her one man show on the other end of the phone. "Morgan? Morgan. Morgan! If you want me to come over just ask. You don't have to make up stories."

"Forget it, I'll be right over. I can't be around this cat." He heard a door slam through the phone and the sound of her car's engine starting.

Kaleb rubbed his temples. "Should I call Nick?"

She sighed into the phone. "No, he'll just think I'm crazy."

Kaleb took a moment to recall all the insane bandwagons Morgan had jumped on year after year. She was all over Y2K, she even bought enough canned food to fill half her trailer. Then there was the documentary she watched about aliens shaping ancient civilization that she made him watch thirteen times. After that, there was the DVD she bought saying our galaxy was going to be colliding with another galaxy and that earth would end up with a second sun. And then there was the time she told everyone she had multiple personalities just so she could go around talking in a bad British accent. Kaleb rolled his eyes. "He wouldn't think that."

•T•

Morgan arrived at his house in a huff. He tried multiple times to get her to talk, but she just stared at her hands. They sat in a long drawn out silence before Morgan finally spoke, "She told me to clean her litter box, you know."

Kaleb decided to go with it. He shrugged. "You really should. It's disgusting."

She looked down at her hands and wrung them. "That's what she said." He let the silence drag on until she finally spoke again, "It's one thing to hear it from you, but she's mean about it."

Her eyes pleaded with Kaleb to placate her failings. When Kaleb didn't offer any empty words of encouragement she continued, "I mean, I don't know how you manage to keep this place so clean."

Kaleb patted her on the knee. "You know the only reason it's ever clean in here is because Austin is totally OCD. Now, I don't know what to think about this whole talking cat thing." He thought for a moment before continuing. "I guess that whatever happened last night could make you ..." He trailed his vowel as he tried hard to find the best way to make her feel better without accusing her of being schizophrenic or a liar. "your cat start talking to you."

She crossed her arms and stared at him. "Really? That's the best you can do? You couldn't lie to save your life."

He slapped her thigh. "Hey! No fair!"

She grinned. "All's fair in love and magic."

⁕

The trio decided to meet at the Thirteen Steps Cemetery after midnight. Kaleb and Morgan spent many of their nights here consoling the dead. They would rather have been consulting the dead but they often found themselves providing counseling services to the deceased instead. On a few occasions, they had to remind the ghosts that they were dead and the dead can't date the living.

The cemetery was called the Thirteen Steps because it was said during the day there were fourteen steps and at night there were thirteen. Somehow they always managed to count twelve. Most people avoided the cemetery because it was notoriously haunted. Despite this fact, or perhaps because of it, the cemetery was their favorite hangout spot.

It wasn't a popular cemetery for burials. There was the occasional newer grave, but mostly it was an old cemetery. Most of the gravestones were at least a hundred years old, some older. Families preferred the larger cemeteries in town to the small roadside cemeteries that dotted the rural countryside.

Nick pulled a bottle of vodka out of his bag and mixed it into a bottle of blue Gatorade. "So." He took a timid sip and nodded his head in approval. "Your cat can talk?"

"Yes, now can we please move on?" Morgan lit herself a cigarette and leaned back on a headstone. They all held their breath as a car drove past on the road down the hill from their sanctuary. The cemetery was closed after nine, but the hill and the line of trees provided nice cover from passing cars.

Unlike the state park they visited last night, they were constantly getting thrown out of the cemetery. As time passed and no state trooper pulled up the short drive, they resumed their conversation. Nick sighed dramatically. "Honestly, Morgan, this is what we're here to talk about. So, if you don't mind, tell Auntie Nick about Mercedes."

Morgan recited what she and the cat had spent their morning talking about. She spared no detail, causing Kaleb to flinch at a couple of great zingers that he would never have had the nerve to say to Morgan's face.

Nick nodded after she had finished. "You know, it does make sense. Witches and their cats have always been connected. Never thought about cats as telepathic before." He shrugged. "But it makes sense."

"It does?" Kaleb quickly corrected himself, "It does."

She smacked Kaleb and Nick. "Don't patronize me. I know you're just being nice."

Nick raised an eyebrow. "Seriously? When have you ever known me to be nice?" Kaleb gave him a skeptical glance, but Nick appeared to be sincere.

"Point taken," Morgan conceded. "Mercedes said we need to figure out this new magic." She felt encouraged for the first time all night. "I was thinking there's really only a couple of options."

Kaleb was puzzled. "What do you mean?"

She smiled and explained. "Well obviously we're talking about stuff that has been burned out of the past by the people in charge of history."

"You mean the Christians," Nick snorted in disgust.

"Exactly. So we need to know where there could be lost knowledge. I've been thinking about that a lot. We've only got a few options. We could hunt down other witches and ask them to share whatever grimoire has been passed down from generation to generation, but the trouble with that is we can't be sure if the spell book was written before or after this new magic."

"Merlin called it high magic." Kaleb stopped and so did everyone else. "What? He did."

Morgan rolled her eyes. "Problem is we don't know when *high* magic left the world. He said the Ladies of Avalon have fallen so it must have been around their time."

The trio looked over to the dark woods that fenced in the cemetery. A few feet into timber a shadow ran from one tree to another. "Yeah, I sense her too. She's been eavesdropping for the last few minutes," Nick said nonchalantly.

Morgan continued from where she left off. "Anyway, that method would have its obvious problems. We'd have to track down a lot of witches, narrow them down to which ones were raised witch or had witches in their ancestry, and then convince them to let us see their spell books. May not go over very well." A shiver ran down her spine as she felt the ghostly presence draw nearer. "You're getting on my nerves! What do you want?"

Nick leaned back onto a headstone. "Just ignore her. I've been asking her to spy on my ex. She's probably here to file her report with me." Once again, they a flickering shadow saw out of the corner of their eyes. Nick reached out with his mind to see what she had for him.

She fed an image into his mind of his ex. Nick and Jess had dated almost a year ago. Jess had been physically abusive. Nick had decided it was time to end their relationship when Jess decided the best way to say "I love you" was by throwing him across the living room. Nick had sent a few curses his way.

"How'd you convince her to be your spy?" Kaleb asked.

24

"Told her I'd help reunite her with her dead husband."

Morgan looked over at the tree line. "How's that going for you?"

Nick shrugged. "I'll get around to it eventually. Sorry, you were saying."

"Right. Where was I? Okay, yes, so what would our other options be? I was watching this documentary the other day about Edgar Cayce. He's the guy that they called a modern day Nostradamus." When no one interrupted her, she went on to say, "Anyway, he said that there is this hidden vault at the feet of the Sphinx. He said that it contained the lost knowledge of Atlantis." Her excitement was apparent. Her companions did not appear to share the same enthusiasm.

By her inflection she expected them to be more curious and excited than they felt. Kaleb was the first to let her down. "Come on, Morgan, I don't mean to disappoint you, but there's no way the Egyptian government is going to let three Americans visit the Sphinx with a backhoe. I really hope your next theory is at least plausible cause this is starting to make my head hurt." He rubbed his temples as Morgan withdrew into herself visibly. "Not at you, at the situation. Merlin came to us to say that high magic was back in the world, and we're sitting around grasping at straws figuring out how to use it."

"I think what Kaleb is trying to say is we need a way to learn about high magic that doesn't involve joining the census, going to door to door asking how many people live in their household and if their grandmother was a witch. Or wandering the desert with shovels," Nick added with more diplomacy than normal.

Though she still didn't feel very encouraged she provided her last suggestion. "Well the only other idea I could come up with would be to break into the Vatican Library." Kaleb threw up his hands. Nick pressed his palm against his forehead. Morgan slumped her shoulders in defeat.

Nick sighed. It would seem it was up to him to reign in the daydreams of Morgan. "All right, so none of those ideas are going to work. I have some ideas of my own."

Morgan looked to Kaleb, but he refused to come to her rescue. She said quietly, "I thought they were good."

"Right," Nick replied coldly. "So, I suggest we use what we know to learn more. I mean, maybe we could use low magic to help us learn how to use high magic. I have a few spells we could try."

As much as she didn't like her ideas getting shot down, she welcomed any opportunity to back up Nick. "I wrote a few over the years too. That love spell that we did." She looked to Kaleb. "It wasn't really a love spell. It was more like a 'come to me' spell. A compulsion spell, maybe?" She waited for Kaleb to agree.

The stillness of the cemetery crept over them as they considered their options. It felt incredibly appropriate to use what they knew about magic to learn high magic. After eternity reminded them they had prior obligations, they snapped out of their reverie and focused on the task at hand.

"So we use the spells we already know?" Kaleb asked skeptically.

Nick tapped his lips with his index finger. "Not quite. We rewrite the spells we already know to get them to do what we need them to do. I like the idea of using Morgan's love spell."

"You do?" Morgan and Kaleb asked in unison.

After a dramatic pause, Nick rose from the grave he was sitting on and began to pace. Their eyes were fixated on him and he smiled. He luxuriated in their bated breath. "I do."

"I have my spell book in the car. Do you want me to grab it?"

A smile crept across Nick's face. "That would be ideal."

Morgan scrambled down the stone stairs and to her car. Dotingly she obeyed. In a flurry she dug through the discarded cigarette packs, empty cans of energy drinks and fast food bags that decorated her car's floorboards. Her hand finally fell upon the soft leather-bound tome that stored her personal spells.

She rushed back up the stairs and stopped. Nick and Kaleb were talking quietly. Most likely about her. Her feelings fell into her feet and they became as heavy as lead. She wanted so much for Nick to like her, and now she was just their spell-runner.

Even though she knew their history, she couldn't help but read into their body language. Kaleb nodded in agreement with whatever Nick was saying. Nick stood above the sitting Kaleb, his seductive features on display. She fought the thought that they were working to eliminate her from the group.

Kaleb knew how much she loved Nick, and by now Nick must also know. They laughed. The frown she wore deepened as she teetered between frustration and tears. Morgan set her jaw and strode back into the cemetery.

They didn't hear her approach and she caught the tail end of their conversation before she was discovered. "Breaking into the Vatican? Come on! She needs to stop sniffing paint," she heard Kaleb say.

She threw the book down at Nick's feet. "Found it." Morgan started to storm back to her car defeated when Kaleb leapt to his feet and began stammering an apology.

Nick was less apologetic. He knew their conversation had been overheard by Morgan and he knew she was upset by it. "What?" He interposed himself between her and the gate. "Morgan, seriously? You can't expect us not to laugh."

She tried to walk around him but he stepped in front of her. "You were laughing at me."

Nick chewed his bottom lip for a moment which she found to be adorable. She had a hard time staying mad at Nick. He reminded her of a deranged Robin Hood. Massacring the rich to feed the poor. She could see the wheels clicking through his eyes and he finally replied with a shrug. "You got me."

Kaleb picked the book up out of the grass and began thumbing through its pages. He recognized several of the spells from the years they had been casting together and a few new ones. Her handwriting was difficult to decipher. The letters ran together and sloped upward as they reached the edge of the page, but eventually he found what they were looking for.

They each drew their blades and held them to the sky. Morgan began the consecration of the circle by calling upon the Guardians of the South and they again congregated at the northern point of their circle. When the circle was complete, they looked to Nick for guidance.

"What?" Nick asked as he sat back down. "Don't look at me, this isn't your first time re-writing a spell. Go ahead Morgan."

Her spirits were once again lifted. It wasn't very often that Nick trusted her to guide the casting. "Well, we don't have any of the spell components, but I think we've been doing this long enough not to need any."

Nick smiled. "They're only to help focus after all. What were the components and I'll be sure to use the appropriate energy?"

"Lodestone to draw them in, rose petals to signify love, lavender because I like how it smells, and rose quartz to hold the energy while we cast." It sounded too simple now that she voiced it. Morgan decided that later she'd have to beef up her love spell.

Nick began, concentrating his mind to the task at hand. He envisioned a lodestone and its magnetism. His hands reached out while his mind searched for the magnetism of the earth. Once he found his center he began in rhyme. "As above, so below. The truth I wish to know. Bring to me one who will be a teacher to me." He repeated the words three times and fed his words with the magic that he could reach. His mind heaved at currents of mystical power and molded them to his will. They wrapped around the words and he could feel them taking form.

At the end of his third repetition he changed the words, "A power beyond this world. I call upon thee. With these words I summon thee. Show me what I need to see. By the powers that be, I summon thee." He put the strength of his will behind his words as he repeated them three times. After he reached his final repetition he let the energy he had been collecting burst free.

Next was Kaleb. He felt uncomfortable, but couldn't understand why. Something within him stirred restlessly as he started his incantation. He envisioned a rose quartz in his mind, collecting the energy of his words and his emotions. He pulled the magical forces to him as he spoke in rhyme, "Heavens above, I bid thee do my will. Let my heart be still. Bring to me a teacher, to show me the way."

Morgan closed her eyes and put her own emotions into the spell. Quietly she mirrored his words, but with her own flair. She twisted his words to her own will. Austin wasn't good enough for Kaleb. Though Kaleb was blinded by love, she could see through Austin and his lies.

For some reason, Morgan and Austin never got along. From the day they had met he didn't like her. Kaleb tried to get them to spend time together, but Austin always had somewhere else to be. He was always either at his brother's or his cousin's. Morgan didn't trust Austin. No one spends that much time with family.

She also didn't like the fact that Austin had a drinking problem. After being arrested for driving while intoxicated and then again for driving Kaleb's car while his license was suspended, Kaleb decided it would be easier to sell the car than worry about Austin being tempted to get behind the wheel.

Aside from his luscious black hair, dimples, and biceps, she didn't know what Kaleb saw in Austin. Since they were casting love spells tonight, she would see to it that together they called someone who could not only help Kaleb grow, but also be someone he deserved.

Kaleb recited the words to his spell, oblivious to Morgan's intrusion. "By the gods below and above, I cast this spell with love. Bring to me the one who will be a teacher to me." Despite Kaleb's platonic intentions Morgan helped to ensure the spell that emanated from Kaleb bore more than a hint of love.

It was Morgan's turn next. She looked at Nick and her heart fell. She wanted him to love her, but she knew it would never happen. He was her dark prince. There were only a few things stopping her from having what she desired, and they were all anatomical.

She could try to use magic to force him to love her. Her heart said go for it, but her head told her to stop. There was only way to free herself from the torment. She had to find someone else to pine over. Someone else to love. Someone else to discard her like yesterday's newspaper.

"Good goddess of the hearth, and of fire. I call upon you, Hestia. Bring to me a flame to light my way. Bring to me a mate who will show me the way. Good goddess Hestia, bring him to me." She felt the forces of the earth stirring below her and the energy of the sky circling above her. She reached out with her mental hands and guided them to her.

"Let his mind be enticing, let his soul be ensnaring. Hestia, let his heart be my home, let his passions be my catacomb. May his eyes be as deep as the sea, may his spirit be free, may he teach me all that I need to know, may he show me what I need to grow." She let the spell explode from her.

She opened her eyes and saw Kaleb with arms crossed and an eyebrow raised. "That sounded more like a love spell to me."

Morgan grinned from ear to ear. "I can't help it if I was the only one who thought of finding a lover *and* a teacher."

Lessons in Reality

Snow crunched under Kaleb's feet as he made his way home from the bus stop. He was exhausted. Work had been terrible. He caught himself fantasizing about sending a current of electricity through the phones lines to maim and destroy. If one more person called to yell at him about their cell phone bill he was going to lash out.

Magic was supposed to solve all his problems. He and Morgan had dreamed of this day since they were casting their first spells. They said someday magic would be their life. They wanted to read tarot or help the police find missing persons. So far all magic had given them was a headache.

They had tried countless times to get high magic to work, but really had no idea where to start. Morgan had managed for one night to change her eyes from green to brown, but Kaleb knew her eyes had always been hazel. It was depressing. They couldn't even manage to conjure a simple ball of light from thin air. The only one who had experienced high magic so far was Morgan, but Kaleb wondered if her talking cat was just another way to get attention.

Kaleb loved Morgan like a sister, but at times her antics got annoying. On occasion, she was amusing with her crazy stories and wild theories, but for the most part, Kaleb ignored them. He didn't think she was a liar. She believed in every conspiracy theory she ever spouted out.

The walk from the bus stop was freezing. He huddled within his coat to conserve body heat. Kaleb hated December. He hated the cold, but he also hated the holidays. It always felt like an excuse for people who were miserly to pretend for one night that they were generous.

What bothered him most was Austin's family. He got to watch all the girlfriends of Austin's brothers open their presents and after almost three years there still wasn't one for him. It wasn't the gift that was important, it was the feeling of being singled out.

His own family wasn't much better. As much as his mother had accepted Austin as a part of his life, his father still referred to Austin as his roommate.

The relationship he had with his father was awkward at best. Kaleb always had a lingering feeling that he was a disappointment. His mother said that his father just didn't know how to handle Kaleb being gay.

He decided last summer, when he gave his father the car he could no longer afford, not to mention the pride bumper stickers all over the back. After his dad spent a few months driving it around town, his sister finally explained to him what "God Save the Queens" really meant. His father never spoke of the incident, thought he knew it bothered him.

Originally the revelation that he was gay sent his mother into a tailspin. As difficult as it had been, Kaleb had decided to cut his family out of his life. For several years he distanced himself from them. Luckily, his siblings and his mother had finally come around to accepting him for who he was.

His mother had made leaps and bounds since he had come out. It was the same year that he met Nick that his mother had invited him home for the holidays. It was the first time they had spoken since Kaleb had finished high school. The only condition he had to joining his family for Christmas was that his boyfriend, Nick, was also welcome. His mother was open to the idea. Unfortunately, Nick was not.

Every year he would invite Nick to join him for Christmas dinner with his family, but every year he was turned down. Lately the excuse had been that Nick couldn't stand to be around Austin, but Kaleb thought there was more to it. He knew that Nick was a loner, but he never understood why.

Kaleb never liked being alone. He jumped from relationship to relationship. Austin was his longest. They had been together for two and a half years and were still going strong. Prior boyfriends had only managed to last from three to six months. No matter what the reason for the relationship ending, Kaleb was always the one getting dumped.

His relationship with Austin had been pretty good so far. Kaleb loved Austin. Even when fighting, they always managed to work it out in the end. They had a pretty good life. Kaleb provided financially and Austin took care of the house. Austin worked a part-time job as a waiter so they would have more time to spend together, yet for some reason there never seemed to be enough time.

As Kaleb walked the frigid streets he reminisced about the night they met. Kaleb had gone out to the bar by himself because Morgan was working and his friendship with Nick had yet to bloom. Austin was sitting at the bar. He looked at Kaleb and said, "Help me." It turned out that Austin was on a terrible blind date, and Kaleb was his savior.

From that moment on they were inseparable. Within three months they were living together and by their fourth they were taking midnight strolls through the suburbs howling like cats in heat to see how many of the neighborhood dogs they could infuriate. Even though he was a couple of years older than Kaleb, they both shared a youthful humor.

But humor didn't hold its own against the tide of depression that came naturally to Kaleb. The season to be jolly was always the hardest. He felt like a failure. Magic had returned to the world, yet there was nothing he could do with it. His heart sank into self-loathing. If only he could remember the visions he had when Merlin came to him. If only he were a better witch.

Something rolled inside of him. He felt as though his mind were being pulled apart from within. He let the feelings overtake him. He didn't notice the patch of ice he stepped onto. He remembered falling, but not hitting the ground. He could barely make out the figments of light poles rushing past him. Kaleb was falling in slow motion as the ground sped past under his feet.

Whatever he was feeling was taken over by panic when the ground did not rise to meet his face. All of his vigor was drained away and he felt a deep sleep greet him. He let his face fall on the pillow of darkness before him.

···

Morgan parked in front of Kaleb's house. The fog of her breath was thicker than the cigarette smoke. The heater in her car only worked when it wanted to. She banged on the dashboard but it still refused to spit out anything warmer than polar. Morgan looked through the barely scraped windshield and couldn't see any sign that Kaleb or Austin were home.

Work had been frustrating. She hated her job. Though it was nice to work at the same place as her best friend, she only got to see him on breaks that the gods of scheduling would allow. Today their overseers saw fit to allow them lunch together. They spent their dinner break discussing what the world will become now that magic was returned, or at least how it should be.

Whatever happened to magic solving all their problems? She was still single, still fat, and still depressed. Wasn't life supposed to be easier now? The only thing magic had given her was a cat that had a lower opinion of her life than she did.

She never had any luck with men. Her last boyfriend had been in high school, and Kaleb ended up being gay. Sadly she was still a virgin. She had a knack for falling for gay guys. Her crush on Nick had become an unhealthy obsession. She knew it, but had no intention of doing anything about it.

She loved this time of year because it gave her an excuse to buy Nick a nice present. Yule was a week away and she still hadn't decorated her trailer. Winter solstice had always been her favorite holiday. She tried to get Kaleb into the spirit, but he was always too distracted by opposing Christmas to actually enjoy Yule.

She was supposed to pick him up after her shift ended. Morgan looked at her phone. He should have been home two hours ago, but there was no sign of anyone. For a second she wondered if he and Austin had gone off to do something together, but dismissed that as ridiculous. "Like Austin would take Kaleb with him," she said, laughing to herself.

Morgan gave up on waiting and knocked at the door, but didn't get an answer. The lights were off so she let herself in. She justified her actions by equating it to the cold wind. "No reason for me to freeze my ass off while I wait," she said to no one.

She hummed to herself Morgan made her way to the fridge. She idly clawed through the contents: some cottage cheese, a quart of milk, and some deli meat that wouldn't be missed. Morgan opened the milk, caught a whiff of the contents and cringed. After putting the milk back in the fridge she grabbed a bottle of beer instead. She turned back to finish making herself a snack. Her foot caught on something and she tripped.

"Kaleb? What are you doing on the floor?" There was no response. "Oh my god, are you okay?" A bottle of beer crashed to the tiled floor, its contents forgotten.

.˙.

The machines monitoring Kaleb's vitals sounded their alarm as he woke with a start. His sudden movement almost yanked the IV out of his arm. Morgan was asleep in the chair next to the bed and Nick was on his other side holding his hand. His head throbbed with pain and he felt like he had just ran a marathon.

His eyes fell first on the electronics monitoring his vitals. There was someone holding his hand. Fear gripped his heart as he struggled to remember where he was and how he arrived. The last thing he remembered was struggling to regain his balance as the cold night attempted to steal his warmth.

Kaleb's body contracted involuntarily. "Oh good, you're awake," Nick said as he quickly released Kaleb's hand. As much as he hated to admit it, he still cared a great deal about Kaleb's well-being.

For several minutes Kaleb tried to form words, but his throat wouldn't cooperate. Nick handed him a glass filled with ice. Kaleb looked around the room in a stunned silence. He saw Morgan half dozing in a chair across the room, and a television playing the last few shows of Adult Swim. When he managed to speak his voice was hoarse. "What happened?"

Morgan awoke at the sound of his voice. She shook her head to clear the fatigue. "I should be asking you that. What do you remember? I found you sprawled out on the kitchen floor passed out." Morgan's eyes were red and blotchy. "You've been unconscious for three hours. You scared the crap out of me. The doctors have no idea what's wrong with you."

"Last thing I remember was walking home from the bus stop. Where's Austin?" Kaleb rubbed his forehead.

Morgan exchanged a glance with Nick. "We tried calling him. I'm sure once he checks his phone he'll be here. I'll try calling again."

"And I'll go let a nurse know you're awake," Nick added.

"Did you try texting?" Kaleb asked, but they had already left the room. He picked up his phone from the tray table and began texting.

When Morgan and Nick were far enough from the room Nick turned to Morgan and grabbed her arm to stop her from calling. "We both know he's at the bar. I say we go find that asshole and drag him back here by the ear." Morgan sighed but nodded.

After stopping by the nurses' station to let them know the situation, they made their way back to Kaleb's room. Morgan beamed at him. "We're going to go grab a bite to eat. They want to hold you overnight for observation, so we'll be back in an hour or so. In case they ask, I'm your sister and Nick is my husband." Nick smacked her in the arm.

It was approaching midnight when they pulled up to Alexander's Garden. They stopped several people to ask if anyone had seen Austin. For the next half hour they searched the dark corners, the patio, the upstairs bar, the dance floor, and the bathrooms. Eventually they gave up and went back to the hospital.

Nick smiled at a nurse as they turned the corner and entered Kaleb's room. They walked right into Austin. Morgan pumped her fist in silent fury and smiled. "Glad you could make it."

He ignored her indignation and sat by Kaleb's bedside. "Baby, I came as fast as I could. I'm so sorry. I was over at my cousin's. I didn't realize my phone was on silent. I'm so sorry. Are you okay? The nurse said you were unconscious when they brought you in. What happened?"

Kaleb sat up in bed. "I think I figured out what happened. I think that I teleported."

Austin dropped his hand. "Be serious! I heard you were in the hospital and I got so worried. Don't make jokes. I read that text you sent me and took the first cab I could get. You had me so worried."

"I am being serious. I stepped on some ice a block away from the bus stop and hit the kitchen floor. What other explanation is there?" Kaleb looked pleadingly into Austin's eyes.

Austin smiled as he looked down at Kaleb. "The only thing I care about right now is that you're okay. I'm here now, and I'm not leaving your side until you're ready to come home."

Kaleb tried to protest, but Austin's lips met his and he forgot his words. "I love you."

"I love you too." Austin replied.

"It's getting late, I think we should head home," Morgan said as she nudged Nick towards the door.

"How was dinner?" Kaleb asked.

Morgan's stomach growled. "Light."

•⸪•

"All right, show us how it's done," Nick said to Kaleb as he huddled inside his black winter coat. The silver faux fur that lined the hood was more for show than warmth, but it did its job well enough. The wind cut into their hands and faces as they stood at the street corner where he first teleported.

Morgan refused to leave her car, but cracked the window so she could add her two cents. Her fingers were rosy colored icicles which she rubbed together furiously. "Can we just get this over with so we can all go home?"

Kaleb wasn't too excited about what they were about to try. The last time he teleported he ended up in the ICU. There was a strange feeling inside him, as though his subconscious was rolling its eyes at him. Kaleb stepped out onto the ice. Nothing happened.

"Maybe if you try falling," Morgan said from her relatively warm vantage. Kaleb lost his footing and fell flat on his back. "Or not."

Nick offered Kaleb a hand which only served to pull Nick out onto the patch of ice as well. His arm flailed as he tried to maintain his footing, but Kaleb hadn't let go of his other hand and they fell together. Their feet tried to find footing as their legs slipped and slid, and knocked them back down. Their arms rotated like windmills in their desperate attempt to find tractable ground.

After a few failed attempts at standing, Kaleb crawled back off the ice on his hands and knees. "You guys know I'm not really into back-breaking labor, right? I'm too fragile," he said as he reached the edge of the ice patch and stood up. He rubbed his aching back and whimpered.

"I'll have to second that motion," Nick added, as he rubbed his elbow.

Morgan turned off the ignition and stepped out into the frigid air. "You boys are going to give up after one try? I'd say stop acting like women and grow a pair, but that'd give women a bad name." She put her hands in the pockets of her yellow parka giving her the appearance of an angry lemon.

Kaleb stretched his back while Morgan stormed up to the patch of ice. "Go ahead, put us boys to shame."

"If you can do it, any of us should be able to. You just have to have the right motivation, conviction, and power," she said confidently, despite the lack of confidence in her eyes. She rubbed her hands together before she stepped out onto the ice.

Her feet fell out from her. "Oh shit, oh shit!" she cried as her feet flew out from beneath her and she cracked her head on the sidewalk. While she lay prone on the icy ground she asked innocently, "So, how does hot cocoa sound?"

•¦•

Winter solstice was upon them. Morgan had decorated her trailer with all the traditional Yuletide amenities. There was mistletoe hanging above the door. A small pine tree decorated with flowers, fruits, and ornaments stood stoically by the entryway. Its slender, frail branches tried in vain to shoulder the burden, but slouched instead in defeat.

Austin sipped at his rum and eggnog while Kaleb opened his gift. Despite their mutual distaste for one another, Morgan and Austin were being fairly civil toward one another.

"Austin," Kaleb squealed in delight as he opened his gift. "You are so sweet." He wrapped his arms around his boyfriend, but never let go of the quartz sphere he had unwrapped. "It's beautiful."

"I thought you'd like it." Austin responded. His voice was sweet but he made a face at Morgan that conveyed his advantage. The tarot deck she had bought for him was partially unwrapped and sitting at Kaleb's feet. He knew what Kaleb liked, and he loved to rub that knowledge in Morgan's face every chance that he was given. His gift to Morgan was less inspired. The wrapping paper was more exciting than the six books of logic puzzles he had gifted her.

Their presents for Nick were still neatly wrapped beneath Morgan's sad tree. As was tradition, Nick could not join them. He was spending Yule elsewhere. Morgan never really knew where that elsewhere was, but Kaleb appeared to be fine with it and that she trusted Kaleb's judgment.

Mercedes peered over a pile of dirty laundry on the kitchen floor. The cat watched as Kaleb kissed Austin. Her eyes narrowed to slits. "*I think I'm going to be sick,*" the cat said, mostly to herself.

Morgan glared at her from the living room. She reclined in her chair, trying to ignore the foul-mouthed feline. In her mind she replied to the cat. "*If you have such a problem with two men showing affection for each other, then you can go be a stray.*"

The cat stretched and walked across the kitchen floor. She walked into the living room and considered her options for seating. Daintily she pawed her way across the coffee table. Her head tilted back to look at Morgan before jumping into Austin's lap. "*I don't have a problem with gay people, I have a problem with the fact that you're so pathetic. I mean really. Every year, it's the same shit. You invite Kaleb and Austin over, and when they leave, you get all mopey because you can't get a man.*"

Morgan picked up a squirt bottle and began to advance on the feline. Austin put up his hand to stop her. "She's just being friendly." He petted her and the cat arched her back. "You just want to be loved, don't you?"

The voice in Morgan's head laughed. "*I'd prefer a romp, but a good scratch will do.*"

Morgan swatted the cat on the head and she jumped from Austin's lap. "Bad kitty!"

"*Hey, it's not like you weren't thinking it too.*" Mercedes licked her imaginary wound from the safety of the coffee table. "*I think the only reason you don't like Austin is that he's fucking Kaleb, and not you.*"

"I will have you spayed," Morgan spat, furiously squirting water at the cat. The cat fled into the dark reaches of Morgan's bedroom. She plopped back down in her armchair.

"Don't you think that was a little uncalled for?" Austin asked, the corner of his mouth raised in disgust.

Kaleb exchanged a glance with Morgan. Despite his near-death teleportation, he was still unconvinced that Morgan had developed the ability to speak with animals.

"You hang out with gay guys because you're a fat slob that no straight man would fuck," the cat called from the safety of Morgan's bedroom. The boys only heard an angry yowl, but Morgan threw a pillow in the cat's direction.

"You have no idea what I put up with," Morgan said as she picked up her glass of eggnog and took a drink.

"I was thinking of getting a cat," Austin offered, trying to change the subject. "There's this adorable Persian at the Animal Rescue League. I thought he was the cutest thing ever."

"When did you go there?" Kaleb asked.

Mercedes flew out of the back bedroom and into Austin's lap. *"Persian? I love me some Persian tail. How old is he? What's his name? Is he neutered?"*

Morgan picked up the cat by the scruff of the neck and hurled her back toward the bedroom. "You just don't quit!"

Austin stood up and crossed his arms. His anger was inspired by the rum that he'd been drinking. "Just be nice to her Morgan. I happen to like cats."

Two months of being belittled and constantly cussed out had finally gotten to her. Morgan threw her hands in the air and shouted, "If you like her so much, than you can have her!"

"*What?*" The response from the bedroom was full of fury. "*I cannot believe you would just throw me away like that.*" Mercedes slowly climbed her way to the top of the laundry heap on the kitchen floor and her pupils dilated to become saucers. "*After all that we've been through together? After all that I've done for you? This is how you repay me? Wow. You are such a bitch. Just when I was about to tell you what I knew about magic.*"

"Wait, what?" Morgan said to the cat.

"I said, I like cats," Austin replied, oblivious to the other half of the conversation. "Kaleb doesn't like cats, which is why we don't have one."

"*Hold up, Kaleb doesn't like cats?*" Mercedes asked indignantly. "*You've got to be fucking kidding me. Don't tell me, he's a dog person.*"

"You do not get off that easy." Morgan scowled at the cat.

Kaleb dragged Austin back down onto the couch. "I never said I didn't like cats, it's just that I'm allergic. Why didn't you tell me you went to the Animal Rescue League?"

Austin pulled away from Kaleb. "Am I supposed to get your approval now? Should I put together a schedule for you to sign off on? Fuck, Kaleb. You're starting to really piss me off. Stop being so controlling."

"*Oh, this is going to be good,*" Mercedes said as she avoided another pillow being thrown in her direction.

"I wasn't saying that," Kaleb replied. "Why are you doing this?"

"Oh please," Austin said as he got up from the couch. "Why don't you tell me why you're spending so much time with your ex? Maybe I should ask him why he never seems to be around when we're together."

"Are you kidding me with this shit?" His own fury of rum was starting to build. He had been accused of many things in his life, but there was one thing he never tolerated, and that was being accused of being a cheater.

"Yeah, I get it. You guys are 'friends,'" Austin said snidely as he made quotation marks with his fingers. "I'm leaving. Morgan, thank you for a lovely evening." The sarcasm was palpable.

"Um, no problem." It was the best Morgan could get out before the chaos erupted.

"This isn't over," Kaleb yelled as he grabbed Austin's wrist. Austin had already managed to put on his coat and was heading for the door when Kaleb stepped in front of him. "I am not sleeping with Nick. I am not having an affair with Nick. Hell, I'm not even interested in Nick."

Austin pulled his hand away from Kaleb. His lips spewed the pain and disdain he felt in his heart. "Sure you aren't. You two are just hanging out every night. Sure. Nothing's going on. We haven't had sex all week because you've been too tired. I bet Nick's been keeping you up late, hasn't he?"

"Nick and Kaleb are just friends," Morgan tried to interject.

"*Let the grown-ups fight, honey. You're interrupting my entertainment.*" Mercedes curled up on the couch to watch the discourse.

"Just stay out of this, Morgan. We're not friends! Got it? You've never liked me, and I've never liked you. I don't know why Kaleb is friends with you. And by the way, this wasn't a lovely evening. Your house is a mess and the only redeeming thing about you is your cat. I'd rather walk home then be here!"

Austin slammed the door behind him. Kaleb's mouth was still open. He slumped his shoulders in defeat. Morgan drew Kaleb into a hug. "I'll get some blankets for you."

Kaleb let Morgan hug him, but didn't return the embrace. His mind was still reeling at the rapid change of events. "Where did that even come from? We were having a good time, and them I asked him about adopting a cat."

"Which I still approve of," Mercedes interjected from the sofa.

Morgan shot the cat a death stare. As much as she disliked Austin, and as much as she wanted to point out his many flaws, the spirit of Yule was about being thankful. Despite being thankful that Austin was gone, she managed to say, "I'm sure it was just the rum talking. I shouldn't have agreed to give him any. I'm sorry."

Kaleb was still dumbfounded. Their relationship had been strained ever since magic's return. Austin was raised Baptist, and he had deep reservations against anything occult. For years that never had been an issue, but now that magic was becoming a larger part of Kaleb's life he wanted Austin to be a part of it, but Austin didn't want the same.

"I just don't understand why he's mad at me," Kaleb finally said. He sank back down onto the sofa defeated.

"I think the best thing you can do is give him time," Morgan responded. She put her arm around Kaleb as he started to cry. Kaleb's body shook as the sobs overtook him. "Let it out," Morgan said gently.

"I think the best thing you can do is give him a Xanax and call the shrink. That boy has issues. Are you just going to sit around and encourage this shit, or are you going to do something about it?" Mercedes asked, curling up into Kaleb's lap.

"Mercedes has a point," Morgan said while Kaleb cried on her shoulder. "She thinks Austin has issues, and they aren't yours. He needs medication."

The cat purred as Kaleb petted her. *"I meant Kaleb."*

Kaleb wiped the tears from his eyes with his sleeve. "I wish you would stop with the whole talking cat bit. You don't have to talk through a third party, Morgan. Or should I say, Bernadine." It was the name of one of her falsified personalities from their youth.

"Don't take this out on me," Morgan said as she pulled away from him.

Mercedes started cleaning herself and added her two cents, *"He's got a point. You aren't really the sanest crayon in the box."*

Morgan glared at the cat. *"I hope you get mange."*

"Wow. This is the thanks I get for being honest. Well I'd wish herpes on you, but you'd have to get fucked first!" The cat yowled as she leapt from the sofa and ran to the back bedroom, a pillow on her heels.

Morgan took Kaleb's hand and knelt before him. "I know you don't believe me, but I wouldn't lie to you. Not this time at least. Mercedes is an evil cat, and apparently my familiar. Nick believes me, and I hope that you can too."

"Don't bring Nick into this. Austin already thinks I'm sleeping with him," Kaleb said as he fell back into hysterical tears. His voice broke and he couldn't say anymore. His body convulsed as he sobbed.

After calming Kaleb down and making a bed for him on the sofa, Morgan went to her bedroom to confront the cat. Though Mercedes wasn't anywhere in the open, she knew that the cat was hiding somewhere in her room. *"I am not finished with you, cat!"*

Without sound, it was difficult to tell where the cat's "voice" was coming from. *"Well, that's too bad, because I've had enough of you. Go away. You're interrupting my beauty rest, something you know nothing about."*

"You are going to tell me everything *you know about magic! Do you think I'm going to feed you, shelter you, and listen to your rotten mouth without getting something out of it?"* Morgan lifted the bed skirt and peered into the darkness under the bed.

The cat shot out from below the bed and was caught by the scruff of her neck. *"I'll tell you everything I know on one condition."*

"What's that?" Morgan asked, pinning the cat to the floor.

"Don't have me spayed."

Morgan considered her options. *"I promise."*

She let the cat go and it jumped onto her dresser. *"I will tell you about magic when you are ready. For now, I will tell you that we are bonded, and that I am your familiar. A witch's familiar is a very powerful ally."*

"All right, fine. So what can you do?"

The cat raised its head to its full regal height. *"I will reveal my powers to you when the time is right. For now, I would like a bowl of cream."*

Morgan rolled her eyes and began to get ready for bed. "Yeah? I'd like a date. Looks like neither one of us are getting what we want."

Tides of Change

Despite the cold breeze, it was the first warm day of spring. Overhead the sky was clear and the sun was shining bright. The trio converged at the picnic bench just down the hill from the Thirteen Steps Cemetery. As much as they enjoyed the cover of darkness, Kaleb had insisted that he and Morgan call in sick to work so they could enjoy the beautiful day.

Kaleb had yet to duplicate his teleportation, and his inability frustrated them all. "So what all have we tried?" Kaleb asked as he stared into the trees. The trees hadn't begun to bud, but he was still hopeful that winter was finally over.

Morgan crushed another cigarette beneath her shoe. They'd been at this for over an hour and the pile of butts was beginning to grow. She let out a painful groan. "We've tried summoning a teacher, and we all know how long summoning spells can take."

"I've been writing new spells," Nick provided. "Still no visible results, but I'm still hopeful."

Nick provided no further explanation. Kaleb tilted his head and gave him a sideways stare. "Evil spells?"

"No, of course not. I'm on a diet. All the great taste of regular evil, with half the karma." Nick radiated the demure of a southern belle.

"Good, because I've been trying some new spells too." Kaleb had bought every spell book he could find online. Despite having a brand new occult library, he was still no closer to figuring out high magic then he was in

November. Kaleb retrieved several of the books from his backpack and began thumbing through them.

Austin was not pleased that he had spent the majority of his tax return on books, but Kaleb made up for it by having a dozen roses sent to his work and a day of pampering. After their fight on the winter solstice, Kaleb had become more attentive to Austin. Regardless of how doting Kaleb was it didn't seem to matter, when Austin wanted a fight he would bring up Nick. He even found a way to tie Nick into the sudden influx of books.

"Okay, let's go back over what Merlin said." Morgan said.

Nick shook his head. "We've been over this a thousand times. I doubt we're going to find any clues. It was vague, and it was totally unhelpful."

"Well, he said what we call magic is as feeble as a single rain drop. I mean, that has to have some significance. Right?" Morgan countered.

Kaleb closed the book he was reading and sat it down on the table next to him. "I'm sure it has some significance to Merlin. I really don't know what to do, guys. I know you're looking to me to be the leader, but I'm really lost right now."

Nick laughed. "You're the leader? I mean, really? You can't even go to the grocery store by yourself. What qualifies you as a leader?"

"Well, somebody's gotta be in charge. I don't see any of you stepping up." Kaleb crossed his arms defiantly.

Morgan's stomach growled. "I have to agree with Nick on this one. You like being in control, but that doesn't make you a good leader. I'd like to think of us as a democracy. Right now, my vote is that we pack up for the day and get some food."

Kaleb sighed. With sullen reluctance he packed his books away and shouldered his backpack.

"What's wrong, girl? Did your husband not pack you a sack lunch?" Nick asked sarcastically.

Morgan shot Nick a glare that said to drop it. It wasn't that Nick hadn't been made aware of the Yuletide fight, it was that he hadn't been made aware who the fight had been centered around. "I think we need to go easy with the husband jokes."

Kaleb ignored the comment and replied to Morgan, "I think you're right. I'd like to get home anyway. Austin should be home soon, and he's been moody lately."

"That's an understatement," Morgan replied. "I guess you'll have to find some new friends that he approves of."

Kaleb rubbed his temples. "Could you both lay off? I get it. You don't like Austin, but do you have to constantly remind me every time I see you guys?"

Morgan put up her hands. "Sorry. No more Austin bashing. I wasn't the one that started it, but I guess that doesn't matter to you."

"Just take me home," Kaleb said softly as he walked toward her car. He was done with fighting. His friends hated his boyfriend, and his boyfriend hated his friends. His head hurt. Something within him stirred. He assumed it was indigestion.

•⸙•

Mercedes huffed for the fourth time in a row. Morgan stared blank-faced at the TV. She was watching a documentary about the Moth-Man. Mercedes got tired of waiting and jumped up on the couch knocking Morgan's drink into her lap.

Morgan jumped to her feet. "Hey! What the hell, cat?"

"*Great. Now that I have your attention, would you mind turning the TV onto something productive?*" The cat circled her spot on the couch and lay back down.

"Are you kidding me?" The cat glared at her. Morgan sighed in exacerbation; she had yet to win an argument with the cat. She paused the DVR and crossed her arms. "Fine. What do *you* want to watch?"

The cat looked up at Morgan from her spot on the couch. "*I want to watch* The DaVinci Code."

"So now you're having a laugh at my expense?" She sat back down and resumed her documentary. Morgan tried to ignore the cat, but Mercedes was staring at her. "What?"

"*You should probably invite Kaleb over, too. I mean, you said he could shadow-walk.*" Mercedes jumped onto the coffee table and pushed her paw down on the remote shutting off the TV.

She was too stunned to react to the cat usurping her remote. "I'm sorry, shadow what?"

"*Shadow-walk. With all these books laying around you'd think you'd pick one up once in a while instead of watching ridiculous documentaries.*" The cat jumped off the couch and crossed the living room to a pile of books lying on the floor.

"You can read?"

"*I think the problem here is that you don't. Besides, what else do you think I'm going to do with my time while you're at work?*" The cat used her paw to swat several paperbacks down the hill of books. "*Here's the one,* The Watchers of Avalon. *Says that's how Merlin used to get around.*" Mercedes sighed. "*Are you even listening to me?*"

"You can read?"

The voice in her mind mumbled some incoherent things, Morgan only made out a couple of random expletives. "*Yes, I can read. I can't write because I don't have thumbs and can't hold a pen, otherwise I would. I'm not stupid! Do you see me chasing cars because they are shiny and move?*" When Morgan didn't respond the cat continued, "*Besides, you were the one that told me about Kaleb's teleportation experience otherwise I wouldn't have brought it up. It's not like every fictional book you read is really fiction.*" Mercedes looked at her with a mental eyebrow raised.

"You mean like Dianetics?"

The cat's eyes narrowed and her tail flicked sharply. "*How did I know you'd say something stupid like that? No, not like Dianetics. Scientology was invented by a science-fiction writer to avoid paying taxes. Honestly, I'm a cat and even I'm not that dumb.*"

"So you think Kaleb's a shadow-walker?"

"*No, I think Kaleb can shadow-walk. What the hell's a shadow-walker?*" Mercedes stared at her for a moment before continuing, "*Did he try focusing on the shadows and then stepping to where he wants to go? Of course he didn't, because who would ever think that shadows were anything more than a lack of light.*"

"Okay, so let's just assume for a minute that Kaleb is a shadow-walker." Morgan corrected herself as she saw the cat's eyes narrow. "Sorry, *can* shadow walk. Why are we watching *The Davinci Code*?"

The cat lay back down on the couch. "*Because he's going to need a mental image of where he's going.*"

"But that library scene wasn't the real library. He'll end up on the back lot of some Hollywood movie set."

"*Are you daft?*" Mercedes didn't give her a chance to respond. "*He's not going to shadow-walk to the library, he's going to shadow-walk to Rome.*"

"But there are plenty of other movies that are set in Rome."

"*I know.*" Mercedes began cleaning herself. "*But I like that movie.*"

·ꞏ·

Kaleb hated working weekends. While his friends got to lounge around at home he was stuck trying to talk a woman off a ledge over a thirty-cent surcharge. Kaleb got an email that asked him to "please come to the office on the second floor by the security desk." His heart jumped to his throat and the floor fell out from beneath him at the same time.

He arrived at the office and saw someone he had never met before and beside her on the long conference table was a box of tissues. He took a deep breath. "I'm Katie from HR, do you know what this is about?" the heavyset woman asked politely.

"Actually, I have no idea," he answered truthfully.

She looked down her nose at him. "You've reached the maximum allowed unscheduled absences."

He breathed a sigh of relief. "Actually, right now I should be at seven. I've been keeping track."

She pulled a single page out of a brown folder in front of her. "Are you familiar with our attendance policy?" The woman slid the page in front of him.

"Yeah. Which is how I know I have one absence left before you can fire me." Kaleb said while trying to mask his irritation behind diplomacy.

"I show that you missed work on Thursday and on Friday," she said as she read another of her loose leaf forms.

"Yeah, but I had PTO scheduled for Thursday." At the start of the meeting Kaleb assumed this had been a mistake, but he was growing increasingly aware that he was being fired and there was no talking his way out of it.

"When you have scheduled a day off and call in sick the following day, both days become unscheduled. Putting you at eight absences. Do you have any personal belongings at your desk?" She appeared to be enjoying herself, which infuriated Kaleb.

"No, I think we're done here." He threw his badge on the table and stormed out. Kaleb walked to the bus stop and checked his watch, the next bus wouldn't be arriving for another half an hour. He called Austin's phone but there was no answer.

He tried calling another few times during the bus ride home, still no answer. Kaleb walked home in silence. He texted his family and friends and told them he had been fired, but ignored them when they tried calling. He was in no mood to talk. For a moment, he wished he could figure out how to teleport, but he was too tired to care.

The door was unlocked. He called out for Austin, no response. Kaleb looked around the house, still no Austin. The phone rang and Kaleb jumped out of his skin, it was Morgan. He stared at the screen before deciding if he wanted to answer. "Yes Morgan?"

"So you finally decided to answer me."

"I just got fired from work and I have no idea where Austin is. I'm really not in the mood to feel worse. I could use a friend right about now. Could you come pick me up?"

"I thought you'd never ask."

•¦•

Mercedes and Kaleb eyed each other suspiciously from across the living room. *The DaVinci Code* was playing on the TV, though the only one who was really watching it was the cat. Morgan was mixing drinks in the kitchen while they waited for Nick to arrive.

"It was nice of you to get her a catnip toy. Mercedes says thank you."

"*No I didn't,*" Mercedes said, not taking her eyes off Kaleb.

"So I got a text from Austin. He's apparently at his brother's and won't be able to get a ride home for another three hours," Kaleb announced. "I really wish he'd just come home. I mean don't get me wrong, I love your company, but it's not the same."

Morgan handed him a vodka gimlet and put her hand on his knee. "I know. Don't worry about it. Mercedes says to make yourself feel at home."

"*I really wish you'd stop putting words in my mouth,*" Mercedes chided.

She smiled sweetly at the cat, and Mercedes huffed in defiance. "Besides, if you need me to give you a ride over to the east side so you can see if he's at his brother's I won't mind. It's not like you wouldn't do the same."

"You've really been a great friend to me. I don't tell you that enough." Kaleb's voice cracked as tears welled up behind his eyes.

"Oh, now, don't you go crying on me. You've been a great friend to me too, Kaleb."

"Sorry, it's just so hard. I busted my ass at that place for the last six months and do they care? Of course not, they were just looking for a reason to fire the freak." He started sobbing. Morgan hugged him tight.

The door opened and Nick saw Kaleb wiping his eyes and immediately crouched down on the floor in front of him. He gave him a peck on the cheek and hugged him. "Don't you cry; pretty people don't cry."

"No." A slight smile emerged on Kaleb's face as he said, "We don't."

"Besides, we've got to plan your revenge," Nick said, pulling a bottle of vodka out of his bag and pouring it into a bottle of orange juice. Kaleb raised his eyebrows. Nick didn't miss a beat. "Well of course we need to plan it. Did you think we'd just storm in there and set the place on fire? Of course not. We need to plan this one out."

"How are we supposed to do anything if I can't even figure out how to teleport without breaking my nose?"

Morgan rushed to the opportunity. "So I know that this will probably sound crazy, but Mercedes showed me this book."

Nick and Kaleb burst into laughter.

"Stop that. She did." Morgan crossed the room, picked up the copy of *The Watchers of Avalon* and threw it at Nick's head. She missed.

"Oh come on," Kaleb replied. "We're just having a laugh. I'm sure Mercedes is a very nice kitty, but are you really going to expect us to believe that she's literate." Nick and Kaleb fell back into laughter.

Mercedes jumped down off her perch on the windowsill, "*I am not putting up with this.*" She jumped up on the coffee table and knocked Kaleb's drink over. She wrote in vodka with her paw. "Fuck you."

The laughter ended immediately. Mercedes eyed them. The silence was palpable. Morgan picked up Kaleb's glass and asked with feigned disinterest, "Do you need a refresher?"

"Um. Yes. Thank you. That would be ... Yes. Um. Thank you." Kaleb stared unblinking at the cat.

Mercedes didn't move from her spot on the coffee table. She licked her paw clean while Kaleb and Nick scooted towards the edges of the couch to increase their distance from cat. Eventually, Nick picked up the book that was tossed at him. "You have very good taste in literature, Mercedes. This is one of my favorite authors."

"She says thank you," came the response from the kitchen. Mercedes head swiveled to glare at Morgan. "Okay, she said something close to that, but I really don't know where she got such a filthy mouth."

"If you keep putting words in my mouth, I'm going to take a shit in your coffee. Now, tell the boys what I really said."

Morgan returned to the couch and locked her jaw. "She says she'll take a shit in my coffee if I don't tell you what she really said. Nick, she says she thinks you're an ass-hungry fairy who couldn't read the back of cereal box let alone a novel. Kaleb, she says you're a whiny little bitch with as much backbone as a ninety-cent hooker with scoliosis."

"I'm sorry if we offended you, Mercedes," Kaleb said while reaching his hand out to pet her. She allowed herself to be petted. Her back arched as she leaned into his hand. "I'm sure you can understand how we would be a little skeptical at first."

Mercedes mind-voice rumbled as she purred. *"Well, just don't let it happen again."*

Morgan didn't allow Nick time to respond to the cat's taunt. "So, Mercedes said that Merlin had this ability the book called shadow-walking. Merlin could step into a shadow and step out from a different shadow. Apparently he could cover huge distances."

The cat returned to her perch and resumed enjoying her catnip toy in the shape of a mouse. The Vatican Library scene of *The DaVinci Code* had just started.

Morgan pointed at the screen. "Which is why she asked that we watch this movie."

"*Well that and I love Tom Hanks.*" Mercedes mind-voice began to slur as she rolled and chewed and played with her catnip toy. Mercedes rubbed her body against the toy and moaned with pleasure. "*Feels so good.*"

"So she thinks I'm a shadow-walker?"

Morgan cringed and looked over to the cat on the window sill. "Don't let her hear you calling it that. She's very particular about it. It's an ability. She thinks you *can* shadow-walk." Morgan relaxed a little when she saw that the cat's eyes were beginning to droop. "Thank you for getting me that catnip toy. She's the worst roommate ever."

They all looked over at the sleeping cat. Kaleb finally asked, "So what's up with us watching *The DaVinci Code*?"

"Oh, right, sorry, so she thinks you could use this shadow-walking to break into the Vatican Library. It seems I was right after all." Morgan finished, beaming.

"Right?" Nick asked.

"I said our best option would be to break into the Vatican, and I was right," she said, still smiling.

Kaleb responded as kindly as he could manage, "You forget, I still have no idea how to shadow-walk. We have no idea where they are, I've never been to the Vatican. Our only resources at the moment are a Tom Hanks movie and a cat with the mouth of a sailor."

"We could go online," Nick retorted.

"Oh yeah, I'll just type in the search engine 'how to break into the Vatican' and see what comes up," Kaleb replied sarcastically.

Nick tapped his nose. "It's not a bad idea. I mean that won't be what you put into the search bar. I think we should start doing some research about the Vatican Library. Any information is better than what we have at the moment and, as you so eloquently pointed out a moment ago, we don't have many resources."

Kaleb crossed his arms. "Fine. But that doesn't solve my problem."

Nick looked up at Kaleb. "Which problem is that?"

"I'm still unemployed," he said as he slumped back into the sofa.

•⁊•

"What a surprise," Austin muttered as he came home from work.

Kaleb was surrounded by a collection of discarded cans of soda. He stared blankly at the television as Austin stormed around the house cleaning up Kaleb's mess. "I would have gotten those."

Austin abruptly turned and yelled at Kaleb, "When? Like when you said you'd get a job? You either sit around here watching TV or you're off with your friends."

Kaleb retorted, "Oh, don't even pretend to know how I've been spending my time! You work five hours a day and I only end up seeing you for three! That's a lot of unaccounted for time, wouldn't you say?"

"Do you blame me for not wanting to come home to my lazy boyfriend who won't even pick up his own pop cans? You said you'd have a job in two weeks, it's been four. So where's this new job?"

"You said you'd have a second job in one week, looks like that didn't happen either," Kaleb said with a smirk. "And it seems like even though my income has been seriously slashed, you still drink the same amount. If not more."

"I guess it's no surprise I'm going out with Jamie tonight," Austin shot back. He skirted around their coffee table and stormed up the stairs.

Tension formed in Kaleb's jaw as he yelled up the stairs, "Well, maybe I should join you!"

Before he even realized the turn the argument had taken Austin yelled back, "Well maybe you should!" He stopped, but it was already too late. Kaleb was invited.

••

Kaleb stared sullenly out the backseat window. Motes of snow hung in the air and melted when they hit the warm ground. Winter's last dying breath held the world in limbo. The trees could not decide if it was safe yet to return from their seasonal slumber. Though winter had officially ended weeks ago, it once again reared its ugly head to torment them.

Morgan and Nick couldn't come out to the bar, so he was stuck with Austin and his friend Jamie. Kaleb hated Jamie. She was the friend whose car Austin had been driving the night he was arrested for driving while barred. Kaleb was fairly sure she was into some serious drugs, but even if that were untrue he was certain she was still a bad influence.

Tonight would be different. He had convinced Austin to go to a bar that Kaleb liked. It was the only gay bar in town that actually felt like a bar and not a club. He hated clubs. He hated music that was less like music and more like a massive drum beat that pounded your spine. Kaleb hated the press of people. He hated how the only thing on anyone's mind was who they were going to sleep with next.

"I'm glad we're doing this," Jamie said from the driver's seat. "You never come out with us." She stared at him through the rear view mirror.

Kaleb didn't respond so Austin did for him, "It'll be fun."

Though the car ride was awkward it wasn't long before they were at the bar. Austin gathered drinks while Kaleb found a table in the corner. The bar was a single square room with pool tables at the center and a bar on the far wall. Most people came for the patio, but it was still a little too cold to be enjoying the outdoors.

There weren't many people, which suited Kaleb just fine. His corner table provided him plenty of room for lamenting. "Dancing Queen" was playing on the jukebox and three of the twelve people at the bar were doing just that.

He hardly noticed when the topic changed to leaving. "I want to go to Alexander's Garden, but Kaleb won't want to," he heard Austin say to Jamie.

"Damn right I won't. What's wrong with staying here?" Kaleb crossed his arms. When no answer was provided Kaleb stormed to the bar to refill their drinks.

Austin stepped behind him and put his arms around Kaleb's waist. He whispered sweetly into Kaleb's ear, "I want to go dancing."

Kaleb thought back to the last time they went dancing. The bar had been overcrowded, the music was so loud it hurt his chest, and the people he tried to talk to snubbed him. So he sat at a dimly lit table, by himself, overlooking the dance floor while Austin danced with other guys. Kaleb had no desire to repeat the experience.

He turned to face Austin. "But I hate that bar. We can go anywhere else but there."

"But I want to go dancing." Austin's bottom lip stuck out as he pouted.

He ignored Austin and walked back to their table. He handed Jamie a bottle of beer and sat back down. Kaleb sipped his Long Island Ice Tea and waited for Austin to return to his seat. Instead, Austin stood next to the table pouting.

Jamie broke the awkward silence. "We don't have to leave right now, but I definitely agree, I want go dancing."

Kaleb took Austin's hand and pleaded, "I'm serious. I really don't want to go there. Please don't make me go there."

"We're going to go out for a cigarette. I'll talk to Austin," Jamie said as she flashed him a smile. Austin and Jamie sat their drinks down and left through the front door.

Kaleb sipped on his drink. Several minutes went by and he reached the bottom of his glass. They still hadn't returned from their cigarette so Kaleb went to check the parking lot. They weren't in the parking lot. Anger welled up inside him. He pulled his phone out of his pocket; it was ringing.

"Where the hell did you go?" he screamed at Austin.

"We decided to go to Alexander's. I called you a cab." Austin's voice was completely lacking any remorse.

"I can call my own damn cab, that's not the point, the point is you *left* me at the bar." Kaleb wanted to throw his phone across the parking lot, but his phone wasn't the one being an asshole.

"Well you didn't want to go, so I called you a cab."

"*You left me at the bar!*" Kaleb screamed and hung up. The phone rang several more times and he ignored it. He walked to the street and sat down on curb. An unknown number came up on his phone. Kaleb had no desire to take Austin's cab, and he wasn't done fuming.

When his fury wore off, depression set in. He couldn't seem to do anything right. He hated fighting with Austin, but they always managed to find a reason. He missed the long walks and the laughter. It seemed like they were in a never-ending cycle of fights.

The building across the street was empty brick shell. The warehouse had long ago been gutted. Kaleb felt the same way. The broken windows mirrored his shattered confidence. He felt empty inside, like all his feelings had been drained out of him and he was just a husk of a man.

No matter what he said or how hard he tried, Austin was still convinced that there was more going on between him and Nick. Nothing he did or said made any difference. He was powerless.

His despair deepened when he started to think about his failings with magic. Out of the trio Morgan was the only one who could manage to perform real magic consistently, though he was pretty sure if he asked Mercedes he would hear how the cat was the one performing magic. He considered what he would do with a disparaging talking cat. It didn't matter how magical the cat was, Kaleb would definitely have her spayed out of spite.

No matter how much he tried to shake his morose mood, he couldn't. He just wanted it to be over. Magic was back, and he couldn't even manage a simple incantation. He was a failure. His indigestion was back. It felt like his stomach had rolled over. Chills passed through his body.

Out of the corner of his eye he saw three men exit a club down the street. The neon lights lit their way as they proceeded down the sidewalk in his direction. Kaleb kept tabs on them as they approached. They were noticeably drunk. The one in the middle was kind of cute, he had a nice face and slim body. Kaleb looked down at the street to avoid eye contact.

The one closest to Kaleb was the first to speak. He was a bigger guy with receding blonde hair and a tribal tattoo on his arm. It might have been a trick of the light but he thought he saw the man flex his entire body. "Whada we got here boys? Looks like we gotta a little faggot."

Kaleb remained silent. He was not in the mood to be harassed. If he just ignored them, they would go away on their own. He wrung his hands and looked up the street away from them.

"They throw you out for bein' too faggy?" the man with the tribal tattoo chided. His friends chuckled.

When it was apparent that they weren't going to leave him in peace Kaleb got up from the curb and walked toward the alley between the abandoned brick buildings. They followed him. His stomach was in knots. He felt his internal organs trying to break free. He resisted the urge to run.

"We weren't done talkin' to you, faggot." The man with the tribal tattoo was on his heels as Kaleb walked away.

He was pushed from behind. "I'm really not in the mood for this," Kaleb said to himself, his anger building up again. He stumbled deeper into the darkened alley. When he regained his footing, he picked up his pace. Still they followed. Kaleb reached inside himself for strength and was met with a surge of confidence. For a second he thought he saw the alley flicker into a darker version of itself.

The tank of a man stood threateningly at the mouth of the alleyway. "There's nowhere to run little faerie."

They were farther behind than they had been moments ago. Without so much as a conscious thought, Kaleb started pulling at the shadows. Up ahead was the chain-link fence that barred the alley. He had to figure this out and figure it out now.

Kaleb closed his eyes and stretched his mind outside of himself. Something within him pushed his mental hands into a stream of magic he hadn't felt before. The power was deep within the earth. He summoned the energy to him and stepped forward. He imagined himself entering the shadows. Darkness flowed upward.

He was standing in what appeared to be the bottom of a muddy aquarium. His surroundings hadn't changed, but they no longer felt as though they held any substance. Kaleb passed his hand through the wall of the building he had been standing next to a moment before. He pulled his hand back and it trailed a thick black smoke.

His own shadow had morphed into a monster of darkness. The world looked stretched out, yet the darkness all around him was compressing him. His heartbeat boomed in his ears; it was the only sound he could hear. Fear gripped his body and he felt its cold fingers working down into his core.

He saw the vague outlines of the men who were chasing him. Kaleb watched as they walked to the end of the alley and stopped at the black lattice had once been a chain-link fence.

Beyond the fence were two shadows moving like grain in the breeze, swaying to a silent song only they could hear. Their limbs were long and twisted. They reminded Kaleb of inflatable tube-men that the car dealerships would often adorn their lots with, but a more gothic style of tube-man.

Cautiously Kaleb approached the shadowy forms. They lurched toward him. Kaleb nearly jumped out of his skin. For a split second he thought about taking his chances with the homophobes. Unfortunately he had no idea of how to exit the dark realm of shadows. He started running.

What he thought must be streetlights cast a dim radiance on the ground. While he ran globes of light sped past him faster and faster. There was no wind to gauge his speed, only the lights that passed by him so quickly he felt as though he must be under a strobe. The rest of the land was a blur to him as he ran. His heart was beating out of his chest, but he was too afraid to stop.

After running for several minutes he was winded and had to slow down. Kaleb realized he had no idea where he was. He started to panic. Not only was he lost, he also didn't know how to return to the real world. Exhausted and afraid, he sat down on the ground and put his face into his hands.

The sound of his own heart began to drum in his ears. Kaleb closed his eyes and willed it to stop beating so quickly and with such force. The complete lack of sound was unnerving. He pulled his phone out of his pocket and put in his earbuds.

He wasn't sure how long he sat on the ground. The only gauge of time was the length of time it took for the songs in his ears to play. Kaleb knew that he was in trouble. No one could come get him, even if he knew where he was. As many times as he considered ending his life, he had never actually meant to follow through with it. Mortality stared at him and all he could do was look away.

"I'm not going to die here," he finally said to himself. He could barely hear his own voice over the loud music playing in his ears, but it was better than the alternative.

He remembered how it felt to move into the shadows and decided it must be the same, except in reverse. Kaleb reached out with his mind and found that same source of magic as before, except on this side of the night it was everywhere and not locked away deep within the earth. He closed his eyes and stood up. He imagined himself walking out of the shadows and took a large step forward.

The world materialized around him. As he moved forward the scenery moved with him and slid back to its natural state. It was still dark and hard to see, but he could tell that he was in the middle of a cornfield. What he had thought looked like large black eels on the other side were actually the remnants of last year's crop.

He heard a crow in the distance and sighed in relief. He closed his eyes and searched for that new magical energy. Once he found it, he pulled into himself and threw it at the shadows, bending them to his will. The ability to move back and forth made it less terrifying. For several minutes he practiced stepping in and out of the real world and the shadow world.

Kaleb decided he didn't care if he was home when Austin got back from the bar. He was eager to show off his new trick. He called Morgan. "Hey girl, what're you up to?"

"Mercedes and I are watching *Sleepless in Seattle*." Kaleb could hear the disgust in Morgan's voice. "You wanna come over? I've got ice cream and crème de menthe."

"That sounds awesome! I'd love to come over." He did his best to keep the excitement out of his voice.

"Should I come get you?"

Kaleb closed his eyes and reached out his mental hands to the energy around him. He channeled it to his core and shifted into the shadows. The darkness deepened and he concentrated on his destination as he ran. When he finally arrived he stepped out through Morgan's open bedroom door. As he strutted into the hallway he said to Morgan, "No, I think I'll find my own way."

Morgan jumped off the couch. "Holy shit, Kaleb! That was awesome! Do it again!"

Kaleb gathered magical forces to him, shifted the shadows and stepped through. He knocked on her front door. When she opened, it Kaleb was grinning from ear to ear.

Morgan clapped her hands together like a kid who was just told that the candy store was having a half-off-everything sale. "This is so freaking cool! We have to call Nick."

While they waited for Nick to arrive, Kaleb recounted the events of his evening, sparing no detail. "Can you believe he called me a cab?" he finally asked.

"What a jerk. You deserve so much better. I bet there's someone else out there who will treat you right. Should be arriving any day now." Morgan smiled, thinking about the love spell she cast for Kaleb earlier that year. "Any day now."

Kaleb gave her a sideways glance when they were interrupted by a knock at the door. Nick arrived and Kaleb excused himself to go to the bathroom. He stepped into the darkness and reemerged through the front door. "Sorry, I forgot my drink," Kaleb said as he picked up his glass and headed back to the bathroom.

Nick shook his head, and said to Morgan, "Did he just?"

Morgan nodded. Kaleb reemerged from the hallway wearing a huge grin.

"Shit dude! That's so cool. How does it work?" Nick was giddy with excitement. "You have to show me how."

"I was being chased by these three guys. Then I closed my eyes and started searching, and I found this energy. It's like it's beneath the stuff we normally work with. Like it's deep within the earth almost. I brought it to me and imagined myself walking into the shadows. Crazy, right?"

"I have to try this," Nick said. He stood at the entrance to the trailer and closed his eyes. He searched for this magic to which Kaleb had referred to. His mind probed deep within the earth. He smiled when he found it and pulled it into himself. Nick opened his eyes and focused on twisting the shadows. He took two steps and stumbled down the wrought-iron stairs. He managed to keep himself from falling flat on his face by turning his stumble into something between figure skating and hopscotch.

Morgan and Kaleb resisted the urge to laugh. Morgan got up and strutted to the door. "Okay, my turn."

Morgan closed her eyes and reached with her mind. She found the channels of power that they normally worked with, but this time dug deeper. In her mind she felt as though she were descending into a cave. When she reached the bottom she could feel an aquifer of energy unlike anything she had ever felt before. It felt old, and primal. A shiver ran down her spine and she clapped her hands again.

Following Kaleb's instructions, she channeled magic to herself and flung it at the shadows. She willed herself to step into them. She took a step forward and tumbled down her stairs. Her legs were still on the steps but her face was on the sidewalk.

Nick and Kaleb laughed as she picked herself up off the concrete. "Not funny guys. Kaleb, what else do we do so we can shadow-walk?"

"*I told you, it wasn't something that everyone could do. Nobody ever listens to the cat. Merlin could shadow-walk. It's an ability,*" Mercedes said as she pawed her way to the door.

"So why didn't you say something before we tried?" Morgan asked aloud.

"I wanted to watch you fall on your face." The cat ran as Morgan chased her back into the trailer.

"You know what this means, don't you?" Nick asked. "It means that you can go anywhere you want. You could break into bank vaults, and no one would know where you went or how you got in. Well, at least in theory."

Morgan tapped an unlit cigarette to her lips. "It also means that we might be able to test out my theory." They both looked at Morgan with confused stares. "You know, the one about the Vatican keeping the truth about magic hidden from the public."

"Yeah? And while I'm at it, I should also stop over at Area 51," Kaleb said sarcastically.

The sarcasm didn't register. "Now we're talking. Might as well find out what our government is hiding from us while you're at it. You we should also hit the Pentagon. I've heard they're planning to stage a terrorist attack."

"Okay, wow, Morgan." Nick rubbed his forehead. "So, as much as I hate to agree with Miss Conspiracy, going to the Vatican isn't a bad idea."

"You've got to be kidding me," Kaleb groaned.

Nick put his hand on Kaleb's shoulder. "They have the oldest library on earth right now, Kaleb. Like it or not, you're going to the Vatican."

•ᵀ•

A heavy metal band played in his ears as he stood at the edge of the shadow version of the Atlantic Ocean. The trees along the coast stretched clawed hands to the gray sky above. All around Kaleb were vague outlines of the physical world. Houses and cars were wisps of black smoke. His feet began to sink into the black sand. He pulled his feet out of the sand and they trailed the inky black smoke that was the substance of the nocturnal world.

The ocean stretched out before him. There was no breeze, just a sea of black and gray. He had never been out of the Midwest before except for a trip to Disneyland when he was eight. Kaleb considered stepping over to the material world so he could see the actual ocean, but decided against it. His friends were waiting for him.

Kaleb took a deep breath and closed his eyes. According to the cat he could travel anywhere in the world through the shadows. He laughed at how ridiculous his thoughts sounded. "According to the cat," he said to himself.

"No time to get freaked out." Kaleb couldn't swim, and the thought of just walking out into the ocean terrified him. He opened his eyes and stepped into the black waves. The 'water' had just as much substance as everything else.

He stood waist deep in the dark substance that was the sea. While he stood in place he began to sink. Kaleb's heart started beating faster and he was paralyzed with fear. As the shadow-sea reached his neck something broke inside of him. Panic overcame him and began thrashing around to reach the surface. With every heartbeat he rose closer to the surface. It was as though he was clawing his way through molasses and with each terrified grab at the surface he pulled himself closer to the surface.

Waves passed through him as he worked to catch his breath. After a moment he looked down and realized he wasn't on the beach; he was sitting on the surface of the water. He reached his hand down and played with the inky darkness that was the ocean.

Kaleb stood up and took a confident step forward. He was walking on the surface of the ocean. The fear inside him abated and he inhaled deeply. "Okay kids, next stop, Rome."

•⸬•

The sun was rising over the cobbled streets of Rome as Kaleb stepped from the shadows. He really had no idea where he was going, but it didn't matter. Before tonight, he never had the chance to travel, and for the first time he was getting to see Rome in all its glory.

The streets were packed with buildings, some old, some very new. He was wide-eyed as he made his way through the city. Kaleb was a tourist and he didn't care. The mission was lost to exploring the city and taking pictures of all the beautiful buildings.

Kaleb wasn't the type to get lost in architecture, but he loved history and this city was jam packed with ancient structures and beautiful sculptures. He wandered for several hours before he remembered at home it was getting very late at home.

Begrudgingly he found the nearest shadow dark enough to take him. It took him some time to find one, but as soon as he was back in the realm of night he ran. He ran as fast as his legs would take him.

Leagues of the Mediterranean and then the Atlantic sped below him. He focused on his destination and continued to sprint. The east coast of America passed by so quickly he almost missed it. In little over a half an hour he had run all the way back to Morgan's.

Kaleb slipped back into the dimly lit trailer, exhausted but exhilarated. Nick was asleep on the couch and Morgan's bedroom door was closed. He looked at the clock and saw that it was close to four in the morning. Kaleb cursed to himself and stepped back into the shadows to walk home.

•⸬•

"Where the hell have you been?" Austin asked before Kaleb even had a chance to close the front door.

Kaleb's good mood was immediately shattered. He responded defiantly, "You left me at the bar, asshole! Or don't you remember that?"

"So you ran off to Nick's?" Austin stumbled across the room and stood scowling in front of Kaleb.

His mouth dropped open. "Are you freaking kidding me with this shit? I thought we were past this. There is *nothing* going on between me and Nick."

"I really doubt that. You spend an awful lot of time with your ex, Kaleb. You spend more time with him than you do with me!" Austin's breath reeked of liquor. He pushed Kaleb against the door.

Kaleb calmly looked into Austin's eyes and said, "You're scaring me."

It took Austin a second to realize he had just pushed Kaleb for the first time. He quickly released Kaleb's arm and looked down. "I'm sorry."

"You should be! This is absurd. I don't know why you think you have anything to worry about. I love you." Kaleb drew Austin into an embrace. "Are we okay?" he asked.

He kissed Kaleb gently before responding, "Yeah. We're okay. I love you too."

·⁛·

It was mid-afternoon before Kaleb woke up. Austin had already left for work and he was grateful. He didn't want to have to talk about last night. Austin's jealous outbursts were getting more severe. Lost in thought over last night's altercation, Kaleb shadow-walked to Morgan's.

They were still asleep when he arrived. Nick was laying on the couch, and Kaleb didn't want to wake him. Nick was a very attractive man, so he understood why Austin would be concerned over the amount of time they had been spending together.

Kaleb looked away uncomfortably. There was no truth in Austin's delusion. As cute as Nick was, there was nothing more going on between them than simple friendship. Kaleb had never cheated on Austin, and he didn't plan on it.

The bedroom door opened and Morgan made her way down the short hall to the kitchen. On her heels was Mercedes, her head and tail held high. Morgan's hair was a tangled mess. She yawned and waved at Kaleb as she opened the freezer and grabbed a box of thin-mint ice cream.

Her arrival roused Nick from his sleep. He stretched, yawned, and groaned. Nick rubbed his back and said, "I am never sleeping on your couch again. I will never be rid of these knots. Oh, hey Kay. How was Rome?"

"Oh, you know. It was okay." Kaleb said, trying to do his best to hide his excitement. He felt guilty that he was the only one of his friends that could enjoy this new-found ability.

"Just okay?" Morgan asked, talking around a mouthful of ice cream.

"Okay, so it was freaking awesome." Kaleb pulled out his phone and started showing them all the pictures he had taken of Rome.

"So I take it you didn't manage to find the library?" Morgan asked.

Nick rose to Kaleb's defense. "Can you really blame him? It's Rome! Magic can wait, I want to send him shopping!"

"*Oh you would,*" Mercedes added reproachfully. "*Morgan, are you going to let these little queens derail our plans?*"

Morgan hated having to disagree with Nick, but the cat was right. "I think we can wait on shopping. We need to get into the Vatican. It's been six months since magic came back and the only one that can do anything is Kaleb."

"*I can do a lot of things to you,*" Mercedes said into her mind. The cat's eyes narrowed. Morgan ignored her as she shoveled another mouthful of ice cream into her mouth. "*That reminds me, aren't you forgetting something?*"

"The Animal Rescue League is a phone call away," Morgan said under her breath as she lifted herself out of her armchair and went to the kitchen. Pouring a bowl of cat food she replied to the cat, "*Better?*"

"*It's a good start.*" The cat stretched and walked to the food. Mercedes looked at the bowl of dry cat food. Her head rotated and she locked eyes with Morgan. "*Is this the cheap shit?*"

"Oh, dear goddess," Morgan said, putting her bowl of ice cream on the floor. "I hope you get sick."

Nick waited for Morgan to return from the kitchen. He grinned at her, his mind was already made up. "Then it's settled, he can do both."

•ᵛ•

Kaleb spent the next two weeks running back and forth from Rome. He managed to find presents for both Nick and Morgan. After three days of shopping, his credit card company finally called to ask about the "suspicious" purchases. With no record of him leaving the country, Kaleb responded by crying fraud.

Eventually, he found his way to the Vatican itself. Kaleb attached himself to a group of tourists. He learned a lot about the history of the church and a few different popes, but found that the tour group was really not going in the direction he wanted.

Kaleb was frustrated and exhausted. He shadow-walked back to Morgan's trailer as soon as he was sure he wasn't being observed and had a dark enough shadow. After a long run he arrived in her bathroom. Kaleb took a moment to catch his breath and then went to find Morgan. He plopped down next to her on the couch. "I give up."

"You've been at this forever. Take a break if you need to, but come on, you've only just started." She handed him the cup of jasmine tea she had made for herself and went back to the kitchen to make another.

He drank down the tea in a big gulp. "All right. I'm off. Wish me luck."

Morgan wished him luck as he stepped into the darkness. The run was a lot longer than he remembered. He rested several times along the way to let his side stop aching. When he finally arrived in the shadow version of Rome, the only shadows he found were surrounded by people.

He still hadn't seen any of the shadow-creatures he ran into the night he discovered the alternate world, but didn't want to wait around for one to show up. There was no way he was going back to Morgan's to wait it out, so instead he extended his senses.

His mind extended out and away from himself. He felt the darkness of the catacombs. He hesitated for a moment. There was no way to know if the catacombs were part of a tourist attraction, if they were closed off to the public, or if they were completely sealed off. Kaleb held his breath and closed his eyes, he decided to risk it. He envisioned himself walking down stairs and descended into the halls of the dead.

It was pitch black inside the ancient burial chamber. Kaleb decided he would wait for at least half an hour before trying to find a shadow on the surface. The screen of his cell phone lit his face as he played Sudoku. The air turned cold and he looked around and felt a group of ghosts watching him. As best as he tried to ignore them, they didn't leave.

"What?" he snapped angrily. He put his phone back in his pocket and addressed the nosy ghosts. There were three of them. He got the feeling that they were curious about why he was in the crypt and how he arrived. "Sorry. I'm just passing through."

Kaleb turned away from them and was going to find another place to sit and wait when he felt a ghost standing in his path. He couldn't see any apparition, but he could sense its presence. The air was cold and the hairs on the back of his neck stood on end. A male voice spoke into his mind. "*Quomodo haec fiant?*"

"Look, I don't want any trouble. I'm just passing the time." Kaleb turned to walk the other direction but the ghost was now behind him. It was a long walk but he resigned himself to going back to Morgan's to wait.

As Kaleb merged with the darkness, the spirit grabbed his hand before he could take his first step. Rome, Spain, the ocean sped past him. He ran faster than he had ever run before. When he finally arrived in Morgan's trailer he was out of breath and the spirit still had hold of his wrist.

The ghost had passed to the material world. It was a semi-luminescent wisp of a man in chain mail. There was a red cross on his chest, the symbol of the Templars. It spoke to him in broken English, "*Sorcerer, lend us your, what is word?*" The ghost searched for the right word before it finally turned to him and said, "*Aid?*"

Kaleb yelled, "Morgan!"

She yawned as she exited the bedroom door. Her eyes were still half closed. "It's six in the morning. What do you ..." Her mouth hung open, but the sentence didn't finish. The Templar spirit bowed his head to her.

"Shit, it's six?" Kaleb cursed. "Austin is going to be pissed. Be a dear and look after our new friend for me." Before Morgan could protest, Kaleb had already vanished.

•¶•

They met at the Thirteen Steps Cemetery shortly after midnight. A thick mist clung to the forest that surrounded the small cemetery. Nick reclined on the stairs as Kaleb stepped from the shadows with the Templar ghost.

The trio had worked with ghosts for years, but whenever they interacted it was less about seeing a ghost and more about sensing it. On occasion they had seen spirits out of the corner of their eyes but for the most part had never seen a full-on ghost.

For most, the visual appearance of a luminescent see-through man clad in chain mail would be deeply disturbing. Nick greeted the Templar with a nonchalant wave and a nod of his head. "So, why are we meeting at the cemetery and not at Morgan's?" Nick asked.

"Because Mercedes wouldn't shut up and it was giving me a headache." Morgan huddled inside her coat as a cold April wind ripped through her jacket.

"Besides, it's a much better ambiance, don't you think?" Kaleb interjected. A distant owl hooted. Kaleb smiled. "See. Ambiance."

Nick pulled a bottle of Gatorade out of his bag and mixed himself a drink. "So what's this ghosty got to say that was so important to drag me away from my stories?"

"*Sorcerer, we Templars never rest 'til Holy Roman Church has fallen,*" it spoke into their minds.

79

Nick spit vodka out his nose. "Ow! Oh. Wow. I was not expecting that."

"Well you see, that's going to be a bit tough," Morgan replied to the Templar. "It's not just the Catholics anymore. Now there's the Lutherans, and the Baptists, and the Protestants. Not to mention the Anglican Church, and the Church of Christian Science."

"And don't get me started on the Mormons," Nick added.

The specter looked confused, *"I not understand."*

"The other major obstacle is the only magic we know is our little Kaleb here's shadow-walking," Morgan said. Her hands were cold and she rubbed them together.

"Sorcerer, if not you to destroy, why to go to death beds of Templars?"

"Um, well, you see, I wasn't so much meaning to go to any death beds as I was just trying to wait until there were more shadows to walk between," Kaleb said uncomfortably.

"You are only hope. I take you to Bibliotheca Saint Patrick. You take his magic."

Nick froze mid-sip. "Wait, what?"

"I'm pretty sure it's Latin; it means library," Morgan provided.

"No, I got that," Nick said dismissively to Morgan. "Saint Patrick was a druid that turned on his people and sold them out to the Christians. Are you saying he stole their magic and gave it to the Christians?"

The Templar shifted uncomfortably. His image blinked in and out several times before he responded. *"Templars, is keeper of secrets. Sent to recover Ark to bring back magic and Saints."*

"You've got to be kidding. The Ark of the Covenant? Why on earth would that bring back magic?" Nick asked. His disgust with Christianity was evident in his voice.

"When we discover truth, Templars find magic was taken from world to protect it. Those who claimed be of Christ want sink land of Ire into the sea. That why Merlin remove magic."

"You were sent to find the Arc of the Covenant, and then what? God showed you a big vision of the past? This all seems really fishy to me guys." Nick crossed him arms.

Morgan leapt to her feet. "Kaleb, this is our big opportunity. I don't really care about history, Nick. If Kaleb's little friend can take you to Saint Patrick's Library then high magic is finally ours!"

"*I will show you way*," the ghost said into their minds as he extended his hand. "*Promise you must, when you have magic you destroy church and lay us rest.*"

"Yeah, sure, whatever," Kaleb said, taking the ghost's hand.

They traveled through the shadow world at a rapid pace that only slowed down as they approached the Vatican. The two began to descend below the streets. Darkness deepened as they came to a stop.

Shades unseen by the pair rode in their wake. Their dark figures held back as Kaleb and the Templar returned to the physical world. Silently they watched, silently they waited.

Kaleb squinted into the immense room. He grabbed a flashlight out of his back pack. Trunks of trees were cut up into sections and stacked like columns throughout the room.

Kaleb's mouth dropped. "What the hell?"

.·.

Nick and Morgan had been sitting at the cemetery for well over an hour. They started off excited about what Kaleb would be bringing back but as they waited, and waited, their excitement abated. They had tried to talk about what they thought the secrets of high magic would be, but that topic soon trailed off.

Nick sighed. "Do you think we should head home?"

Morgan chewed on her bottom lip. She really didn't want to be around Mercedes by herself, but she had a hard time saying no to Nick. "We could, but maybe we should give Kaleb a little bit longer."

Nick mixed himself another drink. Despite the knowledge that Morgan was infatuated with him, her company wasn't unwelcome. Her mixture of angst and self-loathing was a cocktail that had no peer.

As a psychic vampire, he always welcomed the opportunity to feed, and his favorite emotions were the negative ones. Nick lounged on the steps as he sipped on his drink and Morgan's abundant negative emotions. They had already exhausted all their conversation topics, and without Kaleb around they just didn't seem to have anything to talk about.

They watched from their vantage on the hill as a police car rolled onto the gravel road leading up to the cemetery. The police car rolled to a stop at the top of the hill and shined the bright light in their direction. They focused their minds and magic on being perceived as gravestones. The light passed them over. The officer pulled into the parking spot next to Morgan's car.

"Can't be up here," said the cop as he stood at the base of the thirteen steps.

"Sorry, officer, we've been up here for hours. What time is it?" Morgan attempted a seductive stance and failed miserably, looking instead as though she was constipated.

The officer was young and attractive. His age was difficult to tell, but Morgan guessed mid-twenties. She stared at his chiseled jaw-line and bright green eyes. He was taller than Morgan, yet shorter than Nick, but Nick was pretty tall. He had a lean build, and strong arms. Morgan was in love.

He pointed his flashlight at Nick as he was packing up his bottle of vodka. "Drinking in a graveyard? Don't you think that's a bit disrespectful? You're not thinking of driving are you?"

"We're sorry, officer, we really didn't realize it was that late. Our friend went for a walk in the woods and we were waiting for him to get back."

"I can't let you guys stay up here." He thought for a second, "Look, I'm not a bad guy, here's what I'll do. I suppose one of you was his ride?" Morgan nodded. "Well I don't know how much your friend here has had to drink."

"Nick." The officer shined his light in Nick's face. "My name is Nick."

"Well Nick. I don't want you drinking and driving, so I'd prefer you ride with the young lady. I'll wait for your friend, and if he hasn't been drinking, I'll have him take your car home."

"Keys are in the glove-box," Nick responded with a salute.

They left the officer to wait for Kaleb's return. Morgan wasn't sure if Kaleb could see where he was going while shadow-walking, but she desperately hoped he didn't give the handsome officer a heart attack when he got back from Rome.

•¶•

Kaleb stared into the dark room. Motes of dust hung in the air. His footsteps echoed through the chamber. Kaleb ran his hand along the bricks in the archway that must have long ago been the entrance to this secret chamber. Like the catacombs this chamber was carved out of the earth itself, though by more skillful hands.

His flashlight illuminated cross sections of tree trunks piled one on top of another. He walked to the nearest and examined it. The bark had been stripped away and along the circumference of the trunk were engraved words that he didn't recognize.

The Templar standing beside him said, "*Gaelic. You not speak?*"

"Can't say that I do," Kaleb replied. He ran his fingers along the carvings. They were deeply etched as though the words were burned into the tree. There were other markings as well, runes and symbols that didn't appear in any of the spell books he had ever seen. "It's beautiful though. I have no idea where to even start."

"*Sorcerer, we to start with these.*" The spirit walked to a table where some of the tree trunks had been left. The ghost examined the inscriptions. "*You want read magic elementares? That is word?*" When Kaleb nodded the ghost the Templar pointed to a word on the engraving. "*It mean baculus.*" When Kaleb looked confused he pointed to the staves lining the wall. "*Baculus, yes?*"

Kaleb shined his flashlight in the direction the ghost had pointed. There were ten in total. Each had been propped up into a small recess that appeared to be carved specifically for that staff. Half of the staves were carved to be straight and half were gnarled and bent. They each had a gemstone at the top secured by copper wire.

He walked to the nearest staff. It was a smooth ash staff topped with a blue stone, possibly a sapphire. Kaleb ran his hand down its length before picking it up. He took the staff into his hand he could feel the currents of magic around him. He felt the power being channeled into the staff. The blue stone atop the staff began to glow. He dropped the staff in surprise.

"*Danger?*" The Templar was immediately at his side.

"No, I'm fine." He picked the staff up off the floor and the gemstone again began to glow with a soft blue light. After another moment in his hand the light slowly dimmed and then was gone.

"*Staff is, what is word? Cubiculum olla? No, not right word. Vessel? It say those with ...*" The ghost paused straining for words. "*ability?*" Kaleb nodded so he continued, "*Those with ability draw magicis first to baculus, then with words of power build spell.*" The Templar walked around the table to read the other side of the inscription. "*As sorcerer grow in power they make magicis without baculus, but apprentice must learn make through vessel.*"

"Sounds like a good place to start." Kaleb ran his hands across the other staves as he examined each of them. The wood was smooth and exquisitely carved. One was topped with what could only be rose quartz and another was obsidian. Nick and Morgan would love them. "Great work, um, I guess I never did ask your name," Kaleb said, feeling rather embarrassed.

"*I called Geoffroi.*"

"Thank you, for all of your assistance, Roy, I think we should bring those inscriptions and some of the staves back to Morgan's and figure out what to do next. Oh, shit, they're still at the cemetery."

Kaleb tried for a moment to get a grip on a staff and an armful of the engraved cross-sections. He tried to grab as many small pieces as he could but kept dropping them. Kaleb gave up trying and stacked the cylindrical trunks on the floor next to the staves.

He stepped into the shadows empty-handed.

•፣•

Officer Walter Graham hated this part of his job. The two that he had kicked out of the cemetery seemed harmless enough, but rules were rules. What he really didn't like was being at the gates of an allegedly haunted cemetery in the middle of the night jumping at every sound.

He shined his flashlight into the woods and paced the distance between his car and the stairs. Officer Graham really hoped that their friend wasn't a runner, he really had no desire to go traipsing off into the woods after a drunk kid with warrants.

The hairs on the back of his neck began to prickle. He had shut the lights of his car off about ten minutes ago and was now regretting it. He regretted telling them he would wait for his friend, but he did promise, and one thing he could say was that he was always a man of his word.

Something moved in the woods. He quickly shined his flashlight in that direction but could see nothing. He approached quietly. It was his second month on the job by himself and he wasn't sure if he was following the correct protocol but he preferred to let his morals be his compass.

As he turned to walk back toward his car, he saw a semi-transparent man in chain mail materialize in front of him. That was the last thing he remembered before his head hit the pavement. He wasn't normally a fainter, but in this case he'd make an exception.

Kaleb was right behind Geoffroi as they arrived at the cemetery. He saw the cop car and the man passed out on the ground. "Aw hell, officer down."

.⁊.

Walter had no idea how long he had been unconscious but he was definitely leaving this out of his report. He opened his eyes to find himself staring into two of deepest, most beautiful, softest blue eyes he had ever seen.

"Officer, are you okay?"

He had a hard time forming words. It took him several moments to look away from those eyes and find his composure. "I'm Walter. I mean, Officer Graham."

Kaleb laughed and smiled. "I'm Kaleb. You have a pretty nasty bump on your head. Let's see if we can get you on your feet." Kaleb gave his hand to the fallen officer. His hands were soft and strong. It took him a moment to find his feet. "You know, you might have a concussion. I don't know if you should be driving."

Officer Graham sat down on the stairs. "That's just what I need. Oh god, how long has it been since I last radioed in?" he said as he looked at his watch. "Okay, less than ten minutes, I should be fine. I don't need the whole station coming up here."

"Well you should at least wait a while before driving." Kaleb said, kneeling down beside him. "So do you mind telling me how you ended up on the ground?"

"Oh, um, I don't really. It's kind of embarrassing." He paused to rub the massive goose egg forming on the back of his head. "I thought I saw something. Do you mind telling me what you were doing in the woods in the middle of the night?"

"Okay, turnaround is fair play," Kaleb responded.

Walter nodded. "Good."

Kaleb tilted his head. "Yeah, that's a concussion talking."

Walter massaged the lump on the back of his head. "I had to ask your friends to leave. Your friend Nick said that the keys are in his glove box."

He frowned. "Nick knows I don't drive."

Kaleb thought he saw a smile cross the officer's face, but if it had been there it was quickly replaced by the mask of duty. "Okay, well, I guess I can give you a ride back to your place." He stood up and stumbled.

"Well I don't think you should be driving anywhere right now." Kaleb helped him over to the steps and they sat down together.

"I guess you're right. My shift will be over in twenty minutes or so. I'll let the station know that I'll be up here for a little while longer." He grinned. "In case their friend is still in the woods."

"So do you know why I had to pick you up off the ground?" Kaleb said, trying to pull off a cop impression. He was trying to be cute, but it just ended up sounding silly. Walter didn't seem to notice.

Walter considered his choice of words very carefully. "I don't know whether or not you'll believe me if I told you. It still sounds crazy to me. Do you believe in ghosts?"

Without hesitation, Kaleb replied, "Of course I believe in ghosts."

"What if I told you I saw one? Here. Tonight." Walter ran his hands through his sandy blonde hair.

"I would tell you that it wasn't the first time someone has seen a ghost out here. People come out here to see if they catch a glimpse of one. That's what first got us coming up here, but now it's just because we love the view and the tranquility."

Kaleb looked over at Officer Graham who was staring intently at him. Kaleb had to clear his throat and remind himself that Austin was waiting at home for him. "Tell you what. If you can get past fainting, I just might know where we can see a ghost," Kaleb said with a calculated smile.

"I don't know. I really should get back to the station and then go home. I'm still giving you a ride home, aren't I?" His vibrant green eyes were searching Kaleb for something.

"Yes, that would be very nice of you. If you ever decide you want to see a real haunting, give me a call."

Walter looked puzzled. "But I don't have your number."

He smiled and patted Officer Graham's hand. "Well, I'll be sure to fix that."

They sat in silence for another few minutes. Walter kept rubbing the bump on his head and looking at Kaleb. Walter smiled timidly, but Kaleb was admittedly glancing back just as much. Their arms brushed and awkwardly they chuckled and sat a little farther apart. Kaleb was staring up at the moon and Walter did his best not to stare at Kaleb.

Walter hadn't dated in years. He never had a problem meeting people, he had just never met anyone who he connected with. For the most part, he was a loner. He had no problem with being single, and he was never the type to sleep around. There was something about Kaleb that he really liked. Or perhaps it was just the concussion.

"Okay, I think I'm okay." Walter stood and checked his balance. He gave a hand to Kaleb and helped him to his feet. He opened the passenger door for Kaleb.

He had never been arrested, so this was Kaleb's first time being in cop car. The radio kept the silence from becoming awkward. Kaleb caught Walter looking over at him a few times and smiling. It was a short ride back to Kaleb's house.

They arrived to a scene straight out of a frat house. All the lights were on, music was audible from inside the car and people were outside drinking on the lawn. As soon as they saw the cop car stop in front of the house, they dropped their beer cans and took off running. Kaleb sighed and slouched down in the seat.

Walter looked back at him. "Is this where you live?"

"Yes, and believe me, it doesn't always look like this." Kaleb sighed. "That would be the handiwork of my boyfriend, Austin." He hadn't meant for it to come out the way it had, but there it was. Full of disdain and displeasure.

This wasn't the first time that Austin invited random strangers home for an after-hours party. Many hours of sleep were lost because of parties that Kaleb had no way of stopping short of calling the police. "Would you mind shutting it down? Please. I'll wait in the car."

"I really don't want to have to charge you with disorderly house," Walter said. Kaleb's eyes pleaded with him. "Okay, okay, I am off duty so I guess I can let it slide this once. Let's go meet this boyfriend of yours."

Kaleb watched as Officer Graham strutted his officer walk and knocked his police knock on the front door. Kaleb hunkered down in his seat while short work was made of the partygoers.

Walter returned to the car and said to Kaleb, "I told him that we had a noise complaint and that if he didn't break up the party, I'd have to charge him with disorderly house."

Kaleb smiled his most gracious smile. "Thank you for not fining us. I lost my job and I'm still looking for a new one. Between my unemployment and Austin's part-time job, we can't afford a ticket."

"Well, if you're looking for work you should head down to the station. It was really nice meeting you, Kaleb. I hope I get to see you again sometime."

Kaleb smiled as he handed him a small piece of paper with his phone number. "I'd like that too."

Kaleb waited for the cop car to drive away before he stormed into the house. If he'd had had a chance to translate any of those inscriptions he would be casting spells right now. He was furious. He only recognized a few people in his house. At the center of the maelstrom of drunks was Austin.

"Oh, here we go," Austin said, talking to no one in particular. "First the cops, now the nagging boyfriend. Where've you been all night? Out with your other boyfriend?"

Kaleb eyes became wide with anger. "Get these people out of my house. I'm going to bed." No one moved. "Now!"

"I guess that's who called the cops. Heard us from down the street? Whatever, that cop was totally checking me out." Austin wasn't wearing a shirt and admittedly looked very sexy.

Kaleb pursed his lips, but said no more.

"Fine, whatever." Austin turned to address the press of people. "Hey guys, got to go, ball and chain's back. Everybody out. Miss Party Pooper is home." As the drunks began filing out the door Austin stormed upstairs. "There, are you happy now? If you can't have fun, no one can."

Kaleb waited for the last of the strangers to leave before storming up the stairs and into the bedroom where he assumed Austin had passed out. He was ready to yell and scream some more, but when he opened the bedroom door all he saw was Austin lying above the covers, naked.

"Are you just going to stand there, or are you going to take your clothes off?" Austin grinned to himself and closed his eyes. "I'm so warm. Aren't you warm?"

Kaleb sat on the bed next to him and ran his hands along Austin's bicep. He kissed Austin's arm. "Am I still mad at you?"

Austin pulled Kaleb down next to him and unbuttoned his shirt. "I sure hope not. I was just having fun. I was lonely. You've been gone so long. But you're home now."

Guilt replaced anger. Kaleb hadn't been spending very much time at home lately. Secrets were the most dangerous poison to relationships and Kaleb knew it. He also knew how Austin felt about magic.

Austin unbuttoned his pants and slipped his hand into them; he lost his train of thought. Tomorrow was as good of time as any to come clean with Austin about how he'd been spending his time. A gasp left Kaleb's mouth as Austin helped himself to what he had found.

•꙳•

Kaleb turned off the shower and dried off. He wanted to prove to Austin that magic was real. It was the only way to stop the argument about Nick once and for all. Once he understood what they were working on, it would be clear that there was nothing going on between them.

He crawled into bed next to Austin. Kaleb's mind started to wander back to that vault of knowledge. There was so much to do. First thing he wanted to do was learn Gaelic. Then he would go through and catalog all the "books" and try out a few spells.

He rolled over to look at the alarm clock on the nightstand. It read four thirty and Kaleb still couldn't sleep. He rolled back over and froze. Looming over Austin's side of the bed was a shadow, darker than any of the others in the room. Its arms ended in long, snake-like fingers.

The creature walked slowly to his side of the bed. Kaleb lay paralyzed in fear. The icy fingers of terror ran through his entire body. He tried to scream out but he couldn't. It lunged at him. Survival broke the spell of fear and he fell out of the bed in his attempt to get to the lamp. He must have cried out because he woke Austin.

"Baby, are you okay?" he said, rubbing his eyes.

Kaleb picked himself up off the floor. "Bad dream. Go back to sleep honey," Kaleb responded soberly. He hoped it was a dream. The shadowy figure was gone and he had no idea if sometime in the night he had managed to actually drift off to sleep. Insomnia was a strange bedfellow; sometimes sleep snuck in without you even knowing it.

Austin leaned over and gave Kaleb a kiss and fell back to sleep. Kaleb quietly got out of bed and went to the bathroom. He plucked the nightlight out of the wall socket and brought it back to the bedroom, reawakening Austin back up in the process.

"Must've been pretty bad," Austin said, half asleep. At an almost inaudible volume he mumbled, "I know I'm not the best boyfriend in the world. I love you."

"I love you too. I'm fine. I'm going to go get a glass of water and maybe stay up for a while. Go back to sleep, handsome." He gave Austin a kiss on the shoulder.

Austin fell back into a deep slumber and began snoring. Kaleb quietly made his way down the steps to the kitchen and in between the sixth and seventh step shadow-walked to Saint Patrick's Library.

•¶•

Morgan woke up to a semi-transparent ghost looming over her bed. "Ugh, I just laid down, what do you want?" She pulled the blankets up to her chin.

93

"*Kaleb ask me tell you he is ...*" Geoffroi paused, puzzling out if what he was about to say was really a word. "*Okay?*" When she didn't correct him the ghost nodded. "*We arrive at death beds. Offizier down? Kaleb said come here.*" He smiled.

Morgan sat up and turned on her lamp. "Well, thanks for the report. You can go now." The Templar didn't move. She shook her head. "Can I help you?"

The ghost stared down at her. "*I see how you look to him.*"

This was going to be a long day. Morgan sighed. "Kaleb and I are just friends."

"*No, I mean the other. I die hundreds of ages ago, but still know look of amare in young maiden's eye.*" The ghost smiled at her.

Morgan sat up in bed. "Oh, him. Look, sorry, what's your name?"

"*Geoffroi.*"

"Right. Look Roy, Kaleb and Nick are ... what's the best way to put this in terms you would understand? They like the dick!" she said as she ran her hands through a tangled mess of hair.

The ghost looked puzzled, "I not understand."

"Are you serious? Okay, let me try putting it another way. They like boys, not girls." Morgan's patience was running low.

"*Eunuch? Yes, I know this. It not unheard of in my time.*" The ghost loomed over her bed.

"Okay, sure, whatever. So you see there's no way for me to ever be with Nick. He doesn't like my lady parts." Morgan rubbed her eyes. It was six in the morning and this ghost just cost her four hours of sleep. She slumped her shoulders; he still wasn't leaving.

The Templar shifted from foot to foot in discomfort. *"Amare should not abandon so easily. You sorceress, no?"*

Morgan got out of bed. "Wow, Roy, wow." She made her way to the kitchen with the ghost in tow. Mercedes peered at her from the living room. She stretched before she jumped from her perch on the back of the sofa. "Great, now we woke up Sleeping Beauty."

"Well it's nice to be finally recognized for my beauty," Mercedes added, jumping to the kitchen counter.

Morgan pulled out a box of ice cream from the freezer and sat down on the couch. She talked around a mouthful of cookies-and-cream, "Let's just suppose for a moment that I could magic myself into being a boy. What if I make an ugly boy?"

Mercedes chuckled in her mind. *"With all of the things you could do with magic, you want to be a boy?"*

"No. I mean, maybe. Roy here was telling me that I'm in love and should do whatever is in my power not to let it get away," Morgan replied around another mouthful of cookies-and-cream.

The ghost sounded confused. *"That not what I say."*

Mercedes huffed. *"Are you really going to listen to his nonsense? There are so many great things you could do and all you can focus on is an infatuation. And you."* Mercedes gave Geoffroi a very nasty look for a cat. *"Stop filling her head with ridiculous delusions."*

"I not say be boy," the ghost muttered; they still weren't listening.

"Morgan, this is complete crap. You aren't taking this seriously, are you?" Morgan's face had a detached look that Mercedes had seen a million times before. Morgan was fantasizing. *"Oh great. Look what you've done. We've lost her."*

"*With no disrespect, you are cat.*"

"*Disrespect taken! You're walking a real fine line here buddy. I don't want to hear any more of this nonsense. Got it? I'm going back to my nap. I suggest you get out of here and go lurk somewhere else.*" Her tail flicked back and forth.

"Mercedes, be nice," Morgan countered. Her face still held a vacant expression. "He's only trying to help."

"*This is not the kind of help you need. I've been watching out for you for years. Remember the time I killed that mouse? That bastard was stealing your food! And then there's this guy. This guy just walks in here and tells you to swap genders so you can run off into the sunset with Kaleb. I say bullshit!*"

The ghost shifted from foot to foot. "*I not say Kaleb.*"

They ignored the ghost. "No we were talking about Nick."

The cat tilted her head to one side. "*Oh. Well, in that case never mind. I say go for it.*"

Her eyes brightened. "Really?"

"*No, not really! Fuck, Morgan! What you need is a good step aerobics class, a dietitian, and a shrink. Changing genders so you can snag a gay guy? I don't know why I stick around here.*"

"*Lady Cat—*" Geoffroi started, but Mercedes' head swiveled around to give him another piercing look.

The cat's mind-voice was cold and harsh. "*I don't want to hear another word out of your incorporeal mouth or I will roll the salt shaker across every door and windowsill and you will never step your ghostly feet in here again, you got me?*"

"*I say no more.*" The Templar bowed and faded from view.

Morgan was crying into her box of ice cream. "You think I'm fat."

"Oh, Morgan, I didn't say you're fat." Mercedes curled up into her lap, *"You are fat."*

Last Respite

The Templar Geoffroi howled out in pain. Three shades pinned the Templar to the floor of Saint Patrick's Library. A demon stood on the other side of the veil between realms. It had no way to pass physically through to the other side so it ordered the shades to pull the ghost back to the nocturnal world of the dead.

"Tell me, how did you cross over?" The demon's voice sounded like the rumbling of a volcano. It towered nine feet high over the ghost, its fingers ended in sharp black talons, and its body was covered in red thorny spines, but it wore nothing else. The demon's snakelike red eyes bore down on the ghost.

Geoffroi's voice cracked as he replied defiantly, "*I not afraid of you.*"

The demon laughed. "Yet you cower like a child. There aren't many creatures of the night that can pass to the realm of the living. Legion seem to be under the impression that there's a new shadow-strider."

Kaleb sprinted past them, oblivious to their presence. Immediately on arrival he stepped into the physical world. Geoffroi had tried to call out to him but his passing was too quick.

"How perfect," the demon said to itself. "Right on time." The demon watched from the other side of the veil. It was like trying to read the label at the bottom of a bowl filled with water and ink. It wasn't impossible, but required a lot of squinting.

As it watched him, the Templar used the distraction to wiggle free of the shades and escaped. The demon raised one of its massive fingers and silently ordered the shades to follow the ghost. The demon quickly calculated its options.

Kaleb took three staves into his arms, the demon smiled. It cut open the fabric of the shadowy realm with a massive claw and created a world within the darkest of the staves. The focal point of the rift was the obsidian orb at the top of the staff.

With an outpouring of magical power the demon created a place inside where it could wait and watch in secret. Once the demon was safely within the staff its lips curled into a smile. The last time it had smiled was a thousand years ago; it hurt.

•╤•

Kaleb brought the first load of dissected trees to Morgan's living room. "Get out your laptops kids. We've got a long day ahead of us."

After the initial shock of the "books" had faded, they had started to realize the size of the endeavor. Morgan and Nick both called in sick to work so they could all start their new pet project together.

Kaleb had brought back all ten staves; each was beautiful in its own way. Nick immediately gravitated to the oak staff topped with a sphere of obsidian. Morgan pawed through them before settling on a cherry staff topped with a chunk of rose quartz the size of her fist. Morgan took the remaining staves and left them propped up against the wall in her bedroom.

Even Mercedes was enjoying her gift from Kaleb. He had brought her a catnip toy, for which Morgan was extremely grateful. Though she wouldn't tell the boys why, she secretly enjoyed watching Mercedes go crazy for catnip, and it was even more enjoyable now that she knew what the cat was thinking.

Kaleb ferried the "books" from the library to the trailer. If it were left up to Morgan they would be haphazardly strewn about her living room, but Nick had seen to it that while Kaleb was running back and forth from Rome, he would clean her trailer and organize the cross sections into neat columns arranged by size. Morgan had to move her TV to the bedroom so they could have more space. When the stacks of giant coasters filled half the living room Kaleb decided they had enough work to do and sat down to join them in translating.

Kaleb was surprised that Roy hadn't shown up to help translate, but they copied as best they could and would translate later. They worked for hours. Every now and then, the repetition would be interrupted by Nick reading one of the inscriptions out loud. Morgan and Kaleb braced themselves each time, but luckily, his pronunciation was terrible. By four in the afternoon they each had about twenty "books" worth of transcriptions.

"Once the sun goes down I think you might be able to take the neighbor's wheelbarrow if that'd help," Morgan said, taking a sip of her tea.

"I appreciate the thought, but Austin got off work two hours ago. He's been texting asking where I am."

Nick smirked. Kaleb crossed his arms. "What? I know you don't like Austin, believe me, I know. So what? Just spit it out."

"I really doubt he cares where you are," Nick replied while trying not to look too smug.

"Yes, he does. You haven't had a boyfriend in over a year? So don't try and give me relationship advice."

Nick interrupted, "Seriously, Kaleb, when are you going to wake up? Let's see. I don't want you, I don't want Austin. Men are pigs, and you can do so much better."

"Thank you for sharing, but need I remind you this is my life. I will spend the rest of my life with that man. So you best start getting along with him now, because he's going to be around for a long while."

Nick muttered to the drink in his hand, "Whatever you say."

"I don't know what made you so bitter. You never would tell me, but come on, Nick, open up your heart. Mister Right is out there. You're just going to let him walk right by because men are pigs?"

"Well, if he were Mister Right he wouldn't walk right by. Now would he? He'd sweep me off my feet and onto his shiny white horse, or fire-breathing hell horse, whatever. The point is, Mister Right isn't here *right now* and I'll end up being some old biddy collecting cats and safety pins, no offense," Nick said, punctuating his statement with a gesture to Morgan.

Morgan shrugged. "None taken."

"You never did tell us if you ended up meeting Officer McHottie the other day." Nick licked his lips. "Always did love a man in uniform. Not to mention that ruggedly handsome look he was sporting, total scruff-muffin."

Morgan jumped on the opening. "I can at least say I see Kaleb's point. You didn't even try to flirt with Officer McHottie. I should know, I was there."

"Oh my god, Kaleb, you should have seen Morgan trying to flirt. It was *hilarious!* She put her hand on her hip like this." Nick did his best impression of Morgan's attempt to flirt. Morgan threw a pillow at his head but her aim left much to be desired.

Kaleb was smiling sheepishly. "You thought he was cute?"

"Who? Oh, Officer McHottie. Yeah! Totally! Oh my good goddess, you did meet him. Did you see his arms? What happened? Lord and Lady, you made out with him!" Morgan was practically on the edge of her seat with excitement. Kaleb flung the pillow back across the room, which Morgan dodged. "I don't know why I even ask. No one appreciates me."

"Yes, I did meet him. His name is Walter." Kaleb was blushing slightly.

Nick gravitated to drama like a bug to a zapper. If he weren't sitting in a cross-legged position, his feet would have been kicking in the air with anticipation. "You did make out with him, you little minx."

"We did *not* make out. We didn't even kiss. He was …" Kaleb trailed off and smiled.

"So, are you going to make out with him?" Nick asked.

"Nick, be serious. I have a boyfriend. Besides, I gave him my number. Told him to call me and we'd go see a haunting. Figured I could get Roy to rattle some chains or something."

Nick's voice went up an octave. "Oh my goodness, our little Kay-kay has a crush-crush!"

"Stop it, Nick. I just thought it'd be nice to have a friend that wasn't a complete bitch," Kaleb said, hitting Nick in the face with a pillow.

•᛫•

Kaleb stopped by the house to find Austin had already left. He sent him a message to see where he had gone and got a short reply saying that he was at his cousin's playing cards. Kaleb shrugged and took a frozen pizza out of the freezer before shadow-walking back to Morgan's.

He arrived to find Nick and Morgan on their computers copying and pasting into an online Gaelic-to-English translator. They knew it wasn't going to be a very accurate, but it would at least give them a rough idea about what the spells could do.

It wasn't long before they realized what their problem was when trying high magic on their own. The teachings of the ancient druids talked about rivers of magic they referred to as ley lines. Those lines all connected within the earth in a kind of wellspring, a sea of magic.

Spells required them to first draw the power from the sea of magic through these channels. The staff could be used to hold that magic while they recited the incantation that would form the spell. With enough practice, a sorcerer could be free of his staff, but they were still a long way from trying that.

"Well now, what do we have here? Oh, Kaleb! I think I'm going to like this spell," Nick chimed. "A spell to locate a person." He grinned up at Kaleb who came to read over his shoulder. "Who should we find first? That douchebag boyfriend of yours or Officer McHottie?"

"Just stop it! I don't need a spell to know where Austin is. He's at his cousin's house," Kaleb said.

Nick crossed his arms and looked up into Kaleb's eyes. "He seems to spend a lot of time hanging out with his family. Seems a little unnatural to me. Morgan, do you happen to have a city map?"

Kaleb was no longer playing. "Stop it!" Unfortunately, it didn't stop his friends.

Nick added relentlessly, "If he's at his cousin's, then you have nothing to worry about. I'm just curious to see if the spell works," he lied. Nick was certain that the reason Austin was accusing Kaleb of cheating was because he was cheating.

Morgan went out to her car and came back with a map of the city. When she returned she took Nick's laptop and read over the translation. "Okay, the spell says that you need a pendulum and power. Direct the power through the staff and into the pendulum. Clearly state the name of the person you are trying to locate and have an image of the person firmly in mind. After that you're a short incantation away from locating them."

Nick picked up his oak staff and reached out with his mind to the nearest stream of magic. Morgan handed him a necklace with a teardrop-shaped smoky quartz hanging from it. He tried to pull it into his staff, but he couldn't get it to come to him. Whenever his mind touched the magical currents it ran through his mental fingers. He couldn't get any to go into the staff. He tried again.

A female voice spoke into his mind, *"You're not doing anything wrong, you're just different."*

Nick jumped a little causing a few raised eyebrows, but no one said anything. Nick thought if Morgan could have a talking cat, why not a talking staff.

He pretended to concentrate on the task at hand. "I got this, I just need a minute," Nick said to Kaleb and Morgan. *"I'm sorry. Who're you?"* he responded to the voice in his mind.

"You are the first person I have spoken with in centuries. Are you from Avalon?" Her voice was silky and sweet and Nick was certain she could easily have a career as a phone sex operator.

Morgan tried to take the pendulum from his hand but he batted her away. "I've got this," Nick said as he closed his eyes. Morgan shrugged. She lit a cigarette while they waited. In silence he resumed his conversation with his staff. *"Um, no ma'am. Not to be rude, but did you have something to do with why I wasn't able to cast that spell just now?"*

She laughed softly and politely. *"I'm afraid not. From what I saw it appears you are not a sorcerer at all."*

Nick kept his skepticism in check. *"No offense, but I've been casting for years. Granted, we didn't call ourselves sorcerers. I don't know, is witchcraft the same thing as sorcery?"*

"Is a painter the same as a sculptor? Each is an art, but very different results. You may be a witch, but you are certainly no sorcerer. Your key ability will keep you from casting spells of high magic. I should know, it was the ability I have," she mused.

"How did you get trapped in the staff?" Nick asked.

"I was powerful and I was feared. My ability, you see, was vampirism." Her mind-voice was as smooth and soft as silk.

A slight smile crept onto Nick's face which he immediately hid from his friends with a yawn. *"So I'm a vampire?"*

"Yes, and strong one I'd wager. Our kind is so limited when attempting spells of high magic. The only way to hold onto high magic's forces is when we feed."

"I knew it! I told them I was a vampire!" Nick composed himself. The woman in the staff was guarded, he couldn't feel any emotions from her. He would have to be careful. He hesitated, but finally asked, *"Will you teach me?"*

The voice contained a smile when it replied, *"I would be honored."*

The expressions of his friends looked to be on the border of indifference and boredom. "Sorry, guys, looks like I'll need more practice. Morgan, why don't you give it a shot?" He handed her the pendulum.

Kaleb got to his feet and walked over to Morgan. "You really don't have to do this. I'm sure there're a lot of other spells we can try out."

Morgan shrugged. "But I want to try this one." She took her staff in one hand and the pendulum in the other. Her mind reached out to the nearest stream of magic and pulled it to her staff until the stone glowed with a rose light. She beamed at Kaleb and Nick. "Neat!"

She read the words in Gaelic and formed an image of Austin in her mind. Morgan finished by saying the name of the person they sought, "Austin."

The pendulum circled around the length of the map of its own volition. It circled high and fast. The stone of her staff pulsed a soft red light as the pendulum swung around and around.

In the blink of an eye, the pendulum shot out of Morgan's hand, hovered for a second over a small section of the south side and slammed into the map.

"Um, Kaleb?" She looked to Kaleb who was clenching and unclenching his fists. "I take it that's not his cousin's house."

•┇•

Nick arrived at his dorm. With his laptop under one arm and his staff in the other he confidently walked down the halls. Several people gave him sidewise glances which he ignored.

The one thing he hated most about living in the dorms was how stupid and repulsive some people were. Nick had to pay for his college on his own. The people he hated the most were the kids who thought they could ride through life on their parents' dime.

Nick had no parents. He had gone from foster family to foster family and then to the streets when he finished high school. The foster parents he had been placed with last saw him as a meal ticket. Their two biological children could do no wrong, and he could do no right. When high school ended so did his relationship with that family. It had been hard to be alone at first. Trust was a luxury. Nick learned quickly that a pretty face and a fit body could pay for anything he needed.

He wasn't proud of his life, but he was living. Kaleb and Morgan were good friends, but they didn't need to know where his cash came from. He let them believe he was a trust fund brat who could have whatever he wanted. Everyone had a price, sadly he knew his was two-hundred dollars an hour.

Occasionally, he would meet someone who actually was a decent person, but for the most part they only wanted one thing. College was no different. He smiled as he realized that from now on they would be his experiments. If he was to learn how to become a true vampire, what better place to start than here?

The dorm room was empty when he arrived. Their room was shaped like a Tetris block, a long room with a small bathroom off to the right of the entrance. Nick had the front half of the room, and it was decorated with black and grey silk hangings. Devin had the farther end of the room and decorated with sports posters and pictures of bikini-clad women. In the middle of the room was their shared space: a TV, a small fridge, and a desk.

Nick sat his laptop down on the desk next to his roommate's computer. He propped his staff up next to his bed and lay down. He cleared his mind and extended it to the staff. *"I'm ready to learn."*

•¶•

Walter paced the length of his living room fighting his indecision. The slip of paper was in one hand and his phone was in the other. It had been three days; was it too soon to call? Today was his day off, so if he wanted to spend time with Kaleb it would need to be today.

He couldn't stop thinking about those eyes and it felt like every time he closed his own there they were. He took a deep breath and dialed the number.

A timid voice answered, "Hello?"

Walter's stomach fell out from under him. "Hi, um, is this Kaleb?"

"Yeah. Who is this?"

Walter began pacing the length of his living room. His nerves were getting the best of him. "I don't know if you remember me from the other day—"

Kaleb interrupted, his voice conveyed a smile, "Is this Officer Graham from the graveyard?"

A nervous laugh escaped Walter, "I'd prefer Walter, if that's okay. I'm off duty today and was hoping you might be—"

Again, Kaleb beat him to finishing his sentence. "Interested in taking you out for lunch and then stop up at the thirteen steps for a ghost hunt? I'd love to."

Walter gulped. "Dinner?"

Kaleb's voice was nonchalant and pleasant. "Yeah, sure, I mean if that's okay with you. I haven't eaten yet."

"That'd be great, it's a date!" he meant to stop himself, but it was a little too late.

Kaleb didn't seem to notice his choice of words. "Pick me up at six?"

Walter let out the breath he forgot he had been holding. "I look forward to it."

Once the phone was hung up, the facade of calm was replaced by a rush of things he needed to do. He only had an hour to get ready and he was nowhere near presentable. He took a quick shower and shaved. He sampled a few scents before deciding on his most expensive Calvin Klein. He tried on a few outfits and tidied up his car before he was on his way.

He pulled up in front of Kaleb's house at six on the dot. Kaleb was sitting out front as he drove up. As much as he had tried to forget, Walter painfully reminded himself that Kaleb was in a relationship.

"I hope you don't mind Greek. I made reservations at The Oracle," Walter said as he opened the passenger door. Walter's spirits sank as a frown came over Kaleb's face.

"That sounds great, but I couldn't afford that place before I got fired."

Walter chose his words carefully, "It would be my treat. You're going to be taking me on a ghost hunt after all. What're friends for?"

Kaleb cheered up. "In that case, it sounds great. But you'll have to let me take you out for lunch sometime to make up for it."

"You won't hear me complain," Walter said as he caught himself putting a hand on Kaleb's knee, and quickly turned it into a pat. "So, is Austin okay with this?"

"Well, he knows I made a new friend and we're going up to the cemetery for a ghost hunt. He doesn't approve of anything involving ghosts or magic, so he didn't question it any further. Besides, he's at his cousin's tonight playing poker." Kaleb's voice quivered a little.

"Everything kosher in paradise?"

"Yeah, it's just that I see him less now that I'm unemployed than while I was working full time." Kaleb shrugged. "Enough about me, I want to know about you."

"Well there's not much to know. I moved here about five years ago from a small town in Texas. Two older sisters. Joined the force. Doesn't give me much time for a social life."

"Why'd you move all the way up here?"

"One of my best friends growing up, she's a lesbian, came up here with her partner. They had a baby, broke up, and now she's up here all by herself. Her family doesn't approve of her 'lifestyle,' so she decided to stay. I came up here to help."

"Wow, that's really noble of you." Kaleb grinned.

Walter smiled back. "It was supposed to be mine, but they went with another donor." An involuntary frown crossed his face. "The kid is adorable, so I guess they made a good choice."

"I'm sure you would make beautiful babies," Kaleb said, patting him on the knee. "I take it you want kids?"

"Absolutely! I love kids. My nieces and nephews are great, but it'd be nice to have some of my own someday. It's scary though, after what happened to Connie. I don't know how she does it. They were together for four years."

Kaleb cautioned a question, "What happened?"

"One day after work, Amy sat her down and told her she just couldn't do it anymore. Told her she was going to take a week to clear her head and never came back. Connie's been really strong through it all. That kid's got a great mom."

"Sounds like it's been pretty hard on you." Kaleb could tell that this was a subject Walter didn't enjoy talking about. "So what's keeping you from having kids of your own?"

Walter shrugged. "Haven't met the right guy. I'd rather have the whole package: nice house, good job, and a great husband. Without that, I don't think I'd be ready for kids."

Kaleb thought for a second before responding. "Well you seem like a really nice guy. I'm a firm believer that there is someone special for each of us. I'm sure you'll meet yours soon."

"Is Austin yours?" He didn't know why he asked the question. Walter scolded himself for not bringing any tact with him.

Kaleb masked his feelings under a veneer of tranquility. "Some days more than others."

•፣•

It was an odd sensation for Nick. He was halfway between meditation and a true out-of-body experience. Within the staff was the strangest cathedral he had ever seen.

The benches and walls appeared to be made of a dark marble, and the stained glass windows let in a blood-red light. Where a cathedral would normally have an altar instead was a voluptuous woman in a crimson robes sitting on a marble throne.

Her skin was milk white, and her hair was as black as the obsidian on his staff. When he approached she began to speak, "The first lesson of vampirism is that we don't drink blood. We drink the vitality of our victims. Obtaining the energy can be challenging. You must first get past the target's personal shields. Most vampires prefer fear or seduction, but other means exist."

"Okay, that seems easy enough. Oh, Teacher, what name shall I call you by?"

She thought for a moment. "My name may be difficult for you to pronounce. You may refer to me as Lifedrinker." The demon held in a laugh. This had been easier than she had thought.

Given her nature, she had always been fond of the vampires. She had even schooled some of the earliest vampires in the art. It certainly suited her perverted humor for her first human subject to refer to her by her preferred name.

Lifedrinker resumed the instruction. "Now, once you have broken down their shields, you are ready to feed. There are seven chakras which are the converging points of vitality within the body: the crown, the third-eye, the throat, the heart, the solar plexus, the sexual or sacral, and the base or root chakras. Each is tied to a different bodily function. Do you understand?" Nick nodded. "Good."

Nick looked around the cathedral and then back to the dais. "So what do you think of the name Lucian?"

She wheeled around to face him. "Excuse me?"

"Well, I mean, Nick isn't a very good vampire name. So I've been thinking, I think I want my vampire name to be Lucian."

Lifedrinker scowled. "Have you been paying attention?"

"Yeah, of course, break down shield with fear or sexy-sexy, drain life through chakras. Got it. Pretty self-explanatory. So do you think Lucian would be a good vampire name?"

Lifedrinker glared at Nick, and scolded, "I am sure I can wait another hundred years for a pupil who will take this more seriously."

Nick waved his hand at her. "Sorry, don't mind me. You were saying?"

"You can pull energy from any of the chakras, but the easiest is the heart chakra. You can obtain different results by disabling different chakras. The throat chakra can disable the voice, shredding the sacral chakra can render a man impotent. Destroying all seven can paralyze."

Nick interjected, "So you like the name?" Her lips became a thin line on her face. "Sorry, never mind. All right, I got this. I even have a perfect test subject in mind. So, you said disabling chakras can get different results?"

After learning what he could from Lifedrinker, Nick began to focus on his actual body. He started with his fingers and toes and felt them tingle. One by one he felt his muscles expand and contract. He felt his breathing and his heartbeat. Slowly he worked his consciousness through his entire body until he could open his eyes and sit up.

A smile formed on his face and he patted his staff. He called his ex, Jess. It had been a pretty hard breakup. There had been screaming, physical violence, and a visit from the police. If anyone was worthy of being his test case it was him.

"Hey, Jess, it's Nick. Yeah, I'm sorry for calling." Nick feigned some tears. "Would you mind if I stop over? I've had a rough couple of days." He hid his laughter behind fake sobbing. "I was hoping I could see you. Really? I mean, just like that? I didn't think you'd ever want to see me again after everything that happened. No, you're right, that's all ancient history. Okay, I'll be right over. Should I stop and pick up anything? Okay, I'll grab some beer."

Nick grabbed his keys and headed out the door. The staff was left propped up by his bed. He wasn't worried about anyone trying to steal it. Lifedrinker would see to it that it was returned if someone was foolish enough to try and take it.

Unlike sorcery, vampirism didn't require the use of a staff. It required skill and training. With Lifedrinker providing the training, he would hone his skills and suckle the forces of life itself.

.٭.

Nick arrived just after dark. He used a bottle of eye drops to give the impression that he had been crying all day. He looked in the mirror and commended himself. He hadn't taken acting classes before, but considered adding it to his schedule for next semester.

He walked to the buzzer and rang Jess's apartment. When the door opened Nick threw his arms around Jess. He was a bodybuilder; his chest puffed out like a song bird while he held Nick in his anaconda arms. Jess's blonde crew-cut hair ran down his sideburns and into well-groomed facial hair.

Nick wove a tale of cheating and heartache. He embellished a little on Kaleb's relationship. To hide his laughs he put his face in his hands and feigned sobs. Jess rubbed his back.

"Can I stay with you tonight?" Nick asked, rubbing his eyes to try to coax out a few more tears. Seeing Jess again was making him angrier than he had anticipated. It took a great deal of restraint to continue the ruse.

The physical abuse wasn't the only trauma delivered by Jess's hands. Their relationship had ended over a year ago, but the scars of the emotional abuse never healed. Tonight he'd get his revenge.

"Of course you can." Nick had counted on Jess's libido to do the trick. He could tell from Jess's eyes that he was expecting more than just a cuddle.

With his mind Nick could feel the forces that surrounded Jess. There was a shell of energy around him that was the shield Lifedrinker had mentioned. Nick wasn't sure why he had never noticed shields before. It was like the thin membrane of an egg yolk that shifted and flowed around the person it was protecting. With a little more pressing that shield would come down.

Lifedrinker said that one of the tricks was using seduction. Lust wouldn't drop those shields, so just dropping his pants wouldn't cut it. Nick had to be cunning. He drew Jess into a hug and fake-sobbed on his shoulder.

He conjured up some fake tears before looking into Jess's amber eyes. "He said he didn't find me attractive anymore."

Jess pulled Nick into a tight embrace. "You are the most beautiful man in the world."

If it weren't for the physical abuse and the torment he endured at Jess's hands he might have fallen for it. Nick held onto his resolve. This man was a monster, and tonight he was going to find out what real monsters can do.

Nick leaned in and kissed Jess. He moved his hand under Jess's shirt and pressed their bodies together. The shield came down. Nick lunged with his mind and shredded Jess's sacral chakra, the chakra associated with sexual function.

There was a taste and texture to it. It was like drinking vanilla-flavored silk. He felt invigorated, as though he had just drank seven cups of coffee but without the jitters. His body was alive and afire. Colors radiated with inner light, sounds were sharper and clearer. He felt powerful.

Lifedrinker said it could take months for a chakra to reform after being destroyed by a vampire. Nick knew the kind of libido Jess had and it was insatiable. Jess was about to see what it was like to be the impotent one.

•፨•

The Oracle was overflowing with patrons. They were seated in a small corner table near the fireplace. The floors were all hardwood, and the tables were of the same wood. They gave the impression that they were carved out of the floor itself.

The dining room was decorated in blues and whites. Greek columns were spaced evenly through the length of the dining hall. Lining the wall were bronze busts of all the major Olympian gods. From their table he could see the busts of Zeus, Hera, and Apollo.

Kaleb could smell baking bread coming from the kitchen and the lavender that graced their table. Their table was lit by three white taper candles, and despite being crowded the spacing of the patrons gave them some semblance of privacy. Kaleb wondered if they had installed a sound dampener in the ceiling.

Kaleb took a drink of his water and finally gathered enough courage to ask, "How on earth did you get this reservation on such short notice? I mean, there's got to be a waiting list for this place."

Walter smiled. "What can I say, I have connections."

Kaleb raised an eyebrow. "An officer perk?"

"No, not like that. I know the owner. I was her 'maid of honor' for her wedding," Walter replied. "She'll probably want to come meet you. I don't ask her for favors very often. That, and I kind of told her I had a date."

Kaleb took a sip of his water. "I take it that's why we got the good table."

"Yeah, I don't go on dates very often. I knew it'd get us seated, I really hope I'm not out of line. On second thought, fast food would have probably been more appropriate. I'm sorry."

"Don't be. If the food is as great as I've heard, then I should be thanking you. As long as you know this isn't a date." Kaleb cocked his head to the side to await Walter's response.

"Oh, I totally know that. This is just a casual dinner between friends." Walter looked around nervously around at the other diners whose clothing was anything but casual. "Well semi-casual at least. Did I mention I'm friends with the owner?"

Kaleb laughed. "You did."

Walter bit his lip as he stared at Kaleb. "So I have to ask, are you a natural blonde? I mean, you hair is almost white."

"I am, and yes this is my natural color. I used to dye it black every once in a while, but Austin likes the platinum look so I haven't done that in a long time."

The food arrived at their table as the conversation shifted to ghosts and magic. Kaleb took over the conversation with exuberance. Walter loved listening to the passion in Kaleb's voice. He loved his job on the force, but he could never claim the level of passion that Kaleb felt about the occult.

"Have you ever thought about dropping the job search and starting up a business?" Walter said before taking a bite of his loukaniko.

"What like tarot reading?"

"Sure, I mean you know a lot about this sort of thing. I'm sure you'd be good at it."

He frowned. "Starting a business takes capital, drive, and skill and all I've got is the skill." Kaleb took another bite of his gyro and closed his eyes in pleasure. "By the way, this is the best gyro I've ever had. The cucumber sauce here is amazing."

"Tell you what, you draw up a business plan, and I'll find you a backer." Walter had no idea where to even start looking but he wanted so badly to help Kaleb make his dream come true.

"A business plan?" Kaleb snickered. "I have no idea how to write a term paper, let alone a business plan. You're sweet Walter, but if wishes were fishes we'd all be swimming in the sea. There's no way I'm going to make a living off reading tarot. I'd still need a day job."

"It was just a thought," Walter said, sounding defeated.

Kaleb was beaming. "And one of the nicest thoughts I've heard all year."

"I know I only just met you, but you just have this passion. I couldn't help it, I just thought it'd be nice to see you doing something you enjoy."

Kaleb crumpled his brow, "Wow."

"What?" Worry lines formed on Walter's forehead. He wasn't off to a good start and he was afraid he finally crossed the line.

"What a line. Does that usually work for you?" Kaleb asked, half grinning.

He tried to defend himself. "I'm serious. You are very passionate about magic. I just think you should do something with it."

Kaleb looked out the window as the sun was starting to set and muttered, "Oh, I am."

⋅⊤⋅

Kaleb and Walter arrived at the Thirteen Steps Cemetery a few hours after dark. Walter hesitated in getting out of the car, but Kaleb returned an earlier favor and opened his door for him, grinning. "I seriously hope you're not scared already."

"It's not that at all. It's just the time. We've only got another hour before we're not allowed to be up here," Walter said, not budging from his seat.

"Well, you had better stop stalling and get out of the car." Walter still didn't budge "Sir, I'm going to need you to step out of the car, please."

He crossed his arms. "Oh, ha-ha. You can't use cop lines on me."

Once Kaleb had finally gotten Walter to leave the safety of the car, they began to make their way to the cemetery's surrounding woods. It was eerie and quiet.

A branch snapped. Walter jumped and grabbed Kaleb's hand. For a moment, Walter considered letting go, but instead Kaleb squeezed it putting his mind at ease.

As they entered the woods, an owl cried out to the night. Walter froze. Kaleb rubbed Walter's arm with his free hand. "There's nothing to be afraid of out here. The living are much worse than the dead."

"I've never really done anything like this before," Walter said timidly.

"Oh, here we go with the bad pickup lines again," Kaleb replied with a laugh. Walter realized with another squeeze of his hand and seeing the impish grin on Kaleb's face, that this was, again, a joke.

Up ahead was a soft glow, but Walter couldn't make out what was causing it. It was a brightness in the middle of darkness. His legs quit working and he froze instantly.

"Don't be scared. I wouldn't let anything happen to you," Kaleb said reassuringly.

"Easy for you to say. What's up there?"

"Just trust me." Kaleb squeezed Walter's hand again before leading him through the dark game trail.

They walked slowly up a small hill and at the crest of the hill Walter saw what was causing the glow. It was the light of the full moon shining off a lake. The woods themselves were alive with its light. Kaleb squeezed Walter's hand again and said, "See? Nothing to be afraid of."

Walter let go of Kaleb's hand and walked down to the lake. "It's so beautiful. Is this where you were the other night?"

"Not quite, but I do come up here a lot to think." Kaleb carefully made his way down to the water's edge. He took off his shoes and put his feet in the water.

Walter stood next to Kaleb and gazed out over the placid water. "Is it dangerous to swim here?"

Kaleb shrugged. "No idea; can't swim."

Walter was shocked. He spent most of his life an hour away from the Gulf Coast. Swimming was a weekly thing for his family. "You can't swim?"

Kaleb kicked his feet in the water. "Nope, I sink."

Walter began to take off his shoes. "I'll protect you. Swimming is great." Kaleb did not seem to be very interested in the idea. "It's okay, you don't have to be bashful." Walter removed his shirt. His muscular body was smooth except for a patch of hair right below his belly button.

"Now you're just trying to get me naked," Kaleb said, eying Walter.

"Would you prefer I turn around while you undress? We are not skinny-dipping. I'm still a law-abiding citizen." Walter stripped down to his boxers and waded out into the pond. "Come on in, the water's ..." He grimaced as a current brought icy water to his nether parts. He smiled a fake smile. "It's great."

"Sure it is." Kaleb hiked up his pants over his knees and began a slow hesitant walk into the water.

"Seriously?" Walter was already chest deep into the water. Kaleb waded out to his calves and stopped. "I'd rather not have my seats soaked. I promise not to peek."

A very unhappy Kaleb made his way back to the shore. "The water's freezing, and I can't swim. I don't like this at all."

Walter pleaded. "I really want to teach you how to swim. I haven't met anyone who can't swim. Please, Kaleb? I did take you out for dinner. It would mean a lot to me if you gave it a try." He played his trump card, guilt.

"Fine." Kaleb said, unbuttoning his pants. "But don't look."

Walter turned around. He heard Kaleb sloshing through the water toward him. When Kaleb reached him he said, "Okay, so fall back into my arms and we'll teach you how to float."

Around the chattering of his teeth Kaleb managed to respond, "Excuse me?"

Walter positioned himself slightly behind Kaleb, placing his hands on Kaleb's waist. "Do you trust me?" Without saying a word, Kaleb fell back into Walter's arms. He held Kaleb above the water and Kaleb's body was rigid.

"You're safe, relax. Just breathe. Close your eyes if it helps." Kaleb closed his eyes and rested in Walter's arms. He could feel Kaleb begin to relax. "Keep breathing. Now start kicking your feet. There you go," Walter said encouragingly as he began to inch his way into the deeper water of the pond.

They reached the center of the lake and the moon was directly above them. Its silver light reflected off the water around them. "Now open your eyes."

Panic. Kaleb clutched Walter. So far, Walter had done a good job keeping Kaleb's head above water, but now Kaleb started to bob in and out of it. "Don't let me," Kaleb tried to say, but his face fell below the surface. Walter tried desperately to remind him to stay calm and to breathe. Kaleb clung to Walter. "Why would you bring me out into the middle? You know I can't swim?"

Their bodies were pressed closely together as Kaleb hung on for dear life. Walter spoke in a calm soothing manner, "You're safe. You're doing fine."

Abruptly the strongest undercurrent he had ever felt ripped them and their world apart. They were sinking.

·*·

"You know, I'm really sorry, Jess. I shouldn't have come over. This was a bad idea." Nick started piecing his clothes back together. "It's probably better this way. We won't have anything to regret in the morning."

Inwardly, Nick smiled. He had never had a problem with rising to the occasion and knew it must be terribly embarrassing. He delighted in Jess's dismay.

Jess interposed himself between Nick and the door. "You're not leaving."

Nick fumed with anger. The power he had been feeding on began coursing through every fiber of his being. "Step out of my way."

"Or what? You'll call the police like you did the last time? I don't see a phone." Nick wasn't a small person, but Jess was bigger. He always liked the muscled men, but his preference had been his undoing. Their last "date" ended with Nick being hurtled across the living room and into the kitchen cupboards.

Mystical forces flowed through Nick's veins, and no matter how large Jess was, he was no longer intimidated. The vampire within him drew upon the vitality he had been drinking. He reached out with his mind and he took hold of Jess's root chakra. "I don't need the police. You won't be hurting anyone anymore." He scowled as he ripped the chakra out.

Jess stumbled backwards. His legs were giving out beneath him. The vampire slowly stepped into the hallway, one foot at a time. Jess crawled backward on the floor into the living room.

"And you will *never* hurt me again." Nick loomed over the cowering Jess. He reached out with his mind and tasted the fear seeping from his ex. It was minty with a slight tang. "What's the matter babe, vampire got your tongue?" He ripped Jess's throat chakra out.

Jess dragged himself across the floor and grabbed the phone. He tried to speak but nothing would come out of his mouth. Jess's eyes were full of fear as Nick loomed over him. He held up his hands, pleading. The fear was palpable as tears streamed from Jess' eyes.

"I'm sorry, I can't hear you. Are you sorry for beating me up? I'm sure you are. It's too bad you had to throw your weight around again. I would have been fine leaving you a Viagra, but you just had to go there." Jess crawled to the door. "As you can see, I am not afraid of you anymore." Nick reached above him and locked the door.

Nick slowly shredded Jess's solar plexus chakra. Jess writhed in pain. Nick was reminded of how he felt after the broken arm and ribs. He shredded the crown chakra and the heart chakra, leaving only the third eye remaining.

Without his chakras he would be trapped within the confines of his own mind. Jess's aura had gone rouge, surging uncontrollably. He was completely conscious but unable to act. All that was standing between paralysis and coma was one last chakra.

"Oh, I almost forgot," Nick pulled out a Ziploc bag containing an assortment of drug paraphernalia. "I wasn't sure if you were going to be a good boy or a bad boy. So I stopped and got you some candy just in case you tried to get all gorilla on me. The police will never believe that these drugs made you comatose if we don't get them into your veins. Who's a good boy? You want some drugs? Yeah? Yeah you do."

Nick grabbed Jess's limp hand and tapped his arm searching for a good vein. He plunged the needle into his arm and pushed down on the plunger. "You're going to like this one. My friend said this one's called Chex Mix. Do tell me if you like it.

"Oh wait, almost forgot, I can't have you enjoying this. Night, night." Nick took Jess's third eye chakra into his mental hands and squeezed. He drank from Jess's aura as he tore the chakra to pieces. Jess's eyes closed and a sadistic smile crossed over Nick's face. "God that felt good."

Once Nick had finished placing Jess in what he felt was a natural position, he made himself a sandwich and watched an episode of *Cops*. He checked Jess's vitals a few times just to make sure he hadn't drifted off to death.

When the episode of *Cops* was over, Nick made his way back to the bedroom. He rummaged for a while through Jess's clothes. "Oh, this is cute," he said to himself. He peeked his head out into the hallway. "You won't mind if I borrow this, will you? No? Oh, you're a peach!"

After an episode of *Golden Girls* and a bag of popcorn Nick finally called 911.

"911, please state your emergency," the woman on the line said plainly.

Nick put on his best panic face and said, "I don't know what happened! I went to go to bed, he said he was going to have a cigarette, and when I came out here he wasn't responding. There's a needle, oh my god, I don't know what to do!"

"Sir, stay calm, what is your address?" the operator asked in a soothing voice.

Nick knew the address by heart; this wasn't his first call. "He said he was done with this shit. I'd have never come over if I knew. Oh my god, I'm not sure if he's breathing." Nick added a few tears to his voice.

"Okay, sir, remain calm, I'm sending an ambulance."

•፣•

Kaleb had a lungful of water. He was sinking fast but he felt Walter sinking faster. Something big moved beneath him. Panic turned into terror. Kaleb floundered and stretched and reached. He hadn't had to hold his breath this long before. Walter was somewhere below him. Kaleb sank like a rock. Something rushed past him in the darkness. Kaleb tugged at the darkness around him and stepped forward into the shadow world.

He fell onto the shore of the pond. Kaleb's lungs burned as he coughed up water. Immediately he started running back into the lake. He had to get to Walter. Tears streamed down his face as he fell onto the surface of the water. Without warning the pond heaved upward, pushing Kaleb back onto the shore.

A mighty dragon rose above Kaleb. Its sapphire scales gleamed in the moon's radiance. Daintily the dragon held Walter in its claws and laid him next to Kaleb. He had no time to faint, though we wanted to; Walter wasn't breathing. Kaleb began to administer CPR.

Walter's world returned to him in a rush. He could feel soft lips. And then coughing. There was pain as mouthfuls of water were forced out of his lungs. When he was finished he wrapped his arms around Kaleb, who had never left his side. "You saved my life."

He pulled Kaleb into a tight embrace and rested his head on Kaleb's shoulder, not wanting to let go. It was cold, but together they were warm. Their bodies rose and fell together with each breath. Walter's chest was pressed against Kaleb's. Walter could feel Kaleb's heart beating fast. Walter rubbed Kaleb's arms for warmth as he shivered in Walter's embrace.

Their eyes met. Kaleb stared into Walter's deep green eyes. Walter pushed a bead of water off Kaleb's forehead before it could run into his eyes. Without thought, Kaleb leaned in and kissed Walter tenderly. Kaleb withdrew from Walter and leapt to his feet. "I can't believe I did that. I'm so sorry."

Walter was still busy recovering from the kiss. "No. No, I'm sorry."

"What do you have to be sorry for?" Kaleb pulled on his pants and started looking for his shirt. The wave had tossed the entire edge of the lake several feet from where they had left it.

"I shouldn't have taken you out to the middle of a lake, in the middle of the night, to teach you how to swim. I'm so sorry, Kaleb, I wasn't thinking," Walter said as he passed Kaleb's soaking wet shirt to him and Kaleb handed him his pants.

Kaleb shook his head, "I'm sorry for kissing you. It was wrong of me."

"Don't be sorry for that." He reached out for Kaleb's hand and it was accepted.

"I have to be. I'm with Austin, and I'm faithful and loyal." Kaleb let go of Walter's hand and put on his shirt. He poured lake water out of his shoes and slipped them on. "I went too far. God damn it. I'm very attracted to you. There. I said it."

Walter smiled. "Don't be too hard on yourself. We all make mistakes. I'm sure Austin would forgive you for a kiss. There a lot worse things," he said as he put on his own shirt. "I'm proud of you."

His clothes were soaking wet. While he wrung water out of his shirt he asked, "And why is that?"

"I taught you how to swim." Walter grinned.

"You just keep telling yourself that," he replied soberly.

•┇•

Blue and red lights danced across the apartment complex. The paramedics had come and gone leaving Nick alone with the police. Nick's eyes were streaming with tears. "I have to go with him to the hospital."

Officer Sully responded, "I'm sorry, we've still got a few questions for you."

Cops was replaying in Nick's mind. His ex was being driven away in an ambulance. One misstep and he could be hauled off to jail. "Of course officer, I'm sorry. I'm just a little tired. I was on my way to bed when I found him."

"Are you okay to drive? I'd like to do this at the station?"

He had played this out in his mind since he phoned the overdose in, and luckily it was still playing out exactly as he expected. "I think so, officer. I'm just a little shaken."

"Well if you're not comfortable driving, you can ride with us. You're not under arrest. We just have a few more questions to go over."

"That'd be fine. Thank you officer."

•┇•

Kaleb saw Austin off to work. Resentment and loathing boiled below his façade of happiness. For the last two weeks he knew that Austin hadn't been going to his cousin's like he said he was. Thanks to Morgan, he knew that Austin wasn't being honest with him. He hadn't mentioned the kiss to Austin, but his guilt for holding that secret in was overshadowed by the suspicion he had about Austin's fidelity.

His phone rang. Morgan sounded upbeat when she greeted him, "I got off work early. Phones were pretty slow so they were letting people go. Are you ready?"

"Yeah, but Nick isn't out of class for another few hours. Can Mercedes type?"

"I'm sure she can, but I won't give her any reason to have a bigger ego than she already has. You remember that whole reading comment she made. She may not say anything, but I can see her judging me every time I turn the TV on. You know she thinks she's the gods' gift to man. Not kidding, Kaleb, it's like she thinks this is Egypt and that we should be worshiping her. Are you there?"

Kaleb hadn't really been listening. "Sorry. I had some crazy shit happen to me last night. I'm kind of glad Nick won't be there to turn it into a joke."

"You mean like you do?"

He buried his face in his hands. "Exactly."

"What happened? No wait, let me guess." Kaleb waited. "I got nothing. I have something to tell you too, and you're not going to be happy about it."

Kaleb sighed, just what he needed, more drama.

"Oh, hold on, call waiting." Kaleb started making himself something for breakfast while he waited for Morgan to come back on the line. "Oh my goddess, Kaleb, you will never believe it."

Kaleb sighed, "No, you're probably right. What is it now?"

"Nick needs me to pick him up from the cop shop."

Kaleb's egg fell into the pan, shell and all. "Shit. What? Seriously? What did he do?"

"Didn't say. But I'll be a little late picking you up if that's okay."

"Yeah, that's fine." He did his best to dig the shell out from his omelet.

"You know you could shadow-walk over. Honestly, if I could shadow-walk, I'd never travel any other way."

"Call me when you're on your way." Kaleb hung up the phone.

•٭•

Nick and Kaleb sat on her couch as Morgan stood above them with her arms crossed. Kaleb still had a stunned look on his face and hadn't spoken. Nick's only answer was that he didn't want to talk about it.

Morgan broke the silence. "Okay, somebody better start talking." When no one began, Morgan threw up her arms and plopped down on the couch between them. "I don't know why I even bother. I guess I'll start. Guess what next weekend is Kaleb?" She paused. Still no one spoke. "Oh, you're not sure. Well that's okay, you may not have gotten the memo. Next weekend is our *Class Reunion!*"

Kaleb groaned. This broke him free of the stupor he was under. "Oh, Morgan, please, please don't make me go!"

"Oh you're going, buddy. You skipped the five-year and made me go by myself. I will not go to the ten-year alone," she said with her arms crossed.

"But Morgan!" Kaleb whined.

"Mercedes says to grow a pair." Mercedes looked up from her perch on the kitchen counter offended. "Okay, I said to grow a pair, but it sounded better coming from her." Mercedes ignored them and jumped from her perch and gracefully walked to the back bedroom.

"I wasn't out in high school. I don't have anything in common with those people. The only person from high school I still talk to is you," Kaleb said, still whining.

"I'm not going by myself. I will drag you there kicking and screaming if I have to."

"You just might have to." Kaleb recalled the people from their school. He had no desire to see any of them. High school was a time for regrets best left forgotten. There were too many for Kaleb to face. He remembered his embarrassing attempt to come out to the one guy in his class he thought might also be gay.

Kaleb had a crush on him since the third grade and during their senior year he decided to risk coming out to see if his crush was also gay. He had suspected that he might be. He wasn't. Kaleb found that out after handing him an embarrassing and telling letter he had written the night before. There was no way he was facing that embarrassment again.

Morgan gave Kaleb the look of a scolding parent and he shrank.

Kaleb threw up his hands. "Fine! I'll go. But I'm bringing Walter."

Nick and Morgan both dropped their jaws and replied in near unison, "What?"

"You heard me. I'm bringing Walter. I'll have to clear it with him first, but I'm pretty sure he'll make time off for me. There's no way Austin will want to go," he said, pleased with himself. It wasn't very often that he had the opportunity to shock his friends.

Nick was on the edge of his seat, "Okay, start at the beginning. Don't skip any of the juicy details."

Kaleb recounted his evening, skipping the dragon and the kiss. Even without the pivotal details, Nick still found enough fodder to begin wedding planning. Kaleb rubbed his forehead as he listened to Nick and Morgan gushing over his not-a-date.

"All right, you've had your fun. I have something serious to talk about." He waited, but they were still spewing nonsense. "I saw a dragon." Their mouths fell open. "No, for real, I can't swim. I panicked, I shadow-walked to shore, and an enormous dragon lifted Walter out of the water and set him down on the shore."

Nick's jaw was the first to be picked up off the floor. "I put my ex into a coma."

Everyone turned to Nick with stunned expressions. Morgan recovered first. "You did what?"

"What?" Nick slumped back into the couch. "I thought we were sharing."

A Darker Shade of Gray

Nick tried desperately to stay awake while the psychology lecture dragged on. For the last couple of days, he felt as though he had no energy. If it weren't for the fact that his neck hadn't swollen up like a balloon, he'd have thought it was mono again.

His eyes slid in and out of focus. He was completely aware of the auras of his classmates and the professor. He could see how they pulsed and swirled. Deep within him, he felt an insatiable hunger.

The girl sitting next to him leaned in and whispered, "You look terrible. Are you okay?"

Nick gave his best fake smile as a reply, though he couldn't help comparing her to a cheeseburger. Her aura was a delicious shade of orange and brown. He reached out with his mind for a sip and hit a shield. Nick's mouth watered as he searched for any unguarded person who wouldn't notice if he took just a little sip.

An aura of red and yellows felt inviting. He carefully moved in, but was blocked by a shield. The man to his left hosted a vibrant purple and sapphire aura. As he attempted to feed, he again ran into a shield.

He had almost given up out of desperation when he noticed that the professor, while pouring his heart out about some inane drivel, was completely unguarded.

Nick pounced with his mind and began to feed on the man's vitality. It tasted like honey-covered strawberries. Nick's eyes rolled into his head involuntarily and his toes curled in his shoes. The life energy flowed from the teacher and into him. He was awake, his body bathed in warmth.

The lecture ended abruptly as the professor fell to the floor. As the rest of his classmates rushed to the man's side, Nick nervously packed up his books and headed back to his dorm.

When he arrived at his room, Nick lay down and meditated with his staff. There was no reaction. He probed the staff with his mind, still no reaction. As he was about to give up, he felt her.

A satin female voice rang into his mind, "*My pupil, I see that you have returned well fed. Shall we continue our lessons of magic?*"

Nick grinned. "Yes, my teacher, I am quite full. I am here to learn."

"*Excellent. Now, relax and close your eyes. When you are at my side we shall begin.*"

He closed his eyes and relaxed. Slowly he slipped back into the trance-like state that allowed him to enter her dark cathedral. Nick fell away from his body and his mind was guided into the staff. The raven-haired beauty stood before him. She wore a simple black gown that made her pale skin even more pronounced.

"Now, where to begin?" she pondered while tapping her long nails to her lips. "I guess it would be prudent to begin by teaching you some defense."

She rose from her chair and approached Nick. The woman sized him up as she circled him closely. "Let's see how quickly you can master this spell. It's a simple concept. Though, as a novice, I'm sure you'll be needing this."

A staff appeared in her hands. It was a near replica of the one in his dorm room. Nick took it in his hands. "Is this—" he started but she raised a hand to stop him.

"It's real enough. Despite the many differences between my prison and your home, you'll find the magic here is quite the same. Reach out and bring it to your staff."

Nick closed his eyes and reached out with his mind. He was already apart from his body, so the movement of his mind's eye was smoother and simpler. He could feel forces of magic all around him beyond the cathedral Lifedrinker called her home.

Power surged into his staff and the small orb of obsidian glowed with a weak gray light. Nick summoned more magical energy to him and it flared to life. He closed his eyes and smiled at Lifedrinker.

"Very good. Now—" she began but it was Nick's turn to cut her off.

"Where exactly are we?"

Her lips curled up into a sweet smile. "This is my home of course."

"No, I get that. But, where exactly is your home? I mean, when I was seeking power it was like there was this curtain around this place. What's that about?"

Her face was a careful, calculated expressionless mask as she replied, "Some call it Nox, others refer to it as Twilight, and still others call it Limbo. It is a place between places. It has no form except to mimic that of both sides."

Nick shrugged. "All right."

"There are some that can walk between these worlds. Nightwalkers, or shadow-striders. Whatever they call themselves, they are the rare ones. I was trapped in this wretched place by a shadow-strider."

"That sucks."

Her eyes searched him for a moment. As quickly as the scrutiny descended it was just as quickly replaced by the expressionless mask. "Yes. It does. Now, my dear, shall we learn the spell of shielding?"

On what felt like his fifty-first attempt at shielding, Lifedrinker had grown impatient. "It's not enough to simply recite the words. You have to feel the spell. You have to sense the magic and bend it to your will. Perhaps after a light meal you would be refreshed enough to continue. Let's break for dinner."

"I'm not really hungry." Nick cocked his head to one side. "Oh, right, you meant feeding. Yeah. Did I tell you how delicious my professor's energy was? When I was draining him it was like the whole class froze in time and it was just me and him."

Lifedrinker appeared saddened by this news. "Oh, yes. It is quite enjoyable. I myself haven't had the luxury for centuries. I'm sorry, I shouldn't complain. It is so unbecoming. You are the first company I've had for such a long time."

"I'm sorry, I didn't mean to gloat. Is there a way I can bring you a snack? Like, instead of sending high magic to my staff could send you someone's energy?"

An enormous smile grew on her face. She spoke softly. "You would do that for me?"

"Well, yeah," Nick responded. "You're showing me all this cool shit to do with magic; it's really the least I could do. I'll go bag us a meal." He closed his eyes and began to focus on his physical body. He had been in a deep state of meditation for so long he could barely feel it.

Slowly he began to feel his body again. It started with a tingling sensation in his toes. Next he could smell the dirty socks his roommate always left discarded by the computer desk. One by one, his muscles began to contract. Very carefully, he opened his eyes.

With just one eye open, Nick watched his roommate crawl into his bed at the other end of the room. His roommate, Devin, was one of those spoiled trust fund brats he hated. Though they were polite to each other, he could always feel the haughty sense of superiority wafting off him.

Tonight he would try a night-terror spell. In between his attempts at shielding Lifedrinker had instructed him on a few other basic spells. The instructions were to wait until his victim was fast asleep and then to use the spell to slip into the target's mind. From there, he could manipulate the flow of the dream like a puppeteer.

As soon as his roommate had fallen asleep, Nick quietly recited the incantation. He drew on the forces of high magic and the darkness of the room to weave a spell around Devin. Nick closed his eyes as he said the final words aloud.

.¥.

It was raining. Devin was waiting for a bus. Nick wasn't sure how he knew that about the dream. It was like watching a bad movie. The color was all wrong, it was somewhere between color and sepia tones.

Nick could see the edges of the dream. It was like being in a glass jar, where the only thing outside the glass was darkness. Standing inside the dome was like being on the set of a film that was constantly moving. As he stood staring at the edge he saw the bus pull up out of the corner of his eye.

"Let's make this interesting, shall we?" Nick asked aloud as he focused on an image of the interior of a bus filled with corpses.

In a flash he was sitting at the back of a school bus. Devin walked past the dead bodies as he made his way to the back of the bus. It took him a moment to realize that the passengers were dead.

Devin's body was frozen in fear. Nick could taste it. He could feel the paralysis that was choking him. The thought came to Nick's mind about making the corpses rise and begin to grab for Devin.

Directing the dream was easier than he had thought it would be. He merely presented an idea, to which the dream responded. Nick allowed Devin to be free of the paralysis and he ran from the back of the bus and fell headfirst into an open grave.

Nick watched as Devin's mother dropped a single red rose into the grave of her son. The gravedigger began to fill in the hole. A terrified scream echoed throughout the dream. Nick smiled as he wiped the imaginary dirt from his hands.

With little effort he slipped out of the dream and back to his own body. "That was so much fun. You didn't tell me how fun that would be," he said to the staff at his side.

He could smell urine; Devin had wet himself. "Oh, this night could not get any better. Oh, that's right. It can," Nick said to himself as he lunged with his mind. Devin's soul was completely exposed and Nick sank his astral teeth into him.

The world melted away. There was only Nick and his victim. He was the center of the universe in that moment, the most powerful man alive. Devin's vitality coated the burning ache he didn't realize he felt. The sweet nectar of his life made Nick's toes curl in pleasure.

Nick's stomach growled. He took a last sip from Devin and pulled the energy to the staff. "*I'm going to run and get some real food. But don't worry, I'll bring you with me.*"

The reply was swift, "*It has been so long since I've had a decent meal. I appreciate the snack.*"

Nick took one last look at his roommate as he picked up his keys from the desk. The life-force he had stolen still ran through his body. Nick took a moment to enjoy the sensations flowing through him. He knew he should be feeling some emotion, but he couldn't remember what that was. Guilt? Shame? Remorse? No, he felt powerful.

.•.

Nick sat on the hood of his car. He tossed the fast food bag into the grass as he licked mayo off his finger. Like the rest of his senses, his sense of taste was beyond anything he had ever experienced. A burger never tasted as good as it did tonight. He was certain that it was all in his head, but it was like eating prime rib with the texture of burger.

"Lucian, if you're finished eating I have something I'd like to suggest," the sweet voice said into his mind.

"Aw, you remembered. It's a good name, right?" Nick said, smiling to himself.

"Of course I remembered. And yes, it is a great vampire name." Lifedrinker paused, letting her words sink in. *"I was thinking, since you were having such a rough time learning how to shield. Perhaps I could ..."* she started to say then stopped.

"What is it? Do you think it would help?" Nick's excitement carried through his mind-voice.

"I was thinking, perhaps I could show you how. You understand the concept of possession, right?"

Nick jumped to his feet, bringing his staff with him. He spoke aloud, while also projecting his thoughts into the staff, "Whoa, lady, slow down. I don't think I'm ready for you to get in my pants quite yet. Cash up front, if you know what I mean."

"I didn't mean to imply I was going to possess you, but it's like possession. You see, I have a physical form, so I wouldn't be able to possess you. We'd just be joining minds. I'd be projecting my mind into yours. But it requires that you give control of your body to me. Would you do that?"

Nick had channeled spirits before. It wasn't a foreign concept to him. Most of the ghosts he dealt with just wanted to talk, or drink, or have a cigarette. Lifedrinker was suggesting that she use his body to show him how to use magic, but her explanation of how this wasn't possession because she had a body didn't sit well with him.

"Okay," Nick replied. *"I've done this before, so don't think I'm going to give you complete control, and if I see you start making for Mexico I'm pulling the plug."*

Nick closed his eyes and opened his mind. He relaxed his body and invited her to join him. A cold darkness entered his mind. It wrested for control, but Nick pushed her back.

"Hey now, I told you that I'm not giving you complete control," he said aloud. He gave her control of his arms. For now, that was all she was getting. They would share his voice. With years of experience channeling, he gave his body to her, but only those places he permitted. The rest was still under his control.

A more feminine version of his voice responded, "I understand your reluctance. Don't worry, my dear, I am not offended. Now, if you wouldn't mind bringing some high magic to the staff, we can get started."

The staff glowed with a pale gray light as high magic filled it. Lifedrinker drew the staff before her and made a complicated gesture with her hand.

She spoke in a guttural language that was completely foreign to Nick. She grabbed the staff in her hands and wove the magic into her spell. Before Nick could ask what she was doing, or for her to slow down, they rocketed into the night sky.

At first, Nick was petrified. But no matter how afraid he was, he refused to give up control of his body. Together they ascended through the clouds and the horror of not being in control lifted as he saw the moon and the stars above him.

The night sky was beautiful above the city lights. He could see stars and galaxies that he would have never seen from the streets below. Nick smiled as he looked at the moon with wonder. It was brighter and its features clearer. He could see the craters and crevices in crisp detail like never before.

The world seemed miniscule in comparison to the billions of stars that were casting their light on him. His eyes were wide and his heart was as light as a feather. He had never been a fan of stargazing, but he had never seen them in such vivid detail before.

A pillow of clouds stretched out below them. The air was cold and he felt a little lightheaded from the lack of oxygen, but he still smiled at the beauty all around him. *"This is so amazing,"* he said into the staff.

"Yes, I thought you'd enjoy it."

Without warning Lifedrinker released the flight spell and they plummeted. Nick's heart raced as a fear he had never known before gripped him. *"What are you doing?"*

"Teaching you how to fly," she replied calmly.

The air rushing past Nick's head was too loud for him to think. He had always wanted to go skydiving, but would have preferred to have a parachute.

"You went too fast," he thought back to her. His anger was overflowing in his mind's voice. *"How am I supposed to cast a spell if you don't even slow down to let me learn it? You just want full control! I'm not going to let that happen. If I die, I'm going to land staff first and no one will know you even existed!"*

"Come now, Lucian," she said with coyness. *"Why would you think that I want your body?"*

The lights of the city were getting closer. The only other light was from his staff. Nick stared into the gray light and shouted over the noise of the rushing wind. *"I will not die tonight! I'm going to fly."* In desperation he drew the remaining magic from the staff and willed it around him like a robe. *"I'm going to fly!"*

The freefall ended abruptly. A wicked laughter filled his mind. *"Well done, my dear. You see, the words only help you form intent. It's your will that forms the spell. With a strong enough need you don't need fancy words."*

"That's what this was all about? To get me to think you were going to kill me so that I would cast a spell?" Nick was furious.

"It worked, didn't it?" she replied through his voice.

⁘

141

They landed near a river just outside of town. Nick lay down on the sandbar and stared up at the sky. As much as he hated Lifedrinker for tricking him, he had to admit she had finesse.

A hysterical fit of laughter overtook him. "That was a dirty trick, Superman." He beat his hands into the sand and laughed.

Nick jumped to his feet as a branch snapped nearby. In the moonlight he could see a man watching them from the tree line. His clothes were threadbare and his beard was unkempt.

"I smell dinner," Nick heard himself say.

"Show me a spell, and I'll feed you," Nick responded.

Before the transient could run, Nick had already closed the distance between them. "Going so soon? We were just about to have a snack."

Lifedrinker spoke through him the words to a new spell and Nick supplied the magic to the staff. A white fog poured out of Nick's mouth and as she spoke the final word it surrounded them.

With ease, Nick ripped the root and throat chakra from the old man and he fell to the ground. Lifedrinker and Nick lunged with their minds and began to feed. The old man whimpered and cried, but without the focal point of his vocal energies he was speechless.

Nick could feel the old man dying as they fed upon him. His life-force tasted like licorice and coffee. With every second he got closer and closer to death's doors. Nick stopped himself before the last dregs of the man's vitality was gone.

"How sweet of you to offer me the last bite," Lifedrinker said through his voice. "It would be shame to rob you of your first kill. You haven't experienced anything until you taste the life-cord."

Nick eyes were wide. "Life-cord?"

The higher, more feminine version of his voice responded, "It's truly the best part. Once you've drained all the life-force away, you can feel it. Sitting right there between their body and their soul. Get a good grip on it and yank it right out of them."

Nick finished drinking the man's life away, and when there was nothing but an empty husk he felt it, a tether between body and soul. He took hold of it and tugged as hard he could. A wave of pleasure rolled over Nick. Every fiber within him was alive. He could feel parts of his body that he never gave a second thought to before. It was the top ten orgasms of his life happening simultaneously. The man's last dying breath wasn't heard over Nick's cry of ecstasy.

A Fine Day for a Felony

Walter parked his car in front of a dilapidated house. "This is where she grew up?"

The house appeared to be holding itself together with superglue and imagination. One corner of the roof was drooping down over a porch that hung precariously from the side of the small two-story house.

Walter and Kaleb walked from the gravel driveway to the porch. From his vantage, Walter could see a small garage and beyond that was a line of trees. The nightly lament of insects and animals filled the air. When they reached the porch Walter feared if he stepped on a wrong floorboard the whole house would come tumbling down around them. It creaked and swayed with every step.

Morgan and Mercedes were sitting on the swing when they arrived. Morgan called out to them as they approached, "Mercedes said that she hates riding in the car and you have to shadow-walk her back."

Kaleb tried to shush her, but it was too late. Walter turned to Kaleb, "Shadow-what?"

He scrambled for a decent lie. "Shadow-walk. Morgan's writing a book. She's basing a character off me; it's actually pretty good. Maybe if she's in a good mood she'll let you read it." Kaleb glared at Morgan.

Morgan crushed out her cigarette and gestured for the boys to go inside. "Well, come on in."

On the other side of the door was an episode of *Hoarders*. The kitchen table was covered in newspapers and magazines. The sink was the same graveyard of dishes as in Morgan's trailer. Gnats buzzed around the kitchen and the entire house smelled of dirty laundry.

Kaleb found the nearest surface free of debris and sat. "I see the brownie is still on strike," Kaleb said with feigned sweetness.

Morgan glared at Kaleb.

Walter turned to Kaleb. "Brownie?"

Kaleb crossed his legs and began explaining to Walter, "Again, part of her book. A brownie is a type of faerie. They're house faeries you could say. Her book has this family of crazy witches that believes they have a faerie that cleans up after them. Though, obviously from the state of the house, you realize pretty quickly that it's a joke."

"Right," Morgan countered. "I was just working on the scene where Jon and his boyfriend are about to split up because his boyfriend is a piece of shit douchebag."

Kaleb pursed his lips together. "You'll have to let me know how that goes."

"Well I'm pretty sure it ends up with Jon meeting someone else. Maybe an EMT. Someone in public service seems like a good fit for Jon. Somebody who is a selfless, honest, loving person. Someone who doesn't lie about where he spends his time," Morgan said through her teeth.

"Did you finish the scene where Samantha finds a way to magic up her own personal life?" Kaleb asked sweetly.

Morgan said through a locked jaw, "It's a work in progress."

Walter cut the tension. "Can't wait to read it."

•T•

Morgan waved as Kaleb and Walter pulled out of the drive. Her mother was working late at the nursing home so she was on her own for the evening. The best part about visiting her family's house was the acres of timber that spanned the property. She was still furious at Kaleb for chiding her about her lack of a personal life. She decided to take a night stroll through the forest.

It was a warm night, and she had no one to impress. She wore her most comfortable gray sweatpants and cutoff t-shirt. She carried with her the staff and a handful of spells she had printed out the day before. The crystal atop her staff shed a pink light on the ground as she walked through the thicket of trees.

Morgan wanted to try out a spell of empowerment. From what she could tell it was supposed to awaken more of the caster's inner potential. The spell was vague in its wording, but it sounded like it might be worth trying.

Deep within the timber was a massive oak tree that she and Kaleb used to climb when they were young. It was the one place she felt most connected with the power of the earth. The tree sat atop a low hill in a clearing in the woods. She huffed as she climbed the hill and sat beneath its branches.

Morgan breathed in the earthy aroma as she began to lay out her circle. The spell didn't require a circle to be cast, but some habits die hard. After she finished calling on the Watchtowers, she lit a cigarette.

The magic she had called to her staff was overflowing and yearning to be put to use. After taking her last drag off her cigarette she started casting. The words were difficult and she stumbled in her pronunciation. They had copied the spells down in their original Gaelic and then again in English, just in case the spell was language specific.

Following the instruction of the spell Morgan raised her hands to the moon. "Power of the moon, fill me. Bathe me in your glory. Let my power amplify in your light."

She read aloud the spell she brought and poured the magic from her staff into it. Her heart pounded with anticipation. The rubbing didn't say what she should expect, but her imagination was teeming with ideas for how it would end.

Morgan said the final word of the spell and lowered her staff. Its rose-colored light faded completely. She felt no different. "Well, that was great."

Despite the results of the last spell she had no intention of leaving empty-handed. She grabbed the next spell out of the pile and read it over. Her staff flared with light again as she channeled more mystical energy into it.

The next spell was fire. She looked up at the tree and decided it best to try the next spell somewhere less flammable. Morgan walked back into the woods in search of the small stream that passed through her mom's land.

In the distance was a bleating, soulful cry for help. At first she wasn't sure she had heard it, but there it was again. She started running in the direction of the voice. A tangle of blackberries impeded her but only for a moment. Morgan ran with determination.

"I need a personal trainer? Screw you cat! I'll show you who's out of shape," she said to no one in particular. She was soon panting. Her legs ached, but she found the brush from where the cries for help were issuing. She pushed back the brambles and saw it. A baby rabbit.

"No, oh no, HELP!" the bunny screamed.

"Don't be afraid," Morgan replied, falling to one knee beside the trapped bunny. "I'm a friend." She loosened the wire wrapped around its leg. It didn't run.

The bunny looked up into her eyes. *"You can hear me?"*

"Well, I guess so." Morgan stroked the fur of the shaking baby rabbit. It was no bigger than her two hands put together. Her heart melted.

•˚•

Morgan spent the rest of the night trying to find the bunny's mother. When her stomach started to growl she decided to bring him home with her instead. "Mercedes!" Morgan stormed back into her mother's house. "You have some explaining to do."

"What the fuck is that?" Mercedes asked, drawing out each word as she spoke in Morgan's mind. She stared at the bunny in Morgan's arms with disgust.

"I haven't given him a name yet, but would you mind explaining to me why it is that this little bunny and I can talk? You said the reason you could talk to me was because you are my familiar."

Mercedes padded her way gracefully through the graveyard of dishes and came to the edge of the counter looking reproachfully at Morgan, *"I said that I was your familiar? Oh, yes, right, about that."* She licked her paw and began to clean behind her ears. *"Well, I believe that the reason I am such an intelligent, and might I add absolutely exquisite, exception to my feline friends is that I am your familiar."*

"Oh you better dance, cat! Now as far as the reading and the spelling of certain curse words on coffee tables is concerned, yes, you are a very smart kitty." Mercedes preened. "*But, that does not grant you the title of familiar! And it certainly doesn't give you the right to say awful things to me!*"

Mercedes lay down on a clean spot of kitchen counter and moved her paws together in a sort of mock clap. "*Well done. Now if I could see more of that out of you, I wouldn't have to remind you what a filthy mess you are.*" She leapt from the kitchen counter and approached Morgan and the rabbit. "*As far as your new friend here, I think you may be a druid.*"

"Excuse me?"

"*Well I thought you might have skipped over that book as well, so I made a point of rereading it recently. A druid, my dear girl, has the ability to commune with nature.*"

"Okay," Morgan said, still cradling the frightened bunny, "I think I understand."

"*I'm glad you do.*"

"Yeah, I get it now." She smacked the cat on the top of her head. "You just make this shit up as you go! You better start telling me the truth cat, or I swear to god I will send you to the Animal Rescue League."

Mercedes eyes narrowed, "*Well played, Morgan, well played. If you must know the truth, you had better have a seat.*" Morgan moved a stack of magazines off the nearest dining chair and sat. "*You're right, I'm not a familiar. In fact, I have no idea what to call me. One afternoon I was content chasing a light on the wall and then, all of a sudden, it was like this awareness struck me. I was alive. Do you understand what I mean?*"

She stroked the bunny's soft fur. "I think so."

"*Good. It was like waking up from a dream I suppose. A bad dream that I never knew was bad. I had ideas. Some of them not really the best ideas, but I don't really want to get into that. Then I started reading. I never knew that I could. I saw a book lying open on the floor one day and I just sort of knew. So you tell me, miss fancy druid lady, what am I?"*

Morgan leaned down to pet her. The cat arched her back and began to purr. "That is the most vulnerable and charming you have been since you started talking." Morgan smacked her on the nose, "So no more swearing. And you need to stop acting like a high and mighty know-it-all."

Mercedes looked up at her with saucer-like eyes, *"I can't promise anything, but I will try. You are an awfully big target for sarcasm."*

She swatted at the cat. Mercedes bounded for the windowsill and began cleaning her imaginary wounds. Morgan looked to the rabbit, who was staring up at her with awe and fear. "We're going to have to come up with a name for you."

.•.

Walter parked the car in front of Kaleb's parents' ranch style home. A feeling of foreboding met him as he opened the door. Instead of the awkward reunion he expected, he was greeted with hugs. Kaleb was an image of his mother: they both had high cheekbones, both with timeless beauty, and both only weighed under a hundred and thirty pounds, wet.

"So you finally traded up," she said to Kaleb. "Let me have a look. Oh, he's handsome." Walter blushed as Kaleb's mother looked him up and down. "Nice butt."

"Mother, this is my *friend,* Walter," Kaleb said sternly.

"I know, I know, just like it was your *friend* Austin, or your *friend* Tom. I get it, I get it. A mother always knows." She touched her nose and winked at Walter. "Well don't worry about your father. I told him he's just going to have to deal with it. I said, 'Hamilton, he's your son, and if he's happy, so am

I.' Well he didn't agree, as I would have liked him to, but I don't care. Oh, Kaleb, he is handsome. Hope he's not like that *Austin* fellow you were with, sure he was pretty, but he sure was pretty dumb." She laughed in Walter's direction.

Kaleb sighed. "Mother, if you would ever read my text messages, you would know that I'm still dating Austin, and Walter is just a friend."

Walter held out his hand, "It's very nice to meet you."

•ᵛ•

Walter couldn't sleep. He was happy that he had been invited along to Kaleb's class reunion but wished that the circumstances were different. Kaleb's mother encouraged them to share a bed. For some reason she still would not believe Kaleb's insistence that they were just friends.

The rooms in the basement had deliberately been left unfinished. Kaleb said it was so his parents wouldn't have to pay higher property taxes. According to Kaleb, the house originally had two bedrooms upstairs and would have five bedrooms if his dad would ever finish building them.

"Kaleb?" Walter called out to the darkness. His thoughts had been going in circles for the last half hour and there was no way he was going to get any sleep.

"Yeah?" came the reply from between "walls" that were in reality two-by-fours covered with sheets.

"I'm wide awake and was wondering if you were." His thoughts kept going back to their kiss. He couldn't get it out of his head. The only reason he had agreed to this trip was because they were staying at his parent's house. Nothing would happen here.

"Can't sleep either. What did you have in mind?"

"I just wanted to talk." There was silence. Eventually Walter garnered enough emotional strength to ask, "I know you're still with Austin, but …" he couldn't bring himself to finish the question.

Kaleb finished the sentence for him "But why?" When Walter didn't make an effort to correct him he continued, "I'm with Austin because I'm committed to him and the life we've built. He's actually a really great guy when you get to know him. He makes me laugh. We play, we have fun, and we go on these amazing walks. Things may not be great right now, but I believe they'll get better."

"You know what?" Walter choked down the words that tried to betray his true feelings. "I want you to know that I respect you. I have made no attempt to get you out of your pants. There's just one thing I still don't get."

"What's that?"

Walter took the opportunity to redirect the conversation, "What the hell is a brownie, and what's the whole shadow-walker thing?"

Kaleb wrung his hands. "I don't know that I should do this but, Walter, can I tell you a secret?"

Walter pulled back the sheet separating the two rooms. "Oh, please don't tell me you're some felon, or a drug dealer."

Kaleb laughed. "Nothing like that." Kaleb let out another slow breath. "I don't know that I can do this. I don't want to lose your friendship. I'm afraid to tell you."

Walter climbed out of bed and carefully made his way to Kaleb's room. He sat down on the edge of the bed. Walter could see Kaleb's struggling with whatever this secret was. "There is nothing you could tell me that would make me think less of you."

"Magic is real," Kaleb said quickly. He pulled his blanket up to his chin.

"I'm sorry?"

"Magic is real," Kaleb repeated.

Walter looked at Kaleb sternly, "Yeah, I caught you the first time. Um, would you mind telling me what you mean by that?"

"I just mean that magic is real. I mean real magic, high magic." When Walter didn't respond Kaleb continued, "Okay, so you know about witchcraft, right?"

Walter scratched his head, "I guess. I mean, not really, I only remember what I heard in church growing up." Kaleb's body stiffened, "And I'm sure that is a very biased opinion, and I'm a lot more open-minded than that."

Kaleb sat up. "Okay, so witchcraft is all about 'the goddess helps those that help themselves.' So magic was put here so we could do just that. What we've been working with is called low magic."

Walter shifted uncomfortably. "What do you mean 'been' working with?"

"Simple stuff, that's what low magic is. High magic." Kaleb thought for a second. "High magic is a little bit more active."

Walter scratched his head. "I don't think I understand."

Kaleb crawled out of bed and began dressing. "I think I'm going to have to just show you."

"Are we going somewhere?"

"No, you just wait right there. I'm going for a little walk. Do you need anything from home?" Kaleb looked up at him as he laced his shoes.

"Um, Kaleb, that's a bit more than just a little walk."

"Well if there isn't anything you forgot then I'll just grab a trinket." Kaleb said as he stepped into the shadows and was gone.

Walter squinted into the darkness. "Okay. Not funny. Wherever you're hiding, you can come out. I'm not buying it." Walter began feeling his way around the room for the light switch. He turned on the lights in that room and proceeded to the next, searching each room for any trace of Kaleb.

Walter reached the stairs as Kaleb was coming down them. "Now why'd you have to go and turn all the lights on?" He was holding something in his hand.

"That was a great trick, you'll have to tell me how you managed to sneak away so quietly." Kaleb placed something in his hand and he looked down. He was holding his class ring, which he was sure had been sitting on his nightstand at home when he and Kaleb had left. "So you pocketed my class ring before you left my apartment? Kaleb, what the hell?"

Kaleb sighed and shut off the light. He stepped into shadows and disappeared again. This time there was a knock at the basement door. Walter opened the door and Kaleb was on the other side. Again Walter was unimpressed, "I've seen street magicians before. You're going to have to do better than going outside and knocking on the door."

"What the hell will impress you? Do you want to lock me in your trunk? What do you want me to bring you to prove that I can travel through shadows?" Kaleb was getting frustrated.

"Oh, is that what the whole shadow-walking thing is about. Okay, let's see, what would be impressive enough?" Walter thought for a second and then replied, "The comforter off my bed."

"Done." Kaleb stepped off into shadow and when he returned he was holding Walter's comforter. Walter's jaw dropped. "So this isn't some trick?"

"No. I've been trying to tell you. It's magic."

∙⫶∙

Kaleb's palms were sweating as he reached out to open the door to the Rainy-Day Lodge his former classmates had rented. Morgan exited her car and join the boys at the door. She cleared her throat, and when he still made no move to open the door, she did the honor for him.

"You okay?" Walter asked Kaleb under his breath.

Kaleb nodded and let out a slow hissed sigh. Deep down, he wished that Austin were with him, but as expected Austin said no. "I'll be fine."

His eyes circled the room. They graduated from a small school, their class had been forty-three people in total. From what he could tell, less than half decided to attend. The lodge was decorated in their school colors, green and black. Banners lining the wall read "Fighting Clovers."

Someone had decided on a nineties theme. One of the decade's many boy bands was playing. Kaleb rolled his eyes; he never liked any of their music. The buzz of talking ceased abruptly as the three entered. Kaleb put on his best fake smile and the buzz of conversation resumed.

Standing by the buffet of assorted lunch meat sandwiches and bowls of chips were the two people Kaleb never wanted to see again. There was no avoiding it. He was here now and Morgan wouldn't let him leave.

The two men hovered over the food table, beers in hand. David had once been Morgan's secret crush. The years hadn't been so kind to him. His mousy brown hair was thin and receding. His dull green eyes had wrinkles around the edges that were premature for his age. The muscle he was once so proud of had turned to flab.

Morgan had been obsessed with him. It was during their sophomore year that she decided that it was time to vocalize her affection. Had Kaleb

155

known what she was planning he would have derailed her crazy train before it left the station, but by the time he found out what happened the damage was already done.

It started innocently enough; she wrote anonymous love letters to him and left them in his locker. As the year went on, she started to hang out in the same areas as him after school. When he took up smoking, Morgan took up smoking.

Eventually she was caught stuffing letters into his locker, and then the school found out about her unrequited love in a very crushing, very public way. David managed to convince one of his friends on the yearbook committee to publish one of her love letters and included a mocking response.

For the rest of their time in high school, David mocked her relentlessly. She was the butt of a thousand jokes. As much as Kaleb tried to shield her from the ridicule, it didn't end until after graduation.

To David's left was Kaleb's crush, Alex. Though there hadn't been any overt signs that Alex was gay, Kaleb had convinced himself that he was. He still wore the same style jersey shirt that he did in high school. The years had been less destructive to Alex's looks. He still had a full head of light brown hair. His face was clean-shaven and his hair was the paragon of bed head. His body hadn't changed much either, his athletic build hadn't been lost to the years.

Kaleb, having learned nothing from Morgan's misfortune, wrote his feelings down in a letter to Alex. That letter circulated the entire high school before the day was over. To Kaleb's credit he waited until the last week before graduation to make his feelings known. The mocking and ridicule was shorter-lived than Morgan's torment.

Morgan saw the two at the table and grabbed Walter's hand. "You won't mind if I borrow him?" she said, and without waiting for a response dragged Walter to the buffet table. Walter nervously glanced back at Kaleb.

"David? Alex?" Morgan said, trying to sound surprised. "How have you guys been? This is my husband, Walter."

The two men laughed under their breath. "Nice to meet you, Walter. If that's really your name," David said. "What Craiglist add did you she get you off of?"

"I'm surprised he's not here with the fag," Alex chimed in.

Walter didn't know who to defend. He decided to try both at once. "Well aren't you both just shining examples of masculinity? Morgan has told me so much about you." Walter gave the man a piercing glare. "As for fags, they say the guys that are the most homophobic usually have a bit of homo in them."

David coughed and puffed out his chest. "Well aren't you the big man. Yeah, I'm sure you married this psycho lard-ass because you like her personality. Right. Well, let's see the wedding ring." Morgan's face was turning crimson. "Yeah. I didn't think so."

Kaleb walked up and put his arm around Morgan. "I think we should go. I didn't want to come here in the first place."

"If I had my staff right now, I'd destroy every one of you!" Morgan screamed.

"Just as insane as high school, huh? You never were right in the head," David said, antagonizing her further.

"Back off her," Kaleb demanded.

David spat on Kaleb. "I don't take orders from faeries."

Morgan picked up a lunch meat sandwich and threw it at David's head. She missed.

"That's weird, I always figured food just got sucked in your mouth when you picked it up," David mocked.

Morgan was halfway across the table before Walter could pull her back. The punchbowl wasn't saved in time and was kicked from the table, shattering on the floor. Morgan managed to crawl to the middle of the long fold-out banquet table, but it gave out under the pressure of her weight. The table crumbled onto itself bringing with it plates of pastrami on rye and a fruit tray.

"Whoa Morgan, calm down. Kaleb, we're out of here." Walter took Kaleb's hand and together they dragged a kicking and screaming Morgan to the door. A slice of kiwi that was stuck in her hair fell out as she thrashed against Walter and Kaleb. His classmates stared in shock at the carnage Morgan wrought.

•⸎•

After following Morgan home, to ensure she wouldn't go back to crash the party further, they began the long drive back to the city. Kaleb stared out the window of Walter's car in silence. They passed fields of corn and thickets of timber on their drive without speaking and then abruptly Walter asked, "So how long have you been a witch?"

"I thought we'd already gone over that," Kaleb replied sullenly.

Walter's eyes never left the road, "No, I mean, when did you know you could do real magic?"

"Oh. Back in December was the first time I shadow-walked. The first time it just sort of happened. I've got better control over it now. We've only cast one spell really. Last week we cast a locate spell on Austin."

Walter raised an eyebrow. "How did that go for you?"

Kaleb sighed. "Well he wasn't where he said he'd be. But I'm sure there's a logical explanation for why he was on the other side of town. I'd ask him about it, but how do you explain to someone that you were magically spying on them."

Walter chewed on a fingernail. "Do you think we could try a spell later?"

Kaleb got a little excited. "Yeah? Really? I thought you were freaked out by the whole magic thing."

"I am." Walter corrected himself, "I mean, I was. I will admit it's a little exciting."

Kaleb patted Walter's knee. "What would you like to try?"

Walter thought for a second. "A truth spell. I mean, if that sort of thing possible."

Kaleb grinned. "Oh, I'm sure it is." Kaleb rubbed his hands together. "This is going to be fun. Who did you have in mind? A boss? Some cute boy that you've got a crush on?"

"Austin," Walter blurted out without taking his eyes off the road.

"Wait, what?"

"I'd like you to cast a truth spell on Austin. It's pretty apparent that you have doubts about him."

Kaleb stared out the window. "Why do you think that?"

"You wouldn't have asked me to come with you to your class reunion if everything were okay at home. Don't get me wrong, I'm glad I got to come with you, but you talk about your relationship like the only reason you're with him is because you hope it'll get better."

Kaleb thought for a second. The butterflies in his stomach began doing somersaults. Anxiety built within him and he responded softly, "I don't like where this is going."

Walter gripped the steering wheel tightly. "I'm sorry. It's not my place."

"No, it's not your place." Kaleb crossed his arms.

"That's why I think you should cast a truth spell. I really enjoy your company, and I don't want to come between you and Austin." He glanced over to Kaleb who was still staring out the window. "I just don't want you to be unhappy."

The car rolled to a stop in front of Kaleb's house. All the lights were on. Walter took Kaleb's hand into his own. Kaleb withdrew his hand. He stepped out of the car, but before he walked away he turned back to say, "Thank you for coming with me. I really enjoyed your company."

Despite what his heart told him, a truth spell was certainly warranted, though he was afraid of what the results would be. His friends had been trying to get him to do something like this for months. If a relative stranger could see there was trouble, then it was time to act on his fears.

"I'm so sorry. This really wasn't how I wanted to end our weekend, but I really thought you should know the truth," Walter said with genuine sympathy in his voice.

"I know that. I'm just afraid that you could be right. I've dedicated the last three years of my life to this man. I'm just scared."

Walter reached out to Kaleb before he could step out of the car and gently squeezed his arm. "Promise me one thing."

"What's that?"

"No matter what you find out, please promise me you'll still be my friend. I've really enjoyed the time I've spent with you. I'll respect your relationship with Austin. Please don't think I was trying to break you guys up. I just ..." Walter couldn't seem to finish his own thought.

"No, it's okay. I understand." Kaleb leaned across the car and hugged Walter. "I'll let you know what I find out."

The house was empty. Kaleb gathered the loose papers that contained the spells they had been copying. He went to the coat closet and grabbed his staff as he leafed through the spells. The second spell from the last was just what he was looking for.

The sapphire atop his staff glowed with a blue light as magic collected in it. He retrieved a punch bowl from above the fridge and filled it full of water. The spell seemed simple enough. He exited through the back door and placed the bowl on the patio table.

Into the punch bowl, he began chanting. A film began to form across the surface and he chanted more fervently. Overhead the clouds parted and more silver light from the moon streamed down and filled the bowl.

The pale blue light from his staff pulsed and went out as Kaleb pushed its magic into the spell. His voice dropped an octave as he finished with the final words of the spell, "Truth be seen."

Kaleb peered into the bowl of light as it reflected for a second his face, and then his lover's face. There was no sound. He waved his hand over the bowl and the scene expanded. Kaleb squinted his eyes to see in the darkness what was on the other side.

Blood boiled in Kaleb's veins as he saw where Austin really was tonight. Austin lay in bed, his armed draped over some boy. Kaleb's nostrils flared as anger welled up inside of him. All the anxiety he had been feeling bubbled up to the surface and was replaced with rage.

His hands clenched and unclenched as he pulled the scene back further. Kaleb saw the street name for the house that held the bed that sheltered the man he had once called his lover. Shadows parted around him as Kaleb stormed into them. Once on the other side, his throat opened and he let out a shriek of rage.

•¶•

Morgan was still furious. After trying for several hours to concentrate on translating spells she gave up and decided to go for a walk. She imagined all the terrible things she could have done to David had she been permitted to take her staff. Kaleb had refused to let her bring it.

After twenty minutes, she had calmed down and began to enjoy herself. She always loved hiking through her parents' property. They had miles of cypress and ash trees. From an outsider's perspective, the land wasn't very valuable. Other than the trees, there were no natural resources, and the ground was too poor for farming.

She heard a crow call from the trees above her.

"*Doom!*" cried a voice in her mind.

Morgan froze. It was difficult to pinpoint where the call had come from. There didn't appear to be any animals in distress. She stopped walking, but after waiting for a few minutes she shrugged and walked on.

Once again came the ominous mental shout, "*DOOM!*"

She saw the crow in the tree above her. She focused her mind and sent a mental query to the bird, "*I'm sorry to bother you, but are you shouting doom?*"

"Shaman? Shaman! No doom!" the bird called in response.

A great murder of crows rose from the field just over the hill and flooded into the tree next to Morgan. They called to each other, a score of different mind-voices all speaking at the same time, *"Shaman? Shaman! No doom? Doom! Doom? Doom Shaman?"* They talked over one another. *"Yes, Shaman! Doom! Good Shaman? No, doom? No Doom!"*

Morgan rubbed her temple and thought back at the group of around thirty to forty birds, *"This is getting a bit ridiculous."*

A large crow disengaged from the group and flew down to Morgan's level. It landed next to her and eyed her warily. Morgan approached cautiously. "Are you in charge here?"

"Stop, Shaman, come no closer." It eyed her suspiciously.

Morgan scratched her arm. "Why do you call me Shaman?"

The crows in the trees began to repeat the word. Morgan sighed and began to turn away when the crow on the ground spoke to her mind, *"You are Shaman, for you speak with us. Tell us Shaman, why do we know?"*

She looked back to the large bird. "Excuse me?"

"Why do we know?" The rest of the birds repeated the question from their vantage in the tree. The crow on the fence hopped closer to her.

"Oh! You want to know why you woke up. Like from a dream?" She remembered all of what Mercedes had told her. "You *know* because magic has awakened you."

"Very good. Shaman may join us."

Morgan looked up to the crows in the tree and then back to the crow on the fence post. "No, I'm good. I think I have enough animals to take care of at the moment. I don't need a whole group of them to feed. No offense."

The crow hopped closer to her side. *"No, Shaman. We do not join you, you may join us. Be with us."*

Morgan's eyes locked with the coal black eyes of the crow. A swell of magic flowed between them. It flowed from the earth, from the crow, and from Morgan all at once. There was a tranquility in those dark eyes.

"Be with us Shaman," it said peacefully into her mind.

Her world contracted to those dark eyes. Morgan felt as though the wind and the heat of the sun were coursing through her being. Morgan's eyesight became sharper, she felt lighter. A weight she had never recognized before began to lift from her shoulders. She closed her eyes and let the feeling overtake her.

The world dropped away as they sped through the sky. There was a freedom to it, the shackles of mundane life fell away. The wind was like the tides of the sea pushing them toward the sky.

Forever, they were locked in embrace: the sky, the wind, the heavens, and the earth. Together they rose. They fell. They flew. Together they soared. It was a dream. A silence. A noise rushing around her but not overwhelming her. Life was a distant fantasy. All that mattered was the experience. It was poetry. It was fate. The air was a symphony and they were the chorus.

.⋅.

Morgan let out a sigh. The crows had taken roost in the barn next to her mother's house. She was still a virgin, but she thought for a moment that even sex would not be as satisfying as her experience flying with the crows. Mercedes was content in her lap. A deep rumble emanated from the cat as Morgan stroked the length of her body. They sat for over an hour enthralled in their own pleasure.

In a moment of realization Morgan asked, "Where's the bunny?"

"*Oh, the bunny? Um. I'm sure he's around here somewhere.*" Mercedes' body tensed beneath her hand, betraying her. "*Have you checked the cupboards? I think I saw him trying to sneak out a box of Chicken and a Biscuit.*"

Morgan's blood turned to ice. "What happened?"

"*What do you mean? I'm sure he's just hiding somewher*e," Mercedes looked up into her eyes, trying as hard as she could to convey innocence. "*He'll be around soon enough. What? You don't think something happened? No, you just watch, you'll find him hiding in some pantry chowing down.*"

"If you killed Bonbon, I'm going to kill you cat!"

"*Are you serious? You named him Bonbon? Shit! You really need a shrink lady. I think you might have some food issues.*" Mercedes leapt down from Morgan's lap and tried to inch back toward the house.

Morgan picked her up by the scruff of her neck. "Don't you dare try to turn this around on me! Did you eat Bonbon?"

Mercedes squirmed in her grasp, trying unsuccessfully to get free. "*I'm insulted that you would even consider such a thing.*"

Morgan's staccato words hissed between her teeth, "Did you eat Bonbon?"

The cat stopped trying to struggle. "*I won't justify that with a response.*"

"I can't believe you. Shit! I leave for a couple of hours and you have to eat my new friend. You really are a bitch you know that?" Morgan released Mercedes from her grasp and the cat fled to a dark corner of the deck.

Mercedes licked her imaginary wounds. "*I'm sorry.*"

"I'm sorry? What was that? I don't know why I even keep you around! That asshole from the class reunion was a better friend than you are, cat! He made me feel worthless for my entire high school career, but you. I don't know why I even put up with you!"

"What if I help you get even?"

Morgan ended her rant. "What?"

"Okay, hear me out. What if I helped you get revenge? You deserve revenge, right? Well, what if I helped? Would that make up for me eating Bonbon?" Mercedes' mind-voice added quietly and quickly, *"He was delicious by the way. Just saying. Not that you would ask."*

Morgan considered this for a moment. The cat made a good point. She did deserve revenge, especially revenge that couldn't be traced back to her. As mad as she was at the cat for eating her new friend, Mercedes was a cat. Could you fault a lion for eating a gazelle? Leaving them alone in the same room together was her mistake. She conceded, "What did you have in mind?"

The cat approached her apprehensively, *"I was thinking, what if I could help you find the glamor spell you've been looking for? You could look hot."* The cat added under its mental breath, *"Even though that's a stretch."*

Morgan ignored the rudeness, "That's all well and good, but how is a glamor spell supposed to help me get even?"

The cat jumped onto her lap and kneaded her thigh like a loaf of bread, *"Okay, hear me out. Once you had him in your clutches, so to speak, you could do whatever you wanted to him. If he inflicted pain on you, then pain he gets in return."*

Morgan considered the logic of the feline and she began to stroke Mercedes' black fur. "You're right, you know. The only payment for pain is pain in return. You're a good kitty." Mercedes began to purr under the petting of Morgan's hand. Morgan struck the cat on the top of its head, "That does not give you the right to eat Bonbon!"

.·.

Kaleb found himself on a side of town he had never been before. A brick bungalow stood before him. It would provide no sanctuary for the man that had lied one too many times. The shadows themselves bowed out of respect for the power that was Kaleb. For a moment he thought of taking the anger from his veins and blowing the brick house sky high.

He walked through the shadow-version of the front door and passed through it as though it had little more substance than a wisp of smoke. He slipped back and forth from the physical realm and Limbo. Whoever lived here was not providing opposition. Kaleb walked unchallenged into the nearest room. He found Austin spooning the man from the vision in the punch bowl, oblivious to the fact that Kaleb stood at the foot of the bed watching them.

Slowly, Kaleb drew back the covers and exposed their nakedness. Lies were laid bare for Kaleb to see. His stomach retched as his rage built. Kaleb wanted to die. His entire world was ripped from him and turned upside down. Tears stung his eyes. Deep within him, he could feel a rumbling, something begging to be freed. He gave into that feeling.

He gave into the force within him. Kaleb could see symbols and runes flash before his eyes. He let go of his body and his hands closed tightly around his staff of their own accord. The staff flared to light.

The men didn't rouse as words began to fall from Kaleb's lips. The force within him was strong. He could feel the words to a spell just behind his lips before they formed, but didn't know where they were coming from.

167

A dark fire erupted around Kaleb as he clenched his fists and then placed his hands, palms down, onto the bed. The black fire slowly inched its way across the bed.

Ancient runes and words poured through Kaleb's mind and off his tongue. The man Austin was spooning awoke but the damage was already done. Coiling around his body was fire and at the foot of the bed was a pillar of darkness.

Kaleb turned his focus to Austin. The black fire enveloped them both. A stream of magic nearby yearned for Kaleb's touch and he molded it to his will. "May the world see you for the snake you are," Kaleb cried.

Austin and his lover began to writhe in pain. A surge of energy hit Kaleb in the chest and he passed it along to the spell that was already in motion. The men began to transform.

•⁊•

Walter crawled into bed. It had been an exhilarating and exhausting weekend. He was glad he had told Kaleb what he thought about Austin. Deep down he knew Kaleb would do the right thing. Kaleb would find the right spell to get his answers and there wouldn't be any doubt left. Perhaps then they could be a little more than friends. He hoped he was acting out of selflessness and not out of a desire to be with Kaleb.

Magic did scare him. His entire world had been thrown off a bridge. There wasn't really a choice to deny it. Everything that he believed in was gone. He tried desperately to tie his recent experience up in a nice little ball with his religion but kept failing. There was no escaping it. Either Kaleb was a sorcerer or the Anti-Christ; Walter hoped for the former.

If he tried hard enough he could tie his world back together without too much of it falling on the floor. If what Kaleb had told him was true, then the Catholics were to blame for the cover-up, but perhaps they didn't even know they were covering anything up anymore. It was a secret wrapped up in a lie and buried with denial.

As Walter thought about it, he connected a few of the pieces himself. There were very few references to miracles in modern times. All of the miracles had been performed either before or during the time of the Saints. Were the Saints merely sorcerers? That was a question for the Catholics. Walter was a Baptist, or did it matter anymore? What if Jesus was a sorcerer? That last question made his head reel.

Thoughts spun around in his head. There was no way he was getting any sleep tonight. The cemetery truly was peaceful. It was no wonder why Kaleb enjoyed spending time there. It was a place one could be completely alone with their thoughts. Walter grabbed his keys.

The drive was longer than he remembered. When he rounded the last bend in the road he could make out the glimmering shapes of headstones and a faint glow that didn't belong there. Walter groaned. He was off duty so he shouldn't have to kick whoever was up there out, but he wanted some tranquility.

As he approached the turnoff, he shut off his lights and approached the gravesite slowly. There were no other cars parked at the cemetery, but at the top of the steps was a strange, pale blue glow. He calmly took a deep breath, got out of the car, and climbed the steps.

Geoffroi waited patiently as Walter finished climbing the stone staircase. The ghost spoke into his mind, *"You know Kaleb, yes?"*

Walter stared in stunned amazement. He wasn't sure if he had truly seen a ghost the night he met Kaleb, but tonight there was no denying it. Standing before him was a luminescent, transparent man in chainmail. He counted to three and reined in his fear. "You know me?"

"*I, Geoffroi. Please, great danger.*" The ghost became agitated. "*You speak with Sorcerer or no?*"

Walter shook the stupor out of his head, "Yes. I just got back into town with him not too long ago. Is something wrong?"

"*Must speak to Kaleb.*"

"Well, hold on. I may be new to all this, but maybe I can help you?" He didn't know why he had offered, but it felt like the right thing to do. If nothing else he'd have a story to tell Kaleb in the morning.

The spirit eyed him suspiciously, "*You are sorcerer?*"

"I'm not sure, but I'd like to give it a try. What do you need?" Walter shuffled from one foot to the other.

The Templar's eyes bore into Walter soul. "*I escape demon. It have shades. It want Sorcerer. I told nothing.*"

Walter realized his mouth was open and snapped it shut, "Yeah, we should probably call Kaleb."

•⁘•

Kaleb was in a state of panic. Whatever he had just done transformed his soon-to-be-ex and the home-wrecker into serpents. He was pretty sure one of them was poisonous. His phone rang. "This really isn't a good time."

Walter's voice greeted him, "Um, Kaleb, I'm really sorry to bother you, but I'm out at the cemetery. There's a ghost here that wants to talk to you. Goes by the name of Gee-of-roy?"

"Oh, Roy? Yeah, tell him I'm a little busy," Kaleb replied as he considered his options.

"I would have taken a message for you, but this sounded a little important." Walter's voice betrayed his fear.

Kaleb's voice quivered. "Please don't hate me forever, Walter, but I've got a couple of things to deal with at the moment."

"Okay, sorry, I'm sure he can wait if I tell him you're busy. You will come as soon as you can, right?" Walter's voice conveyed the hurt he was feeling.

"No, I mean, please don't think I'm an evil witch and try to burn me at the stake." One of the snakes began rattling its tail at Kaleb and weaving ominously back and forth on the bed. Kaleb yelped and jumped back.

"Oh my god, are you okay? What happened?"

Kaleb steeled himself against Walter's reaction. "I sort of, accidentally, turned my ex into a snake," he said quickly.

"I'm sorry, what?"

"Don't be mad. I didn't mean to. It just sort of happened." Another involuntary yelp erupted from Kaleb's throat as one of the snakes lunged at him.

"Kaleb? Are you okay?" Walter yelled into the phone.

Kaleb backed away from the bed slowly as they hissed their dissent at him. "Yeah, I think we should probably talk in person."

"Do you need me to come get you? Where are you?" Walter said into his phone as the call was lost. "I think Kaleb's in trouble," he said to Geoffroi.

Kaleb stepped out of the shadows, ran to Walter, and threw his arms around him. For a while, Walter just held him as Kaleb wept on his shoulder.

Occasionally he muttered something incoherent or profane. Eventually he stopped crying and just held him.

"Better?" Walter said, looking into his eyes.

Kaleb dried his eyes and broke free from the embrace. "Yeah. Sorry about that. I found Austin in bed with another man."

"You don't have to apologize, it's not every day that you find out your boyfriend is a despicable, cheating snake *and* turn him into one." Walter said with the corner of his lips raised in a smile. "I'm sorry, too soon? I just don't want you to be upset."

Geoffroi cleared his throat. *"Sorcerer, there is matter of importance."*

Kaleb made one last sniffle and turned to the Templar. "What is it?"

"A demon take me. It try to find you, but I no say."

His head spun around, "I'm sorry, *what*?!"

"Not safe." The Templar became frustrated with his broken English. He stopped and started several times before saying, *"Demon want you."*

Kaleb rubbed his temples. Not only did he have to deal with finding a way to fix what he did to Austin, but now he needed to be on the lookout for demons as well. "Walter, how long do I have before someone can file a missing person report on Austin?"

The implications sunk in; Walter began to hyperventilate. "I'm aiding and abetting, oh my god, I'm going to get fired. We're all going to go to prison for kidnapping or whatever they decide this is similar enough to. Oh my god, a cop in prison? I can't go to prison! Kaleb, I can't go to prison!"

Kaleb shook Walter. "Snap out of it." He went to the steps and sat down. "Okay, just think." He got out his cellphone and called Morgan. "Morgan? What do you mean this isn't a good time? Well you should probably make some time because I really need your help. Yes, Walter is with me. Why?" Kaleb handed the phone to Walter. "It's for you."

Walter took the phone in his hand and placed it up to his ear. "Hello?"

Morgan calmly stated, "What do I do if I accidentally killed someone?"

He was already in such a state of shock that he replied just as calmly, "Well, that depends. How did you accidentally kill said person?"

"I think he may have had a heart attack."

Walter sighed with deep relief, "Well if that's the case you should call 911."

Morgan paused for a moment. "Yeah, that's not really going to work. Kaleb told you about the whole book thing, right?"

Walter chewed his thumbnail. "How it was code for high magic?"

There was another long pause. "So, yeah, I'm not supposed to be in here. I flew in an open third story window."

Walter sat down next to Kaleb and put an arm around him. "You flew. Okay. So he died of a heart attack when a five foot tall woman flew in through his window. Were you riding a broom?"

Morgan laughed and repeated his question out loud and then laughed some more. "No, but that would have been *hilarious*. I didn't ride a broomstick, I shape-shifted into a crow. You sure are taking this all pretty well."

"I'm fairly certain I'm having a nervous breakdown," Walter said nonchalantly. "So a crow flew through his window. I don't see how that would scare someone to death."

Morgan's side of the phone was quiet again. "Well, I'm not really sure if it was a heart attack. It also could have been the waterboarding that killed him."

He jumped to his feet, nearly knocking Kaleb over. If Walter had a drink in his mouth he would have spit it all over the thirteen steps. "Waterboarding?"

"Yeah, it's when you—"

Walter cut her off, "I know what water boarding is! What the hell were you doing?" Walter paced the top of the stairs, his hand rubbing his forehead.

"About that." Morgan briefly trailed off. "It just sort of got out of hand. I mean one minute it's harmless fun and then, before you know it, I'm poking him with silverware that I heated up on the stove."

He ended his pacing and said plainly, "Morgan, you know I'm a cop right?"

"Mercedes said to tell you, if you think anyone downtown will believe you when you tell them a three-hundred pound woman ... how dare you cat, I am two-hundred and ten pounds! Okay, sorry. If anyone at the station would believe you when you tell them that a *two-hundred and ten pound* woman flew into someone's locked third-story apartment in the middle of the night and tortured him to death well then you can ... I will not say that!" Morgan paused again. "Anyway, I was told to talk to you so I know what *not* to do."

He held the phone away from his face and screamed into it, "What *not to do* is kill a man!"

"Yeah, well that's already been done. So, how do I make sure they don't find fingerprints?" Walter hung up. Morgan called right back but he handed the phone to Kaleb. "Did he just hang up on me?"

"I may have only heard one half of that story, but you can't expect him to help you cover up a murder. Besides, we've got a couple of other issues. So there may be a demon out to get me." He braced himself for the next revelation. "And I accidentally turned Austin and his new boyfriend into snakes," Kaleb said it as fast he could, hoping Morgan wouldn't pick up on it.

She was angry. "Oh sure, he'll help you cover up ... well, whatever crime it is you committed, but won't help a friend out and tell her how to cover up an *accident*. Well I guess that's what you get for having tits. I really need to find some straight friends."

"Um, I really don't think this has anything to do with you being a girl, it has to do with the fact that you're a *murderer*, which would make us *accomplices*. Shit, Morgan, you really screwed up this time. Okay, let me think." Kaleb fervently ran his hands through his hair. "Okay. I'll come get you, we're going to the library. I've got to find a spell to break an enchantment, and you've got a spell to resurrect the dead to find."

"I didn't think you could take others with you when you shadow-walked."

"I think this deserves a try." Kaleb ended the call, took Walter's hand and stepped into the world of shadows. It made Kaleb think of how a tractor would feel trying to pull an elephant riding on a whale through a lake filled with molasses. With all his strength he pulled and ran and pulled. He didn't have the courage to look behind him to see Walter's face.

They arrived at Morgan's mother's house. Kaleb was furious with Morgan. He didn't say a word to her as he took her hand, and she grabbed hold of Mercedes by the scruff of her neck. He took Walter's hand in his other and tugged the three of them across the Atlantic Ocean to Saint Patrick's Library.

⁖

The group arrived at Saint Patrick's Library. While the living busied themselves with searching for keywords, the Templar patrolled the aisles. There was a darkness lurking here. He could feel it but he couldn't tell if it was the lingering evil of the demon or if it was still lurking in the shadows.

Kaleb handed staves to Morgan and Walter from those that lined the wall. He filled them with magic so they would glow. Morgan gave him a look suggesting she could do better.

Taking the staff in her hands she recited the words to a spell she had recently memorized. Balls of floating light erupted around her. She pointed to spots on the ceiling and they flew through the air and shed their light. "That's much better. Shall we?"

"What words are we looking for again?" asked Walter for the third time. He stood staring at one of the sections of trees. He had taken the shadow-walking and the strange library very well.

"Vida or morte, preferably both together, and voltar forma. Shit, where's a librarian when you need one? I'd give anything for Dewey right about now," Kaleb said as he stood on a pile of 'books' to read the higher-up ones. They had been at this for hours and he was exhausted.

Walter scratched his head, "Dewey?"

Morgan responded as she walked past him to another column of spells, "Have you never been to a library before? It's how they sort books." She kept walking and ran her hands along a section of tree carved with runes and writing. "You know, this place is massive, Kaleb. When you were bringing them over to my place I didn't imagine there would be this many."

Kaleb replied through his teeth, "Sure is great. Especially when the needle in the haystack is written in Gaelic. Roy, stop sulking and help us."

"I not sulking, Sorcerer. Must have vigilance. Demon want you. I keep protected Sorcerer."

Kaleb rolled his eyes, "Well, at least try to be less dramatic about it."

"Shouldn't we also be trying to find something to take care of the demon problem while we're all here?" Walter tried to contribute.

"One problem at a time please. Well two problems." He sighed. "We are never going to find anything ..." Kaleb froze mid-sentence. Walter joined him as he stared at a large section of tree. Kaleb whispered to Walter, "I recognize these runes. They appeared in front of my eyes while I was casting."

The engraved cross-section was toward the bottom of a large pile of dissected tree. There was no doubt that wherever these had come from it was a very large tree. He had no way to dislodge it without moving the entire pillar.

Walter rubbed his shoulders as Kaleb considered his options. The answer seemed simple enough to Walter, "You should get a roll of paper and some charcoal."

Kaleb leaned forward as he enjoyed the back rub. "Why?"

Walter stopped rubbing and Kaleb nearly fell forward. "Are you serious? You hang out in graveyards and you've never done a grave rubbing?"

"Okay, yes, but where am I supposed to get charcoal and paper? Do you want me to shadow-walk into an art store and leave an IOU?" Walter and Morgan shrugged. "Fine. Does anybody have any cash? I'm not stealing." Kaleb went around and collected what he could before shadow-walking away.

Morgan and Walter searched for their keywords for what felt like an eternity. Mercedes was the first to complain of thirst and that was the moment they realized they were trapped. Thankfully, it was such a large space they didn't feel confined, but they became all too aware of the lack of exits.

Walter turned to Morgan, "So, can you shadow-walk too, right? I could really go for a burger right now." His stomach protested its emptiness with a loud rumble.

Morgan stared through him. "No, Kaleb's the only one of us that can do that. I'm thirsty. I wonder how much air is in this vault. I mean, it's all bricked up." They looked at each other and their level of distress increased significantly. A hollow laugh emerged from Morgan. "How long could it take?"

.٦.

Midway across the Atlantic Ocean, Lifedrinker chose to strike. She wore her true demonic form. Her wings made no sound as she trailed him. The shadow-walker hadn't noticed her following him. A smile crossed her face as she attacked.

The demon pounced on him and attempted to sink its ebony claws into his shoulder. Kaleb wailed in agony. He rolled to the left. They fell like stones together into the inky waters of the shadow-ocean. He slipped from the shadow realm and into the true waves of the sea.

He would have to return to the shadows if he wanted to live, so she waited. The demon watched and waited for him to emerge. Kaleb erupted into the darkened sky of the plane of shadow. He hovered fifteen feet above her.

"So I take it you're the demon that Roy was talking about." Kaleb held his hand to his shoulder to slow the flow of blood. She flung herself into the sky after him but found that he had rocketed to another spot in the sky. "I can see why Roy was worried about you, but I'm not."

The demon unfurled her black and red wings and lunged after him. Once again he wasn't where he should be.

"I'm a shadow-walker, demon," he said mockingly. "What are you?" Shades crowded his position in the sky. "Oh, right, demon. Gotta go." Kaleb rocketed through the sky and was gone.

The demon opened its mouth and let out a cry of frustration and anger. It cried out to the shadows floating above her. "Find him!"

•٠•

Nick's morning lecture on biology aggravated him to the core. Deep down he wanted to eat of each of his fellow class mates and the teacher. The worst part was knowing that he could. He felt around for any lowered shields to take the edge off but found none.

It had been a few hours since he last fed, but he was already hungry again. If only he could find someone to sip from. The words of the professor buzzed in his head as his mind scoured the classroom.

His mind was searching the sheep for a victim when he found another wolf. It had the unmistakable sign of psychic vampire, an aura imploding on itself. With a fake yawn he took a moment to scout the room. In a far corner he saw her. She had a mane of fiery red hair, her face was pale and freckled, she was tall and frail, and her green eyes caught him staring.

He turned back to the lecture and was torn between playing cat and mouse with her and taking her as his pupil. He thought for a second about how it would taste to eat another vampire's life-force.

The redheaded woman felt Nick's presence and sat upright. The lecture carried on in the background as their awareness centered to a point in space. He refrained from batting her mind away like a cat toy.

He had never tried telepathy, but he knew how to dream-scape. He would mark her mind and wait for her to fall asleep. Patience was a virtue. Nick wished, for a moment, that he could bring his staff with him to class. Surely Lifedrinker would have known a spell to make her fall asleep.

A smile grew wide on his face. Who needed spells? All he would have to do was drain her vitality just enough to make her fall asleep. Her shields were weak and he was stronger. Pulling on all his strength he battered, his mind against her shields. Once he had finished bashing his mind against her shields, he felt as though it had been beaten with a bag of oranges. There was a reason Lifedrinker insisted on tearing down the shields before attacking. He was going to have a headache later.

He had recently fed, so he found the energies of high magic and was not concerned that they would drain away at his touch. He called upon the nearest wellspring and resumed his assault. Within a matter of seconds he was in. Slowly he began to drink her life-force until her eyes started to droop. With a small push of the magic and a force of will he entered her dream.

The dream started off innocently enough. They were in a small grotto of trees with a trickling stream flowing through it. Nick twisted it to his will. The grass started dying and the stream became black filth. In her robe of gossamer she looked around in disgust.

Nick allowed himself to be seen. He wore the guise of a winged demon, complete with black horns and claws. His body was half man and half goat. His torso was red and muscled. A fresh corpse lay at his feet and he played with the entrails as she approached.

The woman's red hair became flames that rose and fell about her head. As she walked her mind spoke into his, "*You think I should be impressed?*"

Nick was impressed at how easily she took control of the dream. He closed his eyes as he licked a drop of blood from his finger. "I am called Lucian. I will forgive you for not groveling."

She spat at his feet. Nick's demon guise grew in size until he towered above her. The woman took an involuntary step back. The dark energies of death swirled about his form as he glared down at her.

"You will show respect, *child*!" the faux demon shouted. "I have called you here. You will obey!" His eyes flared blood red. She fell to one knee. "That's better. If you wish to feed you will obey, and you will listen."

Her eyes were fixed on the ground, and her jaw was set. "Your words are my gospel," she responded.

The twelve-foot tall demon raised its head to the sky and laughed as the ground trembled. Nick realized he was losing his grasp on the dream and spoke quickly, "You shall be called serf, and I shall be your bread. If you wish to truly feed then be at the clock tower at the witching hour." Nick had always felt a connection with the old clock tower at the center square of the campus. The dream fell apart as the bell rang.

.॰.

Walter and Morgan had given up on searching for spells hours ago, now their sole focus was Kaleb's return and the lack of ventilation. Mercedes was the only one not fazed by the dire situation and enjoyed what she felt was a fantastic new world to explore.

When Kaleb finally returned with a duffel bag and fast food, both Walter and Morgan met him with arms crossed. Morgan was the one to ask the question on both their minds, "You stopped for fast food?"

Kaleb sat his baggage down and stumbled. He winced in pain. "I would have been back sooner, but battling the demon over the Atlantic took a bit more time than I was anticipating."

Geoffroi appeared at his side. *"The demon find you? Sorcerer, I say nothing."*

Walter and Morgan ran to his side. Kaleb's shirt was torn and Walter helped him remove it. His shirt stuck to his wound as Walter pulled it slowly over Kaleb's head. The gash was deep and the gauze that Kaleb had taped to his shoulder was already drenched with his blood.

Morgan stepped to his side with her staff. She put a hand on Walter's shoulder and said, "I've got this." The rose quartz atop her staff flared to life. Morgan chanted in a soft voice and placed her hands inches above the gash in Kaleb's shoulder. He moved away from her involuntarily as her hand neared his skin. "Stop moving."

Kaleb sat still as she chanted. His shoulder had been burning for last hour, but now it felt cool. The pain he had been tolerating melted away. When Morgan finished her casting Kaleb looked up at her and said, "Thank you. I was pretty scared when she attacked me, but I managed to outrun her. You should have seen me, I don't think I have ever ran so fast in my life."

Walter put his arms around Kaleb. "We're just glad you're okay."

Kaleb smiled and went back to the duffle bag on they had all forgotten. He began to pull their food from the bag. "Walter, no veggies, extra ketchup. Morgan, plain add pickles and mayo."

It took them a moment to realize he was talking about the food. Walter smiled. Morgan was preoccupied with whether or not he had gotten fries with that. Mercedes sniffed the bag.

"Yes, Miss Kitty, I got you something too. I wasn't sure if you preferred dry or wet food so I got both." Kaleb slumped down on the floor.

Mercedes sniffed his hands and said to Morgan, *"I've always liked this one."*

Morgan said out loud, "You like anyone who will feed you." Two sets of eyebrows raised as she dug into her meal with a ferocity. "Okay, okay, we're like twins. There, I said it. Happy?"

Kaleb smiled smugly. He got out his own dinner and dug into it as well. Kaleb waited until his mouth was no longer full and said, "I'm really sorry it took so long. I bet you guys were freaking out."

Walter and Morgan shared an embarrassed glance and said in unison, "Not really."

"We were more worried about you," Walter added.

Kaleb looked down at Mercedes and asked, "Are they serious?" The cat shook its head. "Well at least one of you is honest." He put up a hand to Walter's retort. "I was scared for you. When that demon attacked me, the only thing I could think about was getting back to you guys and getting you out of this vault."

Walter put his hand between Kaleb's freshly healed shoulder blades and attempted to offer comfort. Morgan was still lost in her food. Mercedes stared up at him, still waiting for her can of Fancy Feast.

•❦•

The clock struck three. Nick had been surprised at Lifedrinker's reluctance to add a new member of their little family. He cared little whether or not she liked it. He began to worry that he had been stood up, but then a fiery redhead strutted across the commons.

Nick had rehearsed this in his head all afternoon. There wasn't much life energy to act as a buffer this late in the day, but it was enough. He called upon the forces of high magic and his staff glowed. As he spoke the last words of his spell a fog cloud flowed from his mouth and surrounded them.

Her steps became more hesitant, and he could feel her blood pressure rise as fear grew in her heart. When she stepped into the space where they could see each other, she stopped. Nick took a step forward into the fog-covered courtyard. They stayed rooted to their respective spots for several minutes before they began to circle each other, sizing the other up.

"So you're the one from the dream? I thought you'd be ... I don't know, a little bigger." Gwen planted her feet, ending their dance. "I'm Gwen. You will either tell me how you got into my dream, or I walk."

"Quite demanding, aren't we?" A malicious smile grew on Nick's face. "Especially when I'm the one that knows, and you're just the student."

"Oh please. Don't even try that bullshit on me. I know that you are a freshman. Your name is Nick. My friend Mark said you're a drama queen."

Nick tried to remember who Mark was. Regardless of where she was getting her information, Gwen wasn't winning any points with him. No one knew who she was planning to meet, assuming she told anyone she was going to meet a demon from her dream. She was alone. Nothing would trace this back to him.

He called magic to his staff and it flared into life. Gwen backed up a pace. Nick's intent was strong. If Lifedrinker's instruction was correct he needed to focus his will on his goal, the words didn't matter as much.

"Let the darkness be free of its bounds and show her terror." Nothing happened. Nick rolled his eyes. He wanted the shadows to turn into people and start circling Gwen, but they wouldn't budge. The buffer of energy that kept high magic from spinning the drain of his abyss was depleted.

"Are you kidding me with this?" Gwen asked.

Nick quickly closed the gap between them in a single leap and drew in a breath an inch from her face, "Don't *ever* challenge me child!"

Her hand reached for something in her pocket. She was already terrified, even though she would never admit to it. He made quick work shredding her chakras. She fell to the concrete beneath them.

Casually, he walked away. "Not so powerful now, are we child?" He took his time draining away her life-force. Slowly, he strolled back to her side. With a smile he reached into her pocket and grabbed the can of pepper spray. He could feel her heart pounding in terror.

The staff flared to life as he once again filled it with magic. With great care Nick formed a tiny shield around the nozzle of the pepper spray and pretended to spray it into his mouth. Nick leaned down and said to her, "Minty."

Nick pulled a bottle of Hawkeye Vodka and a bottle of Diet Mountain Dew from his satchel. He took his time since Gwen could only watch. He sat on the concrete, sipping at his drink, and said to Gwen, "And what to do with you? I'm sure by now you realize you're up against someone much more powerful than yourself. Oh, was that a nod? No, of course not. I can taste your terror by the way. Do you want to know how it tastes?"

He crossed the space between them whispered in her ear, "It's delicious."

Nick stood above her, Diet Dew and vodka in one hand and his staff in the other. "Now, what am I to do with you? Defiant, yes, but I like that. I could kill you now and no one would be any the wiser. They would think it was a tragedy, of course. Do you have family, Gwen?" He took a sip of his drink. "Oh, how silly of me, I can tell by your sudden increase in fear that you must."

Nick looked at his imaginary watch. "But how, my dear, do we resolve this? I could kill you here and now. What would be the point in that though? I'm no monster." He looked down at her. "Oh wait, I am a monster. But I bet a fellow wolf would be ..." He added another dramatic pause. "Tasty." He smiled. "I'm sure you're wondering. Why, oh why, does this psycho call me a wolf? Well my dear, let me tell you about vampires."

As Gwen stared at him with fire in her eyes, he explained what he knew about vampires to her. He explained how he felt her pulling at the life-force of their fellow students. He left out a lot, but he made his point.

"*Lifedrinker, can you tell me how to heal her chakras so we can get on with this,*" Nick said in his mind to the staff. There was no response. "*Lifedrinker?*" Still no reply. "*Hello?*" He shook the staff in his hand and knocked on the wood. "You've got to be kidding me. Nobody's home. Well I guess I'll do it myself."

Nick kneeled over Gwen. He drew on his desperation. His hands were inches from her as he channeled high magic through them and focused on healing her chakras. One by one they began to reform. Once they reached the point of functioning properly she was released from the paralysis.

She fought the urge to run. "What do you want from me?"

"Call me master and I will teach you what I know."

.᠇.

The day had been more profitable than they expected. Three spells included the keywords they were looking for. Morgan rubbed them with charcoal onto the parchment. They were exhausted. Morgan had always wanted to see Rome, but she didn't expect to see it from the inside of a vault. When Kaleb had finally shadow-walked her back to her mother's house she never wanted to go back.

They made a hasty, sleep-deprived translation. Kaleb decided they would start with Morgan's problem. The spell they were using included both Gaelic words for life and death, so they moved forward quickly. In order for this to work they would need a powerful gemstone attuned to the forces of death.

They had argued for a while about what type of gemstone would be best when with great pride, Mercedes chimed in. "*We need the Hope Diamond.*"

Morgan ended her argument and stared at the cat. "You realize that we can't just borrow the Hope Diamond."

Walter exploded, "You have got to be kidding me! So in order to fix you're little 'oops, I murdered an old high school classmate,' you want Kaleb to steal from the Smithsonian?"

Kaleb rested a reassuring hand on Walter's shoulder. "She's right. If we're going to bring this guy back from the dead we need the Hope Diamond." He drew in a deep breath. "I'm not okay with this either but Morgan's my friend, and I know she didn't mean to hurt anybody. Magic just gets the best of you. I don't know if you realize how tempting it is. I didn't mean to turn Austin into a snake, it just sort of happened."

Walter groaned. "I don't doubt that, Kaleb. But you turned a snake into a snake, Morgan killed a man."

Morgan objected, "I resent that."

Kaleb interrupted their argument before it began, "I know but, you have to understand that if a death spell had come to mind instead, both Austin and that little home-wrecker he was sleeping with behind my back would be dead."

Walter rubbed his back soothingly. "You might not believe this, but I don't think it would have happened that way. You're a good person Kaleb, I don't think you would have killed him."

"Oh, so therefore I'm not a good person?" Morgan muttered under her breath.

"You weren't there," Kaleb said as he shied away from Walter's reassuring hands. "Morgan, I am incredibly mad at you. I will get the Hope Diamond from the Smithsonian, but I will only do this once. If you go on a killing spree I will *not* be there to bail you out."

She hung her head, "I know. I'm sorry. It won't happen again, I promise."

"All right, so it's settled, we will bring him back from the dead. Walter, do you forgive Morgan?" He took Walter's hand and put it in Morgan's.

A month ago Walter would have only expected this question on TV or in a movie. Somehow, he was thrust into a completely different world and his morals hadn't yet caught up. Deep down, he was afraid that they never would. He knew the difference between right and wrong. This didn't seem right, but magic had never been part of the equation before. "I guess so."

"This may take me a while, but according to the spell you have some work to do as well. Morgan, you'll need to anoint the corpse in spring water.

Walter, I'm sorry, but could you please consecrate us a circle please. You'll need salt, sage, and a sense of piety."

Mercedes glared. *"Oh, he has plenty of that."*

Morgan didn't translate. Kaleb finished assigning their roles and once he was sure they had a firm grasp of what was required of them he shadow-walked away. Morgan grabbed the iodized salt from the kitchen and handed it to Walter.

"I'll only be gone a few minutes," Kaleb said. Walter didn't respond. Morgan shrugged, got in her car and drove off down the gravel road.

Walter muttered and mumbled to himself as he poured the salt into a circle in Morgan's backyard. The cat watched for a while and only came down to join him at the center of the circle when he had finished. She crawled into Walter's lap and began to purr. "These people are crazy," he said to the cat. Mercedes bit his hand and ran off.

Waves of Despair

A fog covered the ground as twilight approached. The creature struggled to breathe. Its body was writhing in pain. It collapsed halfway across the road. Two pinpoints of light shone through the fog. Its senses were overwhelmed and it was disoriented. Before the creature could react, the strange object struck it. The car crumpled around its form.

A man was flung into glass and metal and into the trees beyond. His ribs were bruised and he was bleeding. The world pulsed around him. His heartbeat pounded in his ears. Time crawled as pain was the only thing alive in the world. Darkness descended on him. His eyes would no longer stay open. He was certain that death was sure to follow. Shock and pain stole his mind away.

His eyes blinked open one last time as the forest came alive with red and blue lights. He heard a man's voice shouting near him, "We've another one over here! Must've been thrown from the car."

•╥•

The sun was lazily beginning to rise as Kaleb returned with the Hope Diamond in a gloved hand. Morgan had still not returned with the corpse. The birds began to sing their morning dalliances. Walter and Kaleb sat in awkward silence.

Walter couldn't bear the silence any longer, "I'm sorry, I know you want to help your friend, but you just stole the Hope Diamond!"

"Come on, do you really think I want this damned thing? I'm sorry. Neither of us has slept yet, I'm sorry."

Walter's offense grew, "No, this has nothing to do with how much I've had to sleep! Do you realize that I have just been an accomplice to murder and first degree burglary?"

He eyed Walter warily. "You realize that I have no desire to be the next owner of the Hope Diamond, don't you? Any individual that owns the Hope Diamond dies an early death."

The sun peeked over the hill. Walter's frustration wasn't going away. "I don't know how that matters. You stole the Hope Diamond and your best friend is a murderer."

Kaleb took Walter's hand in his own. Walter tried to pull away but Kaleb placed it to his heart. He said sweetly, "Seriously?" He looked into Walter's eyes pleadingly. "I really hope you don't feel that way. I have every intention of returning this damn rock to the Smithsonian when I fix Morgan's problem."

Walter regretted his earlier statement. There was no denying that he was well beyond the academy or even the law's rules at this point. Magic didn't care about jurisdiction or forensics. This was a new beast whose moralities were yet to be defined. He could feel in his heart that Kaleb was trying to do the right thing, but was it right?

"Walter?" Kaleb clenched his hand. "I want you to know, I didn't mean to hurt Austin. I was hurting and I wanted him to hurt, too. I admit that. I didn't mean to hurt him." He shook his head. "Please don't judge me."

His eyes stared at their joined hands. "I'm not judging you. I know you didn't mean to."

"But I can see it in your eyes, I can feel it in your hands. You don't agree with what I did. I'll make it right, please believe me when I say that."

Their conversation ended when Morgan pulled up the drive. They dragged the body out of her trunk. They maneuvered the corpse into the center of the circle.

Kaleb took up the reins. He summoned the nearest stream of high magic to his staff. He anointed the corpse with the spring water Morgan had furnished. Words fell from Kaleb's mouth has he circled the corpse. He traced runes with his staff into the ground and the Hope Diamond began to glow a sickly red color.

Walter felt uneasy as the corpse began to stir. Morgan joined the chant that Kaleb had started and Mercedes joined as well. She howled along as their voices joined in unison. The voices met in a strange unsettling harmony. Morgan's voice rose and fell with Kaleb's as though they had practiced this song all their lives, yet it was a song without notes; only inflection and the staccato rhythm of their words.

A halo of eerie red light clung to the ground, the sky, and the corpse. The world had transformed as though it was being viewed from rose-colored glasses. Only the trio and the cat held their original color. The temperature dropped further until their breath fogged. Kaleb and Morgan continued their chanting.

As the chanting intensified Morgan's phone began to ring. *La Cucaracha* played from inside her purse. At first they tried to ignore the sound as they concentrated on the work at hand, but it began to ring a second time. Morgan looked at Walter. He retrieved the phone from her purse and answered it.

"Hello, Morgan's phone," he said as politely as possible.

The voice on the other end of the line was an older man, "This is Officer Gomez from the Jasper County police department. Is Morgan

Daniels available?"

Dread washed over Walter; it took him a moment to respond, but he managed to keep his composure. "She's in the shower, officer. Is there something I can help you with?"

"There's been an accident." Walter held in a sigh of relief. "Please have her give me a call. Do you have a pen and paper?"

"No, but can she call you at the number that came up on her phone?"

"Yes, that should be the right number. Please have her ask for Officer Gomez."

"I will officer, thank you." Walter hung up the phone and held onto it as the ritual was reaching completion.

Kaleb's voice had dropped an octave and they were beating the ground with the base of their staves while chanting to the beat. The Hope Diamond pulsated with ruby colored light. A moment ago, the diamond had been a beautiful shade of blue and was now emitting a sickly red light. Walter found the change to be highly unsettling.

The spell reached its climax and the red light that had built within their circle was sucked into the corpse. It sat up. Walter wore a startled expression as he jumped back several feet. Morgan laughed with delight until she realized a sane person shouldn't be laughing.

Her delight faded as she realized he wasn't jumping to his feet and freaking out over being tortured to death. There was nothing. He stared forward into the distance expressionless.

Morgan let out an awkward chuckle. "Um." The head of her former classmate turned slowly to face her. "Did it work?"

Kaleb cautiously approached the sitting man. He felt the neck, the wrists, there was no pulse. "Not sure how to put it, yes the spell worked, but

I'm not sure it was the right spell." He walked back to where Walter was standing in case of sudden fainting. "He's a zombie."

Panicked words began to spew from Walter and Morgan's mouths simultaneously. Kaleb rubbed his temples and took in their situation. A zombie wouldn't fool forensics. The body would already be in some state of decay, cause of death would still be the same. They were, in one word, screwed. Kaleb couldn't focus on this right now; he had a priceless artifact to return and a boyfriend to break up with.

"Guys, we'll figure this out in a minute. I've got to return this to the Smithsonian before someone notices it's gone." He picked the diamond up in his hand. It was still a beautiful blue color, thankfully.

.ᵛ.

It was Jeremy's first day as a security officer at the Smithsonian and the place was in a complete state of panic. The security footage wasn't much to go off of. One moment the Hope Diamond was resting in its case, in the next section of the tape a man dressed in all black broke the glass of the case and walked away.

There were no tapes showing where he came from or where he went. One second he was there and the next he wasn't. Jeremy knew what they thought. It was only a matter of time before they accused him of it being an inside job.

The police and the FBI were called and were on their way. They had been keeping a close eye on him all night. He had to use the bathroom and for the first time in over an hour he was allowed to go off on his own. He turned the lights on in the men's room and almost fainted.

The Hope Diamond sat beneath the glass of the bathroom mirror. The priceless relic sat on top of two twenties. On the mirror, written in lipstick, "Sorry about the glass."

That day the Smithsonian was "closed for maintenance." Jeremy was questioned by the FBI, the police, and many more whose job titles he didn't know. There were forensics, handwriting experts, police dogs, surveillance experts. It was a circus.

There was no trace of the perpetrator. No sign of forced entry, no sign of exit. The Hope Diamond was determined to be the original. Jeremy had been left in an empty back room for hours. He knew his story was preposterous and full of holes. He was patrolling by himself when it went missing and he found it in a bathroom.

A man in a black suit entered his holding room. "So, you have no idea how the diamond got in the bathroom?"

This would be the tenth time that he told his story to different people. He was tired. The man sat down at the table across from him. Jeremy finally nodded in confirmation and looked away.

"I bet you want to get home and get some sleep." The man stood up and held the door for him. He flashed a pristine white smile.

Jeremy was confused, he was certain he was going to prison. "Yes sir. Let me know if there is anything else I can help with."

The tall man in the black suit patted him on the back, "Oh, we'll be in touch. For now, don't mention tonight to anyone."

After Jeremy had gathered his belongings and was well on his way the man in the black suit turned to his colleague and said, "He'll slip up eventually. For now we watch and wait. We don't have anything to convict him on, but we'll get him eventually."

•⸙•

Geoffroi trailed the Sorcerer in secret. He hadn't lasted this long as a ghost without learning a few things about remaining unseen. The goals of the Templar seemed to have flown out the proverbial window. Morgan was in distress, Nick was unreliable, and the Sorcerer desperately clung to the status-quo. None of this would do.

While Walter screamed his displeasure at Morgan, he took matters into his own insubstantial hands. Before him was a moving, if not breathing, vessel. The body was a bit out of shape, but none of that mattered. Possession was frowned upon by the members of his order that still haunted the catacombs but this did not involve the subversion of the governing spirit. The governing spirit of this vessel had very much departed.

Though it was more of a display more than anything else, Geoffroi took a deep breath and leapt into the corpse. The sensation that greeted him was entirely new. The power that was invoked that morning clung to his spirit. It was no longer a lifeless corpse made animate, this was once again a person.

Unfortunately, the body was still dead. There was no heartbeat and no warmth of its own. Geoffroi concentrated on the magic suffusing him. With subtle changes to the flow of the magic, he was able to convince it to make his heart beat once again. He did not know, however, whether this small change would count him among the living or still among the dead. He did feel warmer, though that could be all in his head.

Morgan sobbed as Walter berated her for her impulsive recklessness. Mercedes drew herself up to her full height as she arched her back, hissing her displeasure. Geoffroi realized after jumping into the vacant body that he could no longer hear Mercedes and was rather disappointed. He cleared his throat, which was more painful than he would have expected. They froze.

"May I be of assistance?" he said formally. From out of nowhere the English language came naturally and no longer presented a challenge. Morgan and Mercedes were startled; Walter passed out. "Not again."

⁂

Kaleb returned to an unexpected scene. When he left Walter and Morgan alone, he assumed they'd be at each other's throats. Instead he found Morgan carefully nursing a nasty cut Walter had on his forehead. A conclusion scampered around like a mouse in a house full of cats and he pounced.

"What the hell Morgan!? I can't leave you alone for one minute without you and Walter fighting! What'd you do, push him down the stairs?"

Someone was trying to get his attention, but he ignored the strange man, he was on a roll. "You never like any of the guys I date ..." He froze. Realization was a strange thing. Sometimes it hits you on the face at sixty miles per hour, but sometimes it creeps up on you like a seventy-year-old lady on a Sunday. He stood, mid-sentence, finger extended to point out Morgan's injustices, frozen in time. Geoffroi waited patiently for Kaleb to regain his composure. "Uh, Morgan, did the zombie just clear its throat?"

Morgan jumped on the opportunity with a string of words. "Now please don't freak out. I think this is actually a great middle ground and I had nothing to do with it. Actually, it was all Roy's idea but honestly I think it's great and I'm sure Walter will agree once he wakes up."

Kaleb's finger danced between pointing at Morgan and pointing at the zombie called Roy. Morgan beamed at him. Kaleb gulped. "Roy?"

197

Geoffroi took this as his chance to interject, "Well actually, Sorcerer, the name is Gee-of-roy. I haven't really corrected you and Morgan calling me Roy. I truly mean no harm, I just wanted to see if I could help."

"He talks, oh my god he talks!" Kaleb was ecstatic. "You know, Morgan, they can't prove you killed someone if he's walking and talking. This couldn't have worked out better. Gee-roy are you, by chance, able to remember anything about the host?"

The zombie scratched his head, and after a moment nodded. Kaleb clapped his hands in excitement.

Morgan had been absentmindedly stroking Walter's forehead with a damp cloth, and when he began to stir she jumped causing him to groan in pain.

Walter looked up and through half-blurred eyes asked, "Kaleb?"

She patted him on the shoulder. "No, baby, but Kaleb is here. We'll fill you in on the rest later, okay?" She motioned to Geoffroi to exit the room via the stairs to the upstairs bedroom. "Kaleb, darling, I think Sleeping Beauty is awake."

For once her tone was sincere and not mocking. It almost caused Kaleb to stand for a moment in shock, but he realized she was moving and letting Kaleb take her place. "I'll give you two some privacy."

They lay on the floor together for a while, Walter's head lovingly propped up in Kaleb's arms. Walter was the first to speak, "I thought I could handle all this. I mean, as a police officer I'm going to see some pretty crazy stuff, right? I don't know if I'm cut out for magic being a part of my life." Kaleb's heart sank, but he let Walter continue uninterrupted. "I really like you, Kaleb. I just don't know if I should *know*. You know?"

Kaleb smiled and looked down into Walter's eyes. "I really like you, too. If the magic stuff bothers you than you will just have to trust me to make sure everyone plays by the rules. I've got a snake to take care of."

"Oh shit, what time is it?" He looked at his watch in panic, "I've had no sleep, barely anything to eat, and I have to be to work in three hours?"

Kaleb drew him into a kiss. It came out of nowhere and Walter returned it. When their lips parted Kaleb grinned, "I think this warrants a sick day, Officer Graham."

•٧•

Morgan and Geoffroi waited patiently upstairs until she heard the front door close. She was in high spirits. The man she killed was now only sort of dead, Kaleb and Walter were dating, and Mercedes hadn't said one nasty thing to her in over an hour. She remembered that Walter had taken a message for her before everything had gotten so heated and she decided it was time to return the call.

A gruff voice answered, "Officer Gomez."

In her bright, sing-song, customer service voice she identified herself, "Hello, Officer, this is Morgan Daniels. I understand I missed a call from you, how can I help?"

"Miss Daniels, I regret to inform you that there has been an accident."

Her heart hit the floor. Up until this moment she had been caught up in the excitement of the day; it hadn't dawned on her that her mother was now four hours late. "An accident?"

"May I call you Morgan?"

"Miss Daniels is fine. Accident?" Morgan sat down on the stairs.

The voice on the other end of the line drew a deep breath. "This is never easy, Miss Daniels. I'm sorry to inform you that your mother has been involved in an accident on Highway 9. The ambulance arrived and there was nothing we could do. The passenger with her—"

Morgan interrupted. "The passenger?"

"Yes, there was a man with her that was thrown from the car. He's stable, but he hasn't woken up. Actually, Miss Daniels, we were hoping you could come down to the hospital and see if you can identify him."

"Is Mom okay?" she said, dreading the response.

"I'm sorry, but she didn't make it."

The line went quiet. Numbness insulated her from the pain that was building inside. "Okay. It won't be until later today."

There were some more words exchanged that were more reaction than conscious conversation. She vaguely remembered the heartfelt words of condolence offered, and the embrace of a zombie when she finally hung up the phone.

Morgan stared at Geoffroi. The wheels in her head were clinking around an idea. She began to talk to herself, "Okay, so I can use up to seven days of bereavement. I don't know if that'll be enough time. I'll have to ask the crows how long a trip like that would take. I could ask Kaleb to help. No. He won't want to help, besides he's got other things going on. I'll do this on my own."

She turned and acknowledged Geoffroi, "Roy, you're going to need to go back to David's apartment and live there for a while. Take Mercedes with you. You can use my car. Just ask Mercedes how to drive."

Geoffroi watched in stunned silence as Morgan picked up a jacket, set it down, picked it back up, set it down once again. She walked around in a daze, and he wasn't sure how to respond. Mercedes looked up at him with a pleading look in her eyes and he wished he could still hear her.

"I have to get to the hospital. That can wait. No, I think it would be best if I took care of that now. I should probably leave someone in charge of the funeral arrangements while I'm gone. I'll just leave that up to the aunts and uncles. I should probably call them. They'll expect me to call." She set her keys down on the kitchen counter and walked out the front door.

•٢•

Kaleb stepped into the den of vipers, literally. Luckily for Kaleb, it did not appear that the man Austin left him for had any roommates and apparently preferred a nice dark bedroom. He carefully lifted back the bedspread and jumped when he heard the rattle.

A nervous laugh escaped his throat. "Okay, Kaleb, they're just snakes. You're an all-powerful sorcerer now." His personal pep talk did little to alleviate him of his fear of snakes.

There was movement in a corner of the room and he squealed. Kaleb took a firm grip on his staff and planted his feet. He did his best to recite the spell of shape-reversal from memory but gave up and pulled the charcoal rubbing out of his back pocket.

He took the rubbing in one hand and his staff in the other. He let the magic drift into his staff and it glowed with blue light. "Corpo min antes. Selado co poder da terra e do ceo. Cambios no corp."

The spell went on for some time. He waved his staff back and forth. Their eyes never left Kaleb as he worked his magic. They followed his motions with their bodies. "Devolver o que foi." The mamba lunged at him and he jumped back several feet.

There hadn't been time to translate the spell into English, so he was afraid he had done something wrong with the pronunciation, but before he could decide to give up and come back later the magic took hold. Kaleb could feel it growing and taking form behind the words. He began repeating the incantation.

He chanted with fervor, waving his staff in front of the snakes for good measure. The spell reached its climax and broke through Kaleb like a tidal wave's first crash onto shore. Kaleb barely managed to shadow-walk away as their forms twisted and grew until they returned to their original shapes.

Just before he left he was certain he heard one of them say, "I am never doing shrooms again."

⁙

Morgan was guided through the halls of Saint Luke's Hospital. It had been modernized several years ago, but a few of the wings still held their rustic charm. The tell-tale sign that the hospital had once been a smaller rural hospital instead of the megalithic modern facility was its labyrinthine design. In order to get to the wing they needed to first travel through a maze of hallways and take an out-of-the way elevator before they would arrive at their destination.

They walked down the corridors in a silence that reflected the silence in her heart. She was dead inside. Her mother was her lifeblood. Even after her father's death she always considered her mother invulnerable. Morgan always wanted her mother to outlive her. "*Tough old bird,*" she thought to herself. "*Why did you have to go and die on me? You would have loved magic. I'll find a way to bring you back.*"

The crows had created quite the stir. Nurses and patients were huddled at the windows to watch them swarm. She heard one patient mumble that it was the end of the world. Officer Gomez led her to the ICU and showed his badge at the nurse's station. A camera man and a news reporter stood at ready by the nurse's station. They were escorted to a room at the end of the hallway.

He wasn't a pretty sight. There were bruises, cuts, and scrapes all over his face and arms. Yet there was something within him that Morgan could feel. He knew what happened to her mother. "Officer, I'm sorry, I don't know him."

He took her by the crook of her arm and with a comforting gesture began to show her back to the door. She planted her feet before he could usher her out. Quietly she added, "Do you mind if I stay with him for a little bit? I'm sorry I couldn't help, but he was the last person to be with my mother."

He smiled and nodded, "I'll be in the waiting room when you're ready to go."

She returned a half smile, "That's very nice of you, but I can see myself out." She turned back to the only person who knew what happened to her mother and sat down by his side.

"Take your time. I'd still like to wait for you. Come and find me when you're ready, okay?" He waited for her reply but received none, so he silently retreated to give her some space.

Morgan sat next to the man. Despite a few unfortunate acne scars he had a handsome face. His hair was shoulder length and a deep auburn color. He had a goatee that surrounded supple lips. He was the most handsome man she had ever seen. She was in love, again.

She cleared her mind and inhaled deeply. As she slowed her breathing she allowed her mind to drift away from her body. Without the aid of her staff it was a lot more difficult to reach the sea of magic. It felt far away and reluctant to come to her mind's hand. She used her desperation and tugged on the wellspring of power. She grabbed what she considered just a handful. The energy pulsated within her; she had no idea how to make it do what she wanted it to. Without opening her eyes, Morgan took the man's hand in hers and focused on healing his wounds and waking him.

She pushed the magic into the unconscious man. It didn't seem to go very far and her mind quickly returned to the nearby stream and tugged harder. The effort of pulling magic without her staff was harder on her spirit than she would have thought. She flung the magic back to the room in which her body sat and told the magic to heal and wake.

Over and over she flung handfuls of magical energy back at the hospital room. After several minutes, she could no longer keep her focus and opened her eyes. He was sitting upright and staring at her. He looked confused, and lost.

Chaos erupted outside the door. A man began screaming and then being chased. An old woman across the hall poked her head out of her room, her IV still hanging from her arm.

Morgan was entranced by his eyes. There was a depth within his blue-grey eyes like that of an ocean right before a storm.

"Who are you?" He asked and then his body clenched with pain. Morgan helped him lie back down.

Officer Gomez peered through the door. "Miss Daniels, are you okay?" He stopped dead in his tracks as he saw her helping him to lie back down. "I don't know what happened, but the hospital is in an uproar. This whole side of the recovery unit just woke up, the ravens flew off and ..." he froze midsentence, staring at the man in the hospital bed. "Is he awake?"

She slowly looked away from those intense eyes that had her transfixed, "I was just sitting here and the next thing I know he's sitting up."

Quickly Officer Gomez pulled a chair up to the other side of the bed. "You didn't have any identification on you, do you have any family you want me to notify?"

Morgan added, "What happened to my mother?"

Officer Gomez spoke sympathetically to the dark-haired man in the hospital gown, "We want to know what happened, but for right now I want to make sure your family is notified of what happened."

It took a moment to recover his voice. He squeezed Morgan's hand and in a soft baritone voice he spoke, "My name is ..." His face scrunched up as he tried desperately to remember. "Matthew." He smiled and sighed. "My name is Matthew. I'm sorry, but I don't remember anything else. I can't remember."

A rush of doctors and nurses came into the room and politely asked them to leave while they checked Matthew's vitals. Reluctantly she allowed Officer Gomez to lead her from the room.

They made their way from the room and saw more doctors rushing from room to room. The cameraman and reporter were being forcefully escorted to the elevator. Officer Gomez stepped in and helped see them to the lobby. For a second, Morgan thought about slipping away, but decided against it.

When things had finally calmed down they sat in the hospital cafeteria. Morgan sipped on her tea and Officer Gomez on his coffee. They hadn't said much to each other. She picked up some of the conversations going on around the cafeteria and learned that shortly after they left in the elevator, the patients had one by one passed out and couldn't be roused.

After what felt like an eternity of silence Officer Gomez finally spoke, "I've never seen anything like that in my life. Do you mind if I ask you a personal question?" She nodded. "Are you a Christian, Miss Daniels?"

She tried not to choke on her tea. "Why do you ask?"

"Well, with everything I just saw, it makes me wonder if this is the beginning of the tribulations." She didn't respond so he went on to say, "The end of times?" She nodded her understanding and he kept talking, "I didn't know if it'd happen in my lifetime, but now I start to wonder how good of a Christian I've really been. I mean sure, I'm a cop, and I get to help people, but is that enough?"

Morgan patted his hand. He was an older man, certainly old enough to be her own father, but she felt so much older than him in this moment. "I think so too. I think it's definitely the end of the world, at least as we know it."

•⊺•

Kaleb shadow-walked home and began packing his things. He was still uncertain of where he would go. Would Walter take him in, or would he have to crawl on his knees back to his parents' house? At his age, there was no way he would live with his parents again. Perhaps Morgan would let him stay with her for a while, at least until he found his feet again.

The three suitcases he could find were already filled so he started to fill a blanket with his belongings. He had no intention of being sentimental. While he was going through the clothes he found the ticket stub from the first movie they had gone to see together, he shredded it. On the dresser was a picture of him and Austin; he shattered it on the floor. Destruction felt good.

The thought crossed his mind to shadow-walk the TV over to Morgan's but then he thought better of it. He finished his thought aloud, "I've already taken a lot of risks with that."

He would wait for Walter to wake up from his nap. If Austin came home sooner, he would take a cab with his meager belongings, go to Morgan's and shadow-walk them inside. "It's not like she gave me a key," he said to himself in an attempt to justify his thoughts.

The last of his clothes and incidentals found their way into the blanket that would make his last suitcase. He found his mind drifting to Walter. "He's nothing like Austin," he said aloud as he remembered the care and compassion in his eyes. Anger set in. "He's nothing like Austin!" Kaleb resisted the urge to topple the TV and dance on its remains.

Instead, he turned it on. It was the morning news. A blonde woman stood out front of Saint Luke's Hospital. Hundreds of crows circled the building. Kaleb's eyebrows couldn't help but rise. "Morgan?" He turned up the volume.

"We're standing outside Saint Luke's Hospital, Tom, where thousands of crows have taken to circling the building. As you can see behind me, they have come here en masse. What isn't clear yet is why these birds have taken a sudden liking to the building." The camera panned to the swarming black mass.

"It's really sad what passes for news at this hour," Kaleb said to himself as he watched with disinterest. They interviewed a boring doctor who had nothing important to say. Kaleb was about to turn the channel when he heard someone scream. The cameraman and reporter heard it, too. The doctor became suddenly nervous. His eyes kept darting back and forth from the camera to the halls behind him. He tried to dance his words to distract from the scene playing out behind him.

A man dressed in a hospital gown burst from his room screaming. The cameraman zoomed in and Kaleb immediately recognized him; it was Nick's ex, Jess. His eyes were crazed and his words were nonsensical.

The reporter latched onto what was clearly the more interesting story. It was a short run that ended in an orderly tackling him to the ground, while the doctor being interviewed tried desperately to get the cameraman to turn off the camera.

Kaleb turned off the TV and called Nick first, voicemail. He called Morgan, voicemail. Kaleb paced the length of the living room and toyed with the idea of shadow-walking to the hospital himself. "I can't," he said to the now dark television set. Austin could be home at any moment. He sat down and his knees started bucking; he stood up and his foot started tapping. Kaleb felt helpless.

This was the first time since December he couldn't do as he pleased. His hopes for a future with Walter depended on a clean break from Austin. The bags were all packed and he was ready to go.

"I could dump it all out and start again later," he said to himself. "No, I need to have a reason to leave him. He's been gone all night; it's nine in the morning. I'm done with waiting around for him to come home. I'm not a lap dog, I have feelings." Kaleb's motivational speech did little to settle his nerves.

He called Morgan's mom. It rang for quite a while and finally there was an answer, "Mmrrrow?"

Kaleb's eyebrow rose involuntarily. "Mercedes?"

There was a hesitant yowl of reply, "Mmrrroooew."

Kaleb was extremely unsure of how to respond. "Um, so I take it Morgan's not there."

The cat interrupted and he could hear the sarcasm in her inflection, "Mmrroew."

"Okay, yeah, Mercedes, I would be there if I could but I have to wait for Austin to get home before I can go anywhere. I've already packed up and I'm ready to leave him."

"Mmrreoeweow!"

He hesitated. "Now, I'm sure I should be happy that I can't hear your thoughts 'cause I'm sure that was probably pretty vile."

"Mmmrrroooew!"

"Yeah, we could go on like this forever but I need you to do me a favor. Is Roy there?" His legs became restless as waited. His foot tapped and his leg bucked.

"Sorcerer?" the reply came at last.

"Okay, so first of all it's still a little creepy to actually *hear* your voice. Even though I know it's not really 'your' voice. Anyway, sorry, um, so have you talked to Nick lately?"

"I have not spoken with Nick since before the demon attacked me." Most of Geoffroi's accent had been replaced with David's Midwestern accent, which comparatively was lacking accent all together; it was unsettling.

"Oh, that long, huh? Well shit. I can't get a hold of him and thought he may want to know that his ex is awake."

"Should I pass along this message, Sorcerer?"

Kaleb thought for a second about everything he still had to do today, but still decided it would be best for the zombie not to be the one to deliver this to Nick. "Um, could you tell Mercedes that I'll be stopping by the pet store later for her and thank her for picking up the phone?"

"Of course, Sorcerer," Geoffroi's tone conveyed he was slightly offended at not being allowed to assist.

"Oh, and Roy, please stop calling me Sorcerer."

"As you wish, Sorcerer."

•꙼•

The car lurched onto the gravel road. Geoffroi was driving. Mercedes was freaking out. She hated being in the car with Morgan at the wheel, but at least she knew that Morgan could drive.

She went through a list of regrets in her mind: she regretted letting Morgan take that litter of kittens from her, she regretted not saying goodbye to Morgan or trying to comfort her, she regretted not getting to meet Nicolas Cage. She was terrified. Geoffroi tried in vain to calm her with soothing words and reassurances, but she knew deep down she was going to die.

Her life flashed before her eyes several times. Humans always said they got nine, but at this moment she wasn't so sure of that. Gravel turned to highway as they made their way to town. She vowed to herself that if she survived this she'd settle down with a nice tabby somewhere and start a family. At least Geoffroi seemed to know where he was going. He drove them into town, and finally the metal box of death came to a stop in front of an apartment complex.

When the door was opened and she found her feet on solid ground again, she swore to herself she hadn't been scared at all. Geoffroi paused before closing the door to take in the damage Mercedes had done to the seats. "Feeling better my four-legged lady?"

Affronted, Mercedes raised her head and walked toward the apartments.

❧

Austin opened the front door and Kaleb immediately jumped into action. He grabbed the duffel bag full of his things and pushed past Austin. He raised a middle finger to the home-wrecker backing out of the drive. He paled when he saw Kaleb and drove off.

His soon-to-be ex quickly jumped on the defensive, "What's your problem?"

The anger he had been suppressing all afternoon erupted violently. "I am so sick and tired of all your bullshit! It's two in the afternoon! You don't call; you don't tell me where you're going!"

Austin tried to interject but Kaleb pushed on. "This isn't the first time either." He opened his mouth to speak, but Kaleb shut him up, "And don't give me one of your bullshit stories about being at your cousin's, or your brother's. *That* was not your cousin!" he spat.

Austin spewed out his retort, "Don't act like you're perfect! You know how many times I came home and you were gone! You sure do spend a lot of time with your ex these days. I don't know if I'm with you because I love you, or because I don't want to hurt you."

Kaleb's eyes widened. "Excuse me?"

"I'm leaving you." Austin didn't seem too broken up about it which only fueled Kaleb's anger.

"How dare you try to turn this around on me? You don't get to leave me, I'm leaving you! Want to know what my friends say about you?"

Kaleb had backed Austin up against the china cabinet. "My friends say that I'm an idiot for sticking around. You treat me like shit and you're constantly lying to me. How do *YOU* think that makes *ME* feel?!"

Austin's voice raised and he screamed back, "I've never lied to you! You're the one who's been lying to me!"

Kaleb hadn't even come close to exhausting his reservoir of anger yet. "Stop it! You're a piece of shit! How long have you been cheating on me?" Kaleb grabbed his staff and summoned magic into it; the blue stone on top burst with light.

He took a spell out of his bags and read it over. It was exactly what he wanted and a smile crossed his face. Freedom from lies. Kaleb began reading the spell in Gaelic and then again in English. He wove a net of power as the spell directed and threw it over Austin.

Austin backed up to the china cabinet; the porcelain Japanese ladies inside were the only witnesses. "What are you doing?"

"It's magic, *honey bear*." His voice was dripping with venom. "I tried to tell you about it before but you were too busy screwing anyone that would open their legs for you!" Austin went for the door, Kaleb's hand slammed it shut.

"Six months. There were several guys." Austin eyes widened. "What did you do to me?"

"Now listen to me you piece of shit, you will never speak of this to anyone. Magic isn't real." Kaleb drew the magic into himself and once again fueled a spell. "Speak of magic to anyone and being turned into a snake for an afternoon will seem like child's play. I will know, and I will find you. I am going to go live my life and you are going to stay out of it. You will never lie to me, or *anyone*, ever again!" The stone flashed once more with power and then went dark.

.⊤.

A loud knock woke Walter from his fitful sleep. Kaleb never told him where he would go after he broke up with Austin, but deep down he hoped it would be with him. He opened the door and Kaleb fell into his arms. Tears were streaming down his face. At his feet was a duffel bag, a suitcase and a bedspread filled to the breaking point.

In between his sobs, Kaleb finally managed to relay that there were a couple more things still in the cab and that the cab was waiting to be paid. Being the gentleman that he was, he first helped Kaleb to the couch, paid the cab, brought in his bags and returned to Kaleb's side to put an arm around him.

The sentences were barely complete and the words were mostly muffled, but Walter listened intently, "Three years! Cheating! I trusted him." Kaleb began to sob uncontrollably; he was starting to hyperventilate. "I can't ... believe ... how dare ... how could ... why?" When his words finally were overpowered by his tears Walter put his arms around Kaleb and just held him.

Kaleb melted into Walter's embrace. They sat together on the couch. Nothing in the world could touch them. The tears ended and they continued to hold one another.

.⊤.

Geoffroi let himself into David's apartment. For a second, Geoffroi had to remind himself he wasn't David. It took a moment to get past the mirror whose reflection unnerved him. He looked at his knobby nose, his brown hair that was receding and thinning, and his dull green eyes. It was a painful reminder that this was not his body.

Deep down Geoffroi knew this wasn't right, but his Christian morals had been tortured and bled out by the church. It was time for the Templars to take their revenge and he knew he was only the first to be resurrected by the sorcerers that the church tried desperately to destroy.

The crucifix that hung in the bedroom was quickly removed and placed in a drawer. He picked the fan off the floor and replaced it in the open window. There were bloodstains on the sheets and a sense of anger welled up within him. Was it the remembrance of his own torture or was David still within him somewhere?

His stomach growled and he was relieved. Up until this point he was afraid his insides were dead. The magic and his presence were bringing his new body back to life, or at least some semblance of life.

He scratched his crotch as he walked to the refrigerator and paused. That was not a habit he had in life. Something of the original owner of his body must have survived. He stored that thought for later.

There wasn't much to eat in the fridge. He found a block of cheese, two apples, and a plastic Tupperware container full of sliced ham. Geoffroi brought it all with him to the kitchen table. Out of habit he began to say grace, but scolded himself halfway into the blessing. God was no longer a part of his life. He took a bite of the green apple and its flavor exploded into his mouth.

"Mercedes, you must try this." He took a knife and cut a piece of the apple off from the core and placed it next to the cat. She sniffed the apple and then eyed him suspiciously. "It is the most amazing thing I have ever sampled. I did not know the apples of your day were so delicious.

The cat refused her slice of apple. "More for me then, milady." Geoffroi ate the slice and then the rest of the apple. When he reached the sliced ham, he once again erupted into a state of exuberance over the quality of the food and insisted Mercedes try. Instead, the cat raised her tail and perched atop the sofa.

After eating, he took David's cellphone and placed it on the floor next to the cat. "Do you know Morgan's number?" She looked at him sideways, huffed, and went back to scratching herself.

"We are going to need to find a way to communicate more effectively, Lady Cat." He picked back up the phone, "I should at least check my voicemail." He froze. He had no idea what voicemail was. Mercedes stopped grooming and stared at him.

•⁊•

The clock on the kitchen wall struck its angry cords seven times before Morgan finally arrived. She flew through the open bedroom window, knocking the fan from the windowsill and shook off her feathered form. She entered the kitchen and stared in a stunned silence. The man that had tormented her all throughout her childhood stood in an apron that said "Kiss the Cook" making pancakes.

"Um, Roy?" she finally asked.

He wheeled around with a huge grin on his face. "I ordered Mercedes a Speak-and-Spell off eBay. I do hope she likes it. It's been rather hard communicating with her since I took over this body."

Pancakes were stacked high on a plate and presented to her. She reluctantly sat at the table. This all seemed far too close to normal to be comfortable. Giving into the urge she embraced the semblance of normalcy and dared to ask how the drive went.

"*He drives like a fucking lunatic!*"

Absent from the other half of the conversation, Geoffroi responded, "Oh it went swimmingly. Our lady here was a bit of a scaredy-cat though." He stopped and chuckled to himself before repeating the word, "Scaredy-cat."

The voice inside Morgan's mind was highly annoyed, "*He's been doing that shit all day! He thinks he's making up new phrases! Please tell him to stop, Morgan, I promise to be nice to you.*"

"Seriously?" she asked out loud, directing her puzzlement to the cat.

Geoffroi took her query to be amazement. "I just don't know how it is I create such whimsical word plays."

"No, not you," Morgan responded. "I was talking to Mercedes. Seriously? You'd actually be nice to me?"

The cat looked nervous and avoided meeting her eyes, "*Well I guess that wouldn't be entirely correct. Really it's all relative. Nice-er?*"

"Sold!" She turned back to Geoffroi. "You're not making up new phrases, we've been saying them for years." His face fell. "Are you okay?"

Geoffroi sat down at the table next to her. "It's been happening all day, milady. As I shared with you before, I have some memories of the man who once called this body his own, but it seems it is more than that. I drove his car, I checked his email, though at the time I was unsure what email was. It would seem I am beginning to speak as him. I do not know what is left of me."

She placed a hand on his shoulder and looked into his eyes. Though they were the same eyes that she vowed her entire life to destroy, there was a new light within them. "You are nothing like David. I will let you know if I ever think you're acting like him, Geoffroi."

A slight smile formed on his face. "You didn't call me Roy."

Morgan smiled back as he took her hand within his hand. He swooped in and kissed her full on the mouth, but instead of the kiss being returned, she leapt to her feet and slapped him across the face.

"*Ah shit!*" came from Mercedes.

Morgan seethed in anger. "What the hell was that for?"

"I am sorry, milady. I have such a connection with you. You remind me so much of my late wife. God rest her soul." Geoffroi placed his hand to his heart.

Morgan reined in her anger. "Don't let it happen again."

•⸾•

Kaleb and Walter had spent the afternoon nestled together on the couch. Kaleb listened to Walter's heartbeat. Kaleb's face reflected his despair. "Is something wrong?"

"It's nothing," Kaleb lied.

"No really, I can tell something's bothering you." Walter shifted his body, forcing Kaleb to sit up.

"I was just thinking about Austin." Kaleb looked away as he spoke the words he didn't want to admit.

"Anything in particular?" Walter was as nervous to inquire further.

"I'm really trying not to let him get to me, but it just makes me so mad. I gave everything I had to him. At least, I think I did. Why would he cheat on me? Was I not spending enough time with him?"

Walter turned Kaleb to face him. "You can't expect to understand what was going through his head. I'm sure you did everything you could. For some people that'll never be enough. No one is perfect."

"You're perfect," Kaleb said softly.

"I'm not perfect, but I'm glad someone thinks so."

"What time is it?" Kaleb asked abruptly.

Walter looked at his watch, "About seven, why are you getting hungry?"

Kaleb uncurled himself from Walter's warm embrace and stood, "A little bit of that, but I was just wondering if there was anywhere in the world you wanted to visit. Preferably somewhere where its night, but I can work around that if I need to."

"Oh, I don't know. I'm really happy right here," he said as he pulled Kaleb back to the couch and into a loving kiss. Walter's stomach growled its unrest, "Okay, I am hungry." Walter's brow knitted itself in confusion, "Um, so it's still a little bit before seven. Is this watch broken?" He put it to his ear, but it was still ticking. Walter buttoned his shirt and walked to the kitchen, but the clock there also read seven. "Okay, I'm not crazy. It had to be at least a half hour."

Kaleb propped himself up on his elbow. "If not longer. Did you stop time?"

In a daze, he walked back. He ran his fingers through Kaleb's hair as he sat down on the arm of the couch. "Not that I'm aware of. Does that happen? I mean, could I stop time?"

"Well I don't know, have you ever tried magic?" Kaleb said with eyes closed as he enjoyed Walter's fingers massaging his scalp. "I mean, you never really know what you're capable of until you try." Quickly pulling away from Walter, he sat up and added, "Can I teach you magic?"

218

Walter grinned, "You're so cute when you get excited. I'd sure like to try."

.ı.

The small funeral home was packed to capacity. At the front of the room was the open casket of Anna Daniels. All around her were the potted plants that had been left in offering to her memory. Her face held a peaceful expression and her arms were folded over her chest.

Her brother, sisters, family, friends, and co-workers all came to pay their respect. Past the press of family sat Morgan and her friends. The back row of chairs was exclusively her domain.

It felt like forever ago since the last time the trio had been all together in one place. Nick had come with a redheaded woman she had never met before and she felt a pang of jealousy. Kaleb had arrived with Walter, and though it was still extremely awkward between Morgan and Walter, he had at least made an effort to be consoling.

She hadn't been to a wake since her father had died. This time she had more than just Kaleb to offer her comfort. She hated family, so Kaleb stuck around even after Walter had to leave for work.

She had been crying off and on all day. Waves of regret, loneliness, anger, sorrow, grief, and self-pity came over her like the tides. She wanted to cast the spell that they used on David, but her spirit was nowhere to be found.

"Kaleb, thank you so much for being here. You've always been like my twin brother." Tears started forming in her eyes. "It really made being an only child bearable." He squeezed her hand and she cried. "I'm really going to miss her."

"Are you ready to see her?" Kaleb asked.

Morgan nodded and they both stood. Nick came to her other side and put his arm around her. "I'm so sorry. If I can do anything." He gave Kaleb and her a pointed look. "Anything at all." He again gave them a look. "You just let me know."

She gave him a hug and said sweetly, "These things are a part of life. Thank you for offering."

Kaleb whispered into her ear, "We really could try, you know."

"Everyone already knows that she's gone." She began to step forward but stopped in her tracks. The man she had seen at the hospital was here. His deep blue-green eyes scanned the scene of solemn faces and rested on her. "It's him."

She let go of Kaleb's hand as he approached. Awkwardly she smiled. "I see you're feeling better." Silently she chided herself about how stupid she sounded. She made short introductions of Kaleb and Nick; she still had not acknowledged Gwen's presence.

"Hi, I'm Gwen," she said, presenting her hand to the newcomer. She turned to Nick. "You know, you really are an ass. Morgan, I'm sorry to hear about your mom."

Morgan smiled at her and bit back her jealousy, "Thank you. Nick is terrible about introductions."

Nick glanced around nervously. "Yeah, sorry about that. So, everybody, this is my new friend Gwen. I'm really sorry, Morgan, but would you be upset if we took off? We really haven't eaten today."

Kaleb began to realize that Nick's eyes were a little sunken and he was more pale than usual. "Are you feeling okay, have you been sleeping okay?"

Nick waved off the concern. "It's all good. Gwen and I have been hitting up the bars trying to bag her a man." She smacked him with her purse. "I mean find her a man. I really don't mean to be rude, but I'm starving."

Matthew had been waiting patiently and when the pair stepped away said shyly, "I'm sorry to come here, I hope it's all right."

The sweetness in his voice was like honey to Morgan. "Of course it's all right. Honestly I didn't know if I'd get to see you again. I was really hoping you could tell me how you knew my mom."

"I really wish I could, but I can't remember anything. I tried going to the nursing home where she worked, but none of them knew me. One of my doctors suggested coming here to hopefully trigger some memories." Matthew nervously shifted his weight to his other foot.

Morgan felt a twinge of remorse for her earlier self-loathing. Sure she had just lost one of the most important people in her life, but here was a man who had his entire life ripped from him.

He wasn't beautiful in the common definition, but Morgan saw a depth in his eyes that she had only ever seen once before. They were mysterious and inviting, like Nick's. She lost herself in those eyes while he talked with Kaleb about what he could remember. Morgan almost missed the overt probe to hear more about her mother.

"Her name is Anna," Morgan began a very heartfelt retelling of her mother's life. "She was kind of the black sheep of her family, I guess. Dad and I were the only ones that really were there for her." The last statement drew the ire of her aunt standing nearby, but she paid no attention. "Mom raised me Wiccan, which Dad was okay with since his mother was Dakota Sioux and he didn't much care for religion. She would never have wanted all this, but her family wouldn't honor her last requests."

They made their way to the casket while Morgan continued to talk about her mother. Retelling the happy moments helped to hold off her grief, but only momentarily. When she reached the casket, she looked down to see her mother, her knees buckled and she found herself sobbing on the floor. Kaleb and Matthew helped her back to her feet and half-carried her to a nearby chair.

The three sat in relative silence as the procession of family and friends made their way through the viewing and settled in their seats for the sermon. Morgan's mind was a rag doll that had been left out in a rainstorm and dragged through the mud by the neighborhood mutt. She barely registered the words that were spoken or the solemn faces drying their eyes.

Anger replaced her grief. Why hadn't she seen her mother's spirit? It had been a few days and there had been no unearthly visits, no sudden sense of peace and tranquility, no warmth of the sun transforming to a sense of calm and happiness. Where was her mother? She stood up abruptly; all faces stared as she stormed her way to the back of the funeral home.

.⸱.

Kaleb poked his head into the small kitchen that was stocked full of lunch meat sandwiches, cookies, and lemonade. "Safe to enter?"

He knew her too well. Somehow he picked up on it either in her expression or her body language; he knew she was pissed. "Where is she, Kaleb? Why haven't I seen her?" Anger gave way to another round of sobbing. Kaleb sat next to her and rubbed her back. "I mean, why hasn't she come yet? Mom! Goddess dammit, Mom!?"

"Morgan, you're going to need to wait on that," Kaleb said as Matthew joined them. "Wouldn't want to draw any undue attention."

Matthew stopped himself just short of sitting, "I'm so sorry, I just heard Morgan and it didn't feel right in there with all those other people. If you want me to go I will."

Kaleb waved a hand at him and he sat. "Morgan, love, I really don't think this is the best place to be having this conversation."

"I'll have this conversation wherever I damn well please. Those people in there didn't know my mother! My mother was a witch, and a damn good one! So tell me, please, where is she? Don't make me summon you, Mother!" Anger broke and left her with pain. She fell back into quiet sobbing.

Despite Morgan's family having been a second home to him growing up, Kaleb had managed to maintain his composure. Just a he had done when her father died, Kaleb stayed by Morgan's side. He did his best to comfort her during her violent mood swings.

His own family had dropped by briefly to offer their condolences. It had been a while since he had seen his brother and sister. It wasn't nearly as awkward as he expected. After coming out he had distanced himself from his siblings, fearing the worst. Kaleb's father was still awkward to be around, but his sister made an effort to reconnect with her estranged brother.

Kaleb left Morgan with Matthew during one of her more lucid moments to have a word with his sister. As they exited the funeral home, she asked him about Austin. He spent a moment catching her up on his love life and then slipped in a loaded question, "Lizzy, do you believe in magic?"

She crushed out the cigarette she had been smoking. For as much as they looked alike, Elizabeth was completely his opposite. She was rebellious to his reserved and she was religious to his spiritual.

She sighed. "Are we really having this conversation? Look, I can look past the whole 'gay thing' but I really don't want to talk about your crazy 'witch thing.' We were having a nice conversation. Tell me more about Walter."

His voice took an almost whine. "But Lizzy, I really want to know what you think about it. It's a really big part of my life now."

"Oh, so Walter's a witch, too, is he?" she asked, with scorn forming in her face and voice.

"No, but he's at least open-minded about it. Lizzy, do you think magic is possible?" He tried to keep his tone casual, but was failing miserably.

"I believe in miracles and prayer. I really don't like where this is going, so I'm going to go back in and say my goodbyes. It was good seeing you, Kaleb. Stop being such a stranger." She made good on her words and turned to leave.

Slowly Kaleb made his way back into the funeral home and said his goodbyes to the rest of his family. When Kaleb returned to Morgan she was talking to Matthew and they appeared to be getting along.

He grabbed a lunch meat sandwich and almost choked as he heard from Morgan, "If you don't have a place to stay, you can stay at mom's place. I can't since it's too far out of the city for me to commute to work, and I could really use someone looking after it."

This was a joke. There was no way Morgan could possibly be serious. Kaleb turned to give them a half laugh but realized they didn't notice his return. *She's not joking. Oh my god, she's serious!* Kaleb jumped into the conversation, "Morgan would you mind if we had a word?"

"Sure, what did you want to talk about?"

"In private." She excused herself and followed Kaleb out of the funeral home. "Are you serious? You don't even know this guy and you want him living at your mom's? What if he's a thief, or a serial killer!?"

Out of nowhere Morgan burst into fits of laughter. She held her sides as it threatened to overwhelm her. "Kaleb, oh my god you should see your face right now."

He calmed down, it was a joke.

"What would I care if he is a serial killer? If he gets out of hand I could just turn him into a snake or fly off. You still haven't told me that spell by the way, kind of a little pissed that you've been holding out on me."

Kaleb set his jaw while Morgan laughed uncontrollably. "You should really see yourself right now. Oh, you get so cute when you start acting all 'big brother.' Matthew's fine. He doesn't remember anything, so I was hoping that being around Mom's place would help trigger some memories." Kaleb crossed his arms. Morgan didn't let his scorn stop her. "Besides, you've always said it needed a good spring cleaning. Since he doesn't have a job that he can remember, I told him he could stay as long as he cleaned."

"Well you've obviously thought this through."

Morgan smiled, "I knew you'd come around."

"That was sarcasm, Morgan. Obviously, you haven't thought any of this through. First off, who's going to feed him? He has no transportation. He took a cab to get here. Have you always been this impulsive or am I just now noticing?"

She laughed. "I'm sorry, I think I hear my phone ringing, it's the pot and he's calling for kettle. Didn't you just move in with Walter after knowing him for all of a month? Oh and not to mention that little incident with Austin."

"Don't try to turn this around on me. I'm just trying to stop you from making a really big mistake." Kaleb stood his ground.

Morgan rolled her eyes. "I'll have Mercedes keep an eye on him. She's staying with Geoffroi at the moment and I'm sure she'll be relieved to get away from there. He bought her a Speak-and-Spell, you know. It sounds even more evil when operated by a maniacal cat."

An aunt cocked her head and looked their way. "She's writing a book," Kaleb said as he waved in her direction. In a much quieter voice he said to Morgan, "You really should be more careful about what you say."

"I don't know what the big deal is." She finished by shouting in her aunt's direction, "They'll find out eventually!"

"Honestly, Morgan, you've got to stop that. We need to be discreet. I don't need a witch hunt to deal with." Kaleb's eyes were pleading, "Please, Morgan, this world is not going to be able to cope with magic and we really don't know enough spells to keep us safe when they do find out."

"You've been spending too much time with Walter. Where's the Kaleb that wanted to see the world burn?" Kaleb started to talk but Morgan kept going. "We've been waiting our entire lives for real magic, and now that it's here you want everything to stay the same? Last year, you would have hexed homophobes halfway to oblivion and now that you can actually do it you say we need to be discreet? Screw that!"

Kaleb said with more restraint than he usually had, "Morgan, please, volume. We're here to grieve, not fight." She closed her mouth abruptly and allowed him to lead her back inside.

•⁊•

Matthew had been hesitant to speak with Anna's friends and family. This was their time to grieve, not to answer some poor homeless sap's questions. His earliest memory was of being carted away in an ambulance.

For a brief moment he relived the few memories he had. The memory that stood out in his mind was waking up in the hospital room looking up at Morgan who appeared to be lost in a trance.

Kaleb and Morgan returned and broke Matthew out of his reverie. He felt much better about Kaleb now that he knew he wasn't Morgan's boyfriend. When they entered the room, he gave the pair a brief smile.

"So, it's settled. I'm taking you to my mom's tonight. We just have to swing by Geoffroi's to pick him up, he'll be your roommate."

Matthew's brow knitted in confusion. "Did I miss something?"

.ⵟ.

The wake had ended and people were beginning to leave. Another round of hugs and sympathies followed. Morgan retained her composure and was mildly civil to each as they passed. When it was all over the only parties left were Morgan and her two companions, her aunts, her uncles, the funeral director, and her mother's lawyer.

"I know this is a difficult time, but while I have you all together I thought we could go over Anna's last requests. If you would follow me back to the office, I'll try to make this quick." He extended his arm to direct them to a small room in the back of the funeral parlor.

Eight men and women stood or sat around the desk. As promised it was quick, though short might be a better way to describe Anna's will. The majority of her mother's belongings would now belong to Morgan, including the house and the thirty-seven acres of timber around it.

Luckily her family was content with the distribution of their departed sister's belongings. When they were getting ready to leave, her mother's lawyer stopped them at the door. "Your mother asked me to give this to you," he said as he slipped a small key into her hand. "She has a safety deposit box, she told me it wasn't anything monetary just something that has been passed down through the family. That's all she would tell me about it."

Morgan looked down at the key in her hand. What would her mother possibly have that would need its own safety deposit box. Kaleb thanked the man, reminding Morgan of her own manners. She shook his hand and thanked him as well.

•⁊•

Geoffroi returned home from work. He was grateful that in life David had been a stonemason. Not much was different since when he was alive. There were a few modern tools that he didn't fully grasp, but it always seemed like his body knew what to do with them, even if his mind needed a moment to catch up.

He opened the door to the small apartment to find Mercedes carefully stepping on the keys of the laptop. Whatever she was watching, it held her attention as Geoffroi quietly crept up behind her. It took him a moment to realize she was watching National Geographic and what appeared to be a very graphic episode involving mating rituals of the large cats.

Mercedes realized he was standing behind her and jumped on the lid, closing the laptop. She walked over to her Speak-and-Spell, "D-I-D, did, N-O-T, not, H-E-A-R, hear, Y-O-U, you, C-O-M-E, come, I-N, in."

Geoffroi tried not to laugh, "Mercedes, are you in heat?"

"H-O-W, how, D-A-R-E, dare, Y-O-U, you." She stalked out of the room to sun herself in the bedroom.

Geoffroi plopped down on the couch and put his feet up on the coffee table. He didn't understand his fascination with the man in the box but he

228

instinctively pressed the button to turn it on. He idly played with the buttons of what Mercedes called the remote, such a strange name. He was certain Mercedes had pushed the wrong keys on the Speak-and-Spell.

It was strange to him that some things came naturally and others things would not come at all. He could emulate David's moods and social nuances, drive a car and remember most of David's childhood and recent memories. Yet other things, like electricity, he couldn't figure out at all. He just equated it to magic and moved on.

But what really bothered Geoffroi was playing house with a cat while his duty to rid the world of the Christian scourge was still unfulfilled. Geoffroi decided on a new target; his war against those that tortured and executed him and his brothers would be fought against the leaders of the faith, not those that followed. He shook his head to rid his mind of the preposterous idea. Those were David's thoughts, not his. He was certain of it. They all needed to pay for the crimes of their forefathers.

The mindless pressing of buttons and turning of channels came to an end as Geoffroi decided it was another facet of David. He relaxed and let the woman in the box tell him about how the weather would be. He mused for a moment on the notion that she was a sorcerer predicting the ebb and flow of the air.

Life was so incredibly different from what he understood. For centuries he had walked the catacombs of Rome, searching for a way to bring the church to justice. He would never have believed how much life had changed until he actually had one to live again.

His mind wandered once again as the woman on the television discussed the diagram behind her. Could there be peace? Was that too novel of an idea? He watched the inquisitions unfold before his mind's eye. Though it had been after his time, he watched it all in disgust.

Whatever this peace was, there was no way he would stand for it. He had suffered for centuries at their hands. Why should they not suffer, too? Yet something within him stirred and said that not all Christians deserve to be punished for the sins of the church. He squashed that feeling, discarding it as another remnant of David.

He must hold true to himself. Morgan asked him to be at one with the host body to keep her from being persecuted for the crime of murder. She should be punished. Who was he to keep justice from being enacted as he too wished to seek justice for his own murder?

Geoffroi closed his eyes and pressed his palm to his forehead. Were these again the stirrings of David? What feelings were his own? Where did David end and Geoffroi begin?

He tried to abandon the body he found himself trapped within. Geoffroi pushed his soul as far as he could but to no avail. It was as though a chain tethered him to this body and would not let him free. The new woman in the box seemed to be speaking directly to him and he focused on her face.

"Police are looking into a string of unsolved deaths in the metro," she said plainly to him. "Investigations are underway to the cause of death of two metro men. Each of the men were in good health and peak physical condition, according to the medical examiner. Foul play has not been ruled out." She spoke to him as though he alone in this world mattered and he listened.

Whatever was causing these men to die became very important to Geoffroi. Whoever this woman was, she held him enthralled until she was finished and the man at her side took over to discuss some inane high school sports team. Geoffroi hadn't felt so captivated by a woman since the moment he had met Morgan.

Morgan. His mind reeled. Part of him screamed to hold her and dissolve her pain in his arms, another part screamed for revenge. He saw her beauty, he saw revulsion. The words she had last said held him in a limbo of devotion, and yet caused his blood to boil. Geoffroi could no longer think of Morgan without being spun in a dance of love and loathing.

The wake of her mother was occurring this day, and yet he wasn't invited. He was furious, and sorrowful. He wanted to hold her, and to stab her.

He tried again to force his spirit from the body that so greatly contradicted his own desires but found the task impossible. He cursed himself for ever having jumped into the wretched body.

Taking a deep breath Geoffroi marshaled his thoughts. He needed to learn the limits of his new body and its ability to perform magic. If only Morgan would entrust him with a staff. The cat was sent to keep an eye on him, and he would never let her know just how bad it was inside his head.

"Mercedes? What would you say if I adopted a cat?"

"H-E, he, B-E-T-T-E-R, better, B-E, be, C-U-T-E, cute."

•✝•

The bank attendant led the trio back to the safety deposit boxes. Morgan was in no condition to be alone, or to drive. One moment she would be fine, smiling and laughing with Kaleb and Matthew, and the next she would be sobbing uncontrollably.

The attendant left them as they prepared to discover what her mother had taken great pains to keep a secret. Her hand shook as she attempted to place the key in the lock. Matthew put a hand on her shoulder and she dropped the key.

It took several deep breaths and reassurance from Kaleb and Matthew before she was able to unlock the box and open its lid. Within the box was a single note and a large leather-bound book. She read the letter to herself.

Dear Morgan,

If you are reading this then I am no longer with you in the physical. You know better than any that I will always be with you. Dry your eyes and be strong. I have raised you as a witch and your father has raised you to appreciate Mother Earth, but our family has a longer history with magic than I felt was safe to tell you.

The book that has been locked away contains spells dating back farther than even I know. My grandmother told me that these spells were once cast by Morrigan Le'Fey herself. I never did believe the old bird, but loved the stories so much that I named you after our supposed ancestor.

Your grandmother passed the book to me upon her death and asked that I do the same for my daughter. There are spells within this book that are far beyond my limited ability, but perhaps not yours. Other spells are so dark that I wouldn't consider trying.

Remember always that I love you,

Mom

Morgan dried her eyes. Kaleb had been puzzling over the leather-bound book and she took it from his hands. The pages were made of old yellowing parchment. She opened the book to a random page and gasped. She read aloud, "To walk the path of the Fey. Kaleb, do you realize what this is?"

"Your mom had a grimoire?"

She continued reading. "Grandma had a grimoire." She passed the note to Kaleb as she flipped through the pages of the ancient tome. "These look like high magic spells." Their eyes met and they both looked at Matthew.

He looked around and finally responded, "What? I've got no problem with magic, or witchcraft, or whatever this high magic is. I don't even remember what religion I am." He shrugged. "So, whatever."

Kaleb burst out into a fit of laughter. Morgan scolded him. Once he regained control he explained himself. "I'm sorry, it's not funny. I understand your condition sucks, but you're just so nonchalant about it. I couldn't help it." Morgan glared at him. "Sorry."

Morgan began to casually explain the difference between low and high magic to Matthew. He appeared genuinely interested. When she finished he asked, "So can anybody cast spells?"

Kaleb picked up the conversation, "We're not sure, but so far my boyfriend isn't showing any progress in learning magic." He looked over to Morgan. "Please don't tell him I said that, it just slipped out. He wanted me to teach him magic and hasn't gotten any of the basics yet."

She snorted. "Oh yeah, cause Walt and I are besties. I'll try not to let it slip while we discuss how he hates me over tea."

"He doesn't hate you, Morgan, he just ..." Kaleb looked at Matthew. "He just doesn't like some of your methods. I think if you two tried to get along he'd get to know you and then you guys would be friends."

Morgan patted him on the shoulder, "I think he's good for you, Kaleb. I don't care if he doesn't like me, just so long as he makes you happy."

Kaleb stared for a moment, stunned. "Wow, Morgan, that's probably the nicest thing you've ever said about anybody I've dated."

233

She smiled. "Don't get used to it, I may start to dislike him if he ends up being a douchebag. So far he seems like a good guy. Had to pick a cop though." She shook her head. "So, you'd better be on your best behavior. No turning people into snakes."

Matthew let out an awkward laugh. When no one joined him he asked, "I'm sorry did that really happen?"

Kaleb ignored Matthew and smiled at Morgan. "As long as you can avoid starting a zombie apocalypse then I think I can restrain myself. Sorry Matthew, she's writing a book. It's about the end of the world."

"I really wish you'd stop doing that, Kaleb. Matthew already knows about high magic; you don't have to lie to him." What she wasn't telling Kaleb was that she had formed a small crush on Matthew. "Okay, Matthew, so Kaleb and I have done some spells that we aren't quite proud of."

"To say the least," Kaleb interjected.

"Yes, Kaleb, to say the least," she replied snidely. She softened her tone for Matthew. "Now, it isn't that we don't trust you, but we'd rather not talk about those spells. It's all been resolved, but it's still a sore subject."

Matthew backed up slowly. "What did you do?"

"Well I raised someone from the dead, and Kaleb turned his ex into a snake," Morgan blurted out.

Kaleb crossed his arms and yelled, "Morgan!"

"He turned him back. Anyway, what's important is for us is to be a little bit more careful with magic. I want to find a spell that will help fix your memories." She held the book close to herself, "And I think this will help."

Matthew was still trying to piece together everything and made a fatal mistake. "Is that why you were crying out for your mother's spirit? So you could bring her back?" Kaleb shook his head and let out a sigh as Morgan fell to the floor in a fit of inconsolable grief.

•[*]•

There was a knock on Geoffroi's door. His heart was aflutter. It had only been four days since he had taken over David's body. Any number of things could have gone wrong with his impersonation. For a moment he wished with all his might that it would be Morgan on the other side of the door, come to rescue him from his imprisonment in this modern life.

He knew better than to hope for Morgan. At this hour of the night, he doubted it. He climbed out of bed and went to the door. When he opened the door, a voluptuous dark-haired woman pushed through and embraced him.

"David, what the hell? You haven't returned any of my calls and you haven't texted. I've been worried sick! I thought you were dead!"

Geoffroi's mind searched through what was left of David to try and recall who this woman was. Her name was nowhere to be found. While he struggled to find David's memories he improvised, "I'm sorry, I haven't been feeling well. I haven't really called anybody."

She looked into his eyes. "Yeah, you seem a bit off. Your mom's been worried, too." The woman who must be significant to David's life got out her phone and sent a series of text messages. "I've missed you monkey." She put her arms around David and he hugged her back.

Memories rushed to him. "Oh, chipmunk, I'm so sorry. I didn't mean to worry you." This seemed like the right answer as her arms tightened around his midsection. Mentally, he raised an eyebrow at how ridiculous the pet name sounded. He found her name in David's mind, Jackie, and Geoffroi had no idea of why David would equate her to a small rodent.

235

Geoffroi sat down on the couch, just as Mercedes came out of the bedroom to investigate. "Oh! You got a kitty? I thought you hated cats. Or is this little beauty for me?" Mercedes turned her head to Geoffroi and narrowed her eyes.

Mercedes retreated back into the bedroom and soon came the sound, "H-E-L."

Geoffroi rushed into the bedroom, leaving a confused Jackie in his wake. He came back and sat down on the couch without offering any explanation.

"What was that?"

"Oh that, oh, I bought a Speak-and-Spell. You remember those from when we were little? I think the thing is busted, some of the keys are sticking." He didn't sound convincing, even to himself.

She raised an eyebrow. "You're acting really strange."

There was another knock at the door. Dread struck Geoffroi as he wondered what else could go wrong tonight. He felt a rush of relief as Kaleb, Morgan, and a third that he didn't recognize stepped into David's apartment.

Before she had noticed Geoffroi's company Morgan blurted, "Get together whatever you want to bring, we're moving you to my mom's house."

Jackie jumped off the couch and lunged at Geoffroi. "You son of a bitch! That's why I haven't heard from you? You've been cheating on me! You piece of shit!" Kaleb and Matthew did their best to keep her from attacking Geoffroi and Morgan. They held her back while she thrashed violently against them.

"It's not what you think, chipmunk. I'm not cheating on you." He made up a quick story that was the closest thing he could think to the truth. "She's my High Priestess. I'm part of the Church of—"

Without missing a beat Morgan picked up on his lie and completed the sentence, "Church of Gaea's Fist. We believe in restoring the world to its natural state."

"Oh, don't you dare bullshit me! And shut your mouth you tramp. You couldn't find someone better-looking?"

Matthew jumped in with the save; he grabbed Morgan's hand. "No, it's the truth. Morgan is my girlfriend and High Priestess. We're all part of the church. You're free to join us, too, but Morgan's mother just died and she needs someone to tend to the house."

For a moment, she stewed on the lie. At least she had calmed down. "David, can we talk in private?" He led her to the bedroom where Mercedes was still busy cleaning herself. "I don't like these people, David. Where did you meet them?"

"Don't worry. It's okay. I went to high school with them, well two of them anyway. I met up with them at the reunion. It's really great, Jackie. Join us. We cast spells to help the trees and steward the land."

She looked deeply into his eyes. "You hate nature."

"Morgan has opened my eyes. We can really help. I need to help her right now though, so please let me do this." He looked back into her eyes pleadingly.

"Just promise me you won't drink the Kool-Aid."

Enemies and Allies

Country music pummeled Nick as he sat at the bar waiting for Gwen to return with her mark. He rolled his eyes as he saw a skinny blonde girl climb onto the mechanical bull at the far end of the bar. It wasn't long before she was thrown from it and onto the blue, inflatable cushion surrounding it. Though the bar was nowhere near the kind of bar he would normally visit, there was at least some entertainment to be had.

Gwen had really acquired a taste for vampirism, more so than he had. The last few nights she had insisted they frequent the worst bars in town so that she could pick up the worst men in town.

Nick patiently waited for Gwen to give him the signal that she found a man she could safely lure from the bar to kill. He watched out of the corner of his eye as the redhead took a comely man onto the dance floor. Gwen smiled as the man groped and pawed at her. Gwen put both her arms in the air. It was the signal.

Nick ran to his car and grabbed his staff. Moments later saw the man half dragging a staggering Gwen to his car. Nick shrugged; she really should have known better than to accept drinks from strangers.

Nick interjected himself between the man and his car. "Going so soon?"

"Hey man, I don't want any trouble. My girlfriend's had too much to drink."

"You really have bad taste in women, my friend," Nick chided. A smile grew on his face. "This one here's a man-eater." He quickly channeled magical energy into the staff causing it to glow. "Oh yeah," he said. "So am I."

Fog rolled out of Nick's mouth. The man dropped Gwen onto the concrete and attempted to run away. Nick shredded his root chakra causing him to topple down next to her. Next, he ripped out his throat chakra before turning back to Gwen. She stared up at him; her eyes were drooping and she tried to pick herself off the ground but was too weak.

"I thought I told you about taking candy from strangers." Nick redirected some of the man's life essence into Gwen.

Her eyes gleamed with renewed vigor. "Can you believe that asshole actually slipped something in my drink?" Gwen said as she picked herself up off the pavement.

"Yes. Yes I can. I think it's time we found a better way to catch our flies," Nick said as they walked through the parking lot.

"We are not going back to eating homeless people," she said casually as she checked her face in her compact. "They have an aftertaste."

Nick rolled his eyes.

It took them several minutes to find Gwen's car through the fog. They stuffed the man into the back seat. Nick climbed into the passenger seat, and when he was settled he heard Lifedrinker's silky voice greeting him.

"*You have grown strong, my child. You are finally ready for the final lesson of vampirism.*"

Nick raised an eyebrow. "*You mean there's more.*"

"*Only a true master vampire has the ability to drain the powers of the Magi. A true master vampire can drain the life of a Magi and rend the abilities they covet from their soul. Now being that we have none to practice on I will have to do my best to explain the process.*"

Nick frowned. Gwen was talking to him, but he wasn't paying attention. *"You'll have to forgive me but with high magic at my disposal, what's the point of stealing abilities? With all the spells you know, what's left?"*

Laughter filled his mind. *"Oh, how naive you are my child. Yes, you are powerful, but there are things you will never emulate through any spell you find on this world. Shape-shifting, the voice, mirror-walking, shadow-walking; just to name a few."*

"You had me at shape-shifting." A smile formed on Nick's face.

"You have those you call the Atlanteans to thank for shape-shifting. They meddled in what can only be called epic magic. I will share with you what I know."

Nick stammered, "Epic magic?"

Gwen looked over to him. "Epic magic? No, I wouldn't call it epic. Wait, you haven't been listening to a word I've said." He waved at her to be silent.

Lifedrinker cackled, *"All in good time, child. When Merlin removed magic from this world, the shape-shifters were forced back to their human form and have been passing the ability along to their children."*

"So those abilities you named, they're hereditary?" Nick asked.

"Not all, my boy, but some. Other powers are tied to the soul itself from what I can tell. Now to my point. I wish for you to steal the ability of the one called Kaleb. I have been trapped in this wretched place for long enough. It is time for us to rule over these cattle. You shall be my consort and my right hand."

It was Nick's turn to laugh, *"Do you not know? I'm gay! I don't want to be your consort."*

"Enough," she shouted, silencing him. *"You must kill Kaleb, take his ability to shadow-walk. Free me from this prison and we shall rule this world."*

.ı.

The forest was quiet as the group of six climbed the hill. It was the highest point on what now was Morgan's property. It wasn't clear if Morgan had asked the animals for a moment of silence or if they had just somehow known. Even the sun hid itself behind clouds of mourning. The timber line formed a circle around the base of the hill and an ancient oak stood sentry.

Morgan led the procession to where she would spread her mother's ashes. Matthew held Morgan's hand as they made their way to the great oak. Kaleb's eyes were beginning to water as the significance of the event struck him. Walter's hand tightened around his as they approached, hand in hand. Geoffroi was the next in the procession followed by Gwen and Nick.

Kaleb dried his eyes and accepted the urn from Morgan. He spoke the words he had rehearsed all day, "We are gathered today to commit Anna's ashes to the earth and sky. Here we stand at Anna's tree. Growing up, Morgan and I played all throughout these woods, but this tree was sacred to Anna. She told us to respect its ancient boughs. Each summer we would come here to celebrate the Sabbatts."

Nick closed his eyes and bowed his head. His posture was of reverence, but the vampire within him was busy at work.

Tears streamed from Kaleb's eyes, and he wiped them away. "Anna was a second mother to me. She was a guide, a protector, and a friend. I cannot think of another person in this world more dedicated to protecting the earth, or her family. We dedicate this ancient tree to your memory, standing guard over your land, and home, and family."

With practiced patience, Nick's mind slowly approached the pillar of power that was Kaleb. He saw each bright aura in his mind: Morgan's aura was a chaotic blaze of blues and greens, David had two auras intertwined, red and black energy around a core of light blue and gold, Matthew's aura was a mixture of light and dark blues that churned and somehow felt threatening, Walter's was a pure white with flecks of gold. It was a little unsettling how Kaleb's blue-white aura seemed to be watching him.

Nick knew he would have to act quickly as Kaleb was about to begin the spell casting portion of the dedication. Tendrils of his mind probed Kaleb's aura. A face appeared in the aura and the great pillar of energy that was Kaleb suddenly turned toward him.

He could hear that the epitaph had not ended, so he carefully probed deeper. A bright flash erupted and his mind was shoved back into his body. Stars danced in front of Nick's eyes as though he had been punched in the face. He staggered backwards, but his loss of balance was unobserved by the mourners.

Kaleb finished his practiced speech, oblivious to Nick's attempted assault. "I now pass among those gathered the earthly remains of Anna Daniels. As I pass to you the urn, I ask that you each take a portion." Kaleb took a handful of the ashes and passed the urn to Walter who in turn took a handful and passed the urn to Matthew.

Nick regained his composure, but not his magical sight. His ability to see the auras of those around him was completely lost, and he was furious. The urn was being passed along the circle that encompassed the tree and he was out of time. The buffer of death magic that he had collected from his victims was gone. When the urn finally reached him, his jaw was set in frustration. He would be having a talk with Lifedrinker once this was over.

As the urn finally returned to Kaleb, they each held their hands to the sky and repeated the words Kaleb recited. It was only fitting that the spell of protection they were casting came from the grimoire Morgan had inherited. The air was heavy and time held its breath.

The words of power hung in the air like the sound of a gong being struck. Even those without magic of their own could feel the shifting of the world. Nick could feel the hint of fear that clutched each of their hearts. They could not break away from the spell; the words held them captive. As their mouths repeated the words of their own accord, their hearts trembled in their chests.

Two points of iridescent light began to curl around the edge of the clearing. When the two points of light joined, a rainbow-hued light erupted from the ground and into a hemisphere far above their heads.

The spell had not reached its climax and still held them captive. Another ring of white light began to form around the tree and the mourners.

Waves of power pounded the seven to the ground. As each burst of magic passed over them they staggered against its blows. The center circle closed itself and erupted again into a hemisphere of light above them. This time their eyes had a hard time focusing. The tree became distorted. Space and time were thrown out the window.

Nick could not decide if they were shrinking or if the tree was getting larger. As the power of the spell continued to pulse and the words would not stop spouting from his mouth, he looked to his left to see that Kaleb was several feet away from him and that distance was growing. He could no longer see Geoffroi standing on the opposite side of the tree.

The world again began to flicker, but this time Nick realized he was falling. He took in, before darkness overcame him, the sight of the massive tree that had once been just large.

"What the hell just happened?" Nick heard someone ask as he picked himself off the ground. Kaleb sprinted over to where Walter had fallen and helped him to his feet.

The ancient tree reached into the sky like a skyscraper trying to touch the heavens. The trunk had transformed and became as wide in girth as a grain silo. The branches that were once close to the ground now were a football field away in the sky. Despite having an intimidating presence the tree still retained its warm inviting qualities that made it the focal point of so many Sabbatts.

Morgan began to walk the circumference of the great tree as the rest of the group was picking themselves up off the ground. She stared up into its branches with a huge smile on her face. "How is this possible? Mom? Did you do this?" She clapped her hands together as though she had just found out she won a lifetime supply of ice cream.

Nick craned his neck in an attempt to see the top of the tree. He marshaled his emotions to hide the fury he felt. *They're hiding things.* Who was David? Why didn't they tell him Morgan had a grimoire? These weren't his friends, and he wanted their power.

.⋅.

Visions flooded Matthew while he lay on the ground. He was five and running into the arms of a massive lake. His mother was somewhere behind him, lounging on the beach. There were other kids his age playing in the water. He drifted too far, and struggled to stay afloat.

He thrashed around but couldn't keep his head from sinking below the murky water. He was drowning. Matthew's body was now that of a grown man, but he was still drowning. As he sank deeper and deeper, he closed his eyes and waited for death to take him. He no longer worked against the hands of death, but welcomed them.

Matthew woke abruptly, gasping for air. The massive tree stretched out above him. It took him a moment to remember where he was and what had just happened. Panic hit him as he couldn't see anyone else around him, but that panic faded when he saw Morgan coming around the tree.

She looked down at him and smiled. "Isn't it amazing? It's so beautiful." Morgan held out a hand and helped Matthew to his feet. This was the first he had seen her happy and he found it pleasing. He stared into the branches with her. Kaleb and Walter soon joined them, followed by Geoffroi.

Kaleb handed the urn containing the last of Anna's ashes to Morgan, put his arm around her, and stared up into the tree. "A final gift from your mother. It's the most beautiful and remarkable thing I have ever seen."

She looked into Kaleb's eyes, "Did you know this was going to happen?"

"Honestly, I had no clue what it would do. But I have faith that whatever we do, it'll always work out in the end." He motioned for Walter to come closer and the three of them hugged.

"We should probably head back." The edge of the hilltop looked to be much farther away as well. "It looks like we have a pretty long walk ahead of us."

On their way, they met up with Nick and Gwen and slowly made their way back. When they reached the edge of the hilltop, they passed through an invisible barrier that sent shivers down Matthew's spine. Morgan was the first to look back and gasped. The tree had resumed its original size atop the hill.

She stepped back a few feet through the barrier and disappeared to their eyes. Matthew's heart skipped a beat until he heard the disembodied voice of Morgan say, "This is freaking trippy guys."

After they had gotten their fill of jumping back and forth through the magical barrier, they made their way down the hill and to the line of trees marking the border. They all stepped through together and found that behind them was no longer the hill and tree, but a forest filled with mist.

"Holy shit guys, do you realize what this is?" Morgan asked. She wiped the tears from her eyes and a smile replaced her mask of sorrow. "This was how she protected Avalon."

Nick was the first to respond, "I'm sorry, who?"

"Morgana. The Mists of Avalon. I think the only people who will actually find the hill and the tree are those who know what they are looking for. Everyone else will just wander aimlessly through the mist and end up on one side or the other, but never finding the hill."

"So, when can I borrow that book?" Nick asked, grinning.

Morgan hesitated. "I'm not so sure that's a good idea."

•⸙•

Nick stormed into his dorm room and picked up his staff. His roommate stared at him with wide eyes and the vampire flashed back a wicked glare. He lay down on the bed and relaxed. With a conscious effort, he calmed his breathing and stilled his mind. After he reached a state of peaceful meditation he cast his mind into the staff.

The cathedral opened up before him and Nick stormed to its center. "Lifedrinker! We need to talk."

She rose from her mighty throne and joined him amid the pews. "What is wrong my child?"

"Kaleb is too powerful. He did something that knocked out my ability to see auras." The anger he had felt earlier came pouring back. His image in the cathedral flickered as he marshaled his emotions.

"He is not too powerful, you are simply too weak. Perhaps we need to go over the basics again. You have failed to steal the ability of the shadow-walker, but I'm sure you tried your best." Lifedrinker said mockingly.

Nick steamed inside, but maintained a casual demeanor, "Milady, do you require anything else of me?"

She waved him off. "You have served your purpose for now. I will let you know when the situation changes."

He withdrew his mind from out the staff. Nick took a moment to glare menacingly at his roommate who soon decided it would be better to do his reading elsewhere.

Nick retrieved the grimoire he "borrowed" from his backpack. He wondered how long it would take Morgan to realize he left a textbook in its place.

•▼•

"That son of a bitch!" Morgan shouted as she found a copy of *Introduction to Psychology* from her backpack. Geoffroi and Matthew were unsure who she was talking about until she continued ranting. "I told him he couldn't borrow Mom's grimoire and what does he do?"

Matthew cautioned a guess, "He took it?"

Her frustration and anger reached a boiling point. "I may have been willing to let him look it over, but oh hell no! Not anymore! I tell you, this is unacceptable."

Geoffroi added, "Highly!"

"I'm calling Kaleb. His ex is totally out of control!" It had been such a long time since she had referred to Nick as Kaleb's ex. It sounded weird to her. "No, this is my problem and I will deal with it my way! Get in the car boys, it's going to be a long night."

Matthew and Geoffroi exchanged a worried glance.

•٦•

Walter had finally fallen asleep. He and Kaleb had spent the last hour talking about what happened that evening. Kaleb's mind was still filled with unanswered questions and worries about the spells contained in the grimoire.

He stared into the darkness and let his eyes make shapes out of the shadows. Walter began to snore softly beside him in the bed and Kaleb took comfort from it. So little in his life could be considered normal anymore. A snoring boyfriend was an anchor in reality.

Kaleb had drifted into a restless sleep, but was awakened suddenly. He was being dragged off the bed by his feet. He reached for Walter, unsure if he was wanting to protect him or wanted to be protected.

As he fell to the floor, he saw three shades standing above him and one on the opposite side of the bed. He was paralyzed with fear. It stood above Walter and stared down at him. They pulled him into the darkness of Limbo.

Time slowed down to the point of irrelevance as the shades moved him through the shadow world and dumped him unceremoniously inside a dark

248

cathedral. Kaleb had never seen anything like this before. The stained-glass windows were dark and had images that seemed to warp with the imagination.

When he was finally able to move they had already retreated into the darkness beyond the cathedral's doors. They slammed shut. Kaleb slowly approached the doors. They were locked. He tried to force himself to wake up, but he was fairly certain this was not a dream.

He turned and caught a glimpse of a small child hiding behind a shadow-warped statue. "Don't be afraid," he said soothingly. Slowly, Kaleb approached what turned out to be a little girl. She couldn't be older than seven or eight. "We're going to be okay."

She looked up at him with wide eyes and said in a frightened voice, "The monsters locked me in here. I don't want them to come back." She began to cry and threw her arms around Kaleb's neck.

Softly he patted her, doing his best to console her trembling form. "Shh. Don't be afraid. I won't let the monsters get you. I'm going to get us out of here, you'll see. This is just a bad dream." Kaleb stepped toward the locked door.

He reminded himself that this was the realm of shadows and that the door wasn't real. Kaleb held out his hand to the door and closed his eyes. Darkness twisted and parted. The doors had now become a gaping hole in the wall.

With the quivering girl in his arms, he strode forward and met with an invisible barrier. He raised his hands again and focused on passing through. Nothing happened. He tried backing through the door and found he wasn't the one incapable of passing through the door; it was the little girl in his arms.

A voice boomed from the vaulted ceilings. "*YOU THOUGHT YOU COULD ESCAPE? I'M THROUGH WITH YOUR LIES, LIFEDRINKER! YOU'RE MY PET NOW!*"

The girl's body began to steam and Kaleb dropped her unceremoniously on the cobbled stones of the cathedral floor. It began to writhe and expand until a nine-foot tall creature stood on the other side of the barrier. As it screamed its dissent to the unnamed harasser, Kaleb slipped away back into the shadows.

•٢•

Morgan stormed down the hallway of Nick's dormitory with Matthew and Geoffroi in tow. She had only ever visited Nick twice before in his dorm room. It was quite possible that women weren't allowed in the men's dorms at this hour but no one wanted to stop a two-hundred-and-ten pound woman on a mission.

She arrived, planted her feet within the threshold of Nick's room, crossed her arms, and stared. Nick closed the book he was reading. With a calculated smile he greeted her, "Morgan, to what do I owe the pleasure of such a late night visit?"

Morgan's anger poured from between her teeth, "You know, *exactly*, why I am here. Cut the bullshit!"

Matthew and Geoffroi took sentry positions on either side of her, but she was such an imposing enough figure when crossed that the effort seemed moot.

"This whole thing could have been avoided." He tilted his head. "If you could just learn how to play with others. I sure would love to hear more about how your high-school rival miraculously became your new best friend."

Her eyes narrowed to slits. "I'd sure love to hear more about what you and *your* new bestie have been up to. Where is Gwen?"

Nick sighed. "We can go round like this all night, Morgan. I'm not your enemy. I'm sorry I took your mom's book, but seriously, I feel left out. You and Kaleb are having all the fun and I'm left wondering what else you guys are up to." He handed her the book of spells. "Next time you decide to raise someone from the dead, could you at least give me a call?"

Morgan was caught off guard, "How do you know that?"

"Please, you don't think after a year in nursing school I can't tell when someone has been physically abused. Given what I know about your history." He paused to give her a knowing look. "It was the only logical outcome. I'd really love to hear more about how you managed to pull that one off."

She stared back into his eyes, unflinching. "And what if I'd rather not tell you?"

His voice became hollow. Nick's face contorted to a mask of hurt. "Well there are certainly ways for me to find out. I'd thank you for letting me borrow your grimoire, but that would imply you play well with others."

"What happened to you? You used to be so nice," she asked; her emotions were a carousel between unrequited love and hatred.

"Isn't that cute?" Nick replied to Morgan while staring at her bodyguards. "She thinks I was nice. Let me tell you something about friendship, Morgan. Friendship isn't about when it's convenient for you. I'm done being left on the back burner. Do you think we should call Nick? Hmm, I don't know, I'm sure we can raise someone from the dead all by ourselves."

Morgan's fury was losing steam. "We wanted to—" She was cut off by Nick.

"Oh sure, we wanted to what, leave me in the dark? What a great excuse. You and Kaleb are too busy for Little Miss Nick. Get out of here. Take your mom's book. Thanks for including me." Nick turned his back to the three.

After they left a smile grew on Nick's face. Guilt was so much fun.

•ᵗ•

"He's out of control." Morgan was exercising the most self-control she had exhibited in several months. Her hands were folded over her lap as Kaleb took a drink of his tea. Mercedes watched them from the kitchen. She knew Kaleb would never take her hysterics seriously. "I mean, he *stole* my mother's grimoire."

Kaleb sighed. "You and Nick have always had issues. He has a point, we really haven't been including him, and I kind of feel bad about that. With your infatuation—" Morgan attempted to interrupt but Kaleb rose a hand to stop her. "With your infatuation, Nick probably doesn't take you very seriously. You've been unrelenting in your pursuit of him and now that he has a new friend." He held up his hand. "Don't even ask me what is going on there. He dated women in high school, but so do a lot of gay guys."

It was Morgan's turn to take a deep breath. "I really don't think you see what's happening. Nick is being secretive and I don't like that. Last spell he told us about was putting his ex in a coma. He's dangerous."

"Um, Morgan, do I need to remind you that you tortured and killed a high school classmate and I turned my ex into a snake for a day. I think one-slip up is allowed."

"Kaleb, please listen to me. I get a really bad feeling about this. Have you been listening to the news? There's been all these young guys turning up

252

dead. There was another one found last night. No sign of struggle, no prior medical history. They still don't know how they are dying."

Kaleb rubbed his temples. "Morgan, I am not here to discuss conspiracy theories. Besides, I thought I was coming over to talk about getting kidnapped by shades."

"It has everything to do with your kidnapping! Honestly, think about it. The demon that was after you becomes trapped. Then it has a freakout with some booming mind-voice. It's totally Nick! Who else has that kind of power?" Her eyes pleaded with him to believe her. "He stole my mother's grimoire the same night you get kidnapped by a demon. You can't tell me that it doesn't make you wonder if he found a way to harness demon magic."

"Wow, Morgan, I never thought I'd say this but you just went from concerned parent to *Catcher in the Rye* in half a cup of tea. Is that a new record?"

Morgan smacked him.

Kaleb smiled and finished his jasmine tea. "I've got to get back to Walter's. Promise me you won't start anything with Nick."

"He started it!" she yelled back, but Kaleb had already stepped into the shadows of her bedroom. "Gods!" she exclaimed. Her eyes adjusted to the low light of her bedroom and she realized the staves Kaleb brought back from Rome were missing. "You have got to be kidding me! Now he's breaking into my trailer?"

·⁊·

Swings creaked as they swung empty in the breeze. The night sky was clear and dark. A lone owl watched nervously as three cloaked figures converged on the playground of Lauris Elementary School.

Nick opened the parley, "Gentleman, it is good to see you again."

Two men sat on the merry-go-round as Nick climbed the stairs of the slide to address them. When he reached the top he called out to them. "I have gathered you here to share with you the new world order. I call upon the House of Gray to once again rise and become an instrument of fear and power. Don't tell me you haven't become weak and complacent."

It had been quite a long time since Quincy had heard the name 'House of Gray.' For a short period of time he had associated with Nick and his vampire clan outside of his usual *Vampires the Masquerade* group. He wasn't sure how they had been an instrument of fear and power. They mostly drank beer and watched vintage vampire movies.

From his seat on the merry-go-round, Quincy replied, "We're not weak or complacent. We just want to know why you called us up out of nowhere after three years."

"Do you fear me?" Nick asked, from the top of the metal slide.

The two men looked at each other. Ryan replied, "Uh, no."

Magical energy rushed into the staff and the obsidian glowed with a pale light; Quincy's heart skipped a beat. Nick wasn't finished with his demonstration; he stepped from the metal slide and into the air. While he hovered several feet above their heads he looked down and said, "You should."

Before he could run, Nick pounced with his mind and a searing pain ran through his lower body. Quincy's legs buckled beneath him. He fell to the ground, staring up at the menacing figure of Nick above him.

The headlights shined in their eyes as a car pulled into a space and parked. Nick smiled. Gwen was right on time. "We're going to have a little test tonight. If you are a true vampire, then you'll be able to feed. If you're not." Nick glared at the two men lying prone on the ground. "You get to be lunch for the rest of us."

Gwen stepped out of the car and retrieved her new staff from the back seat. Its wood was birch and affixed to the top was a large sphere of clear quartz. She concentrated magic into the staff and it glowed with a brilliant white light. With a wave of her staff and a short incantation, the rigid body of a man floated from the car and made its way onto the playground.

Telekinesis was the most utilitarian spell Lifedrinker had taught him before their falling out. Though he was always more fond of theatrics. Not to be outdone by his protégée, Nick called a ball of lightning to his hands.

Gwen unceremoniously released the spell and the man fell onto the merry-go-round with a loud clang. "Who's hungry?" she asked. A sadistic smile crossed her face as she looked up to Nick.

"Famished," he replied. Nick descended to the ground. The ball of lightning crackled as he passed it from hand to hand. "Oh dear, where are my manners." He looked down to the two men on the ground. "Who wants to say grace?"

"I'm a true vampire, Nick," Quincy said. "Let me prove it to you."

"Please, call me Lucian," Nick said, smiling a malicious smile. Nick passed his staff over the fallen Quincy and healed his root chakra.

Quincy picked himself off the ground and slowly approached the man on the merry-go-round. His heart raced in his chest. When he reached the old man he pulled a knife from his back pocket and put it to the man's throat.

Nick and Gwen erupted into laughter. Gwen mocked him, "We don't drink blood, you idiot. We drink their life essence."

"Reach out with your mind, my child," Nick said. "There's nothing in your way, this guy's so afraid of us I'm surprised he hasn't had a heart attack already."

Quincy closed his eyes and reached out with his mind. He could feel the man's life-force beneath his hands. The concept of a psychic vampire wasn't foreign to him, but Quincy's own heart was beating so fast he was surprised that he wasn't the one having a heart attack.

He reached with his mind and fed. It was new. The emotions he fed on before seemed so tame compared to drinking someone's life. It filled him. The man's life essence flowed into Quincy and his body became warm. He was no longer afraid. He felt powerful. He was no longer the chubby kid with glasses. He was a mighty vampire.

Nick threw the ball of lightning onto the merry-go-round next to Quincy. The jolt wasn't enough to cause any harm, but it got his attention. "Now, now, my boy. Leave some for the rest of us."

.⁙.

A very bored woman took Morgan's money and handed her a receipt. If Kaleb wouldn't take her seriously, she would find someone who did. She strode into the zoo with a confidence she had never really embraced before. As she walked through the zoo, contempt replaced that confidence. She watched the people rather than the animals. They made her sick. Parents ushered children to point at the animals caged against their nature.

How could anyone enjoy visiting a prison? This wasn't a place of levity, this was a place of sorrow. Song birds caged against flight. Penguins sealed away from the world while their numbers dwindled in the wild.

She arrived at the bear enclosure and wanted to cry. The older bear seemed content to lie in the sun. The bear raised its head and huffed in her direction. A second grizzly walked around behind a strategically placed boulder. "*Well, well,*" the lady bear said into her mind. "*What have we here?*"

"*You startled me. I didn't expect you to recognize me so quickly,*" Morgan replied with her thoughts.

The bear jumped. It jumped more like a startled cat than a ferocious bear causing the children surrounding the cage to point and laugh. "*Who spoke to me? Identify yourself!*"

The she-bear paced in front of the glass. For a long moment she paused in front of where Morgan stood. "*I see. A shaman. Well, it is tragic that you should find me in such miserable conditions. What may I do for you?*"

"*Why do all the spirit animals I have met call me Shaman?*" she asked into the bear's mind.

The chestnut bear locked eyes with her. "*That's simple. It's because you are.*"

Morgan rolled her eyes. "*Not the question. I want to know how you can tell, where you got the word, how you learned to communicate. I want to know about it all.*"

The she-bear stared through the glass. "*Well, aren't you quite the busybody. I will tell you all that I know in exchange for one thing.*"

Morgan pressed her hand to the glass and replied, "*Anything.*"

The bear paced to where Morgan stood and nuzzled the glass. "*Free me.*"

Slowly Morgan nodded her head. "*I will do whatever it takes.*"

"*Very well.*" The chestnut bear strode back to the center of the enclosure and lay down. "*It happened right before the nights began to get long. I remember the day very well. At first, I was excited as I knew the men with food would be arriving soon. Their schedule had been so important to me, before the change."*

Morgan found the nearest bench to sit while she listened. Scores of people came and went past the bear's enclosure, but she stayed. There were several hours before the zoo would be closed and she had finally found a spirit animal willing to tell her what happened to them the day magic returned.

"It was like waking up from a dream that I didn't know I was having. My whole life seemed just fine and only after I awoke did I realize how truly terrible it is. I was born here, you know, at the zoo." The bear raised its head and when no one was looking, nodded at Morgan.

Morgan nodded back. *"That's the way Mercedes described it too. The day magic returned she suddenly realized there was more to life, and that the first half of it she had been in a walking dream. It doesn't really make any sense how you all know that word though. Why do you keep calling me Shaman? Mercedes started off by calling me a Druid, but all the other animals I meet seem to think I'm a Shaman."*

The bear responded with a mental shrug. *"I cannot speak for this Mercedes of yours, only for myself. It was like all this knowledge came to me in a rush. I knew that I shouldn't be caged. I am a symbol of strength and knowledge for my Shamans. I can't explain why I knew this only that I did."*

She reflected for a moment before responding to the bear's mind. *"I think I understand. Mercedes is a cat. There weren't any cats here in America when magic was around, so her 'knowing' would be from Europe.*

That's why she called me a Druid rather than a Shaman." Morgan considered that for a moment before asking her next question. "*Why is it I can only hear some animals?*"

The she-bear looked back at the brown bear. "*That I cannot say. Only that some of us seem to be here for a greater purpose than others. This one seems to be just as lazy and dumb as before the change.*"

"*But the crows all seemed be have been awakened. Any idea why that would be?*" Morgan's puzzle pieces weren't all fitting together as nicely as she would like, but the picture it was painting was starting to become slightly clearer.

"*Crows and ravens are smart animals to begin with. I assume there was only one who was smarter than the rest.*"

Morgan smiled to herself. "The leader," she accidentally said out loud. A woman with a baby gave her a sidewise glance. "*The leader,*" she repeated to the bear in her mind. "*Not only was he smarter than the others, he allowed me to join him and take his shape.*"

"*How very interesting. I believe in exchange for freeing me, I would also allow you to share in my form. It's time for you to set me free.*" The bear walked back to the glass and reared up on its hind legs.

"*I'm sorry, Lady Bear, I can't free you yet. There's a little more to it than just walking over and opening the door. If it were that simple, I'd do it now. I'll be back for you though. You have my word.*" Morgan walked back to the glass and put her palm on the window.

•⁊•

Walter's apartment had become a mess since Kaleb moved in. There were clothes littering the bedroom floor and dishes piling up in the sink.

Luckily Walter was a quick study and Kaleb was an open book. He found the best way to get Kaleb to clean was to do it together.

As he handed Kaleb a dish to dry, he jumped into what had been bothering him all day, "I honestly can't believe you still go to her for help. If there's one thing you need to know about me it's that I can read people. Morgan is self-centered, self-loathing, childish, and sociopathic. I wish you would teach me more so you could come to me with your questions."

"She may be all those things, but she is still my friend." Kaleb did his best not to allow his frustration enter his voice. "I will teach you everything I know but she has experience with this sort of thing. I just really wish you could give her a chance."

Walter's jaw twitched, "I did give her a chance but then she *murdered* someone."

Kaleb paced back and forth while he calmed his emotions. "I agree with you completely, but that could have been me. What would we be doing if I told you my magic went haywire and instead of turning Austin into a snake I killed him? Where would we be then?"

"That is not the same thing! She tortured him before she killed him. You let your emotions get the better of you and you couldn't control your on abilities. She didn't just lose control. She enjoyed it!"

Kaleb's mouth hung open; a plate dripped on the floor. "Wow, really? How do you know that? Were you there? I prefer to give my friends the benefit of the doubt, but apparently you 'can read people.' Believe me when I say that I know she's a basket case, but that basket case is my best friend!"

Walter took the plate out of Kaleb's hand and set it on the counter. He put his arms around Kaleb's waist, "I don't want to fight. You've known Morgan for a long time, and it's unfair of me to assume things."

"Damn right it is," he replied with a pout.

Their eyes met and Kaleb relaxed into Walter's arms. "We both know that she has issues, but someone has to be there to put her back on the right track. I don't know her like you do, so it'll have to be you. She needs help, she needs you."

Kaleb grinned. "Stop it."

Walter smiled. "Stop what?"

"Stop being so cute. Come on, you know I can never argue with that smile." Walter kissed him. "So, you want me to involve you more. Can you promise not to freak out?"

"Oh god! You killed someone?" Walter fell into the nearest armchair and Kaleb took a seat on his lap, once again kissing him softly on the lips.

Kaleb raised an eyebrow, "Do you really think I could kill someone? Come on, I couldn't even kill a mouse. So, serious moment." Kaleb collected himself on Walter's lap and waited for the smile to fade before he ventured forward. "I was kidnapped last night by three shades. Don't freak out. I'm already working on finding a decent protection spell. I've been down at the library all morning looking for one."

"Why don't you just do the spell we did for Morgan? Can't you just borrow her mom's book again?" he asked, trying to express some knowledge of the magical arts.

"She's been a bit guarded about the book since Nick ran off with it. She's convinced that he's using it to steal demon magic. I can't borrow it because she thinks I'll lend it to Nick."

"But I liked that spell, bending space like that. I've always liked vaulted ceilings." Walter was proud of himself for remembering how Kaleb described the spell's effect.

"I doubt we'd have that happen. There is no way that spell should have been powerful enough to do what it did. There was definitely way more going on than we know. I think Anna's spirit had something to do with it."

He leaned in and kissed Kaleb, "Sorry love, it's getting late and I'm not going to be able to stay up with you tonight. They've got me on dredging duty in the morning."

Kaleb raised an eyebrow, "Dredging duty?"

"We're dredging the lake up by Thirteen Steps tomorrow. They think a missing person may have committed suicide there." Kaleb's body tensed. "What's wrong?"

"You can't dredge that lake. There's a dragon living in that lake!"

Walter crossed his arms, "This is not a joke, Kaleb. The family's been waiting a long time and needs closure. They think he may have tried to drown himself there."

"I'm not kidding. The night we went swimming up there, I didn't learn to swim. We almost drowned and a dragon saved us."

Walter frowned. "All right, I can't tell if you're kidding, but if there is a dragon living in that lake you have until ten am to find him a new home."

.•.

Kaleb refused to approach the bank of the placid lake until Nick arrived. To occupy his time he played with a ball of magical light, tossing it between his hands. He had memorized quite a few spells over the last two months. Unfortunately, Walter still wasn't showing any promise as a caster. Despite Kaleb's many attempts at teaching him, Walter was still no closer to being a magical protégé than when they had started.

Kaleb was nervous. He had no idea how Nick would react to his invitation or how Morgan would feel if she found out. The wait gave Kaleb an opportunity to reflect on his own part in the rift that was forming.

He hadn't been a very good glue for their friendship. Kaleb had been spending a majority of his time with Walter, only showing up now and again to check in. He made a vow to himself to take a more active role in Morgan and Nick's lives. The library of Saint Patrick had been exciting for a moment, but it felt like he was the only one wanting to learn magic from there.

Morgan no longer seemed to need or want his help. She was forming realities of her own. At least she had Matthew and Geoffroi to keep her grounded, but he wondered if they really were good influences for her in this state. Matthew had no memories and Geoffroi remembered the dark ages better than the modern era.

He was happy that he would have a chance to talk to Nick alone. Dragon-hunting provided a great opportunity for them to reconnect. Aside from Anna's funeral, they hadn't spoken more than a handful of times over the last couple of months. Magic's return should be bringing them together not forcing them apart.

Geoffroi had been extremely helpful in translating the library, but they were still only a third of the way through with the charcoal rubbings he had brought back. He made a mental note to get something nice for Geoffroi, maybe a sword.

Kaleb was so lost in thought that had it not been for the sound of a branch snapping he would not have noticed the hooded figure stepping into the clearing. Kaleb snuffed out his ball of magical light as quickly as he could.

"Kaleb?" Nick asked.

"Over here," Kaleb called back as they both walked to the edge of the lake. "Thanks for agreeing to do this."

"No problem, that's what friends are for. So what's the scoop?" Nick wrung his hands while Kaleb explained why they had met at the lake. "A dragon? This should be exciting."

Kaleb smiled back. "I know! I've always had a fondness for dragons, and this one is very nice. He saved Walter from drowning."

"Oh yeah, I remember you telling me about that. How is the old officer Wally?"

Kaleb conjured a new ball of light so he could see Nick's expression, "Do you not like Walter?" Kaleb leaned on his staff and gave Nick a piercing stare.

Nick rolled his eyes. "Are you kidding me? Kaleb I have no problem with the guy, but I haven't really heard from you except to hear how sweet Walter is. I'd think with everything that's going on you'd be a little bit more than boy-crazy."

"Well, the road goes both ways. The only reason we have stayed in touch is cause I've been calling you. What's up with you and Gwen?"

It took Nick a moment to realize just what had been implied. "Oh my god, seriously? I haven't dated girls since high school, Kaleb."

Kaleb mumbled, "It wasn't that long ago."

"Okay, sure, I may have only graduated four years ago, but I do not date the ladies; I *am* a lady." He sat on a log at the edge of the lake and crossed his legs. "What's gotten into you?"

Thunder rolled in the distance and it started to sprinkle. "Morgan is what's gotten into me. She thinks you and Gwen are dating. I'm sorry Nick, but we haven't really talked much. I guess part of me was hoping you found yourself a love interest."

"I could fault you for being a hopeless romantic, but you'd still be hopeless. Unlike somebody, I've been more focused on learning magic than making ooglie eyes with a cute boy."

Kaleb pushed him off the log. Nick laughed. "Hey, you set yourself up for that. Guess you shouldn't have told me how you boys like to lay in bed just staring into each other's eyes." Nick batted his eyes at Kaleb.

Kaleb helped Nick off the ground and replied, "No fair, I've been teaching Walter magic."

Nick sat back down on the log next to Kaleb and patted his knee. "And how has that been going for you?"

"Not well," Kaleb admitted. "It kind of sucks. He really wants to be able to and I want to have that connection with him, but it just isn't happening. I think he's blocked, but I don't know enough about high magic to know if that's the problem. We're lucky, we've been using low magic for so long we didn't have to start with the basics. I think it makes him frustrated that he can't."

The rain and wind picked up. Nick made a circular gesture with his free hand and his staff glowed brightly. Without saying a word, a transparent barrier formed in a hemisphere around them blocking the wind and rain. Kaleb's eyes were as wide as saucers. Nick shrugged. "What?"

Kaleb spouted off in rapid fire, "That was awesome! You have to teach me that spell. I'm sorry I haven't been spending time with you. Maybe I should ask you to teach Walter. How the hell? Just a gesture? You're getting good!"

Nick laughed. "Calm down girl! I'll teach you the shield spell, but I don't know if I have time to teach Walter. Between classes and learning magic myself, I really don't have much time for anything."

Kaleb waited patiently for Nick to explain the mechanics of the shield spell. The spell was all about intent and willpower, which was why words weren't important. A hemisphere of faint blue light erupted around him like a glass dome. It came naturally to Kaleb and Nick frowned.

"What's wrong?" Kaleb asked.

"Do you know how long it took me to master that spell? It took you two minutes."

Kaleb patted Nick on the knee. "That's why you'd make a better teacher than me. Spells seem to come naturally to me, but you understand *how* they do what they do. I would kill to have you teach Walter and me."

"What about Morgan?"

"I don't think she'd be very inclined to learning magic from you. She thinks you're stealing demon magic." They both laughed. Kaleb didn't recognize the laugh coming from Nick was an awkward one.

"I mean come on, Demon magic? She makes it sound like you trapped one in your staff and now you're draining its life essence."

"Well, I am a vampire, after all." Nick grinned.

Kaleb continued to laugh but Nick did not join him this time. After another couple of chuckles Kaleb straightened his face and said, "Of course you are."

Nick crossed his arms, upset by Kaleb's refusal to acknowledge him as a powerful vampire. His jaw was set and he responded with resentment in his voice, "Are we going to get this done, or what?"

"Oh, Nick, don't be like that. I didn't mean to offend you. I'm sorry. Of course you're a vampire." He patted Nick's knee. "Bram Stoker would be proud."

A grin emerged on Nick's face. "If you don't believe me, then let me prove it to you. Bring down your personal shields and I'll show you. Don't worry it won't hurt. If you still don't believe me after I'm done, then I'm not a vampire."

Kaleb tilted his head and shrugged. "Okay."

Blue-white light shone from a globe of light that Kaleb conjured in the air above their heads. Kaleb closed his eyes and focused his mind on lowering his shields. It had been a long time since he had consciously shielded. When he examined himself he found there were a lot more on him than he realized.

One by one Kaleb brought the shields into himself and dispelled them. After prodding his own aura with his mind for good measure he opened his eyes and declared himself ready.

The vampire smiled a greedy smile. Rain pounded the protective dome and somewhere beyond, thunder rolled. A tendril of power snaked from the vampire and cautiously approached the unguarded Kaleb.

•ː•

Walter stirred in bed. The bed was cold and empty without Kaleb sharing it. He wasn't used to going to bed this early and tried to blame his inability to sleep on it. Deep down, he was unsettled. Perhaps there was something in what Morgan had said. He was fairly certain that the Bible talked about evil recognizing evil. Thunder pounded the windows.

He didn't want to seem like the possessive type so he resisted the urge to call Kaleb and tell him to come home. As the clock on his bedside table

267

ticked its unhappy concordance, his mind would not rest until he tried. The phone rang three times and went to voicemail.

"Is he ignoring me?" He tried again and this time the call went directly to voicemail.

Nerves were only calmed by pacing, so Walter took to the living room to calm them. After several deep breaths and self-delivered words of encouragement, Walter drew back the curtains to watch the rain. Beads of rain slowly trailed their way down the glass and the comfort he found was fleeting.

Words of encouragement were soon met with words of opposition. A colorful story began to unravel in Walter's mind. Kaleb and Nick had dated and they were off alone together. Nick has something that cannot be provided by anyone other than a fellow witch. "No, Kaleb would never do that. Nick may be charming and handsome but Kaleb loves me," he said to himself.

"But Kaleb left Austin for you," Walter countered himself.

"I was more to blame for that." Walter bit his thumbnail. "I tried to keep it platonic, but I can't help how I feel."

Walter's reflection stared back unhappily at him. "So what happens if Nick does the same thing you did?"

"Stop it," he said to his reflection. "Kaleb loves me."

•፣•

The tendril of power met with little resistance. It wormed its way into Kaleb's aura and was swatted away. Nick opened one eye and saw Kaleb waiting patiently. Nick's mouth pursed in frustration and concentration. There was still a shield, or perhaps a conscious thought protecting Kaleb. But Kaleb lacked one thing that Nick had; experience.

Nick marshaled his resolve, took a moment to evaluate Kaleb's lack of shields, and pounced. A concussive force effectively punched him in his third eye. "Seriously, if you're not willing to let me try, just say so!"

"What? I'm sorry, I thought I had them all down. I've never been good at shielding. It's always been sort of a natural thing for me. I've always been told I'm guarded. Do you want to try again?"

Nick was furious. He couldn't see the magical energies and even his own personal shields had fallen. Rain was drenching them. Kaleb closed his eyes and concentrated. He gestured in the shape of a dome with his hands and the rain stopped.

A part of Nick was still seething with pain. "Forget it. Obviously, it isn't going to work, so you're just going to have to believe me."

Kaleb tried to wink but it just came across as awkward blinking. "You said if you couldn't prove it I didn't have to believe you." Nick's jaw was set and he looked away. "Okay, I'm sorry, it's probably my fault."

"Just forget it. Let's just finish what we came here to do." Nick stood and looked out over the small lake.

"I didn't mean to make you upset. If you want to try again you can; I'll try to keep all my shields from getting in the way." He closed his eyes and put his hands on his thighs, concentrating very hard at lowing his guard.

Nick frowned. "I said forget it. Let's just find this dragon a new home."

•⫶•

Kaleb still wasn't home and it was getting late. Walter had been pacing back and forth across his carpet for a half an hour. He bit his lip and once again tried calling. Kaleb answered.

"Hey, baby! I thought you'd be asleep. Is everything okay?"

Kaleb's voice was reassuring and Walter went back to the bed and relaxed. "I just had a bad dream. How are things at the lake? Did you find the dragon?"

"Not yet. Nick's doing some vampire thing where he's searching for life energy." Kaleb whispered into the phone, "Allegedly." Kaleb went back to his normal speaking voice. "He needs to be able to identify each type." His voice returned to a whisper. "Honestly, I think I'd have better luck from the shadow realm, but I want him to feel like he's contributing."

"Well, don't do anything I wouldn't do." He didn't know why he said that and put his palm to his forehead while he waited for the response.

Kaleb laughed. "Don't worry, love, I won't kill any spiders."

"Har har, you know what I mean," he recovered. "Be good."

"Always am. Get some sleep."

•ʅ•

They prowled the edge of the lake. Nick had tried to sense out the creature while Kaleb skipped back and forth from the shadow realm. The vampire inside Nick was becoming restless. It had been twelve hours since he had last fed and Kaleb was no free meal. There was something odd about Kaleb's shields.

Nick took another moment to examine the protections Kaleb had. They were rudimentary at best, but somehow they thwarted his every attempt to bypass them. There was no sign of a dragon and Nick was beginning to bore of the search.

"Kaleb, this has been fun and all but I'm getting hungry. There's no dragon here. So whatever you saw before was a fluke. If there was a dragon here, he's gone on to another lake or forest to make his home."

Kaleb looked a bit saddened by this but agreed. "You're probably right. I was really hoping to return the favor and get him to someplace safe. He did save my future husband's life after all."

"Oh lord, are we really going there already? You said the same about Austin and look how that turned out." Nick sat back down by the lake. "No offense, but your track record isn't the greatest."

"Hey, Pot, Kettle here, just wanting to check in and see how you've been," Kaleb snickered.

Nick raised an eyebrow at the lowbrow humor. "Refusing to date isn't the same as dating douche-bags."

"Are you calling Walter a douche?" Kaleb asked from the edge of offense.

"That is yet to be seen, really, but not the point. The point is I don't date because men suck, and you date because you like to be pushed down the stairs. So if you'll excuse me, momma's hungry."

•¡•

The clock read three when Kaleb finally crawled into bed with Walter. He was already asleep and snoring lightly. A smiled passed over Kaleb's face as he leaned over and kissed him softly on the cheek.

He turned away from Walter and whispered into the night, "Thank you for being so wonderful."

"I wondered when you'd be home," Walter said as he rolled over and put his arm around Kaleb.

Kaleb's hand caressed the soft skin of Walter's bicep and he kissed it. They had agreed to take their relationship slowly. Aside from soft caressing and heavy petting they hadn't been physical. "I'm sorry I woke you."

Walter pulled himself in closer and kissed Kaleb softly on the neck and ear. "Don't be. I tried to wait up for you, but I guess I fell asleep," he said while slowly caressing Kaleb's stomach with his finger-tips.

The feather-touch caused shivers across Kaleb's body and Walter continued his kisses down Kaleb's neck. Walter's fingers coursed up and down Kaleb's stomach until they met with underwear. For a moment there was hesitation, but as Walter began to remove his hand Kaleb rolled over onto his back and kissed Walter deeply.

With renewed confidence, Walter's hands and mouth intensified their exploration of Kaleb's body. Kaleb returned this attention with exploration of his own. Kaleb's kisses followed the curve of the bicep, down his chest, stomach, and beyond.

They explored each other and pleasured one another. Twice.

Divided We Stand

Geoffroi handed a bottle of beer to Matthew as he returned to the porch of their new home. It had been several weeks since they had moved in, and they could finally call it home. After they had cleared out the clutter they began making minor improvements. Matthew was a pretty good carpenter and the house no longer felt like it was going to cave in on itself.

The summer was beginning to be a hot one. Their new home lacked air conditioning, but Geoffroi wasn't bothered by it, though the part of him that was David was agitated.

Geoffroi was excited for what was to become of his new life. Matthew had made no progress regaining his memories, but was content. Morgan's visits were infrequent at best but neither of the men seemed to mind.

It was a quiet life. Geoffroi tended to the garden, Matthew hunted with a bow that Geoffroi fashioned for him. Their lie about becoming stewards of the land had become their life.

Matthew had proven to be a great companion and Geoffroi had planned something special for tonight. He had been secretly fashioning two wooden shields that he engraved with the Greek letter gamma in tribute to their new community, Gaea's Fist. Tonight, he would declare Matthew his brother in arms.

"Looks like it's going to rain," Matthew said casually.

Geoffroi smiled, thinking on his plans for later, "Rain is good, cleansing. Plenty to do before the rain gets here."

They busied themselves with their chores, and when he felt the first sprinklings of the coming storm, they regrouped on the porch. Matthew sat down just as the storm broke and rain began to pour from the sky. They sat in silence, taking in the sound of the falling rain. It fell lightly to the ground and carried the scent of the earth with it.

Geoffroi took Matthew's hand and stepped to the edge of the porch and out into the downpour. After a moment's hesitation Matthew left the shelter of the awning and joined him on the lawn. Geoffroi retrieved the two shields from under the porch.

"I am not so good with sentimental words, so I made these for us." He handed a wooden shield to Matthew. "You are the closest thing I have to family now," Geoffroi choked on his words for a second. "I hope you like them."

Matthew put his hand through the leather strap fastened to the back of the circular shield. Rain washed over them but neither seemed to mind. It was a warm rain that mirrored the warmth of their faces. Matthew nodded and gave him a quick hug. A huge smile grew on Geoffroi's face. "I'll go get the bottle of wine I've been saving." He patted Matthew on both shoulders and went inside.

Matthew's emotions tumbled. He had no idea who he was anymore. His family and friends were specters haunting his mind but never coming out from the shadows. The revelation of magic threw him into an unknown world.

Geoffroi's gift and promise of a new family was more than he could take and he broke down into tears. As the rain flowed over his body, he lost his sense of self.

.٧.

The roads were beginning to get slick with rain as Morgan made her way home from the zoo. She couldn't believe how many awakened animals called their home the zoo, nor could she believe how many didn't want to leave. Was it her place to free them if they didn't want to leave?

The promise she made to the she-bear still resonated in her mind as she slowed down for a deer attempting to cross the road. The deer froze as it stared at Morgan's approaching car. Another car crested the hill, driving far too fast.

The other driver didn't see the deer until it was far too late and they collided. The deer was flung into the windshield as the car careened into the ditch and toppled onto its side.

Morgan was furious. She parked her car on the side of the road and stormed over to the wreck. The driver, a man in his mid-forties, was trapped by the steering column. Blood seeped from a gash on his forehead. "What the hell is your problem? You come speeding through here like a jackass." Her blood boiled.

The man could barely focus his eyes on her. "What?"

"I can't believe how stupid people are. You deserve to end up in this ditch, but that deer didn't deserve to get hit by you." She stormed back to her car.

He began crying out, "Don't leave me here. Call for help."

She grabbed the grimoire off the passenger seat and flipped through its pages. Her eyes met the spell that Kaleb cast on his ex: transforming an enemy. A grim smile emerged on her face as she stormed back, staff in hand.

She yanked on the man's body and he bawled out in pain, "What the hell are you doing? You're fucking crazy, lady!" Morgan jerked on his arm so hard she felt his shoulder pop out of socket. He wailed in agony.

275

Morgan ignored his plea for an ambulance and began the incantation. Power welled up within her and met her anger. She poured the magic and the words into the man. His body began to writhe and he howled in pain, begging for her to stop.

Morgan dusted off the pretend dirt from her hands as his body warped into the shape of a doe. The doe stared at her for a moment before running off into the woods. "Now let's hope some asshole in a beamer doesn't come and hit you."

She went back to her car and drove off. Silently, she said a little prayer for the soul of the deer whose life was lost. Her phone rang. Whoever was calling was not going to be greeted with a warm welcome. She put the phone up to her ear. "What!?"

"Um, Morgan? I really hope this isn't a bad time." It was Geoffroi. He sounded agitated, but Morgan didn't care. Her blood was still boiling and she would rather drive home in peace and quiet than listen to Geoffroi panic about whatever it was he had to say. "Morgan?" Geoffroi said.

The windshield-wipers flicked back and forth. Her agitation grew steadily. "Yeah, what?"

In the background she heard the Speak-and-Spell, "D-R-A-G-O-N, dragon."

Morgan's eyebrow raised involuntarily. "Did Mercedes just spell dragon?"

"Yes, about that. That's actually why I'm calling."

"Has Mercedes been abusing her Speak-and-Spell privileges again? If she keeps swearing at you, take it away!"

She took a corner a little tighter than she had meant to. Morgan was angry and knew she shouldn't be driving this angry. The one person in this world who truly understood her was gone and she had no intention of leaving this world the same way.

"No. Mercedes has actually been quite the respectful lady, shockingly." She heard the Speak-and-Spell utter profanities it was not intended for. "Alright, fine, I guess you *will* get a bath later."

Morgan wasn't in the mood for this conversation. "Get to the point."

"Sorry, the point is, you need to come here right now. We've got a big problem," he said, his voice trembling.

The sun was beginning to set and the rain hadn't let up. Morgan was furious and her driving wasn't the greatest. "It had better be, because I'm really not in the mood."

He blurted it out, "There's a dragon on the front lawn!"

Morgan slammed on the brakes. The wheels screeched and the car slid across the road before coming to an abrupt stop. "What?"

"I think you should probably be here for this. Mercedes is freaking out. You wish for me to call Kaleb?" Geoffroi's voice was pure panic at this point and his accent was starting to come back.

"No. Don't call Kaleb. I'll take care of this. What is the dragon doing now?"

"Um, a moment please." There was a pause and she heard a screen door slam. "It's sprawled out on the lawn in the rain." The line went quiet. "Morgan?"

She turned the car around. "Yeah?"

His whispered, "I'm afraid."

•٠•

The dragon on the lawn lounged as water pooled around its sapphire body. It seemed content enough left alone to whatever thoughts were running through its enormous skull. Geoffroi had barricaded himself inside. Mercedes yowled in fear as he pushed the sofa up against the rest of what wasn't nailed down.

Morgan was two hours away and Matthew was still out there somewhere. Despite what Morgan wanted, he tried calling Kaleb but only reached his voicemail. His world was spinning out of control.

Mercedes was hysterical. She could barely operate the Speak-and-Spell. Geoffroi was well trained in the art of war but he never had to fight a dragon. Dragons were legend. Saint George killed the last one. He admonished himself for falling back to his old faith and teachings. Clearly, the Holy Roman Empire lied about dragons just as they lied about magic.

Mercedes had calmed down enough to manage a few words, "G-E-T, get, H-E-L-P, help."

He threw up his hands, "I try! I try! It be another two hours for the Lady Morgan. The Sorcerer does not answer his phone."

Mercedes puffed herself up to her full size, "O-P-E-N, open, D-O-O-R, door."

Geoffroi wheeled around at the unexpected response. Mercedes licked her paw and cleaned her forehead. "You must not! The dragon will devour you."

The cat let out an eerily human sigh. *"If he does he'll be hungry in an hour."* He couldn't hear her, but her eyes got the point across.

"As you wish, milady, I will not dishonor you." He moved the furniture and debris from in front of the door.

The cat approached the door with as much gusto and bravado that she could muster. "Will you require your Speak-and-Spell, milady?" She responded with a slow nod.

..

The massive dragon languished in self-pity. He couldn't remember why he was upset, only that he was. The shelter that the strange man had ran into opened briefly. He unfolded his wings, stretching them to their full glory, before refolding them by his side. All four of his legs were curled up beneath him like a cat perched on a windowsill.

Curious, the dragon lifted his head to the full extent his neck would allow to see a small feline pushing a strange box with its head toward the stairs. Amused, the dragon situated himself into a better position to view the spectacle.

A disembodied voice lacking both emotion and inflection spoke into the air, "D-R-A-G-O-N, dragon." He let out an involuntary guttural chuckle causing the cat to back up several paces.

He could not recall the last time he had used his voice, just as he could not remember much of himself. His voice was deep and rumbling like thunder, "Daughter of Baast, I hear your mind, you need not use such strange contraptions."

Mercedes left the Speak-and-Spell on the stairs and approached the dragon. *"You can hear my thoughts?"*

"As a protector of the earth, I can hear all its children." The response came unbidden and the revelation was quite startling to him. Perhaps this was why he was so upset, but still he wasn't sure. The world was different, yet he couldn't remember what it was like before. "Tell me, why have you chosen to speak with me, my feline friend?"

She jumped onto the porch rail so she could look him in the eye. "*We are missing a friend. Would you happen to have seen where he went?*"

He thought for a moment, "There was no one here when I arrived. Was this a feline friend?"

Irritation was evident in her mind-voice. "*No, this was a human. He has as much sense as a turkey in a rainstorm.*"

The dragon tapped an ebony claw to an ivory tooth, "I am certain I did not see this friend." He couldn't remember anything and the amusement the cat had provided was waning.

The rain felt good as it glistened off his scales. His eyes closed slightly as he allowed the sensation to take over his mind. As an informal dismissal, he turned his back to the cat to focus on the sadness still brewing in his heart.

The cat did not leave. Slowly, he raised his head and craned his neck back around until his mouth was inches away from where she stood on the porch rail. He noted that, though her fur stood on end, she did not back away. "Brave you are, or perhaps you too have less sense than a turkey in a rainstorm."

She bit down hard on her fear and retorted with a mental shrug. The books she read said it was impossible to lie when speaking mind-to-mind, but she was going to give it her best shot. "*You're just a bigger version of a cat.*"

•⸙•

Dread filled Morgan's heart and she parked the car halfway down the gravel driveway of her mother's house. Within the dragon's claw was her cat. She flung open the car door and ran up the lawn.

She yelled in her best mind-growl to the dragon, *"Put down the cat!"*

The dragon fell backwards and Mercedes was flung into the air. The cat twisted and turned its body but before she hit the ground was caught in the scaled claw of the sapphire blue dragon. "You startled me. Is this the friend you were looking for Mercedes?"

Morgan ended her charge up the lawn. *"Wait, what? You guys are on a first name basis?"*

Mercedes practiced her cat skills and somehow managed to climb to the dragon's shoulder. *"I guess the question here is, what took you so long?"*

"Where's Geoffroi?"

The cat steadied herself as the dragon shifted to a more comfortable position. "Is this the one who has the same sense as a turkey in a rainstorm?" The dragon craned its long neck to ask the cat resting on his shoulder.

"Well you two sure are chummy, Mercedes, do you mind coming down here and explaining what the hell is going on?"

She looked down at Morgan from her perch on the dragon's shoulder. *"No, I'm good."*

The dragon sniffed at Morgan. "A druid? Now this is truly a pleasure. Mercedes, you told me she was useless and pudgy."

Morgan's eyebrow raised involuntarily. "Pudgy?"

"My exact words were pudgy and useless. No, I guess you got it right."

The dragon was obviously not a threat, so Morgan turned to storm off when the dragon stopped her. "Truly, druid, I did not intend to offend you.

Your feline friend has been entertaining me but I recognize that she has offended you."

"I'm glad to see at least you have sense," she said to the dragon as she shot Mercedes a hateful glance. "What may we call you?"

The dragon pondered this question for a moment. "Names are quite helpful, I am sure. You may know me as Rain, as that is what has brought me here tonight."

"It is a pleasure to meet you, Rain. You'll have to forgive me, I don't really know the proper etiquette for entertaining a dragon."

"*That's okay, she doesn't know the proper etiquette for entertaining a cat either.*" The dragon snaked its head around until one massive eye stared at the cat residing on its shoulder. Mercedes shrank. "*What?*"

Rain responded in a half-growl, "It would serve you well to know when to be polite, daughter of Baast." The dragon returned his attention to Morgan. "Druid, it would please me to know your name."

Morgan responded and answered the dragon's questions about herself. She noted that Mercedes was significantly more polite after being scolded by a dragon. The rainstorm however was leaving her soaked. "I don't mean to be rude, Rain, but I'm getting soaked and I'd like to continue this conversation after I've had a moment to dry off."

The massive sapphire head nodded. "I will be here when you return."

Mercedes leapt off the dragon in order to beat Morgan to the door, she was soaked and extremely unhappy about it. "*I require a towel,*" she said as she reached the house.

Morgan resisted the urge to kick the cat and entered the house to find a fretting Geoffroi. "What's going on out there? Did you find Matthew?"

"Matthew's missing? Why is this the first time I'm hearing about this? I thought he was in here with you!" Morgan threw up her hands and went to the bathroom.

Morgan refused to talk to Mercedes or Geoffroi. She threw a towel at the cat as she changed out of her clothes and into warmer ones. She grabbed her umbrella and stood next to the front door. "We're going to look for Matthew. Mercedes, you're not invited. Geoffroi," she said as she stepped out into rain. "Grab an umbrella."

·Ƴ·

Rain lounged on the grass. He rather liked the druid and the cat. They distracted him from the ache in his heart. The dragon closed his eyes and enjoyed the sensations that the rainstorm had brought. It wasn't long before the door opened. Morgan and a new friend, perhaps the one with the sensibility of a turkey, emerged.

There was something wrong with the new friend. His scent was of decay and although slight, it was still noticeable. Rain backed away from the stranger. "Why do you travel with this abomination?"

Morgan froze. "He's harmless, what's wrong with him?"

"I will not be in his presence! He reeks of death!" The dragon stretched his wings and barred his teeth. "Druid, how can you associate with this zumbi, are you its bokor? You are no druid!" The words came unbidden to Rain. He knew what he meant, but wasn't sure where they came from. The zumbi were undead creatures and a bokor was its master. His only concern now was to distance himself from the crime against nature and he took to wing.

Morgan cried for him to return and he felt a sense of loneliness press itself upon his breast. There was a fog consuming his memories and for a moment Rain wondered if he would ever find any other of his kind. This druid might be his only opportunity to find more like himself. Rain decided to circle for a moment as Morgan sent the abomination back inside.

"Please come back, Rain," she said into his mind. *"I'm sorry about Geoffroi. It's a long story."* Thunder punctuated her words.

Rain descended and landed next to her in the yard. His mighty claws sunk into the wet grass. "I have time and you have a need to explain." Disgust made his already gravelly voice even more commanding.

"I'm sorry, Rain, I don't have time to explain Geoffroi. My friend Matthew is missing. He may be out in this storm. I really care about him, but if you agree to help me look for him I promise I'll tell you everything you want to know."

The dragon considered this. "You intrigue me. I will forgive this transgression, but I expect an explanation."

•⁊•

Morgan and Rain prowled the timber. Several hours had passed and there was still no sign of Matthew. She found Rain's company to be quite enjoyable, though she secretly felt he was hiding something from her.

Every question the dragon asked of her she would answer but it seemed as though Rain's answers were more like those of a politician trying to get through the primaries. Though his speech was eloquent, there was no substance.

The rain had ended an hour ago and the sky had cleared to show the stars. She had noticed that the dragon's breath had become more labored but he didn't want to discuss it.

There were only a few awakened animals in the timber and none had seen or heard Matthew coming through the woods. Her heart was starting to sink. Wherever he had gone he was lost to her.

The dragon's pace slowed to a snail's crawl. Its scales heaved with labored breath.

"Is everything okay, Rain?"

The dragon lifted its head to the sky. "It's so dry." He stopped to catch his breath. "Having trouble breathing."

"You're a water dragon?" It took her another moment for her mind to connect the dots, "You're a water dragon! That's why you can't breathe! We need to get you to a lake. There's one about two hours away. It's a man-made lake and it's big enough that you'll have plenty of hiding places."

The dragon looked down at Morgan. "Where is this lake?"

"The Red Gorge Lake. It's huge. Follow me." She shifted into raven form and led the dragon into the sky. She knew she was losing precious time locating Matthew, but the safety of this water dragon was now her top priority.

They made several stops along the way for the dragon to bathe in the streams and rivers they came across. The lake was situated just north of the city so they took a wide circle to avoid getting spotted.

She didn't care if the dragon had been seen during their long flight to safety. Let Kaleb try and sweep magic under a rug; she embraced it. With a large splash, the dragon dove into the lake.

He raised his head just above water level to address her, "Thank you,

285

Morgan, I am sorry we were unable to find your friend. Your friend may still be lost but tonight you have found a new one."

Morgan looked at her watch and her heart sank. It was already past three in the morning and she had to work in five hours. Matthew was still missing but the search would have to resume tomorrow.

.7.

Geoffroi was furious. The dragon insulted him and Morgan did nothing to stand up for him. Mercedes had been rude to him since she came back in the house, but that wasn't anything new. If they weren't going to let him help search for Matthew, he would do it on his own.

He had been playing the alive card far too long. His body ran on raw magic. No matter how much he abused his body it would still function. The dragon thought he smelled of death now? Just wait until several days of no rest or food had passed. He would find Matthew.

The rain had ended and Geoffroi had made up his mind. "I'm going to look for Matthew, Lady Cat. You're going to have to fend for yourself until Morgan or I return for you."

Mercedes looked up at him, pleading with her eyes for him stay. *"Who will be my thumbs?"*

.7.

The House of Gray converged on the disused playground. Weeds grew around the equipment. It was far enough from the city that no one would bother them. Even tonight, on the Fourth of July, when every inch of space was covered with pedestrians trying to find a place to watch the fireworks, no one would bother them.

Shades, like whips of black smoke taken human form, stood sentry around their perimeter. Nick wasn't bothered by their presence, but the others looked to be a bit on edge. Ever since he had imprisoned Lifedrinker they were ever present.

Quincy proved to be more bloodthirsty than Gwen. Though they each enjoyed their fill of the kills. Quincy took great care in draining their victim's blood and storing it. Nick never asked what he was planning to do with the blood. Some people were just weird.

Gwen was Nick's general. He left the training of his new disciples in her hands while Nick focused on their next goal. The only way he was going to gain new spells was by stealing Kaleb's ability of shadow-walking and going to Saint Patrick's Library himself.

While the others practiced conjuring balls of lightning, Nick sat on the swings, considering his plan of attack. Fireworks began to explode in the sky. Nick took his staff and rose into the air.

"My children," he said, while hovering several feet above them. "Train and toil. Soon we will be strong enough to take that which is rightfully ours. Gwen, show them no mercy." Gwen began to assault her pupils with barrages of electric spheres. Nick flew off into the night.

•℣•

Rain stirred from his rest. Overhead was the noise of a thousand people. Terrified, he sunk to the bottom of the lake. There was an explosion. He needed to escape; they were beginning an attack. Flashes of light and sound stirred his blood and he circled the edges of the lakebed.

A slight current caught his attention and followed it to a wall of stone. There was a river on the other side of the wall that he could feel. A ball of red and purple fire erupted above the water and Rain swam fast to the other side of the lake.

Deep inside of himself he found he could influence the water and used this new gift to speed himself like a falcon diving down onto its prey. The water itself propelled him with enough speed and force to crack the concrete of the wall.

Stars danced before his eyes and his shoulder ached but he rounded the lake for another attempt to free himself from the war that was brewing just above the water. Screams of terror now fueled his mad dash. The concrete wall exploded in a cacophony of water and stone. A great wall of water sped downstream to the unguarded city.

·٧·

The zoo had cleared out hours ago. Despite the zoo remaining open during the holiday, only Morgan and a very small, limited staff remained. She never cared for fireworks, so she chose to spend the day with her friends at the zoo.

She was no closer to finding Matthew than she had been this morning. The tracking spell she had cast in the afternoon was a complete failure. The pendulum she was using continued to circle the map. She even tried with a map of the state, and then of the U.S. She originally thought that she was doing the spell wrong, but it had no trouble locating Kaleb and Nick.

She and the bear had been discussing how someone could disappear overnight. They feared the worst. "*I hate to admit it, but you're right. I can't think of any other reason why it wouldn't have worked. Matthew's dead.*"

The bear began to speak, but her mind-voice went silent. "*Something has happened,*" the she-bear said to Morgan. "*The earth is shaking.*"

Morgan could feel the anxiety of the animals in their cages. She couldn't understand the sense of dread that overcame her. They were in the Midwest. They didn't get earthquakes. She had no choice but to get these animals to safety.

In a frenzy, she rushed through the zoo, freeing the animals. She could feel the tension rising. The she-bear stayed by her side and helped by crashing through some of the enclosures and frightening the animals into running. They made an amazing team.

.▼.

Nick had decided he was going to watch from the tallest of the buildings downtown. Carefully he weaved his flight pattern around the rockets that were being shot into the air.

The show was amazing from his perch on top of the building. Something in the distance caught his eye. He saw the crumbling dam and could feel fear growing in the air.

Nick cloaked himself in shadow and dropped from the building, riding his staff like a broom. Outside his cloak of darkness he was a drop of ink in the night sky.

The crowds were starting to stir as people were fleeing. It was pandemonium as he hovered just above one of the bridges; the sounds of screams covered the growing rumble. Nick turned just in time to see an eight-foot high wall of water speeding down the river. He smiled and said to himself, "Dinner time."

.▼.

Kaleb had been sitting at home worrying all day. He hated that Walter hadn't mastered magic. People got out of hand on holidays and Walter would

289

be right in the middle of it all. *When Bears Attack* was interrupted by an emergency broadcast.

"We interrupt your regularly scheduled programming to bring you live coverage from Red Gorge Dam." The picture shifted to an image of a crumpled dam with water gushing from a gaping hole at its base.

"If you live in any of these areas." The image flipped quickly to a map with half the city covered in red. "You are urged to immediately evacuate and seek higher ground. Police are reporting six to ten feet of water." Kaleb didn't wait for him to finish and stepped into the shadows.

•⁊•

Nick took a moment to project his thoughts into the staff. Lifedrinker was still screaming for her release. "*Silence! If you vow to serve me, you will feast tonight.*" She made a vow that he certainly didn't trust, but in good faith channeled a life cord into the staff for her to feed upon.

She provided him the knowledge of a spell that would sustain the wall of water and allow for more destruction. With her assistance Nick cast a spell like a net around the wave and rode it along the river.

The vampire weaved between crumpling houses and falling power lines as he rode just above the wave on his staff. He was drunk with power as he devoured the lives of the terrified masses.

Some would say they died of a heart attack, some by drowning, but Nick would know they mostly died at his hands. He lost himself to the slaughter. After thirty kills, he stopped keeping track and just kept feeding. Every nerve in his body was alive. He was no longer just the most powerful man in the world. He was the world. There were no individuals; they were all a part of him. The life-cords he severed and consumed were gifts, reward for his greatness.

Lifedrinker amplified his abilities. Together their reach was long, and their mouths were hungry. Her presence joined with him as they flew above the expanding lake that was once a city.

A two story house on a hill was ripped from its foundation along with the three inside. It toppled into the river. He ended their lives before they could die on their own. Rows of cars were stuck on a bridge as the wave crashed into it and flung them into its hungry maw. Nick cackled aloud as he extinguished fifty lives at once.

Water roared beneath him as they twisted around the river bend. He had only been to Red Gorge Lake once and remembered it containing enough water for this to last hours.

His fingers crackled with magic. A ball of lightning had formed in his hands without a conscious thought. He could hear and see and smell everything around him all at once and it didn't overwhelm him with its vastness. He was that vastness.

Fires were erupting from downed power lines and homes were seeing the full spectrum of fire and flood. When they passed by a gas station he threw the ball of electricity at it and lit up the sky with fire. Nick didn't want to watch the world burn; he wanted to strike the match.

•¶•

Kaleb traveled so quickly through Limbo that he felt it was almost instantaneous. People were running. Some had fallen and were being trampled. With great pains, he calmed his mind and focused on Walter.

Magic flowed into his staff. He took to heart the lesson he learned from Nick and let his need guide his spell. As soon as he had a lock on Walter's location, he stepped back into shadow and arrived in his car.

The car was underwater. Somewhere above them was the bridge he was knocked from. Walter jumped when Kaleb popped in out of nowhere but threw his arms around him and started weeping, "I thought for sure I was going to die."

Kaleb put his arms around Walter. "Let's get out of here."

Before they stepped away into shadow Kaleb could see cars filled with people. Some were already dead, but others were screaming and pounding on windshields. His heart cried out for him to rescue them, but his head told him he would expose magic and put the entire world at risk.

With Walter in his arms they shifted into the shadows.

•¡•

Morgan had freed the remaining animals from their cages when she finally saw what had been making them so anxious. The animals were fleeing around her as a seven-foot-high wall of water came careening toward the zoo.

She shifted to her raven form and flew to the dam. The water level of the lake had dropped significantly but still had much farther to go. A whirlpool near the edge of the lake was growing as the water flooded out. The dam itself was under terrible strain and soon the remaining structure would crumble.

She cried out for Rain as tears formed in her eyes. This was all her fault. She had put the dragon in the lake and now he was in danger.

•¡•

292

The wall of water was losing strength. Nick and Lifedrinker released the spell holding it together just as they reached the city limits. He landed on the shore of the river and found a spot to relax. He had never felt more charged or alive before.

He was the world, he was a volcano, he was a tsunami. A mad laugh escaped him. His body was burning with power. He was a supernova in the sky. Nick savored the aftertaste of so many lives. He was the Supreme Being. He was a god. He laughed as he lay his staff next to him and rested against a mud-covered boulder. The boulder was breathing.

•٦•

Walter was furious. "You have to go back and save them," he yelled as Kaleb deposited them in Walter's apartment. "You have the power. Use it!"

"It's not that simple," Kaleb said, falling into tears. "I want to save them, but if I do it could expose magic and start a civil war."

"Kaleb, that's insane. If you have the power, you should use it for good. You're just as bad as Morgan!" Walter made a move for the door.

"How could you say that to me? I am a good person! It's a little more complicated than just running in and throwing spells around! What happens if someone figures out that magic is back and decides to burn us all at the stake?"

Walter counted to three. He knew Kaleb was trying to do the right thing and he wouldn't get anything accomplished by letting his own frustration color his words. "Okay, I get that you're just trying to do what you think is right but we need to think outside the box a little." He thought for a second, "Can you glamor?"

His mouth fell open. "You really have been listening. I don't think I could love you any more than I do right now. Yes, I can glamor. What's the plan?"

•፣•

The car was beginning to fill up with water. Her mom and dad were unconscious and she was trying hard to be brave. She could see through the windshield that there were many more people stuck inside their cars, trying desperately to get free.

Though her life had been short, she thought she had been good, so she didn't understand why this was happening. She started to pray, pleading with God to save her mom, dad, and those that were trapped in the other cars.

Water had filled the car, forcing her to hold her breath, but just before her eyes had closed she saw a bright light and two angels. One took her and the other her parents into its arms. The hands of the angels met and she looked up into brilliant blue eyes. After another flash of light there was darkness.

•፣•

Morgan returned to the zoo to find the animals had all fled and the wall of water that had terrified them so much had already passed. Sitting atop a hill was the she-bear waiting patiently for her return. She flew in to greet the bear and returned to her human form.

"*Your plan was successful, Shaman. The water rushed in and covered our tracks. They are free. It was brave of you to create such destruction, for without destruction we will never return this world to its rightful state.*"

She didn't know how to respond. This may not have been her plan, but it accomplished her goal. "But, I didn't mean to hurt so many."

294

"*There are too many humans in this world. You are merely thinning the herd. Death is a part of nature and it's time for humans to be a part of nature once again. The only way for man to be one with the land is to have a predator. Shaman, will you be that predator?*"

Without hesitation, she answered, "*Yes.*"

"*Then you may join me in my form. Be one with me.*"

•⁊•

It was so dark that Nick could not see on what he had stopped to rest. He held up his staff to shine its cold, gray light on what he had taken to be a boulder. He gasped.

Lying unconscious on the beach was a majestic blue dragon. He was torn. For the last thirty minutes he had gorged on death, but his thirst was insatiable. He wanted so badly to sip on this creature's life. On the other hand, this dragon might just be what the House of Gray needed to be an unstoppable force.

He focused his mind into the staff to address the demon within, "*Lifedrinker.*"

Her words were laced with delirious pleasure, "*I have not feasted so well since the War of Mu.*"

Nick had no idea what she was going on about so he ignored her comment. "*Yeah, whatever. I think I found something you might be interested in eating.*"

She laughed.

"*Did you notice the dragon?*"

The voice in his mind went cold, "*There is no better treat in this world. You will not be able to drink its life while it remains in dragon form. Keep it away from its element and kill it when it returns to human form.*"

"*Human form? Is this another ability that can be stolen?*" Nick's mouth curled into a grin.

"*Oh yes, my pet, dragon form is one of the most powerful abilities. You must steal its ability when it shifts back to human form; only then can it be done.*"

Nick carefully prodded the sleeping dragon with the end of his staff. "*What do you mean, keep it away from its element?*"

Again she laughed. "*You may have the upper hand, trapping me in this staff, but why should I help you?*"

It was Nick's turn to laugh. "*Because if you don't, I will find a way to not just trap you, but to destroy you.*"

The levity in her voice faded. "*Many have tried. What makes you think you can?*"

He grinned. "*Let's just say I've been working on a little spell that would allow me to possess your mind. Every time I channeled you, I got a little bit more of what I needed to make it work. From there it'll only be a matter of time before I find a way to destroy you.*"

Anger and defiance responded, "*I'm not so sure you want in my mind.*"

Nick felt more powerful than ever. His spell to trap Lifedrinker in the staff was strong enough to survive at least until his death. "*Enough of your games, Lifedrinker! You're trapped, or have you forgotten? The only way you will ever feed is by my hand.*"

She was quiet as she considered her options. "*Very well. There are four types of dragons, each associated with one of the primal elements: fire,*" *water, sky, and earth. The transformation is tied to being immersed within their element. If they leave their key element for too long they will transform back to human form. What color was your dragon?"*

Nick scraped the mud from the scales with his staff. *"Blue."*

"A water dragon. I do hope you learn these things quickly or you will never make it without my help. And in the future, I may not be so helpful."

"Whatever," he said out loud.

He wondered how long it would take it to regain consciousness and slip back into the river. He tried in vain to steal the dragon's chakras, but there was a powerful shield blocking him.

In a sudden realization, he scowled. He had never actually stolen someone's abilities. According to Lifedrinker the only time that a vampire could capture abilities was right as he wrenched the life-cord from their bodies.

He was going to need practice. In a stroke of brilliance, he chose his target. Morgan.

•⸙•

Geoffroi woke up, cold and wet, on the banks of the river. He had been traveling day and night in search of Matthew and still had found no trace. His mind was foggy and he could not remember how he ended up where he was.

There were seven bodies strewn along the river bank. He looked down at his hands; they were a whitish blue color. His heart had ceased beating and his lungs were completely filled with water. The magic that kept his body moving had not failed him.

He pounded on his chest to expel the water from his lungs and when he finished took a moment to get his heart started again. This time was more difficult than the first.

When he had finished reviving himself, he went to the nearest body and checked for signs of life. The woman he checked had a faint pulse and shallow, almost imperceptible, breaths. He noticed the cross around her neck. He frowned.

The inner stirrings of David were completely gone. He felt no sympathy for this woman. How many witches and heretics did the church drown? He turned around to look at the other bodies strewn about. Dusting the sand from his hands he stood up and walked away.

The sorcerer and the shaman had abandoned him. It was time to make his own mark in this world. Starting now the Christians would pay for their crimes.

His first order of business was to steal the spell that gave life to the corpse he inhabited. He would steal the Hope Diamond and raise an army. He knew where to find his brothers who also died on that fateful day: the catacombs of Rome.

The Holy Roman Empire had fallen, but her children still lived. Geoffroi's goal now was to fix that. He had no allies in the world of flesh and blood, though once he had his hands on the Hope Diamond he would have an unstoppable army.

Geoffroi turned around and started his walk back to Morgan's. He knew exactly which of the rubbings from Saint Patrick's Library he would steal. Perhaps he would take them all. After all, the others didn't even speak Gaelic. He would teach himself magic and then, when he was ready, he would declare war.

·⊤·

Morgan never walked to her mother's house from the city before, but she knew better than to ask for Kaleb's help. It was going to be a long journey. She said a silent blessing for Rain to be kept safe. Though it was a low magic spell, she hoped it could still make a difference.

The walk was long and arduous but the she-bear provided excellent company. They discussed different means of bringing man back to a peaceful relationship with nature. Morgan had taken to calling her Winnie, though the bear didn't get the reference.

The sun was beginning to peek above the horizon as they finally reached the house. She opened the door to a litter box. The smell of ammonia was so thick she started to cough.

"Geoffroi?" There was no answer. She called out for Mercedes.

"*Where the hell have you been?*" Mercedes said from the top of the stairs. "*I had to eat mice. Mice! Geoffroi took off after you and the dragon went on your walk and I have no thumbs!*"

"I'm sorry Mercedes, I had no idea. I'll get this cleaned up. After I do, I'll go get my things and move in. I doubt I'll be going back to work anytime soon." Winnie poked her head around Morgan to get a look into the house.

Mercedes froze mid-step. She puffed up and arched her back. A yowl formed at the back of her throat. "*What the hell is that?*"

"*Oh, this is my new friend, Winnie. It'll be a nice change to have another spirit animal around here that you can't eat.*"

"*Well, she can't stay here,*" Mercedes said, regaining her composure.

Morgan crossed her arms. "I'm not asking your permission."

·⊤·

As the first light of day reached Nick, he noticed the dragon's breath had become quite labored. It still had not awoken. Patiently, he waited and after another couple of hours his patience was rewarded.

The dragon's body began to shift and mutate and warp. Nick had to look away as to not become nauseous. When it was all over, a man now lay unconscious on the sandy beach of the river.

A smile crossed over Nick's face as he recognized him. "Now isn't this a surprise?"

•⊺•

Matthew woke up in a strange bed. He couldn't move, but he wasn't tied down. The ceiling above him was his only view. It was filthy and had water stains. This was no hospital. Panic rose in his blood as he tried desperately to move.

"I see our little friend is awake," Nick came into view above him. "I do hope you're comfortable as I have no intention of making you any more than you already may or may not be. Oh, I'm sorry, was there something you wanted to say?"

A pressure on his throat was lifted, "You're Morgan's friend," he croaked. "What did you do to me?"

Nick chuckled. "Friend is a word that gets thrown around so loosely these days, wouldn't you agree? Are we friends on Facebook? Sure. Have we known each other for several years and used to hang out several times a week? I guess. Is her death the key to my stealing your ability? You bet-cha!"

"That's ridiculous, I don't have any special abilities. I'm just a high school history teacher." He shocked himself. "Holy shit, I remember."

The vampire didn't seem to notice or care about Matthew's sudden revelation, "I'm sorry, Nick's not here right now. If you'd like to leave a message." He leaned in close and whispered menacingly, "Don't."

Nick walked out of Matthew's field of vision, and then he heard his voice at the foot of the bed. "My name is Lucian. The House of Gray calls me Lord Father but you can call me the last person who will ever see you alive."

"Why are you doing this to me?" Matthew strained against his invisible bonds, but the only part of his body that would respond was his voice.

"You've already forgotten? I just said why a second ago. You really should have that memory problem checked out. Maybe some ginseng will clear that right up, though most likely not. I'm here to kill you my dear boy. I want your power."

"I already told you, I don't have any …" he trailed off. The image of flying above tree tops on a cold cloudy night rushed into his mind. Sharp claws. The feeling of rain on scales. "Power."

"I know what you are," Nick said darkly from the foot of the bed.

Matthew couldn't bring himself to admit what memories came unbidden, "Say it."

Nick laughed. "I'm the one giving the orders here, not you."

He closed his eyes. "Dragon."

Deep down, he had hoped the memories weren't true. Saying it aloud caused the truth to reverberate through his body and more memories returned. "You want to steal my power."

"Why, if he isn't catching on? Yes. I want your ability to shift into dragon form. Before I go trying to yank your little beast out of you, I have to get some practice. These things are delicate, you see. I can't go doing brain surgery if I've never eaten a brain, now can I?"

Matthew whispered, "You're insane."

"I'm not insane." Nick laughed a maniacal laugh. He whispered in Matthew's ear, "I'm eccentric."

•

Kaleb was soaking wet when he finally arrived back at Walter's apartment. He had left Walter downtown to be "found" by a rescuer. They decided that it would be the best way to avoid any suspicion.

Kaleb was exhausted. He had never spent so much time going in and out of shadow carrying people while holding a spell in place.

The television was still on from the night before and the scenes of devastation were terrible. Homes had been ripped from their foundations and carried downstream, mud and silt covered the streets that remained, and a giant putrid lake replaced the downtown.

The news reporter said in a shaky voice, "Some are calling this the most devastating disaster in recent history. Hundreds reported dead while a thousand more are still missing. It is still unknown if this was the result of a faulty dam or an act of terrorism. Back to you, Tom."

Morgan's words from the funeral home reverberated in his mind. She did say she wanted to watch the world burn. Was she capable of something like this? His stomach was uneasy as his head and heart responded in unison with a resounding yes.

The signs were all there. A mysterious explosion caused a dam to crumble on the fourth of July, her least favorite holiday. She told David's girlfriend they were forming a group called Gaea's Fist that was going to bring the world back to its natural state. What if this was her first strike?

This was all crazy. He was beginning to get as paranoid as Morgan. He reached for his phone and realized it had been in his pocket the entire time. It was ruined.

Kaleb sighed. Though he could go visit Morgan now and ask her if she had any involvement, he would rather do it over the phone. He really hated confrontation and was fairly certain that asking her about it could open up to a world of screaming, finger pointing, and accusations.

It really had been a long night. He rubbed his temples at the headache forming behind his eyes and dreaded what tomorrow would bring. Kaleb decided to take a short nap and check in with Walter in a few hours. However he felt, he knew Walter must feel ten times worse.

For the first time, he acknowledged how close he came to losing Walter. He shuddered at the thought that Morgan may have had some part in it. She had always been reckless and impulsive, but there was no way he could sympathize with her if she was involved. This was a blatant act of terrorism and mass murder.

Regrets began to pile on top of regrets. He should have been there more. When her mom died he should have paid closer attention to her. Blame followed blame, placed upon his own head by his own hands. If Morgan was a monster, it was his fault for not being there to catch her before she dove off the deep end.

Was Austin all right? Did he even care? As much as he hated his ex, he hoped that he was okay. He laid out a map of the city and a jade pendulum. Kaleb recited the words to the spell they had cast months ago. As it circled the city he held his breath. It spun around the edges of the map and then left his hand to hover briefly over the west side of town before slamming into the map. Kaleb closed his eyes and let out his breath.

⁙

Brown water stains in the ceiling tiles above him played tricks with his eyes and mind. The Rorschach-like patterns woke up memories in Matthew. After Nick had left, they were rising to the surface faster and faster. He remembered going to the lake by the Thirteen Steps Cemetery where his fiancée had drowned the year before. He remembered writing the goodbye letter to his mother, father, friends and the kids at the school.

He remembered the antidepressants and how they made him feel. The torment that filled his heart every day. The therapists that seemed more concerned with prescribing him medication than helping him deal with his loss. He remembered walking like a zombie through his own life, no longer a man but a prisoner in his own body.

Memories of planning his death, withdrawing into himself, writing the letter. Tears streamed down his eyes as he remembered stepping into the lake and letting it take him down.

It hadn't been until the water hit his lungs that he could finally feel. It was like a sudden awakening and the emotions he had bottled up erupted in a geyser. He remembered his body, wracked with pain and expanding. He remembered becoming Rain.

Matthew could do nothing but allow the tears to roll off his face. He remembered leaving the lake for the first time. Wandering the forest for hours. He remembered his body beginning to change as he struggled to breathe. The bright headlights of the car that came out of nowhere. He closed his eyes. It was his fault Anna was dead. The guilt overwhelmed him. He wanted to die, but the dragon within him wanted to live. He decided the dragon could have his life, after he told Morgan the truth.

Together We Fall

Morgan arrived at her trailer to find that Nick had let himself in. He was standing in the entry, crying. She approached cautiously. "Nick? What are you doing here?"

He sniffled a little and dried his eyes. "It's Gwen. She's dead. We were down by the river watching the fireworks when the dam broke. I'm sorry for coming here, but I didn't know where else to go. Kaleb's not answering his phone." Nick propped his staff up next to the door, dramatically threw himself onto the couch, and began sobbing.

She sighed and sat on the couch next to him, softly rubbing his back. "It's okay. I'm sorry for not letting you borrow my mom's book. Just because I got a little upset over you taking it, that doesn't make us any less friends."

He drew her into a close hug and moaned into her ear. She did her best to remind herself of Matthew. Though they hadn't really become official, she wanted to hold out and see how it went.

Nick's arms felt amazing as they held her. She put her hand on the back of his head and held him. Hadn't this always been her dream? Well except for the part about his girlfriend dying.

"Let it all out, Nick, I'm here."

Slowly, he pulled out of the embrace and stared deeply into her eyes. "I never did realize what an amazing friend you are, Morgan. There's really a beauty in you that I never did see before."

He leaned in and kissed her. Softly at first, and then it warmed into something she had never experienced before. She let herself fall into his arms and lips as she returned the kiss. Her body was wracked with pain and then froze.

Nick withdrew himself from her locked form and spat on the floor. "God, that was disgusting!" She tried to respond but her body and voice no longer functioned. She collapsed into the couch. "Not to toot my own horn, but that was Oscar-worthy, I would have to say. Oh, and don't worry, Gwen is fine. Also, not my girlfriend. I'm gay." He picked up his staff and it glowed with a bright light.

She was furious, but she was now caught in whatever plot he had devised. She chided herself and Kaleb for not trusting her conspiracy theory mind. Nick was evil, pure evil, and she had known it ever since magic returned.

In a desperate attempt, she tried connecting her mind to Rain, or Mercedes, or Winnie, or even Kaleb but they were so far away and she had never tried communicating like this before.

Nick smiled at her. "You should be very happy to know that your death will be serving a much greater purpose. Once I feed on your life and steal your ability to shape-shift and speak with animals, I'll be able to do the same to Matthew."

Though her face didn't express the shock she felt, Nick assumed it was there. "Wait, that's right, you don't know about Matthew." He pouted. "Spoiler."

Morgan struggled against the invisible bonds that held her body. Her mind cried out for anyone. He began to feed. She could feel her life-force weakening. In a last ditch attempt, she flung her mind-voice at Nick, *"You will not have me!"*

The mental shout caught him off guard and she seized upon his moment of distraction. The staff was beneath the couch and full of magic. Within her mind she recited the words to the spell she had been practicing for months. The trailer exploded into an inferno.

The paralysis that had taken hold of Morgan was broken by her strength and her fury. The life force he had stolen was quickly replaced by the power of high magic. The damage he had done to her body was instantly healed.

A ball of fire materialized in Morgan's hand and she threw it at Nick. It exploded against an invisible barrier but managed to knock him off his feet. Morgan grabbed the staff out from under the couch. Red and yellow flames snaked up his shields. She summoned more power to her and battered his shields with another barrage of fire.

The walls of her trailer were blown apart by the blasts. In the trailer park, people were running in a panic as smaller explosions were occurring outside of the war-zone. Nick fell backwards and landed on a pile of burning laundry. Morgan continued the onslaught.

"How dare you!" she shouted at him over the roaring fire. "You think you can play with my feelings like that and not get BURNED!" As she said the last word she moved the staff through the flames, she collected them into a massive ball and hurled it at him. "Hasn't anyone ever told you?" She screamed as she threw another ball of fire at him. "Hell hath no fury like a woman scorned!"

His only choice was to run. He balled his fists and collected magic to them. He threw his fists forward and unleashed a wave of telekinetic force that threw Morgan head over heels to the other end of the burning trailer. Nick put his leg up over his staff and flew into the sky. He looked back over his shoulder to the burning chaos that once was Morgan's home. "This isn't over, bitch."

.٧.

Kaleb's stomach churned as he turned the channel on the television to a new scene of destruction. This time there was no denying Morgan's involvement. The trailer park she had lived in for the last several years was on fire. Two firemen had died in secondary explosions. He closed his eyes and rubbed his forehead.

He took his staff and stepped into the shadows.

.٧.

A lemon-yellow car sped up the drive. Morgan parked and stormed up the lawn. She dropped her staff on the ground. Morgan let out a bloodcurdling scream that cut through the peaceful afternoon like a knife.

Winnie couldn't make sense of the Shaman. She could only feel the raw emotion that was pouring out of her. Her anger was so intense that her mind-voice sounded like a hail storm during a brush fire. The she-bear approached cautiously.

An eruption of fire caused Winnie to run back onto the porch. She had never seen anything like this. The heat was intense but had no source. The grass beneath the Shaman's feet withered and burned. Winnie tried in vain to call out to her Shaman, but it made no difference. Mercedes had fled back inside.

She was terrified of what had become of her savior. The door opened and a man she had never met before stepped forward. The bear reared and growled at him. He raised his hands and backed slowly back into the house and cried, "MORGAN?"

Winnie stuck her head through the door way to get a view of what was happening inside the house and Kaleb backed up further. The cat bounded down the stairs and to her Speak-and-Spell. "F-I-X, fix, H-E-R, her."

Kaleb held his hands out in front of him and backed away from the bear that was now trying to fit through the door. He stepped on Mercedes' tail and she howled in pain.

"Sorry, Mercedes, now I'm not sure if *you've* noticed, but there's a *bear!*"

The cat looked up at him, flicked her tail and narrowed her eyes. "*Put on your big boy pants princess, we've got a crazy lady burning down the neighborhood.*"

Kaleb cautiously approached the bear who was now trying to get out of the doorway. Once Kaleb had made his way through the door, Winnie attempted very carefully to use the Speak-and-Spell, "H-I-R-Q-G-I-T-I-H." The bear gave up in frustration and gestured with its paw to Morgan.

Morgan was burning a circle of grass in the front lawn with her at the center. Kaleb's staff burst into light as he put up his shields and stepped forward. He coughed as the acrid odor of burning grass greeted him. Flames licked his shield and he could feel the heat radiating from Morgan.

"Morgan, snap out of it." Kaleb called over the roar of the flames.

She fumed at him, "Why? Are you here to steal my abilities too? Or are you here to try and sweep me back under the rug?"

When they were an arm's length apart, he stopped and pleaded, "You've got to stop this Morgan. The world isn't ready for magic. You'll put us all in danger if someone finds out."

"I bet you'd like that, wouldn't you?" The inferno intensified. "You get to go on playing house with your little husband and pretend like nothing's changed. Well *everything* has changed! If this world can't handle magic, I say fuck the world."

Kaleb was struck by that comment. "You don't mean that."

"Oh, I do mean that, Kaleb. That dam blowing up was the best thing that could have happened. Maybe people will learn not to try to contain Mother Earth! She's a little pissed! This world is going to burn, Kaleb, and I'll be fanning the flames."

Kaleb closed his eyes and his staff pulsated with sapphire light. He couldn't let her expose magic to the world. His hands rose and began to draw a series of runes into the air. Before he could finish, the fire around Morgan intensified and blasted outward, throwing Kaleb halfway across the yard.

He picked himself off the grass and dusted off his clothes, "This isn't over, Morgan. You need to get a grip, girl." He walked to the darkest of the afternoon shadows and stepped in.

⁘

The shadow realm was more vacant than usual. After that demon had been trapped, there weren't the ever-present shades lurking and waiting for him to slip up. For the first time he took his time walking through Limbo. He never had taken his time to really look around before.

His mind was going in circles about how to handle Morgan, and rather than facing his thoughts, he decided to really examine this world. Taking in his surroundings, Kaleb watched as the darkened wisps of cars passed by. Busy with his inner musings, he didn't notice the sudden appearance of several shades. Only after they had seized him and sped him off in an unknown direction did he realize he had been abducted again. He groaned, "Seriously?"

●፣●

Lifedrinker was ready for the arrival. Her demon form appeared above Kaleb, blocking the cathedral's door. Ebony wings stretched out to their fullest. She snarled at Kaleb, "I won't make the same mistake twice. You will help me escape or you will die."

Kaleb rubbed his temples. "Haven't we already established that I have no intention of helping you?"

"But this time I have the advantage. Lucian has provided me a banquet of death. I will destroy you unless you break down the wall holding me to this prison."

Hearing the name stunned him. "Hold up, what?"

●፣●

Geoffroi arrived at the first place he had ever called home since he had died centuries before. There was a freshly burned circle in the grass next to the house that he disregarded. All he cared about was grabbing as many of the rubbings they had made before someone asked him what he was doing.

A bear guarded the door but he paid it no mind. The door was wide open so he let himself in. Morgan was crying at the table with Mercedes purring in her lap.

No one paid any attention to him and it bothered him. "Do not pay me no mind," he said as he passed by Morgan. Still no one appeared to have noticed his presence. "I do hope my pungent odor of death does not bother thy delicate noses." They didn't even look up. "Well, I'll go sit in a corner until you have need of me again."

Morgan stopped crying to look up in agitation and said, "Stop being a prima donna."

"I don't even know what that means! Or have you forgotten I'm from the *middle ages!*" His frustration at being ignored had bubbled to a head and it started spilling out. "I'm just your little magical mistake, and that's all I've ever been to you! Well, I no longer require your assistance, so you can be without mine."

Morgan set her jaw and stood up from her chair. "You're right! You were a mistake! Next time I kill someone I'll make sure there isn't some insane ghost from the twelfth century lurking around waiting to jump into a new body."

He stepped forward until he was standing directly in front of her and shouted, "I beg your pardon, but if it hadn't been for my *lurking presence,* you'd be rotting in a jail for murder!"

She spoke between her teeth, "You better get out of my face before I do something that you won't like."

He glared back at her and refused to back down. "You can do nothing more to me than you already have."

A rose light flashed at the top of Morgan's staff and Geoffroi's body erupted into flames. The cat jumped out of Morgan's lap and ran for the door. The red and yellow flames licked his body and clothes. His skin reddened, flaked, and fell off. His clothes turned to ash and fell to the burning floor.

"Why are you not in pain?" she asked as she did her best to keep the fire contained to Geoffroi's body and not allow it to engulf her childhood home.

"Must be a zombie thing." He shrugged. As Geoffroi walked along the kitchen floor tiny embers fell from his person. She was losing control of the flames and they began to spread around the house. A tiny spark landed in a pile of dry, dirty laundry and quickly was ablaze.

Barefoot and naked Geoffroi made his way to the bedroom that he had called his own. He took a blanket from the bed to quench the parts of his body that were smoldering before packing his meager belongings into a small backpack. He took the rubbings of high magic spells off his desk, dressed himself, and returned to the kitchen.

"You wanted a monster," he said between burned and cracked lips. "Now you have a monster."

Morgan was still standing with her mouth wide as he passed by her. She had two glasses of water in her hand and the faucet was still running.

"I wouldn't try that little trick again, Sorceress. You may be able to conjure flames but they aren't going to stop me from wringing my hands around your neck, or running you through with a knife."

He strode to the door with confidence and upon reaching it turned to address her for the last time, "I will not be treated with such disrespect, *Sorceress*. It does not serve me to kill you, so consider yourself blessed." Geoffroi walked out into the world, nodded to the bear and the cat, and was gone.

∘⁊∘

"We need to have a little talk," Kaleb said calmly as he sat down on one of the cathedral's pews. He crossed his legs and patiently waited for the demon to stop looming menacingly above him.

Kaleb was more terrified than he would let on. He would have to bet on that something within him. It stirred within his mind and body. Over the last few months, he could sense it more and more. Whatever it was, Kaleb needed it now.

The towering demon glared at him from across the room, "Do not speak down to me, mortal." Kaleb tilted his head and waited. It glared at him, but he was solemn in his resolve. Finally, the demon caved in. "Speak."

"It would seem you need me." While he was speaking, the presence within him was working double-time for a solution to their plight. Kaleb said a short prayer to whatever was guiding his actions. "And it seems you have been burned by this person you call Lucian."

He had already connected that Lucian was Nick's vampire name, though he hadn't used it since before the time they had dated. Kaleb had no intention of letting the demon know he had connected the pieces.

Nervously the demon paced. "What do you have in mind?"

His eyes darted to the exit and back. "You want to be free of this cage? Well, obviously you need a sorcerer to do that. We both know your limits, given your ..." The presence within him surged forth and he stepped aside. "Condition."

An eyebrow the size of a dagger raised slightly. "My condition?"

"Oh Lifedrinker, you poor creature. Time does erode the memories, doesn't it?" Kaleb's body rose from the pew and his head cocked to one side as he looked up at the demon. Kaleb was mortified, but who or whatever had overtaken him seemed to be on a roll.

The demon hissed the name, "Merlin?"

Kaleb approached as Lifedrinker backed away. "Now isn't that cute. You remember me. Though I wasn't always known by that name. They really didn't do so well in making you. Did they?" Kaleb had no idea what he was talking about, but from the way the demon's fanged mouth creased he could tell Lifedrinker did.

"Kronos!"

"You remember! I'm flattered. I don't really care for that name, bad memories. I'm sure you can relate to that, can't you? I will at least commend you for how long you eluded capture after the fall."

Kaleb really wished he knew what he was talking about. Kronos was the Greek god of time, father of the Olympians. He was cast down by his own children. According to the mythology he did have it coming. Gods don't take kindly to being eaten by their father.

He was somehow inhabited by the shade of Merlin, who also happened to be Kronos. His head was spinning. Lifedrinker appeared to be connecting the dots, so Kaleb waited patiently to learn as much as he could.

They circled each other. "What's with the boy, Kronos? Is this how you've been surviving all these years? Passing from one dim-witted kid to the next."

Kaleb felt himself shrug. "You know how things go, not the right time, not the right *spell*!" With the last word Kaleb's hand flung the spell that he had been forming. A cage of thorns sprung from the floor and trapped the demon within.

She laughed and unfurled her ebony wings, tossing off the thorns. "Speaking of not the right time. I just fed you fool! I am stronger now than you have ever seen me before. I will drink the marrow from your bones." She absently rubbed her arm as one of the thorns began to worm its way into her skin.

Kaleb laughed. "Perhaps the boy is more dimwitted than I expected. I could never defeat you before, why should I think that now would be any different?"

Lifedrinker idly scratched her black skin with her clawed hand. Kaleb realized that Kronos was distracting her from the thorns that were now working their way into the demon's body. "Perhaps I should leave this one for you to finish and I will go find myself another."

Her eyes flared with anger as recognition seeped into her mind. "You're the ..." Her voice was cut off by a scream. The pain from the worming thorns reached her black heart. Her body writhed in pain.

"It's been good talking. I'm sure you'll survive my spell, but I'm late for an important meeting. You know how these things go." Kaleb's body strode to the door and back into the shadow realm.

Kaleb was ready to resume control, but it was as though there were a boulder inside his mind that stood in his way. He panicked for a moment. He thought about everyone that needed him, Walter most of all. Kaleb used his love for Walter as a crowbar to push Kronos out of the way and take back his body.

Kaleb shook his head. Nothing of that conversation made any sense. "We're going to have to talk one of these day, Kronos. If you expect to share this body, you've got some explaining to do."

•፣•

Agent Kris Sullivan stepped into the local police station. He wore a black suit and dark sunglasses. His face was cleanly shaven and his smile was pristine. Kris had been reassigned from the Smithsonian case to put his field skills to work on the biggest disaster of his lifetime.

Their leads were limited at best. A woman had been spotted the night of the incident screaming, "Dragon Reign." It wasn't much. The eye witness didn't see the woman very clearly, but their sketch artist was very good. He held the picture up again to examine it closely.

The consensus was to bring in some of the members of the Dragon Reign, but this town didn't have a connection to the notorious New York-based Asian gang, and there had never been an indication that the Dragons were terrorists. Kris had shaken his head during that meeting and put an immediate stop to that line of thinking.

He may not have much at the moment, but these things always had a way of working themselves out. He overheard a young woman in tears telling her story to one of the officers. "Please, you have to help me find David. He joined a cult! I haven't heard from him in weeks, and now this, please!"

The officer told her to fill out a missing person form, but not to get her hopes too high. Before he had a chance to hand her a clipboard, Kris was at her side. "I'm sorry to bother you, but would you mind coming with me?"

Reluctantly she followed Agent Sullivan into one of the rooms set aside for his team. "Please, have a seat, Miss ..." he paused for her to finish the sentence. His hazel eyes implored her.

She reluctantly replied, "Jackie. Jackie Kinser."

"Well, Ms. Kinser, I am Agent Sullivan and I am very interested in hearing about what happened with David. Would you mind starting from the beginning?"

She relaxed quite a bit and recapped what she could remember. "Well, we were engaged to be married this fall, but out of nowhere he started getting distant. He wasn't returning any calls, he wasn't answering his phone. And it wasn't just my calls he was ignoring. Even his mother couldn't get a hold of him."

She pushed back the bangs from her eyes. "I called his work and they said he was still going in, but he was acting a little strange. Nothing major, just saying things that seemed out of character. I decided that I was going to check in on him, so I went to his apartment after work.

"I thought he was on drugs, he was acting so weird. And then she came. Apparently his high priestess. There were three of them that just showed up at the door right after I got there. Almost like they had been watching him and saw me, that's how quick they showed up."

"Do you think you could describe them to me if I got one of our sketch artists in here?" She nodded. "For now, I want you to tell me what happened next."

"At first I thought he was cheating on me with the girl, though she wasn't even close to cute. I mean, she didn't seem like his type, if you know what I mean."

"I think I understand, go on." Agent Sullivan took notes as she spoke.

"Well, they all stormed in and told David to pack his bags. She claimed her mother had died and that they needed someone to take care of the house. Though it all sounded like a load of bull to me.

"They said that he was part of their 'new religion' that was all about bringing the world back to its natural state or some garbage. David never cared about the environment, he was a total litterbug."

Kris jotted down more key details but never lost the eye contact he had been maintaining with her. He nodded and she continued.

"They brainwashed him somehow. There is just no way he'd run off to join some hippie cult. Especially one with such a ridiculous name, the Church of Gaea's Fist."

He wrote down the name of the group and underlined it a few times. "Had you ever seen any of these people before that night?"

"No, but David did mention that he went to high school with them," she offered. "Do you think you'll be able to help me find David?"

"You have been very helpful. We will put our resources into finding him as well as the others you mentioned. If you still have a moment, I'd like you to visit with our sketch artist."

She got up to leave but before she reached the door he asked her one last question, "Oh, Miss Kinser, one more thing. What high school did David go to?"

•٦•

There was a resounding banging on Walter's door. He looked over at Kaleb and cracked opened the door. On the other side were three men in black suits.

"Officer Walter Graham?"

"Yes?" Walter responded hesitantly.

"Please come with us down to the station. We'd like to have a word with you. Do you happen to know the whereabouts of Kaleb Thomas?"

"What's this about?" Walter positioned himself in front of the door so they couldn't see Kaleb sitting just inside.

The man at the door took off his sunglasses and attempted to look inside. "We just have some questions for you. Please be cooperative and this will all go smoothly."

Kaleb put his hands on Walter's shoulder and addressed the men. "It's okay, I have nothing to hide."

The ride to the station was quiet. Walter attempted a couple of times to prod for information about what this was about, but no one would answer his questions. Walter held Kaleb's hand and tried to reassure him, but it was Walter who was more worried about where this was going.

The black van parked in front of Walter's precinct building. They were led to separate rooms. Kaleb's face remained impassive and solemn. He was seated in the middle of the room and was left to wait.

He had watched enough police and law shows to know this was part of the game. He would wait while they observed him. Kaleb refused to play that game. He waited patiently on the wooden chair, no pacing, and no grumbling.

After fifteen minutes of waiting, the door opened and a man with dark sunglasses entered. "Kaleb Thomas," the man stated plainly as he reached out and shook Kaleb's hand. "I'm Agent Sullivan. I bet you're wondering what you're doing here."

Kaleb resisted the urge to cross his arms. He knew a skilled interrogator would see that as being guarded. "Among other things."

"Well I don't like to play games, Kaleb. Do you mind if I call you Kaleb?"

Kaleb smiled. He responded pleasantly, "I don't mind."

"Well, Kaleb, I'm currently investigating the Red Gorge Dam incident and your name came up in connection with a new religious group. I'm sure you can understand how that would raise some suspicions." Agent Sullivan flashed him a gleaming smile.

"Sure," he replied calmly.

"Please don't get me wrong, I know that new religious groups are founded every day. I myself don't really have one that I follow, but I do believe in a higher power. What I'm trying to say is, that while a majority of new religious groups don't turn violent, it's the ones that do that we need to keep an eye out for. Would you agree?"

Kaleb nodded. "Absolutely."

"Would you mind telling me a little bit more about the Church of Gaea's Fist?"

He steadied his nerves. In high school he won state speech for his individual improvisation. This time there was much more at stake. "Well, the Church of Gaea's Fist is a peaceful organization whose goal is to harbor an appreciation for the earth and create stewards for the land."

Agent Sullivan nodded. "Yes, a nice pamphlet answer, but you have to admit, Gaea's Fist doesn't really sound very non-violent."

"Oh, well I'm really just an initiate. Morgan is our High Priestess and she was the one in charge of naming the group. We all thought it had a nice ring to it." He was really stretching now. This was not going well.

"Don't get me wrong, it certainly has a great ring to it. I just have to wonder if this is more of a militant order, with a name like that at least."

Kaleb made a mental note to strangle Morgan for her choice of fake church names. He didn't have much time to think; this was a very deadly game he was playing. If he asked for a lawyer he'd be admitting guilt. He was on his own. "I really hadn't thought of it like that."

Agent Sullivan made a few more notes and changed his line of questioning. "Do you happen to know the whereabouts of Miss Daniels?"

Kaleb chewed on his lower lip. "Well I'd assume she'd be at her mom's house. My phone ended up getting wet when the dam broke so I haven't talked to her since. Walter and I were helping people get to safety."

"That's very noble of you. We sent some cars by, but the place recently burned down. Oddly enough, so was the trailer park she resided in. That's a strange coincidence, wouldn't you say?"

Agent Sullivan gestured to the television at the back of the room, "And there's this." The picture was difficult to make sense of as the video was from four security cameras.

"This is footage from the Baen Park Zoo. It's a little hard to see, so let me zoom in for you." Agent Sullivan pressed some buttons on the remote and paused the footage of a shadowy figure opening the gate to the giraffe enclosure. He magnified the image several times. There was no doubt in his mind that it was Morgan.

Kaleb had to stop protecting her, and right now he needed to protect Walter and the world. "Agent Sullivan, do you have a first name?"

"Kris."

"A very nice name. Kris, I don't like to play games either. If Morgan is involved with something, I am unaware of what that is. I joined the church to do good work. You have raised a lot of suspicions in me as well about what she's been up to."

He tapped his pen on the desk. "Go on."

"I'd like to offer my assistance in helping you track her down. If she has committed a crime, she needs to be held responsible for those crimes. I understand if you are skeptical or hesitant to let us out of your sight, so I want you to know as a show of good faith you may keep a watchful eye over Walter and me."

"A very generous offer." They shook hands. "You have a deal, Mister Thomas, and forty-eight hours."

They were escorted back to Walter's apartment. As soon as the door closed Walter began to panic. "What the hell was that about? That was the FBI. Kaleb, what are you involved in?"

Kaleb raised an eyebrow and motioned with his head to the bathroom. "Let's take a shower, babe. Right now I just want to let my nerves settle down. Will you take a shower with me?"

Walter wasn't sure where Kaleb was going with this, but nodded his head. Kaleb lit two candles and sat them on the bathroom counter. He shut of the lights and got in the shower. Once Walter had joined him they shifted to the shadow realm.

"We can't say anything. There is no doubt in my mind that surveillance cameras and microphones are all over your apartment right now. I don't think they'd be the type to set one up in the shower, but I still couldn't take any chances."

Walter's body and voice trembled. "What do we do? I could lose my job if they even suspect that we had something to do with the dam explosion."

"I promised that I would bring Morgan in for questioning."

"She'll never go for that; you know how she is," Walter responded skeptically.

"You've got to trust me on this." Kaleb leaned in and kissed Walter as they slipped back into the material world.

•⦙•

Agent Sullivan entered the surveillance van. "What's our status?"

"Our love birds are taking a candlelit shower."

Kris put the headphones on. "How long have they been in there?"

"About twenty minutes."

Kaleb was heard saying, "Walter, where's your phone?"

They saw Walter on the main monitor pick up his phone from the coffee table and hand it to Kaleb.

323

"Morgan, it's Kaleb; we all need to get together and work some things out. Meet me by the tree where we spread your mom's ashes at noon."

Kris waved his hand for some help, but no one appeared to know to what that was in reference. The call was repeated, this time to someone by the name of Nick. Again Kris waved his hands for more information and his team scrambled to connect the pieces.

Kaleb and Walter got dressed and left the apartment. They rushed to catch them on the other surveillance devices they had installed but were halted by a loud knock on the back door. Agent Morrison answered the knock.

Kaleb and Walter were standing behind the van. Kaleb addressed Agent Sullivan, "Not sure if you heard, just wanting to make sure to keep you in the loop. We're going to Morgan's mom's house, the one that burned down today. You know the way. I'd really appreciate it if you guys would stay back a little though. I don't want her to get suspicious and make a run for it. She gets very paranoid sometimes."

Walter put his arm around Kaleb's. "Ready, love?"

"As ready as I'll ever be." They walked off together. Kris hurried to get his team prepared for what they were about to do. He was impressed with Kaleb and Walter. Not many people had the audacity to knock on the surveillance van. His men were as prepared as they'd ever be. They held true to their word and trailed Walter and Kaleb from a safe non-threatening distance.

Agent Morrison looked back at Kris. "I have a really bad feeling about this."

∴

The drooping ceiling above him began to drip on Matthew as he stared up at it. Nick had left him here for several hours. He had relived so many of his memories that he was exhausted. The most important thing right now was to free himself and save Morgan. From there, the dragon could have his life and he would fade away.

The rust-colored drops that were forming on the ceiling and falling onto his hand gave him a warm strength. It started in his hand and worked its way through his entire body. The feeling flowed through his veins and to his heart. There was a power in water that he never truly paid attention to before.

Water was the sustainer of life, yet a destructive force. Water could level a city, but without that same water, the city would never have emerged. Water can wear away the most beautiful of things that man can create, yet makes things of its own more beautiful than anything man could make.

He remembered how ice could slowly crack the greatest of walls and an idea struck him. He focused on the water drops that had collected on his hand. He felt them enter his body. Back and forth he willed them frozen and willed them molten. Though it was painful, it could be his only chance of escaping Nick's spell of paralysis.

Slowly and carefully, he conjured up an image in his mind of the Great Wall of China. He focused in on a small section that would represent Nick's spell. As he willed the drops of water to freeze and thaw, he imagined a crack beginning to form in the wall.

After several minutes he found his efforts were rewarded. He had control over his left hand and feeling was beginning to return to his arm. He worked harder and faster. The ice his mind had formed into a glacier that was making its way toward the Great Wall.

The glacier approached slowly, reluctantly. As it moved closer the ground began to groan and the sound reverberated through Matthew's mind. His veins pulsed with effort and just as he thought he could take no more, his body shifted and contorted. The three story farmhouse caved in on itself as a dragon tore its way to the sky.

•٢•

Morgan and Winnie sat on the edge of the barrier between the clearing and the tree. She had no intention of letting Kaleb or Nick near it. After Nick had tried to steal the grimoire it had never left her side. The last few hours she scoured the book for defensive and offensive spells. This was war.

Kaleb arrived, followed shortly after by Nick, Gwen, and seven others she didn't recognize. Winnie and Mercedes stood stoically by her side. Each faction stood their separate ground.

•٢•

Walter sat in the car parked in front of the husk of what was Morgan's mother's house. He reluctantly agreed to stay away in case it got ugly, but was beginning to regret that decision.

A million different outcomes played on repeat in his head. Kaleb could die. Kaleb could be forced to kill and never be the same. They could work out their differences and Morgan could agree to go with Agent Sullivan. That last one didn't seem as likely.

•٢•

326

The surveillance van was parked down the road. They had a clear view of Kaleb leaving the car and Walter waiting behind. No one had any idea why Kaleb had strolled out into the woods. Agent Morrison became more and more vocal about his bad feeling. Kris tried to call in support to surround the woods, but there wasn't enough manpower.

He got out of the van and marched up the street to where Walter was impatiently waiting.

•⁘•

"So glad you called this meeting, Kaleb. My friends and I were starting to wonder when you were going to come out and play," Nick called to Kaleb as he and his friends milled around the clearing.

"I'm not here to play, Nick, and these people aren't your friends. We are," Kaleb called back.

Morgan snorted. "Speak for yourself!"

Nick said with mock sadness in his voice, "I'm sorry if I upset you dumpling. As you can see, Gwen is just fine. I know you were just beside yourself with grief while you were sticking your tongue down my throat."

Kaleb reeled. "Wait, what?"

"Stay out of it Kaleb." Morgan sneered back at Nick.

"I think I've been doing way too much of that," Kaleb said, throwing his hands in the air. "Would someone *please* fill me in?"

"Your *friend* here tried to kill me. He plans to do the same with Matthew and I'd hazard a guess to say he wants to kill you, too." Morgan's staff glowed with a bright rose light.

327

Nick shrugged his shoulders. "You got me. Now if you'd just so kindly submit, this won't have to get messy. Nine to two, doesn't look so good for you. You might as well just give up now."

Kaleb tried to inject some sense of reason back into his friend. "Hold up, Nick, what's gotten into you? You used to be such a good person. You were going to be a nurse."

"I still might. It'd be a great way to get dinner without getting caught."

Kaleb still couldn't grasp what Nick was suggesting. "Please, Nick, come back to us. This isn't you."

"You still don't believe that I'm really a vampire. How many more people do I have to snuff out of existence before you will believe me? What a banquet I had. There were so many terrified cattle running around." He paused and cocked his head to one side. "All I had to do was *feed*."

"Wait, you were behind the dam blowing up, I thought it was—"

Before Kaleb could finish his sentence Morgan snapped back, "Oh, you thought it was me? That figures! I'm over here trying to do the right thing and I'm being accused by my best friend of being a terrorist. You know what, maybe I should be a terrorist! It actually was me, Nick had nothing to do with it. I put a dragon in that lake. There you have it. You said it yourself, Kaleb, the world isn't ready for magic. I say let's level the playing field. Wipe out a few cities, maybe I'll start with New York!"

Nick smiled. "Now you're speaking my language."

"Shut your mouth! I don't want anything to do with you or your ridiculous little vampires. Why don't you go back to being all emo and drinking tomato juice like you used to?"

That apparently struck the wrong cord with Nick. He shut his mouth and narrowed his eyes. "You'll be crying to your dead mommy once I steal your little boyfriend's ability to shape-shift into a dragon." Kaleb was stunned so Nick said with feigned innocence, "Oh you didn't know? Matthew's a dragon. Well, he won't be for long. Not once I get some practice stealing abilities from the two of you. I'd really hate to botch that one. Who knows when I'd get another chance to steal that ability?"

"Stop it, Nick, this isn't you!" Kaleb cried.

"No, you stop it, Kaleb. While you were busy being lovey-dovey with Officer Graham, I made some new friends. This is going nowhere. House of Gray, take them down." Nick stepped back as the others stepped forward.

Kaleb barely had time to draw up his shields as balls of lightning struck both Morgan and Kaleb. The force of the blast rocked them to their knees. He could smell his hair being burned by the surge and Morgan was not faring better. From Kaleb's vantage, it appeared that her pants had been singed by the barrage of electricity.

•⋎•

Walter couldn't take it any longer. He grabbed his handgun from the glove box and got out of the car just as Agent Sullivan was starting up the driveway.

Kris ran the rest of the way up the drive and caught Walter by the arm, "What's going on out there?"

"I don't know, but I'm tired of waiting around to find out."

Walter and Kris ran through the woods. Kris kept trying to get Walter to explain what was going on, but all Walter would say was, "Make sure your safety's off."

•⋎•

Winnie had taken a direct hit from a ball of lightning and was unconscious on the ground next to Morgan. She was barely breathing. Morgan didn't have time to check on her, but she could still sense her mind. Morgan thought to her, *"Hang in there, Winnie."*

Morgan countered the first volley with one of her own. She may not have mastered lightning, but she was getting really good at fire. Anger boiled over within her again and she directed it to the nearest vampire. He burst into flames and she lobbed a ball of it at Nick who sidestepped.

Kaleb was being attacked on three sides: from Gwen, a black-haired girl, and a pimply kid. He and Morgan might not be on the best terms, but right now they were fighting for their lives. Morgan shape-shifted into a bear and pounded down the hill, barreled over the kid, and mauled him.

Nick slammed Morgan and Kaleb with a wave of concussive force, knocking them off their feet and the wind out of their lungs. He was dancing around like a jack-in-the-box. "Oh, this is just so much fun!"

Kaleb saw it before Nick, but it was still too late. Walter stepped out into the clearing and raised his gun toward Nick. Nick turned his head and smiled, the staff in his hands flared brightly. A gunshot ran out, but it was Walter that was bleeding. The gun had exploded in his hands.

It all happened in slow motion for Kaleb. Walter looked down at his hands as they were covered in blood, their eyes met, and he stumbled backwards. The metal of the gun was lodged in his chest as he fell.

"Didn't anyone ever tell you, don't bring a gun to a mage fight?!" Nick screamed as he summoned a ball of lightning to throw at Walter.

Before Kaleb could react, Nick threw the ball of electricity at Walter's already bleeding chest. Kaleb screamed with anger. He called forth as much magical might as he could and conjured four dozen knives of ice from the sky.

Ice shattered as it struck Nick's shield, spraying shards into the air like a broken snow cone machine.

A deafening roar from above halted the melee.

•┬•

Kris had been following close behind Walter, but when they stepped into a mist-covered section of the forest, Walter was gone. Agent Sullivan had seen his share of fog before, but this was so thick it clung to him.

There was something very strange going on and Kris didn't like it. The hair on his arms and neck was standing on end. No matter what direction he thought he was going, he always ended up right in the same spot that he started. He may not have been a religious man, but he did believe in the supernatural and this was definitely supernatural.

A loud sound of beating wings came from somewhere up above him, but he could still see nothing. The blood in his veins turned into ice as fear struck his core. A great roar sounded above him. He bent down to one knee and prayed.

•┬•

The vampires looked up to see a mighty dragon circling overhead. Gwen shouted to them, "Let's get out of here! Nick can fight his own battles. Who's with me?"

Nick concentrated on his shields as Morgan pressed down on him with balls of fire and Kaleb with lances of ice. He managed to glare at Gwen as they turned tail and ran. Nick shouted, "Enough!" The staff in his hands flashed brightly. Nick shot up into the air and barely avoided being chomped down on by the dragon before rocketing off into the distance.

The ground shook as Rain landed next to Morgan. Rain stood stoically as he viewed the carnage wrought by Nick. The dragon raised his head to the sky and roared.

The dead lay in pools of red. Walter, Winnie, and two of Nick's allies. Tears ran down Kaleb's face as he ran to where Walter had fallen. His body shook uncontrollably as despair overtook him. He took Walter's head from off the ground and laid it gently in his lap.

Despite what his eyes told him, he refused to believe what he saw. Shards of metal were buried in Walter's chest, and his blood pooled on the ground below him. "Wake up, baby. I'm here now. You're going to be okay." Kaleb patted Walter's face. "Wake up."

Kaleb drew magic to his staff and began reciting the words of a healing spell. The soft blue light of Kaleb's staff fell softly on Walter's peaceful face. His eyes brimmed with tears as he tried over and over. After the third repetition he threw his staff to the ground and attempted CPR. His lips tried at first to give the breath of life, but ended with a knowing kiss.

"Why didn't you stay in the car like I told you to?" he scolded his fallen lover. "Why couldn't you just listen to me?" Kaleb sobbed uncontrollably.

"I'm so sorry." He wiped his stinging eyes. "I never meant for you to get hurt. I can't face this world without you. You're going to be okay." Kaleb brushed the bangs off of Walter's face. His tears fell on Walter's face. "I'll find a way to fix this, Walter. I love you."

Morgan came up and put a hand on his shoulder. He said through his teeth, "Get away from me." Morgan backed up. "You may not have killed him yourself, but you almost did. When you two blew up the dam, Walter could have died! He was out on patrol and his car got knocked off the bridge when the wave hit."

"I'm sorry, I didn't do it on purpose; it was an accident," she said meekly.

Kaleb's volatile emotions poured from his mouth like venom, "Sure it was, Morgan, is that why you were down at the zoo letting out the animals? Sounds a little premeditated." He looked up at her with eyes red and brimming with tears. "The FBI is waiting for you down by the driveway. I don't really care if you talk to them anymore. I don't have anything left in this world for them to take away."

Morgan wanted to console him, but the dragon that was Matthew lowered his head and backed away. *"Let him grieve."*

Morgan retreated with the dragon as Kaleb's body shuddered with the violent sobbing that overtook him. His anger was replaced by bitter sorrow. "I'll fix this. I'll make this right. I promise. I'll find a way."

Kaleb wailed his heartbreak as he clung to Walter's lifeless body. Anguish met with tears. Fear met with sorrow. A wail of agony met with silence.

A Heart as Black as Mine

Kaleb wandered through the shadow realm in a stupor. He no longer had a place to call home, and no longer desired one. Slowly, he approached a group of wayward ghosts. "I'm sorry to bother you, but have any of you seen this man?" Kaleb held up the eight-by-ten of Walter.

"Are you alive?"

"Yes, but I really don't have much time. Walter just died and I really need to get him back in his body. This is very important to me; he's my rock." Kaleb held up the photo as the spirit of a woman examined it. Several others were now gathering.

"Please help me, I must get a message to my daughter," said a woman in a long white gown. She pressed herself as close as she could to Kaleb despite being insubstantial.

"From the look of you, I'm not sure that would be possible. No offense, lady, but I'm pretty sure your daughter may be long gone."

Suddenly this didn't seem like such a great idea. "I'm really sorry, but if you have someone you're looking for I don't think I'm going to be able to help."

A soldier from the Civil War responded, "So why should we help you?"

Kaleb had already accepted this as a possible outcome and had come prepared. "I'm very sorry to have bothered you. If someone could please point me in the direction of the Underworld, I would be much obliged."

The woman in the white gown locked eyes with him, "What makes you think we know the way?"

He closed his eyes and grimaced. Kaleb didn't know how to broach the subject. Some ghosts had a hard time accepting that they are dead. "Ma'am, I am very sorry to have bothered you. I was just hoping that someone among you could either help me find my friend here or at least point me in the direction of the Underworld."

Several of the spirits began to converge on him. He knew in the physical realm that they couldn't harm him, but was that still true on their side of the veil? He ran.

•⁊•

Morgan stood before the tree with her mother's spell book in hand. Matthew took her hand, but his presence was next to invisible while she worked. Words she could barely sound out flowed off the page and through her lips. Above her, the limbs of the tree welcomed her and the crows found their home.

The great oak's bark parted. A hole began to form as Morgan continued her chant. Her words were joined by Matthew, who tried to follow along. The chant was difficult but he managed somehow to keep up. A corridor opened itself before Morgan; the bark of the tree parted to provide her admittance.

•⁊•

Kaleb knew he had lost his way. He no longer could say what it was that he stood for. Morgan and Nick had made their way and chosen to stand against the world, but he had no place in it anymore. Without Walter he felt more at home with the ghosts and perpetual night.

Without Walter to be his moral compass, would he make the right decisions? Would whatever it was inside him finally step out and guide him, rather than just sitting at the back of his mind? Kaleb was so used to letting his pursuit of love be his driving force. Without it he was lost.

"*What would Walter do?*" he thought to himself. The world wasn't ready for magic. Not like this. There were people in this world who flocked to the apocalypse. What would happen when the fodder was handed to them to start their fire?

Kaleb envisioned a world darkened by the smoke of the next great witch hunt. What happened in Salem would be a candle's flame to the funeral pyre to come. The frown that hadn't left his mouth since Walter's death deepened.

"*What would Walter do?*" If he went to the police they would laugh at him. He gripped his staff closer to his body as he let magic flow into him. With a cry of frustration he released it onto the shadowy realm in a burst of light.

He began talking to himself in the hope that Kronos would answer him, "What now, Merlin? Or do you prefer Kronos? Come on buddy, if we're going to be living in the same body, you're going to have to start talking."

There was no response so he walked to the coast of what was probably Spain. That was the thing he enjoyed most about the shadow realm; no matter where he was in the world he could walk anywhere he wanted. No more cars, or buses; there was no need for them anymore.

"*What would Walter do?*" There was only one person in the world with the power to save it. There was only one person with the resources to keep magic hidden. He nodded to himself. That's what Walter would do.

Morgan distrusted the government, but he embraced it as his best and only option. The president of the United States was the most powerful man he could think of.

Kaleb saw a ball of light in the distance. It was like a small sun in a world of perpetual twilight. There was nothing else for him to do, so he approached.

It wasn't a ball of light. As he got closer he realized it was a long jagged gash from which light was to be seeping. It hovered at the top a massive black tower. He approached the courtyard. The tower was made of black marble and the courtyard housed plants that he had never seen before in the physical world. The colors were vibrant and weren't muted by the darkness of the world.

Globes of magical light floated over marble pedestals, and in the center of the courtyard was a fountain flowing with crystal clear water. He approached the doors of the tower.

His eyes were filled with wonder and his curiosity would not be sated until he went inside. There was no doubt in his mind that this tower had no counterpart in the physical world.

"Hello," he called up the great staircase in the center of the foyer. Only his own echo responded.

.¶.

Matthew and Morgan lay by the small hole that they had carved out of the hillside within their sanctuary. The tree now had a few rooms and at the center, situated around the heartwood, was the beginning of a staircase that would someday lead to more.

He no longer had a life to go back to and now neither did Morgan. They were outcasts of society. A dragon and a shaman. Living off the land. His heart was heavy with the knowledge that he had been the cause of Anna's death. He still could not bring himself to say it aloud to Morgan. It festered within him. Matthew could see that Morgan was unhappy as well. In one foul year, she had lost her family and her best friend. There was nothing he could do to comfort her.

Winnie had been given a resting place at the base of the tree and every now and again Matthew heard her speaking to Winnie and Anna. It was both good and bad to be so close to those that she lost. He wasn't sure if she would ever truly recover.

Only when they were working on expanding their home within the sanctuary was she ever really at peace. Matthew wondered if that was when she felt closest to her mother. This place was so strange and yet so peaceful. So large, yet only the crest of a hill. He would never understand the magic that created their sanctuary.

"Morgan?" he said to the woman sitting beside him. Their feet dangled in the empty hole that would someday be a lake big enough for Rain.

"Yes?" she replied, her voice sounded weary.

"There's been something on my mind. Something from my past, and I'm not sure how to tell you. It's been bothering me for a while now, and I need you to know."

"Whatever it is, I'm sure it's nothing."

He braced himself. "Your mother didn't hit a deer. She hit me."

Morgan froze. She immediately withdrew into herself.

"It was the first time I transformed, I still can't control it. Please don't be upset with me. I'm sorry."

Morgan opened and closed her mouth a few times. She walked into the tree that was now their home. He heard a bloodcurdling scream of anguish and pain that set the crows into flight. Matthew wanted to run to her side but he knew that she would push him away or lash out in anger. Despite what his

338

heart cried out for him to do, he knew he must let her deal with her pain in her own way.

.٠.

Tara scoured the horror section of the video store. It was midnight on Halloween, so it had already been picked over. She had given up trying to find something interesting and was considering renting a terrible movie called *Suburban Poltergeist*.

The door chimed as it was thrown open. A man in black hooded trench coat entered the store. He lowered the hood covering his deformed features. His hair was matted and falling out in patches. His face was covered in burns and scars. She was impressed at how lifelike his costume seemed.

"Nicholas?" the deformed man by the door called.

The employee, whose name tag read "Steve," tensed slightly and turned slowly.

She could see the video store clerk clearly for the first time. His dark features and dark eyes mirrored the somber color of the clothes he wore. Though he hadn't acknowledged the strange newcomer, she could tell this was the Nicholas the man in the trench coat was here to find.

Excitement and fear churned inside her core as the disfigured man approached the counter and bowed. It was like watching a traffic accident, a horror movie, and a reality television show all at once.

There was a trail of blood on the floor where he walked. His left foot slowly trailed the other. Tara started to wonder if this really was an elaborate costume. Something big was happening before her eyes and she didn't know whether to run or watch.

The man behind the counter was speechless. After a long period of silence, Nick replied, "No one calls me that here."

"You must realize by now, you don't know me from here," the hooded figure responded. "The great Nicholas Gray, how have you been reduced to this?"

The man behind the counter backed up slightly and Tara crouched down to remain unobserved.

"How did you find me here? I left that all behind me."

"You were a difficult man to find, Nicholas. Do you not recognize me?" The man in the trench coat paused until he saw recognition in Nick's eyes. "You do recognize me. I am sure you know why I am here."

Tara felt her heart flutter. She felt as though she was privy to a meeting of a secret society, though doubt flickered in her mind that this was a ruse meant to make her into the fool. She considered storming out of the video store that very moment, but froze when she heard Nick's reply.

"I've killed hundreds, maybe thousands. Do you not think that haunts me? I binged on death, and nothing was ever the same. Death is a drug, and I got a clean slate here, David."

"That is not my name," the disfigured man replied. "You know me from before David. Or do you not recall our many nights spent together, alongside the dead? How Kaleb and Morgan placated me, telling me they would help when obviously they only wanted magic for themselves."

"Geoffroi?"

"Give the man a gold star!" Geoffroi thought for a second. "Now that certainly can't be what I meant to say. Stars aren't gold. Give the man a medal! Yes that seems more logical." He sounded like he was talking to himself more than anyone else. "This language is so ridiculous. No wonder it was so hard to pick up while I was a ghost."

"I thought Morgan raised David from the dead after she killed him." Nick appeared to be straining to connect all the pieces.

"She did, but when David's soul didn't return I jumped in. I am here to ask for your help. My Templar brothers will never be at rest until I exact revenge on the church we served faithfully until they day they betrayed us."

Nick crossed his arms and pondered the situation before him. "You see, Geoffroi, it's not as easy for me as it is for someone like Kaleb or Morgan. I'm a vampire." Geoffroi looked as if he was confused. "Let me explain how this works. I'm not dead, no offense. I don't drink blood and I have nothing against the sun or garlic."

The man behind the counter shifted from foot to foot. "The best way to describe it is for me to be able to use magic I have to first feed on the life energies of people. Otherwise the magic I'm trying to use goes right down this drain inside of me.

"But that's all behind me now. I'm clean. After the dam broke I couldn't get enough death. I'd feed here and there, but it was never enough. I tried for months to get more, killed another fifty or so. No matter how many people I killed I never felt full. I can't go back to that life."

Tara strained to hear them. Both men were oblivious to her presence. This wasn't an act. This was really happening. With shaking hands she started recording the exchange on her cell phone. Her heart pounded in her chest.

"I can't help you. I've been clean for months and I'm not going back. You have no idea how amazing it feels. Lifedrinker has been nagging me to feed her, but that's not who I am anymore."

"Lifedrinker?" inquired the zombie.

"Yeah, I trapped her in my staff. Goes by Lifedrinker. That's how I was learning my spells. Were you living under a rock? I mean seriously, where were you for the last several months?" he asked.

"I take insult to that, Nick. I was not living below a rock. Morgan kept me away from the world. Matthew and I lived at her mother's house until he disappeared."

Nick ran a hand through his hair and frowned. "Okay, not a literal rock. I did some bad things. I killed Kaleb's boyfriend, I tried to kill Morgan, and I kidnapped Matthew."

Geoffroi's fist clenched. "You are the reason my only friend in this world went missing? Why would you do that to me? What did Matthew ever do to you?"

"Don't be angry with me Geoffroi. The person I was then is not the kind of person I want to be. I did some really bad things. I was just coming off a death binge and I saw that dragon lying on the river bank, and Lifedrinker said to me 'It's a shape-shifter. Steal his ability Lucian.' So I kidnapped him."

It took a moment for Geoffroi to connect the pieces. "Wait, Rain is Matthew? That can't be. Rain insulted me."

"Wow, you have no problem with the fact that Matthew is a dragon, your problem is that the dragon insulted you?" Nick said as he raised an eyebrow.

Geoffroi glared at Nick. "I am a thirteenth century ghost residing in an animated corpse. I have heard stranger things than people are dragons."

Nick shrugged. "Point taken. Well, I'm sorry for kidnapping your friend. I'm afraid whatever brought you here, I can't help you with it. Without feeding I can't even make an orb of light, and those were easy."

"What do you plan to do with your life? Live in this mundane place until the day you die, work this pitiful job until you tire of it? The world is changing and you can either be a part of it, or you can hide with your tail between your legs. I am sure if you ask Kaleb for help, he can rid you of this vampire problem you have."

Nick cringed. "I doubt Kaleb will ever speak with me again. I killed Walter. He will never forgive me, and I don't think I will ever forgive myself."

"So we must do it alone. With these spells I have taken from Morgan." He retrieved a bundle of papers out of his backpack. "We can find a way to free you of this vampire problem and you will be able to use magic."

"If you used magic to track me down, why do you need my help?"

"I used low magic to find you." Geoffroi held up two metal rods that were bent at an angle to provide a hand-hold. "I used a spell to make them tell me your direction and I kept walking until I found you. I wasn't sure if it would work, but I had faith that I would find you. I am no sorcerer, Nicholas, I need you."

Nick thought for a second. "If I help you, you'll help fix me so I can use magic without feeding?"

"You have my word as a Templar." Geoffroi spit on his hand and extended it to Nick.

With a look of disgust Nick spit lightly on his own hand and shook Geoffroi's. Nick immediately pulled hand sanitizer from behind the counter and cleaned his hands. "You look like shit by the way. How does the whole zombie thing work? Are you going to be falling apart and stinking up my apartment?"

343

"We will be roommates?" Geoffroi made no attempt to disguise his enthusiasm. "I will rest, and the spell that keeps this body functioning will repair the damage I have done to it. It may take a while as I have not eaten or stopped walking for three months."

"Okay, wow, yeah, that would explain why you stink."

Tara had been frozen in place for so long her leg had fallen asleep. She steadied herself on the shelf of videos and knocked one off.

"What was that?" Nick strode around the counter. "Great, just what we need. I'm sure you heard the whole thing." He looked at her phone that she was holding in his direction. "Even better, you got it all on video," he said with irritation in his voice.

Geoffroi approached and she dropped her phone. She fell backward into to the children's section. "We cannot allow this! She will expose us. She must be dealt with."

"Oh believe me, I know. Do you have any spells in that bag of yours that erase memories? I can take a little nibble and I'll be fine." Nick calmly strode past the kids' section and followed her as she crab-walked into the horror section.

Nick had her cornered. Tara shook with terror and tears. "Please don't kill me. I promise I won't tell anyone. You can even take my cell phone, I can get a new one. Please don't hurt me."

Geoffroi finished rummaging through the unbound pages. "No, Sorcerer, there are no spells here that are for memories."

Nick sighed. "Well I guess I'll just have to do what I did to my ex and put her in a coma." He looked down at her and said apologetically, "This is going to hurt."

She screamed as pain racked her body. It felt as though someone was digging a hot poker into her forehead and pulling out her brain. "I guess that's why I always went for the throat chakra first."

Tears welled up in her eyes as she felt the sensation again but this time in her throat. Her scream abruptly ended and she clutched her throat. Tara looked up at Nick; he appeared to be enjoying this.

She tried to plead for him to stop, but no words came out. The pain occurred again and again in various places in her body until she could no longer move. Their eyes met and she could feel him within her.

He bit his lower lip in pleasure as he drained away her life. The sensation was too much for Nick. He couldn't stop. A dull pain he forgot was there was now coated in a delicious shell of sweet red and black energy. The taste of her fear and life essence was intoxicating. He could feel her essence flowing down his core and coating his soul with her life.

She was getting closer to death and he could feel it. A sinister smile crossed his face as he knew he was getting to the best part, the final release of pleasure that was the kill. As he drank the final dregs of her life he wrenched at the cord binding her soul to her body. His body was wracked with delight. His entire being was on fire and alive once again. Nick let out a slow sigh before opening his eyes.

Geoffroi crossed the store and looked down at the corpse. "She's in a coma?"

"No, Geoffroi, she's dead. I couldn't stop. It was too much." Her eyes were still staring at him and Nick turned away. He hadn't tried to stop, and that knowledge bothered the part of him that wanted to be clean, but the part of him that was Lucian was alive again. Lucian was hungry. "Do you have that spell they used on David?"

"Yes, but it won't work. We don't have the Hope Diamond," Geoffroi said coldly as he closed the woman's eyes.

Nick walked to the front of the store and locked the door. "What's the Hope Diamond got to do with anything?"

"Kaleb and Morgan stole the Hope Diamond so they would have a gemstone attuned with death magic. The spell won't work without it." Geoffroi leafed through the stack of spells and handed it to Nick.

He rolled his eyes at Geoffroi. "That's easy." Nick crossed back to the woman whose body lay broken on the floor. He reached down and yanked the diamond studded cross off her neck, "I curse whoever wears this necklace to meet an untimely end as the woman here has today." He used the life force he had stolen from her and locked the words to the necklace.

The lights of the video store flickered. Nick looked at the words on the charcoal rubbing Geoffroi handed him. The words were in Gaelic. "I don't know why you bothered handing this to me. What next?"

•⁊•

Agent Kris Sullivan had never given up on a case before, but the suspects had dropped off the face of the planet. No one had seen or heard from Kaleb and Walter, Morgan, or David. He couldn't believe he fell for Kaleb's lie. He was a fool to have trusted them. The official report was that the incident was caused by a faulty dam. No traces of explosives were ever found.

His phone rang. The Oval Office was requesting him immediately.

Kris was rushed to the Oval Office. Something serious was going on. People were tighter-lipped than usual. When he was escorted into the briefing room he understood why. Standing in the center of the darkened room was Kaleb.

"Finally, someone who will listen. Would you please tell them I need to have a word with the President?" Kaleb said with his arms crossed.

The Secret Service agent in the room with Kaleb was visibly shaken. "He just came out of nowhere. The lights go out and there was no one in the room, then he's tapping me on the shoulder asking to talk to the president. I pulled my gun out and it was gone."

Kaleb leaned on the President's desk. "It's not gone, it's just not here. I really don't have anywhere else to be, so, no hurry."

Kris looked around the room at all the unarmed Secret Service agents. Their faces were somber, and Kris could tell whatever happened in this room had them all scared.

The agent next to him whispered, "He asked for you by name. Do you know this guy?"

"If he wanted the president dead he wouldn't be asking to see him. There was something going on here." Kris narrowed his eyes. He didn't know what game Kaleb was playing, but he was going to find out. "Do as he says. Get the President. There's something going on here, and I'd like to find out what it is."

Kaleb exchanged a look with Kris. "That's what I've been trying to tell them all along."

11705074R00196

Made in the USA
San Bernardino, CA
26 May 2014